Dark Horizon

Dark Horizon

Crossing the Void

David Snellen, Jr.

Book Cover by Ken Howl, www.couchfiremedia.com
Edited by Rebecca Brewer & Kritin Gustafson
Photography by Danny Walls
ISBN 979-8-218-27832-8

1.0 edition 2023

This book is dedicated to my son: David "D3" Snellen. I started on this long before you were born. You've brought joy into my life that I could never have dreamed of. I hope someday, when you're old enough to enjoy this book, you can point to it and say, "My dad did that!"

FORWARD

This book started as a short story for a contest around 2002. It won first prize and eventually turned into the prologue of this book. Years passed—life happened—before I started thinking of an idea for two sequel short stories. However, it occurred to me that making a trilogy of short stories would be dumb.

So, I set about stitching those three stories into one book. Years passed again, as more and more life happened. Long stretches of motivation punctuated even longer stretches of apathy and inaction. It wasn't until the past couple years that I buckled down and finished this 21ish year project.

Creating a new sci-fi universe is challenging. I wanted to emphasize that aliens are, well, *alien.* I wanted to make the aliens look nothing like humans. No funny foreheads here. These are biologically distinctive species with completely different evolutionary histories and genetic material.

They also have diverse cultures that may seem alien to some of our 21[sst] century sensibilities, but that's the point. They're *aliens*!

Finally, I want the Dark Horizon multiverse to be welcoming to others' ideas and stories. I specifically wrote it as a multiverse that any story can be plugged into it. Do you want to write an alternate Flip story? Go ahead! Do you have a license to write Star Trek stories and want to put them in this universe? Do it!

Have your people call my people, and we'll work out the money details. Actually, I don't have people. So just email me.

You are monsters! That is the role it seems you are determined to play, so it seems I must play mine!

The man that stops the monsters!

--The Twelfth Doctor, "Flatline"

PROLOGUE

Phillip crouched in his bedroom closet, clutching his new friend, Rex. His mom gave him the stuffed Tyrannosaurus rex yesterday when he turned five. He was a big boy now and shouldn't be scared. But he was. He was very scared.

His new friend would protect him, though.

A T. rex isn't afraid of anything in the universe. They're from Earth, they're big, and they're fierce.

The bombs came in the middle of the night. He awoke in the air, still clutching Rex.

He crashed to the floor, his ears clogged, but he knew what to do. He crawled to his nightstand and got his mask. This mask was his favorite because it looked like a triceratops head.

"That is *so* cool!" his dad had said when Phillip modeled the mask for him. "I wish I had one just like it!"

"It's for big kids, Daddy!"

Phillip had named his mask Trigger. He knew he had to keep Trigger close because he'd protect Phillip from the Phurlani germs.

His cousin once told him about an ancient Earth monster called "the Boogeyman." His cousin was eleven, and he thought she knew just about everything.

"The Boogeyman especially likes little blond boys," she explained, her lips twisting into a sinister curl. "He grabs your ankles, pulls you under the bed, and eats you!"

Phillip cried and pleaded with his cousin to protect him.

"It's okay," she said. "The Boogeyman doesn't exist anymore."

"Really?" he asked, wiping away his tears with his pajama sleeves.

"Really," she confirmed. She put her mouth next to his ear and whispered, "The Phurlani ate him."

Phillip couldn't get to the bunker in the basement because the bombs had already started falling. The Lysserians should have tached him out by now, but he knew what to do. He wiggled into his closet along with his other friends: Bruno the Apatosaurus, Spike the Stegosaurus, and Bertha the Brachiosaurus.

He peeked out a crack in the door, quivering with fear. He couldn't close it from the inside because Bruno's tail was stuck in the hinge. *Too late now,* he thought. *Time to be still. Don't move. Don't make a sound.*

His closet rocked back and forth. His toys, friends, and baseball equipment rattled around him. The shelf above him fell and landed on some of the dinosaurs protecting his head.

2

The bombs stopped. The ringing in his ears scared him almost as much as the bombs did. He pressed his hands against his ears, but the ringing got even louder. He wanted to claw the sound out of his head.

Where are Mommy and Daddy? he thought. *Did they go to the bunker without me?*

No, Rex said, *they wouldn't do that. They'll come save you. They won't leave you.*

He heard Amelia down the hall, wailing with the sound only a terrified infant could make.

Why haven't we been tached out? Please, Alliance, save us.

He wanted to go to his sister. He wanted to leave the closet and find his parents.

Stay still, he thought. *Don't move even a centimeter unless there's fire. That's the rule.*

Everyone practiced for drills: at home, at the park, at school, and everywhere else on Lysser. The sirens could go off at any time. There hadn't been any sirens this time, though. There'd been no warning at all.

"Loose lips sink ships," his teacher had once said. Phillip didn't know what that meant, but his lips stayed tight. He choked back sobs while his mask filled with tears.

He heard his parents running down the hall. Amy's crying paused for a moment—his mother must have run into her room. It sounded like his father was running toward Phillip's room.

Please, Daddy, save me.

Lights, bright as the sun, came through his window.

Maybe the Lysserians are here? Phillip thought.

I don't think so, Rex said. *Stay still.*

Okay, Rex. His voice shook even though it was only in his head.

His father ran into Phillip's room, calling for his him.

Phillip and Rex peered through the crack. Phillip's breath caught in his throat. He wanted to run to his father, but his legs wouldn't move.

It's okay, Rex whispered. *Daddy is here. He's even stronger than me.*

"Phillip! We have to go!"

Yellow bolts screeched down the hall, and his father ducked behind the dresser. Phillip heard his mother scream and then a thud. Amy stopped crying.

"Phillip." His father's voice sounded hoarse.

The bedroom wall exploded, and smoke poured into the room. Phillip closed his eyes and pressed his hands even tighter against his ears. The shockwave knocked the wind out of him, but the closet door held. Even a Phurlani grenade couldn't tear down a closet door packed with stuffed animals. He let go of his head and embraced his friend.

You did it, Rex! Phillip said.

It's not over, Rex said. *This will never be over.*

Phillip didn't know what that meant, but it sounded like the truth.

4

Shadows came through the hole in the wall and slithered across the floor and ceiling. Phillip saw his father scooting away from the shadows on his butt.

"Don't move!" his father yelled. He held his hand up as if commanding the shadows to halt.

Daddy is strong, Phillip thought. *But those shadows are big, Rex. They have claws and teeth and guns.*

They're Phurlani, Rex said.

"Stay there, Phillip!" His dad didn't look at the closet. He just held his hand out, warding off the inevitable.

"Son! I love—"

The monster sprang and latched its mouth around his father's throat. His dad gurgled as blood sprayed across the bedroom walls.

Phillip locked eyes with his father. Blood gushed from his neck and mouth. The Phurlani's claws gouged through his father's stomach. He could see his father's mouth shape the word "you" before his jaw was ripped from his head.

The monster flung his father into the hall and chased after him. Phillip heard crunching and tearing.

Phillip swallowed the tears pooling near his mouth so his mask wouldn't fill up, but he kept his lips tight.

Please, Rex, save me.

CHAPTER 1

Captain Phillip "Flip" Marsh crouched in a nook on the Phurlani flagship, the *Shoison*. Millennia of warfare had led to one impending battle between the Universal Alliance and the Phurlani Directorate—a battle that Flip intended to start with an intelligence coup.

He glanced at his supply of energy pills and popped one into his mouth.

This is gonna be a close one, he thought.

His Fractal Algorithm Neural Gestalt, or FANG, node relayed this thought to the other members of his Viper Corps team. The node transmitted everything: every perception, emotion, thought, and memory. A Viper Corps team functioned as a single organism.

A deadly organism.

You got that right, Captain, came the collective reply. *Damn close.*

Check your energy levels, he instructed. He knew they already had, but he needed to say it. If not for them, then for his own peace of mind.

They'd need energy to power their nodes and nanites: molecular-sized machines that coursed through every organ and blood vessel. Their supernatural abilities—strength, speed, healing, and more—came from this technology.

Flip slinked down the circular corridor. Yellow bark like that of Terran trees covered the curved walls. Flip and his team had remained invisible in their cloaks, while reptilian Phurlani skittered around these hallways on their long, lethal claws.

Flip, Lieutenant Drete said, *they're on day five of this party.*

We see that. The team laughed.

The information they'd pulled from the *Shoison*'s computer had indicated that this conference room would be empty for weeks. That's why Drete had been creeping through it toward the ship's bridge.

But the Phurlani had other ideas. Much to the team's surprise, dozens of Phurlani stormed the conference room and began a boisterous celebration that interrupted the most important Alliance mission in nearly 3,000 years. Even with his cloaking device concealing him from the enemy, Drete dared not move a muscle.

The Phurlani wore tight blue uniforms over their red and green scales. Their evolution favored the number three: they had three forward-facing eyes on their flat, pug-like face; three rows of sharp teeth in a large mouth that could unhinge like a snake's; three pairs of limbs, each with claws tipped with three long talons upon which they could skitter or walk upright; and a three-forked tail that could be used as a weapon or as an additional appendage. To reproduce, three individuals combined their reproductive broth into a large container. As the fetuses developed, they

7

devoured each other until one remained. From thousands, only the strongest emerged. Every part of Phurlani physiology said, "we make natural selection our bitch."

The Vipers now saw Phurlani excitement and joy. No one else had ever seen such a spectacle. Seen it and survived, that is.

The Phurlani danced and drank. They traded stories and plans for what they'd do after the war. They talked of friends they'd lost and homes they missed. One could almost forget that they were murderous, bloodthirsty xenophobes. Almost.

We'll have to wait for the party to end, Flip said. *Unless anyone has any ideas?*

Why don't you grab a drink, Drete? Houbros said before breaking into a gut-busting laugh through her node. Seven different species returned the laughter.

You guys can fuck straight off, Drete said. *I'm guarding the ship next time.*

Luck of the draw, my friend. Swichef said. *As I've mentioned many times, I'm a very lucky Spibatphon.*

Drete fumed at the team. At that moment, his anger toward the team rivaled his hatred toward the Phurlani.

Focus, everyone, Flip said. *We don't know how much longer the party will last. The new arrivals make me think this is a graduation party for the Ghost Squad.*

The Ghost Squad served the Directorate like the Viper Corps served the Alliance: as elite special forces. They didn't link together with nanites, though—the Phurlani considered that practice abhorrent and saved it for their enslaved prisoners, the Phages.

They're so young, Drete said.

They're running out of adults, Alidth said. *We need to find the hatchery. Running out of energy pills isn't an option.*

Good thing there are plenty of snacks for ya, Drete! Houbros chimed in. *They look yummy!*

Shut up, Houbros, Drete said. *You can fuck off straighter than everyone else.*

I have the fewest pills left, Alidth noted. *I guess I could eat something here, but I was hoping I wouldn't have to.*

Nanites allowed Vipers to digest anything they could fit into their digestive tracts.

Looks like Drete has the best options! Houbros just wouldn't let up. She loved getting under Drete's gelatinous skin.

May I remind everyone, Drete sneered, *that we have to stay on a timetable? At this rate, the eggs will hatch before we even make it to the bridge, and the assault teams will get toasted.*

Good point, Flip admitted. *Are there any Ghosts around?*

Actually, Houbros said, *I think all the Ghosts are at the party.*

The group tallied up the known Ghost operatives and compared that to the ones at the party. They double-checked. They triple-checked.

This can't be right, Alidth said. *Surely, they wouldn't pull all of them for a party.*

They must feel safe here, Flip said. *They think Sandria is impossible to find.*

Still seems risky, Alidth said.

They're complacent, Houbros said. *They believe the eggs are their salvation. That and parties.*

I don't fucking believe it, Drete said. *I'm going to spend the next two thousand years listening to drunk Phurlanian karaoke.*

Two thousand years isn't that long, Houbros said. *That's... what? Four hundred million renditions of* Yellow Submarine*?*

Four hundred million, four hundred eighty thousand, Aldrith corrected. *Err, approximately.*

Oh, come on already! Drete said.

We should go to Ghost Green, Flip interjected.

The chatter stopped.

Agreed, Drete said. *I'll catch up.*

Viper teams used the Ghost Green tactical protocol when they believed the chance of encountering a Ghost was extremely low. They didn't use it often. Almost never, in fact. They'd relax their concealment protocol and move a bit faster to make up time.

Agreed, the group concluded.

Let's move, Flip said. *Bring me some cake, Drete.*

Fuck you, Flip.

Intergalactic civilizations relied on tachyon technology. These strange particles arrived at their destinations a split second before leaving their points of origin.

Slip drive and slip comm, the faster-than-light technologies, were fast. Space was vast, though, and "vast" always beat "fast." No matter how many multiples of the speed of light one traveled, true interstellar civilizations couldn't exist as a single entity. Space was just too... vast.

The invention of tach drive and tach comm solved this problem, and it allowed for galactic and even intergalactic civilizations to rise and flourish. Tach drive took you anywhere in the universe faster than you could even think about blinking your eye. A ship with tach drive could disappear and become untraceable, not due to technological limitations, but due to the physical properties of the universe.

The Phurlani had burned across galaxies for thousands of years. Their religion granted them exclusive rights to the universe, and they intended to serve that directive. The Directorate devoured entire species, systems, and galaxies. Or, worse, phaged them.

Phages existed in a state between life and death. Enslaved by nanites, they mindlessly swarmed Alliance positions, phaging more beings as they went. Alliance forces feared the Phage army more than they did the actual Phurlani. The worst a Phurlani could do was tear you limb from limb.

A Phage, however, consumed you. Its nanites spilled out and swallowed your very being, twisting you into an undead weapon. Trillions of beings fell to the Phages. And those nanite-infested corpses dragged themselves across galaxies, spreading their plague and paving the way for their Phurlani overlords.

The Alliance had barely survived the horror of the Phages. Most species had unlocked the secrets of biological and cybernetic immortality. As such, many lived through hundreds or thousands of years of the Phage Horror. Flip and his comrades fought with the rage of beings who had been threatened with imminent destruction for generations. Trillions upon trillions of beings had been killed or phaged during the war. The potential for eternal life made these deaths all the harder for their loved ones to bear.

Over the past several centuries, though, the Universal Alliance had accomplished what Mother Nature couldn't—they'd made the Phurlani an endangered species. The Alliance had pushed the Directorate back into worlds the Phurlani had already conquered. With no sentient beings to enslave, the mighty Phage army cracked, and the Alliance broke the Directorate's lines.

Phurlani reproduction became a strategic weakness. They needed more juveniles to repopulate their species, and they needed them as soon as possible. Their scientists devised a way for everyone to deposit their broth into one huge pool and nourish all the embryos so they wouldn't have to feast on each other. They created the Great Hatchery where billions of soldiers gestated.

As the Alliance closed in on the Phurlanian homeworld, the Directorate tached their entire population and all their resources to a rare extragalactic star system known as Sandria. Once there, the Phurlani reverted to radio communication lest any trace of their existence be revealed. They meant to bide their time and rebuild their population. They still planned on conquering the universe to please their gods, and they believed their remote location protected them. And for a long time, it did.

The Alliance, however, found the Phurlani and monitored the Directorate for decades. They deployed intelligence teams around the Sandria System—strike teams trained in galaxies throughout the universe. Alliance Command developed and deployed a new tachyon-suppression field around the system. The Phurlani didn't know it, but their tach drives were down and out.

Here, in this star system billions of light-years from the nearest galaxy, the fate of the universe would unfold. The Directorate and the Alliance would meet at the site of their last battle.

The Battle of Sandria.

* * *

Like the corridors, bark coated the spherical bridge of the Phurlani spacecraft. It stretched a hundred meters in diameter, giving the crew plenty of room to control every aspect of the Sandria System.

Pillars spider-webbed across the sphere, stretching from wall to wall with smaller ones branching away from the larger ones. The Phurlani scraped their long claws through deep grooves in the pillars to access the controls. Every member of the Viper team carried detachable claws so they could interface with the Phurlani system.

The Central Pillar stood alone and controlled the Great Hatchery. Flip needed to reach that pillar and directly interface with it to access the data. If all went as planned, he—and only he—would scrape his claws through the control grooves.

The data would be stored as copies in each of their nodes. If a single Viper made it out alive, the Alliance would have all the information it needed to begin the final extermination of the Phurlani Plague. The team, however, planned for everyone to survive the mission.

The team had arrived at their positions three days before Drete arrived at his. They used that time to observe the bridge, catalog shift changes, identify Ghost patrol routes, and refine their infiltration and exfiltration plans.

Drete took his position on the opposite side of the bridge from Flip. He'd provide cover fire if the mission went sideways. The rest of the team held their positions along the egress route.

Drete and Flip spotted seven Ghosts clinging to the interior of the sphere. The plan called for Flip to use the most extremely restrictive movement protocol here. They knew this would be the case; it was part of the plan. But because of the party that had trapped Drete, the two days they'd allotted for this part of the plan were just too long.

Flip had changed the plan: instead of crawling around the interior surface of the sphere and then up the Central Pillar, he'd taken a direct route through the jumble of columns. This cut this mission down to just a few hours.

The problem, as it stood now, was that none of the other pillars intersected the objective. Flip would have to make a dangerous leap to the Central Pillar. Not dangerous in the sense he might miss, but dangerous in the sense that he'd be ridiculously easy to detect.

This isn't a good idea, Flip, Drete said. Most of the team agreed.

There aren't any other options, Aldrith said. *Our schedule is very tight. That's why we chose this method in the first place.*

If we're spotted, we won't make it at all, Swichef said.

We won't be spotted, Houbros said. *Be positive. Drete made it out of his party without a hangover, so luck is on our side.*

I thought we were being serious, Drete said.

We can do both, Houbros insisted. *Plus, you should hear my incomparable wit one last time before you're vaporized.*

Thanks, Houbros, Drete said. *That's a great contribution to the debate.*

Flip cut off the discussion by jumping to the Central Pillar. He froze upon landing, hoping he hadn't been seen.

Damn it, Flip! Drete yelled. *Can't you keep us in the loop?*

They're starting a search pattern, Swichef said. *Sit still for a while. Maybe they'll think it was a stray reading.*

Hold your breath, Flip, Drete advised.

Flip could hold his breath for hours. His nanites could pull oxygen in through his skin, eyes, or any part of his body in contact with air, water, or any other substance that contained oxygen. It wasn't comfortable, but it was worth it in many cases. This was one of those cases.

A Ghost jumped onto the Central Pillar, just above him. Its claws rested a hair's breadth above Flip's head. Detecting a cloaked Ghost at this range was a trivial matter—Flip could see the enemy as if it wasn't cloaked.

The Ghost could likewise detect a cloaked Viper if it knew the Viper was this close. Only Flip's ability to remain motionless could save him. It all felt so familiar.

The Ghost turned toward Flip. It sniffed around him, drawing deeper breaths as it circled the pillar.

What the hell is it doing? Houbros asked.

I don't know, Drete said. *I've never seen a Phurlani do this before.*

No one has seen a Phurlani do this before, Aldrith added.

The Phurlani came back around to Flip. Flip's invisible hand rested in a control groove, his probes still siphoning data out.

This isn't good folks, Flip said.

Stay calm, Flip, Houbros said. *Calm.*

Please, Rex, save me. The thought came, unbidden, from Flip's node.

A gasp rippled through the team. A scared little boy *had* seen this before.

We're here, Drete said.

16

Stay still, Houbros said.

His teammates saw his memories. They heard the crunching and tearing and screaming.

Flip felt the Phurlani's stale breath on his face. It smelled like dank, mildewed cardboard and it conjured a fear in him that he'd not felt in a long time.

Easy, Flip, Drete said. *I've got him lined up.*

Drete knew. They all knew that he was just a scared little boy who wanted to save his family. Who wanted to destroy the Phurlani.

No. He didn't just want to destroy them. He wanted to carve their skin off and bleed them to death. To roast their children on spits over a campfire. He wanted them to beg and plead for their miserable lives. For them to feel the pain and suffering he'd endured. That everyone in the Universe had endured. He wanted to steal back the childhood they'd taken from him—that they'd taken from everyone.

He wanted vengeance. Pure, cold, vengeance.

We all feel it, Aldrith said. *We all want revenge.*

Other childhood memories flashed through the FANG network: phaging nanites flooding the atmosphere of Drete's homeworld; Houbros running from her phaged parents; and Aldrith screaming in terror and hiding from the firestorm of an orbital bombardment.

The team seethed with rage and found strength in their anger.

Flip's eyes flicked to the Phurlani's face.

Don't move, the team spoke as one.

The monster inhaled and tilted its head.

Hold, Captain, the team spoke as one.

The Phurlani stared into Flip's eyes.

I've got the shot, Drete said.

No! Wait! Aldrith yelled.

The monster smashed its claw into the pillar, mere centimeters from Flip's face.

I have to shoot!

No! Aldrith insisted. *Not yet! We need the data!*

It knows he's there!

Flip couldn't move. His eyes locked with the Phurlani's. Purple saliva dripped from its teeth.

Flip glanced down at the claw.

It smashed the relay, he said. *They know.*

Heads up! Swichef said. *We have incoming. A lot of them.*

We've almost got it, Aldrith said. *Hold just a little bit longer!*

The monster opened its mouth. Flip could see its three rows of serrated teeth. Anger burned through his veins. His nanites swelled through his muscles while one thought raced through his head: *those teeth are the last thing Daddy ever saw.*

We have the data, Aldrith announced.

The Phurlani's head exploded.

Flip leaped backward, flipping through the air, as yellow bolts ripped through the Central Pillar.

Blue streaks flashed from Drete's weapon. His shots ripped through three Ghosts; their bodies fell to the bottom of the spherical bridge.

I'm coming down, Houbros said.

No!
Drete and Flip said in unison. *Get out!*

The Ghosts fired in all directions, blasting through their crew, searching for the Vipers.

Straight up! Drete said. *Jump!*

A ledge thirty meters above Flip's head opened to a circular corridor. Not ideal, but it would do for an emergency exit.

Drete peppered the interior of the sphere with fire, pinning down four Ghosts near Flip's position. Three Phurlani huddled at the entrance above Flip. He tossed an antimatter grenade into the corridor.

Pieces of Phurlani rained over him as he somersaulted through their remains. He turned around to kill a pursuing Ghost.

They're closing in on you, Drete, Flip said. *Stop firing and move!*

Drete leaped onto a pillar as the corridor erupted in flame. He was still cloaked, though, and the new Ghosts didn't have the skills to track him. Flip used his wrist harness to fire three rockets at them. The missiles gouged the far wall, shredding the young Phurlani.

Let's move! Flip said.

Good idea, Drete said, leaping between pillars. He dashed across the pillars to Flip's corridor. "You sure you don't want to go back for some cake?"

Scores of Phurlani soldiers swarmed the bridge. They fired indiscriminately, destroying pillars and killing their own crew. They knew they'd been compromised, and their existence depended on finding and killing the Vipers. Nothing else mattered to them.

With the soldiers' arrival, the Vipers' mission became significantly more difficult. They needed to get back to their small ship that clung to the outside of the *Shoison* and to poke along at slip drive before they got outside of the tachyon-suppression field. And they needed to do this before the Alliance strike team left their staging bases.

And, now, they had to do all this with the Phurlani on their tails.

They had to scrap the existing plan—not the whole plan, though. One part still remained.

They would get everyone out alive.

CHAPTER 2

"Welcome to Saganville, Captain Marsh. All of Mars welcomes you."

Flip surveyed the room, noting that "all of Mars'" consisted of this one technician in the Tachyon Dematerialization/Rematerialization station, or "tader" for short. She stood behind a control console examining him, her curiosity likely piqued because Vipers weren't exactly a dime a dozen.

"I, er," she stammered, "I mean, I welcome you on behalf of Mars."

"I'm familiar with the standard Martian greeting," Flip said. "Operator...?"

"Lacy, sir. The integration room is"—she gestured off to her left and then paused—"oh, I guess you don't need that, sir?"

"No, Operator. I don't."

Like tach drive, someone using a tader existed at their destination before leaving their current location. When traveling in a ship, one didn't notice this effect. When taching as an individual, though, the effect was *very* noticeable. The brain had to reconcile the paradox of being in two different places and, unless the being had undergone intense tader training, they experienced a side effect called the "paradox puke." It manifested in different ways for different species but was generally unpleasant.

"Will you be staying on Mars long, sir?"

"No, Operator Lacy, I won't. I'm just here to meet someone at a café called"—Flip consulted his node—"Double T."

Lacy laughed. "There are a thousand of them in the city. Do you know which one, sir?"

Flip pulled up the location on his node. "Oh, yeah. I suppose I do."

"Are you headed to Earth for the ceremony?"

"I am, in fact."

"The Phurlani War Memorial looks quite impressive. I was born after the Extermination. Even though it was only fifty years ago, it seems like ancient history to me."

"You're quite lucky, Operator," Flip said. "It was—" He choked. The upcoming dedication ceremonies had dredged up memories he'd tried to suppress. Focusing on his node helped him keep his composure. "It was a difficult time. For all of us."

So long ago, for so many beings, Flip thought. *Yet it feels like yesterday to me. Sometimes I forget it's over.*

His node, of course, stored every memory perfectly. He could never escape the War.

Flip walked out to the hustle and bustle of Saganville's streets. As the first settlement on Mars, and one of its biggest cities, Saganville served as a center of commerce and tourism. The defensive fortifications had been replaced with parks, businesses, and other symbols of life moving forward. Slender towers seemed to defy Mars's light gravity, reflecting a faint red from the sky. Species from across the universe walked to and fro. The air, terraformed to match Earth's, filled his lungs. Banners and flags waved in the breeze, proclaiming the anniversary of the War's end.

Flip didn't have time to appreciate the sights, though. He had to get to the Double T and meet a kid named Johnny Rogers.

Technically, Johnny wasn't a kid. "Kid" was a nickname for Alliance soldiers who were less than a hundred years old. At thirty-five, Johnny had become a distinguished professor of ancient Terran literature. He specialized in science fiction and ancient Terran interpretation of the future. He'd petitioned Command for a civilian position to conduct comparative research on other cultures' science fiction.

Truth be told, Flip just wanted to meet new beings with new perspectives. He wanted to distract himself from his all-consuming pangs of grief and fear and hate. He had never met an anthropologist before, much less one versed in ancient Earth fiction.

Flip would adapt, as he always did. It would just take time. Operator Lacy, Johnny Rogers, and the billions of other beings coming into Alliance Command had thousands of years ahead of them. He tried to remind himself that he did too.

Flip felt so tired sometimes, though. He'd spent his youth running and hiding from the Phurlani. He'd been shuffled from distant relative to family friend to refugee camp until he reached eighteen, the Terran age necessary to enlist.

Even if he hadn't wanted to join the Alliance, there'd not have been a choice. He would have ended up in the War whether he enlisted, was drafted, or was eaten by a Phurlani invasion force. Enlisting had given him the privilege of applying for a particular career path. And he'd chosen the path that would allow him to kill lots of Phurlani.

Not just kill them, but kill them up close. He wanted to see the light fade from their eyes while blood gushed from their necks. And he had, over and over and over again. It never got old, but it was never enough. His node wouldn't let him run from those memories, and he wasn't sure he wanted to.

I'll never be the same, he thought. *The War changed me.*

He and his other war buddies said that a lot—but what did it mean? He'd enlisted centuries ago. How had he actually changed? Was he still a scared little boy? A refugee fleeing from planet to planet trying to outrun the Boogeyman?

No, he thought. *I've always been the same person. The only thing that's changed is that the scared little boy killed the Boogeyman.*

Flip found the correct Double T and saw Johnny sitting against the far wall. Like most Terrans native to Mars, he'd grown tall and thin. His red hair and dark complexion indicated he'd come from a family who had lived on Mars for eons. An antique green suitcase sat in the booth next to him.

"You must be Johnny Rogers," Flip said, approaching the table.

"Captain Marsh." Johnny toddled out from behind the table. He almost knocked the table over with his awkward moves. He straightened everything on the table as if he was apologizing for the items' inconveniences. He looked like a tower of blocks himself, one small push from being knocked over.

"It's an honor to meet you, sir," Johnny said, sticking his hand out.

"Please, none of the formalities," Flip said, shaking the offered hand. "I've already heard enough of the it's-an-honor-to-meet-you stuff today."

"Oh, er, sorry. Sir." The kid looked a bit embarrassed.

Flip slapped him on the arm, just a bit too hard. "I'm kidding, kid. It's okay. I'm honored to meet an anthropologist!"

They sat down, and Johnny somehow managed to keep his whirling limbs from knocking anything else over. Flip ordered a cup of Thymaxian coffee.

"Thymaxian coffee?" Johnny asked. "How do you drink that? It's toxic for Terrans."

Flip took a gulp and smiled. "It's the only stimulant that works for me anymore. And, yes, without my nanites I'd be dead by now."

"You were a Viper, right?"

Flip winced at the use of the past tense.

"Thankfully there's no more use for my specialty." He took a long sip of his coffee and ordered another.

Am I happy to be obsolete? Flip asked himself. *This kid is our future. I'm the past. Dr. Sbob says I still spend too much time trying to save the future, but that job is done. I'm not saving the future anymore—I'm just running from the past.*

"Your specialty, though," Flip said, accepting a fresh cup from a server, "is quite in demand. Can you tell me more about it?"

"Absolutely," Johnny said. "I studied Terran perception of space travel from the mid-nineteenth to the mid-twenty-second centuries. I compared those stories to how history played out. I wanted to figure out if an emerging interstellar civilization could make reasonable predictions about the future."

"I assume they didn't get it right?" Flip asked.

"Well, sir, you'd be surprised."

Flip shot back the remnants of his second cup of coffee and ordered another. "Give me an example."

"Faster-than-light travel was common in Terran stories. Authors at the time were entertainers, though, not engineers. They vastly underestimated the distances involved in interstellar travel, much less intergalactic. Most of the travel was 'go really fast' or 'go some factor of the speed of light.' Imagine traveling around the galaxy on slip drive alone."

"Glad they got that wrong. What did they do about language barriers between all the different species?"

"They glossed over it," Johnny said, taking a swig of tea. "They had on-the-fly translators like some species have now. No one could have predicted that English would become a universal language or that most species could articulate it. Had Earth not beaten back the Phurlani invasion—"

"Yes," Flip interrupted. "But they did."

"Er, yes, sir," Johnny stumbled over Flip's interjection. The kid shook his head and then continued as if Flip hadn't said anything at all. "They—the ancient Terrans—got some things right just for convenience's sake. Most species, for example, live in similar atmospheric conditions.

"They 'predicted'"—Johnny made air quotes around the word—"that Earth would be the center of government. In reality, the course of the War necessitated the Alliance's move to Earth. But, er, you already know that.

"They didn't, however, go into a great deal of detail about how time works," he said.

"What do you mean?" Flip asked.

"There was a lot of" —Johnny looked around the room, searching for the right words—"hand waving."

"As in...?" Flip prompted.

Johnny chewed on the question. "Our time system, where we use Earth Time—Greenwich mean time—in space but local time on planets? They didn't have that. They almost never discussed relativistic effects due to traveling at sub-light speeds."

Flip decided to just drop the subject. The actual system was confusing enough. He let his node do all the sub- and super-luminal calculations, along with the tachyon travel. There was no sense clouding his mind with fictional versions.

"What did they think other species looked like?" Flip asked.

Johnny chuckled. "They looked like Terrans for the most part. Take a Terran and add cosmetic changes to their head, or stick them in a rubber suit. In the early twenty-first century, they started to play around with computer-generated characters. Obviously, they had to work with what they had."

"And our weapons?"

"They thought we'd be using energy weapons as our primary armament and had the physics completely wrong." Johnny shrugged. "They based most of their fiction on aircraft and nautical ships—that's what they were familiar with."

"We probably couldn't do any better," Flip said. He stared out the window, contemplating the coming centuries and what they would bring. "At predicting the future, I mean."

"True," Johnny said. "But we'll live long enough to see it."

"Well, kid, it's time to go," Flip said, then caught himself. "I'm sorry. That's the second time I've called you 'kid.' Mr. Rogers, are you ready to go?"

Johnny smiled as he tried to slide out of his chair and lift his luggage at the same time. "That's okay, Captain. You've got centuries on me. You can call me Kid."

"You got it, Kid. Call me Flip. If you enlist, we'll change that up. Actually, come to think of it, I haven't been to Earth in a long time. How about we stay a week or so and you can show me around?"

"Sounds great!"

Kid looked at the empty plates and glasses. "You know that you're supposed to fast if you aren't used to the tader, right?"

"I'll be alright."

"Okay, but consider yourself warned."

* * *

Flip and Kid popped into the *Aristotle's* tader station after their vacation on Earth. For the second time in a week, Kid didn't make it to the integration room. He heaved his dinner all over the tader room's floor.

"Uh... sorry," Kid said to the operator. "I'll clean it up. I, uh, fasted before coming this time."

The operator chuckled and spread nanites over the mess with her tail. "No worries. Some beings have to prepare longer than others. Happens all the time."

"'Beaming' isn't much fun in real life, eh?" Flip laughed. "I still can't believe you've never used a tader before."

"I research Terran literature. Never really had to use one."

"Lieutenant Martwen," Flip said, turning to the other crew member awaiting their arrival, "this messy chap is Johnny Rogers. Mr. Rogers, this is Lieutenant Martwen. She'll help you settle into your quarters and give you a tour of the ship. We'll meet at the Toga Party tomorrow morning for breakfast."

"Excuse me?" Kid said. "There's a toga party tomorrow?"

Martwen stifled a laugh behind her tentacle as she escorted Kid into the corridor. "The captain loves that joke. The Toga Party is a restaurant on the ship."

"Ugh, don't mention food right now," Kid said as the doors closed behind them.

Flip retired to his quarters. He settled into his comfy chair and reminded himself, yet again, to mod one for his office. During the War, extra matter could prove hard to find. They used it for weapons, armor, and ship repairs. You could stick matter in the modulator, and it would come out as something else. But ammunition took priority over comfy chairs.

Flip pondered the various acronyms that filled his life, courtesy of Alliance Command. OCDs to read, TPRs to write, PCRs to examine, and TBDs to requisition. His node did all this in his subconscious, but he still found the bureaucratic exercises annoying. He liked to picture one Terran in a room sifting through endless paperwork.

The *Aristotle* cruised on slip drive through ex-Phurlani territory, billions of light-years from the Milky Way, searching for resources for the Alliance's rebuilding effort. It had taken the crew some time to get used to scavenging destroyed cities and ships. They felt like grave robbers.

Sometimes they found refugees hiding from their Phurlani oppressors. Many didn't know the War was over. Many had been in hiding for generations, and some were the last of their species.

Flip envied Kid. A future devoid of war stretched in front of him. His generation, and the ones to follow, could concentrate on rebuilding the Alliance. Flip would adapt, but it would be to a universe Kid would find natural to navigate.

He thought about the diversity among the *Aristotle*'s crew. That same diversity had endowed the Alliance with different tactics, technologies, and scientific insights that had proven too much for the Phurlani to overcome. The Phurlani didn't have the tools to adapt to the War's changing conditions. The xenophobia that had sent them on an intergalactic rampage led to their own extermination.

Flip's muscles relaxed as he reminded himself, as he did every night, that the Phurlani had been exterminated. They'd been purged from sensors, battlefields, and the ruins of Sandria. He wanted to unshackle his mind from the War, though the memories would always be stored in his node. But as his therapist said, with patience, he could get to a place where he didn't have to carry it. Where he felt free.

I miss you, Mom and Dad. And Amy, he thought. *I killed the Boogeyman and he's never coming back. I hope you're proud of me.*

Flip drifted to sleep and dreamed of a stuffed dinosaur, long since lost in the ashes of Lysser.

CHAPTER 3

After breakfast with Johnny, Flip decided to break out his old journal. He'd found it in a matter modulator library during the War and wrote in it on special occasions. Over the years, he'd written about "bad special" things and "good special" things. This was a "good special" thing.

"April 20, 4986. *UASS Aristotle.*" He wrote about Kid's encyclopedic knowledge of ancient Earth lore. Kid didn't have a node, and Flip hadn't any idea how someone could have all that data on the tip of their tongue. He was so enthralled that he decided to look up ancient Lysserian stories. Perhaps he could turn this new hobby into a new career. He put down his pen and strode onto the bridge with a newfound sense of purpose.

"Any new and exciting discoveries, Commander?" he asked his first officer, a Lysserian named Andrea Gibla.

Lysserians moved around on four tails that splayed out beneath them. Four arms extended from their barrel-shaped bodies, with a six-fingered webbed hand at the end of each. Four eyestalks sprouted from atop this menagerie of limbs. These eyestalks could rotate independently, much like a cat's ears, and a mouth pointed straight up between them.

A Lysserian's body coloring reflected their emotional state. This was an integral part of their evolution, and their customs lay bound in the open display of their emotions. They wore garments only when necessary to protect themselves from the elements and used transparent material whenever possible.

Commander Gibla sparkled with pale green dots, letting Flip know she was annoyed. She turned one eyestalk toward him.

"I've found a derelict ship on a scan," she said.

"And?" Flip prodded.

"It's three billion light-years from here."

"I see." Flip understood her annoyance. She wanted to check out the ship, but it was far outside their designated search area.

Johnny, observing the bridge, chimed in. "You might say that it's on the edge of known space?"

The senior officers looked at him.

"What?"

"Do you think anyone might be aboard?" Flip asked, turning to Andrea.

"Well," she started.

"You don't think so, do you?" Flip's wife was Lysserian, and he was fluent in their colorings and vocal inflections. He and his wife had planned on spending eternity together after the War... yet another dream killed by the Phurlani.

"I can study it, Captain," Andrea said. "I've developed some new methods for observing tachyon bursts. It would just be easier if we could pop over there for a little while."

"I understand, Commander. Keep an eye on it if you want to, but keep your other three eyes on the lookout for resources and survivors."

"Yes, sir," she said. Her hue melted into a calming blue, satisfied by the compromise.

Andrea exuded intelligence from the tops of her irises to the tips of her tentacles. She grabbed the universe by the horns each day and didn't stop shaking until she'd loosened another nugget of knowledge.

Flip slid into his chair, and again reminded himself to mod a comfy one. The crew knew their jobs. Kid was about his studies. Anything Flip did would only interfere with the smooth operation of his ship. He relaxed and watched the universe speed by.

CHAPTER 4

Over the next several weeks, more beings joined Flip and Kid for their breakfasts. Kid regaled them with tales of fictional spacefaring civilizations and of the Terrans who had crafted the stories.

Flip decided to leave Alliance Command at the end of this tour and become a cultural anthropologist like Kid. He'd already been accepted at Spirman University on Lysser. He'd have to face his demons there, but at least he'd be working toward a future for himself.

He loved the *Aristotle* and her crew, but flying around the universe triggered flashbacks. He didn't need constant reminders of the tragedies in his life; he intended to submit his retirement after bridge duty. He wanted to go over his letter one last time before sending it. No more putting it off.

Just this last mission, Flip thought. *Then I can start a whole new life.*

* * *

Moments later, Commander Gibla slithered into Flip's office. The yellow stars bursting against her blue skin told him she had big news.

"Captain, I think we should tach to the ship."

"Ship?" Flip glanced at Kid for support but didn't get any. Kid was studying some ancient texts he'd found in the Alliance library—Lysserian comic books by Flip's guess.

"Yes, Captain. Remember? The derelict ship on the edge of known space?"

This caught Kid's attention.

"Oh! Yes, of course!" Flip said, placing his roddenberry on the desk and leaning back in his chair. "Why the change of hearts?"

"It's enormous, Captain. It dwarfs anything we've ever seen. The configuration doesn't match anything in our database either. It must be a species the Alliance has never had contact with!"

It did not escape Flip's attention that Andrea had never stormed into his office. She always gathered an incredible amount of data before scheduling a meeting with Flip and the science team leads.

"It's hard to get a good estimate from this range, but it looks like it's been adrift for two thousand years, based on the degradation of the tach drive. Think about it, Captain! Another tach-capable civilization!"

Flip squinted. She wasn't giving him the whole story. "Is that all?"

"We're very far away. I can't come to any specific conclusions, but—
"

"Flip," Kid interrupted. "Let's do this. This is what I came here to do. You know, to boldly study other civilizations? I might be able to find out something about their culture."

"How exactly would you do that?" Flip asked. "You have no experience with xenobiology."

"That's true, buuut," Kid said, drawing the word out, "perhaps there are convergent ideas about technology. Each civilization has to exist within the same laws of physics, and their fiction will reflect that. The stories they tell may reveal something about them."

"I'm pretty sure you made that all up," Flip said.

Andrea and Kid glared at him.

"Okay, okay. How can I resist the two of you teaming up?" Flip sighed. "We have to make sure it's safe—we have to at least scan for phaging nanites."

Kid froze, his eyes wide.

"Best to make sure, wouldn't you agree?" Flip directed the question to Kid. He wanted him to know that exploring space wasn't like in his stories.

"Space," Flip said, "is a scary, dangerous place, and it will kill you in a split second if you give it a chance.

"The stories we make out there," Flip pointed out the window, "are life and death, and no one will write a happy ending for you. You must always—*always*—be aware of your surroundings or else your ashes will be floating through the universe, and you'll be nothing more than a memory."

Kid didn't move. His mouth hung open. His finger hovered over the roddenberry's screen. His eyes darted from Flip's to Andrea's.

"It's okay," Andrea said to Kid. "He's making a mess of you. It's just a precaution, standard procedure."

"She means that I'm messing with you," Flip explained. "Pretty good speech, if I do say so myself. Maybe I'll be a writer."

This didn't seem to allay Kid's fears. His arm, at least, dropped to his lap.

Andrea turned to leave.

"Oh! Commander," Flip said.

"Yes, sir?"

Flip held out his tablet. "Do you know where this comes from? The name, I mean?"

Andrea approached, lowered all four eyestalks, and peered at the data on it. "Sir? This appears to be an illustrated text from Lysser. I'm not familiar with it, though."

"No, Commander, not what's on it. The device itself. Do you know why we call these roddenberries?"

"No, sir. I don't." Her skin swirled with bright reds, yellows, and greens, signifying intense curiosity.

"You should look it up. In fact, do so before we tach to the new ship. I think you'll find it quite interesting."

"I will, sir! Right away!" She turned and wriggled out of the room.

Kid seemed to loosen up and gave a halfhearted smile to Flip.

"She'll get a kick out of that one," Flip said.

CHAPTER 5

Flip, Andrea, and Kid joined Lt. Ortosodl Islidn on *Aristotle*'s bridge. Like Flip's favorite coffee, Ortosodl came from Thymaxia. The lieutenant served as Flip's interim chief medical officer and was a skilled biologist.

Thymaxians looked like bright pink, meter-and-a-half-tall praying mantises. They possessed enormous strength, speed, and dexterity. When it came to hand-to-hand combat, you wanted a Thymaxian on your side.

Their language consisted of sharp chirps, clicks, and trills. Their anatomy prevented them from even attempting English and, unlike most species, they required a wearable translator to speak to others.

The *Aristotle* floated alongside Andrea's mysterious ship. It dwarfed the *Aristotle* and filled the bridge's viewscreen. A young science officer approached Flip.

"Captain, this damage is consistent with a—"

"Phurlani," Flip exhaled. He hadn't heard the officer. He didn't need to hear what she said to know what had happened to this ship. His node filled his mind with the smell of burning flesh and the sound of gurgling screams.

This will never be over, he heard Rex whispering to him across the ages. His first friend to be lost to the Phurlani Plague. He lost his family soon after, and he'd never forgive the Phurlani. He knew them better than he knew himself.

"Er, yes, sir," the science officer said. "There are no recognizable external markings. There's significant damage to the hull, so they may have all been scorched off in the firefight. It has been adrift for a couple thousand years; some may have faded away.

"Engineering thinks they can bring up the power core. Long enough to retrieve a significant amount of data."

Flip, disoriented by the onrushing memories, stumbled to his chair. He only heard her because his node caught her words and fed them to him after his shock subsided. He had a job, a mission. He had to focus on that. He had to protect his crew and, possibly, the universe. He linked his node to the *Aristotle*'s sensors.

This mystery ship had been a warship. Enormous beyond belief and stocked to the gills with particle cannons, antimatter torpedoes, kinetic weapon tubes, and several unidentifiable systems. But for all its might, this vessel fell to the Phurlani scourge as countless others had. The remnants of a once-proud civilization might be hanging just outside his ship.

"Begin remote Phage sanitization," Flip said.

"Captain!" Andrea shouted. "That could destroy valuable information! We don't know if it was the Phurlani. It could have been some other ancient species. We could run a level three—"

"There are phaging nanites over there," Flip hissed.

"Captain?"

"I know it." Flip's voice shook. "I can *feel* it."

He lowered his face to the floor and clenched his eyes shut. His cheeks pulled back to expose his grinding teeth.

He succumbed to the images bombarding his mind: A closet door. A stuffed Tyrannosaurus rex. Smoke. Explosions. Crunching. Tearing. A Lysserian scooping him up, taching him to safety.

This will never be over. He heard this phrase over and over and over. He couldn't get it to stop repeating in his mind.

The Phurlani were still here, with him. Forever.

Andrea put a hand on his shoulder.

He sprang to his feet.

"Sanitize!" he yelled. His crew remained frozen, appendages hovering over their controls.

"Now!" A tear escaped from the corner of his eye. "Do it now!"

His crew, none of whom had fought in the War, snapped into action.

He turned to Andrea. "You're in command. Get it done."

Purple wrapped around her tan body. Vertical pink and orange lines orbited her eyestalks, signaling surprise, fear, and—most of all—apprehension.

Flip marched to his quarters, where he downed Rockeye lagers as fast as he could.

This will never be over.

CHAPTER 6

The exterminators called an all-clear on the mystery ship's sterilization two days later. To be safe, Flip ordered another seven days of sterilization. During the extra week, the scanning team mapped the interior of the ship to a finer degree; no nook, cranny, nor crack escaped their scans. Flip took the time to drill the boarding teams on basic combat techniques. It wasn't much, but it was better than nothing.

Flip wanted to forestall the mission. He didn't believe in premonitions, but something felt *off* about it. Andrea told him to relax. He'd trained the crew, and they wanted to prove themselves to their captain.

Flip gathered the team leads in the Toga Party. The owner, Ct'lin'ga, had closed the restaurant for the meeting. The space typically erupted with life; the silence felt alien. Ominous.

Kid sat next to Flip. Flip wanted to protect Kid and, more importantly, protect the future Kid represented. He wanted Kid to hear everything he heard, unfiltered. He didn't want to forget to pass on any parcel of information. He could not, under any circumstance, let anything happen to Kid.

"Tell your teams," Flip addressed the commanders, "that I think they're the finest crew in the Alliance. I wouldn't want anyone else..."

He didn't listen to the rest of his speech. He said all of the words he thought they'd want to hear: they were the greatest crew, this was an important mission, yadda yadda yadda. He always hated this part of the job. Commanders throughout history recited this incantation when sending their charges into dangerous situations. It felt worse this time, though, because most of the beings here had been born after the Extermination. They didn't truly appreciate the immense danger that may lay ahead.

Lancman Phcont, a nanite specialist, took over the meeting, and Flip faded into the background. He didn't need to consult his node to see who had been in the War. He could see it in their eyes, the way they stood, the way they shifted around. The Phurlani had taken everything from them, just as they had from Flip. His grief wasn't unique or special; it drifted on an ocean of infinite suffering.

Ortosodl sat on Flip's other side. The Thymaxian's antennae swayed, signifying he was tense. Flip didn't know his lieutenant as well as he should but was familiar with his service record. They exchanged a glance.

"It won't be like that," Flip whispered. "It won't ever be like that again."

"Yes, Captain," Ortosodl said. "I hope not."

Flip listened to Phcont wrap up the meeting.

"Our scanning teams are confident there are no nanites aboard the vessel," Phcont said. "Tell your teams to stay on guard and that I am confident this mission will succeed."

"Okay," Flip said and downed another Rockeye. He didn't want to spend another minute listening to that pompous ass.

"Tell your teams," Flip said, slamming his fist on the glass table. "We leave in three days. Tell them to plan their fasts."

Kid let loose a long, loud sigh.

"Do you want to projectile vomit inside your helmet?" Flip asked him.

"Er," Kid replied, "okay. I'll do a two-day fast this time."

Flip didn't want to do this. He didn't want to walk onto what amounted to a Phurlani battleground, ancient though it may be. He thought he'd left those demons behind. He felt like a shell of his fearless-warrior self from so many years ago.

The Phurlani are gone, he kept telling himself. *This ship is just a graveyard. There's nothing over there but old bodies and dead nanites.*

I just have this one last mission.

CHAPTER 7

Flip, Andrea, Ortosodl, and Kid popped onto the mystery ship's bridge. Every team on every deck dry heaved, or what might be considered dry heaving for their species. Flip turned off his node's connection to the audio feed so the sound didn't make him sick too. Even though Flip didn't have to wear a helmet—a gift bestowed by his nanites—he still didn't want to vomit.

Flip scolded himself for not implementing tader training for his crew. Not for this mission, specifically—there wouldn't have been enough time even if he'd thought of it earlier. In general, though, he should have made it part of his crew's training as soon as they came aboard his ship. During the War, everyone, including children, received extensive tader training. As Flip knew all too well, anyone might have to tach out at anytime from anywhere.

Flip had implemented cursory combat drills out of panic, not a rational assessment of the situation. For all the centuries he'd been a bloodthirsty exterminator of Phurlani, for all the times he'd plunged into battle without concern for life or limb, after the War he'd felt more and more like that scared little boy hiding in a closet. He'd been able to push those feelings away, thanks to countless therapy sessions, until now.

Exploring the Phurlani damage to this ship triggered a flood of memories, not all of them his. FANG nodes relayed all thoughts and perceptions across a team. He knew his teammates' final thoughts, saw what they saw, and felt what they felt. Being a Viper didn't just grant you superpowers; it gave you access to the trauma of your Viper teammates. He wished his node could help with this kind of injury, but it could only heal physical wounds—not psychological ones.

He had to focus on this mission. He'd not had an important one for a long time—important in the sense that life and death could be part of the mission parameters. This ship may be nothing more than a curiosity from a bygone era. Then again, it could be the first clue to an existential threat to the Alliance.

The crew's discomfort subsided, and they all got to work. Ortosodl raced around the bridge, analyzing biological samples. Kid wandered to the back of the bridge and picked through piles of broken equipment. Andrea slinked to the walls, examining every crease, dial, display, chair—anything that wasn't the actual wall itself. Her skin popped with colors; bright red-orange, yellow, green, and pink lines orbited her eyestalks. She was curious, Flip saw, but also worried.

Flip pushed his node away and ignored its input. He wanted to experience this with his own senses. He also wanted to keep it from flooding his brain with traumatic memories. It would notify him if an immediate danger presented itself.

His lungs filled with the smell of an ancient warship; his nanites prevented the toxic fumes from affecting him. The engineering team had restored some power, and red lights bathed the room. Flip thought it was appropriate: an artifact of a lost civilization bathed in blood, albeit that of a Terran hue.

"Report, Lieutenant Martwen," he said. "What's the situation down in Engineering?"

"Sir," she responded through the comm link, "there are dead Phages here. Looks like they may have been viable, maybe in a dormant state. You were right, sir. I didn't realize how long they could live."

Of course, I was right, Flip thought.

"What species are the Phages?" he asked.

"There are several different ones, Captain, but mostly it looks like, umm, looks like Patsolorian. Their home world was pretty close to here, so that makes sense. There are also some Chusiks, Azpols, and Terrans."

"So much for the 'edge of known space,'" Kid said. Flip smiled.

"Very good, Lieutenant," Flip said. "See what else you can find out."

Flip stood in a circular depression in the middle of the bridge. It stretched about three meters across and a meter deep. Consoles lined the interior of the circle. Broken circuitry lay exposed in gaping holes around him. Some chairs remained bolted down, their seatbelts dangling to the floor. Others lay scattered in pieces at Flip's feet.

A set of stairs at the back of the circle led up to the main floor. About two meters from the top of the steps sat what appeared to be the captain's chair. Similar to the depressed circle, broken consoles and equipment littered the walls and floor around the rest of the bridge.

Flip walked up the stairs to get a good look at the captain's chair.

Hmmm, he thought, *these stairs are... comfortable? That's an odd thing to think.* Each step allowed him to bend his knee at an optimal angle, within a small margin of course. He couldn't remember the last time he saw stairs on a ship's bridge.

The cushions on the captain's chair had solidified over the millennia. It looked a lot like Flip's, though it had probably been comfier than his in its prime. (It seemed like every chair in the universe was comfier than his. He made a mental note, again, to correct this deficiency.)

Desiccated organic remains littered the floor. Ortosodl dashed from one sample to another, collecting the material he needed to solve this mystery. Flip noticed pieces of Phurlani claws. This hadn't just been a Phage attack. The Phurlani had taken an acute interest in this ship, yet it hadn't appeared in any Directorate database.

Looking past the battle damage, the bridge was spartan and opulent at the same time. Diamond-shaped symbols of various sizes appeared on chairs, walls, control surfaces—just about anywhere one would fit. There was something odd about all the workstations, though. Flip couldn't put his finger on it.

He walked to a wall. Above the consoles, he saw other items that may have been pictures. The battle damage, though, made it impossible to make out their subjects.

48

Ortosodl had stopped collecting samples and turned his attention to analyzing them. Andrea made her way around the walls, her coloring becoming more and more chaotic. She slapped her roddenberry as if trying to make it work correctly. Kid examined the walls, a look of concern plastered on his face.

"This is bad, Flip," he said. "Very bad."

"We'll figure it out," Flip responded.

"But—"

Flip cut him off. "Hold on. I like a good mystery. I want to play detective and deduce this on my own."

I wish I'd brought a magnifying glass. Maybe a pipe. That would have really completed the scene.

Flip strolled around the bridge looking for more clues. Could that splotch be the remains of a Trflak, phaged and thrown into battle? A stray suction cup from a Millite?

He examined the broken control panels and made out labels next to some of the controls. He didn't recognize any of the words, but they were spelled with English characters. He saw regular Arabic numbers, also.

The odds of this, he thought. *Are impossible. They must be. How can they have the same alpha-numeric characters we do?*

"Commander?" he asked. "Double-check all known records. See if there is anything remotely similar to this ship."

"I already have, Captain," she said without turning an eyestalk toward him. "There isn't anything."

"Have you—"

"I'm working on a hypothesis, Captain. I'll let you know as soon as I can." Her investigation occupied her complete attention.

She's the best commander in the Alliance, Flip thought. He felt fortunate to have her as his first officer, especially when surrounded by a mystery as large as this one.

She'll be a captain soon, he thought. *I'm glad she's not one yet—I need her right now. But soon. Very, very soon.*

Flip scraped his finger along the wall and ran his hand over the chairs. He sat at a console. The controls matched his hands exactly.

Something isn't right, he thought. *There's no variation or customization anywhere.*

"This is a single species ship!" he proclaimed.

"Captain?" Kid said. "This is—"

"Give me a few more minutes," Flip said, cutting Kid off. "I've almost got this figured out."

He walked around the wall and ran his finger across what he assumed was an enormous display screen. Something tickled the back of his brain, an idea insightful and obvious at the same time. It was just slippery enough that he couldn't grab ahold of it.

Andrea found a plaque. She had two eyes on the object and two on her roddenberry. One of her hands scratched a spot just beneath her right arm, a Lysserian habit akin to a Terran stroking their chin while deep in thought.

"Flip," Kid said again. The fear in his voice sent chills up Flip's spine. "This can't be real."

"Don't worry, we'll figure it out." Flip was determined, for once in his life, to not be a Viper. He wanted to just be a regular officer on a mission with other officers. Unless his node activated an alarm, he wasn't going to use it.

"You don't understand," Johnny said, crossing the room. He presented a shred of cloth to Flip. "This can't be here. It can't *exist!*"

"I don't know what that is. I've turned my node off."

"Turn it back on!"

Flip took the cloth in his hand.

A sudden flash of bright orange burst from the far wall. Flip grabbed Kid and dove for cover. He saw Ortosodl hiding behind the captain's chair. Ortosodl peeked from behind his cover and then holstered his weapon.

Why didn't my node activate? Flip thought.

He looked over, weapon drawn, and saw Andrea frozen with all four eyestalks on the plaque. Her skin glowed orange and, through the translucent suit, gave the impression that she'd been engulfed in flame.

"Commander? Are you okay?" Ortosodl asked. He pointed at Andrea. "Orange means fear, correct Captain?"

"Yes, Lieutenant. It does." Flip holstered his weapons and walked to Andrea while signaling Ortosodl to go to Kid.

By Apatoa's eyes, Flip thought. *The chairs, the letters, the consoles, the stairs—*

"This is a Terran ship," he whispered.

"I believe it may be, Captain," Ortosodl said. Next to him, Kid leaned on a console and shakily rose to his knees. Ortosodl rested a reassuring claw on Kid's hand.

"These samples are definitely Terran," Ortosodl said. "Some of them contain no nanites."

"How is this possible?" Flip asked.

"I don't know, sir," Ortosodl replied. "But I've checked dozens of samples multiple times. At this point, any hypothesis would be no more than a guess."

Andrea looked even more orange than before. She held her roddenberry out to Flip while keeping all four eyes on the plaque. Her eyestalks vibrated with terror, one of the few Lysserian emotions that had a physical component along with a skin color.

Flip took her roddenberry and looked at the plaque with its curious English letters. He didn't want to know what it said. He liked his new life, and he suspected what he saw on the roddenberry's display would destroy it. He wished he'd continued with the survey mission. He wished he'd never stepped foot on this ship and had left it out here to rot instead.

He looked at the roddenberry:

Language: Ancient Earth, German

Commissioned this twenty-fourth day of August 4785, this ship is christened in service to the Fürher as Bismarck.

CHAPTER 8

The Alliance sent thousands of representatives to the ship, which the Alliance code-named the "Bismarck System." A bit spot-on, but the public would never guess its meaning, even if they heard the name. Hundreds of ships orbited the *Bismarck* as if it were a black hole. Kid felt that analogy might have cut too close to the bone.

Flip had been sequestered—somewhere—on one of the Alliance's military vessels. They'd arrived within hours of Andrea's discovery. Flip gave her command of the *Aristotle* and left. He said he'd return in a few days.

Kid attended as many meetings and lectures as he could over the next few months. He took stimulants to study through the nights. He devoured everything he could about cosmology, mathematics, quantum mechanics, relativity, and a hundred other fields he'd never heard of. He had specialized in cultural anthropology and tried to turn himself into a theoretical physicist in six months.

Kid was burning himself out chasing a truth that ran further away with each discovery. He concluded that he would never understand the true ins and outs of the *Bismarck*. Andrea, one of the best physicists and mathematicians in the Alliance, still struggled to grasp the ramifications of this situation.

While drinking at the Toga Party, he realized that the phenomenon *did* come within his realm of expertise. The Alliance scientists assigned to the project kept saying that their research had become "stranger than fiction." Fiction, however, was Kid's specialty. The data the Alliance science teams had collected reminded him of stories from ancient Earth's fiction. Well, some of them.

He and Andrea spent weeks nailing down a narrative that summarized—more or less—what they'd discovered. Most of the scientists decided that Kid's cursory understanding of the phenomenon coupled with his penchant for storytelling made him the best choice to give the final presentation. Everyone crucial to the Alliance would be there: political and military leaders, renowned scientists from every field imaginable, and, most importantly, the emperor.

Most beings in the Alliance thought the emperor was no more than the figurehead of their constitutional monarchy. The true head of state was, of course, the prime minister. The emperor provided something intangible to the people of the Alliance though: a constancy of vision, purpose, and direction. He had very little legal authority under the Alliance's constitution, but legislators and the public always considered his opinions carefully.

The emperor had been chosen at the founding of the Universal Alliance. He'd been born in Earth's twentieth century and was thus considered an Ancient. Rather short in stature compared to Terrans of later generations, he appeared to be in his midthirties. He wore his brown hair long and sported a reddish-brown goatee. He moved with grace, comfortable in his toned body. He wore glasses, even though they had been rendered obsolete even within his own natural lifespan.

Kid didn't understand why someone of such a high profile would attend this conference, much less his presentation. How could they keep the project secret with the emperor onboard? And why wasn't the prime minister in attendance?

Andrea pointed out that the emperor often indulged himself with flights of fancy. He'd travel to various worlds to study arcane martial arts. He'd disappear for a decade or more to write terrible poetry that he would later inflict on an unsuspecting publisher.

Now that the War had ended, no one would even notice his absence. If the prime minister went missing for more than a few weeks, however, people would suspect that something important and potentially dangerous had sprung up.

"And," Andrea pointed out, "they'd be right."

* * *

Kid stood at the front of a small lecture hall. He'd just finished giving a presentation that summarized the previous two weeks of conferences. Physicists, biologists, mathematicians—essentially everyone qualified to answer detailed questions—had watched him butcher their life's work into what they considered an incomprehensible, mangled, and downright blasphemous story.

"Okay," the emperor said. "Let me see if I've got this straight."

Everyone straightened and turned their attention to the emperor. He'd been seated in front of Kid, in the middle of the first row. He hadn't said anything during any of the presentations. From what Kid could tell, he just doodled in a paper notebook with an ink pen; everyone knew the emperor liked modding these old items—he had a reputation for eccentricity. Kid hadn't thought the emperor was paying attention at all.

"Because I want to be absolutely clear on this," the emperor continued.

All eyes turned toward Kid. He had to organize his thoughts. The experts had at least known what he'd meant through all those rambling tales of starships and heroes coursing through the multiverse; now, he had to provide a detailed explanation to one of the most important beings in the universe.

"The Multiverse Theory is true," the emperor said.

"Er, yes sir," Kid stammered.

The emperor stood and paced in front of the room, his gaze locked on the floor. All eyes turned toward him. "There are an infinite number of universes," the emperor said.

"Yes, sir." All eyes back on Kid. (The audience's eyes bounced back and forth between them for the entire exchange as if Kid and the emperor were playing the most important tennis match in history.)

The emperor moved faster, stroking his chin and gesticulating wildly. "Every possible universe is represented an infinite number of times."

"Correct, sir."

"And in addition,"—the emperor raised an index finger for emphasis—"there are other universes where anything that could have happened has indeed happened or will happen."

"Er, sir. Yes."

"Every combination of physical laws exists somewhere. Some universes don't have gravity. Some have photons the size of baseballs."

"Yes, sir. The Nazis have sent probes into some of those other universes."

The emperor sat down, leaned back in the chair, and steepled his fingers under his chin. "Even the ones with plot holes?"

Kid nodded slowly. He shuffled from one foot to another. Ancient eyes sized him up. The decisions made here would shape the course of the Alliance's future.

"Yes, sir," Kid said. He stared into the emperor's eyes. Those eyes had marched through history and had seen liberation, destruction, and everything in between.

"The Nazi database proved the Multiverse Hypothesis," the emperor said. He stared back at Kid, presenting an unspoken challenge for him to shape history.

"This has been an idea for millennia," Kid said. "First in fiction, then in mathematical models. Now we know it's true. Thanks to the *Bismarck*, we now know how to cross into these other universes."

"I see," the emperor said. He leaned back and crossed an ankle over his knee. "Go on, Mr. Rogers."

"The math is incredibly complicated, and that's not my strong suit. Professor Lharbin went into great detail about the models." He looked over to the Lotian mathematician.

"That's okay, Mr. Rogers," the emperor said. "We've already had a deep dive on that."

"Er, okay," Kid continued. "Once the basic principles are known, it seems pretty obvious that—"

Aggrieved theorists shuffled in their seats at the perceived slight.

"Each of those universes," the emperor said, cutting him off, "are at different points in their own timelines?"

"Not exactly, sir. It seems each universe exists, well..." Kid looked at the ceiling trying to think of a summary.

"Picture this, sir," Kid walked toward the emperor. "Imagine you could stand outside our universe." He spread his arms wide. "Outside *all* the universes. You can't, of course, as far as we know."

The emperor leaned forward and rested his chin on his index fingers.

"Bear with me," Kid said. He walked to the whiteboard at the front of the lecture hall and picked up a marker—two more antiquated artifacts the emperor had insisted upon.

Kid drew some wavy vertical lines.

"These are universes. They are kind of like"—Kid paused to think of an analogy—"drapes. They sort of hang there, waving back and forth.

"This area around the drapes," Kid swept his arms in a big circle around all the lines, "this whole whiteboard; *this* is the Bulk. All the universes are in it."

He pointed at the emperor. "Pretend you're in the Bulk, sitting outside all the universes. Time has no meaning for you. Nothing happens. But these universes are"—he paused, choosing his words carefully—"somehow waving back and forth. Time and matter exist here." Kid banged his finger on one of the wavy lines.

"But for you," he said, pointing at the emperor again. "All of this is meaningless. The universes move and don't move."

"Er," the emperor leaned forward even more. Kid worried the emperor would topple out of his chair. "So, in this example, I'm outside time and space?"

"Yes!" Kid exclaimed. "And these"—he jabbed at the whiteboard again—"are bridges between the universes. The universes—these drapes—collide on their own sometimes. Or, as with the *Bismarck*, someone punches a hole between the universes. That's when the weird stuff happens."

"Oh," the emperor said, leaning back. "*That's* when the weird stuff happens?"

Kid sighed. He'd been turning this over in his head for weeks, wondering if he could write his own stories about it. He put the cap on his marker.

"Every universe has its own timeline." Kid leaned on the podium. "But those timelines don't really exist."

"Pardon me?" the emperor said.

"Okay, sir, picture this instead." Kid stood upright. "You're in the Bulk. You see all the universes. All of them. Every possible reality stretches before you.

"Those universes have their own timelines. But for you, those timelines don't exist. Time in those universes is just mashed up into this..." He trailed off, trying to find the right words. "This... jumbled up stuff.

"These universes"—Kid pointed back to the whiteboard—"don't move. They don't change. They just *are*."

The emperor's brows furrowed.

"When they touch," Kid said, "they collapse into each other."

The experts in the room looked at each other, displeased at Kid's explanations.

"When they touch," Kid plowed ahead. "Their timelines lock." He interlaced his fingers. "They are fixed in time relative to each other."

Kid put his hands on his head and paced for a few seconds.

"When the Nazis came here," he said, "our universes became fixed at a point two thousand years in our past.

"In *our* universe, Earth's Second World War happened four thousand years ago. For them, it could be ten thousand years ago. Or a thousand years ago. We don't know. But now that our universes have touched, they'll age together."

Kid took a deep breath. "Now here's where it gets weird."

"Mr. Rogers," the emperor said, "you said that was the weird part."

"Well, er," Kid said, "yes. But this is weirder."

Kid took a few moments to compose himself. "When the Nazis came here, they could have intersected at any point in our history. The *Bismarck* could have crossed ten billion years in our future or right after the Big Bang.

"At *that* point," —Kid pounded his fist onto the podium for emphasis—"at *that* instant, our history became real."

"Mr. Rogers—"

"Hang on," Kid interrupted. He didn't dwell on the fact that he'd just cut off the emperor.

"From *your*"—Kid pointed at the emperor—"perspective, in the Bulk, the universes are unchanging. Their beginnings, their ends, and everything in between just... *are*. They're all jumbled up together, like I said.

"But when they touch—" The possibilities crashed into Kid's mind and he became more and more animated. "When they *touch*, that's when they *happen!*"

The emperor chewed on his thumbnail. He looked distressed. "So if our universe had been an unchanging, permanent... thing... did we exist before they came here?"

"I don't follow," Kid said.

"I mean," he said, distress leaking into his voice. "They could have come here a few years after the Big Bang. We'd have collapsed to that point in time. We wouldn't exist. Is our history, before two thousand years ago, real? Did it happen?"

"Yes," Kid tried to say with an air of confidence.

The scientists in the audience looked downright angry.

"We exist infinitely throughout the multiverse," Kid said. "No matter what, our history is real."

"Is it?" the emperor asked. "If they'd come ten thousand years ago, everything would be so different that maybe the Phurlani wouldn't have existed. Maybe they'd have been wiped out by an asteroid or something. The War would never have happened. The UA wouldn't exist."

"Sir," Kid said, "I don't know how to answer that. If our history, as we remember it, had been, er, short-circuited, it would still happen elsewhere."

The emperor leaned back in his chair, chewing his thumbnail down to a nub.

"Okay. Okay. Let's change the subject," the emperor said as he jumped up and resumed pacing, this time with his hands behind his back. "You mentioned earlier about bringing universes into existence by imagining them?"

"Yes, sir. I took a particular interest in this," Kid said. "The Nazis believe—and they've had a lot of experience with this—that imagining a universe brings it into the Bulk in infinite replications and variations. If you create a work of fiction, or even just daydream about something, that becomes reality somewhere. Everywhere."

"I think," the emperor said, "this has disturbing implications." He stopped pacing and looked at Kid.

"Yes, sir." Kid didn't like this part. He didn't like it at all.

"Such that we could be the product of someone's imagination," the emperor elaborated. "That we'd not know our universe to be a fiction that had just now been called into existence."

An uncomfortable rustle spread through the crowd.

"Yes, sir. That is... possible." Kid tried to project some uncertainty into the statement.

"All of our fictional creations," the emperor continued, "all of our daydreams and all of our nightmares... exist out there somewhere?"

"Yes." Kid looked at the floor. "And we could meet them."

The emperor gazed through Kid. His eyes, those ancient eyes, seemed to sink into darkness.

"I think we will, Mr. Rogers," he said. "I think we will meet them all."

CHAPTER 9

To borrow a Terran term, Andrea thought while slithering to Flip's office. *I'm dragging my tentacles. Terrans have such colorful metaphors!*

The large military presence had sparked rumors throughout the fleet about the onset of a new war. The opinions split just about 50/50 between "we have to eliminate this threat" and "we don't have the resources for another war." Andrea figured the rest of the populace would do the same. Perhaps it would lead to civil unrest or maybe even star systems leaving the Alliance.

How will they put the needle on the string? she thought as the door to Flip's office opened.

Flip pointed to a Lysscrian chair across from his desk.

"I have some news," he said.

"Good or bad?" she asked.

"Definitely bad." He looked at the ceiling and put his thumb and forefinger to his chin. "But there is good news too. Which do you want first?"

"It is a Lysserian custom," she answered, "to always take the bad news first. That way you leave with good thoughts." She scowled at him. "You know that, Flip."

He chuckled. "Yeah, I know. But it's a Terran custom to ask."

Her skin turned a bright red-orange, signaling trepidation.

"This is all classified, of course," he said.

She squeezed her forward fist, a Lysserian gesture that indicated she understood and agreed.

"We've already sent probes into their universe. A couple small teams, too," Flip said.

Andrea's skin changed to the light purple of surprise. "Already?"

"We know that opinion is sharply divided as to how to proceed but—"

"That's an understatement!" she interrupted.

He nodded. "We're going to take a middle path."

"How—" she started.

"First," he said, "you aren't supposed to know this yet. But you will soon." He smiled and continued, "So act surprised when you're told."

Mild amusement pierced parts of the red-orange that dominated her body.

"I'm being recalled to Viper Command."

Silver shock shot across Andrea's entire body, mixing into the red-orange. She shouldn't feel surprised—she assumed this would happen. Hearing it, though, confirmed her fears.

"I assume"—she hesitated mid-sentence—"the other Vipers..."

"Yes," he walked to the window near his desk. He always stood there when he felt—how did Terrans put it—wistful? Others couldn't see it, even other Terrans. Lysserians, though, could read Terran body language almost instinctively.

He's going to miss it here. It's so easy to see. Like taking an infant to some candy, she thought.

"So, the rumors...?" Another thing she didn't want to ask.

"Depending on the rumors," he started, collecting himself. "The answer is yes. Or no. It depends on how you phrase the rumor."

"Come on, Flip," she said. "You're not making this easy. What the hell is going on?"

"You'll be heading the research about universe traversal," he said. "Large-scale, I mean. You're one of the best scientists in the universe and, frankly, I'm not privy to what you'll be doing."

Confusion rippled across her body. "Flip..."

"Look. I'm gonna level with ya," he said.

Andrea loved Terran idioms. Flip always said "ya" when he was about to slice through the bull's shit.

"I honestly don't know what's going on," he explained. "I know that all of the Vipers are being recalled, even the retired ones."

"That's not surprising," she said.

"Yes, well. From what I've gleaned" —he leaned in, lowering his voice to just above a whisper—"we're launching a secret war."

Silver overwhelmed her body. It coursed down her arms so fast she thought it might spew out her fingers.

"A—" she started, struggling to get the words out. "A secret war?"

"I don't like it," he said. "You can probably guess why."

She took a deep breath. "I can," she said. "We can't let this threat grow. But how do we engage them with our depleted resources? Either way, if word of the multiverse got out to the public there'd be chaos."

"And—" He tried to continue.

She stood. "By Apatoa's eyes!" She put an arm on Flip to steady herself. "Are they?" She felt as if the room swirled around her. She couldn't imagine the colors coursing around her body.

Flip, ever calm, ever the captain, grabbed her eyestalk: a reassuring gesture among Lysserians.

"I know what you're thinking, Andrea. And I don't know the answer. That's another reason we need to do this."

"Isfym's ass, Flip." She twirled around the room in frustration. "What's the good news?"

"Well, Commander," he said, drumming his hands on the desk, "you are..."

Terrans, she thought, *are so dramatic.*

"A captain!" He spread his arms up, a rough approximation of a Lysserian saying *surprise!* "Well,"—he glanced at his clock—"in a couple hours, anyway."

"What?!"

"Yes, my friend, you are a captain. Sorry we can't have the pomp and circumstance you deserve." He lowered his head. "These are trying times. Or rather, they will be."

"I don't know what to say." She grabbed the back of the chair to steady herself.

"'Thank you' is something you definitely *shouldn't* say." He walked to the matter modulator and ordered a cup of tea for each of them.

"What about Kid Rogers?" Andrea asked. She'd grown fond of his stories and history lessons. They helped her understand Terrans a bit better. "He seems like he may be useful."

"You're right on the nose," Flip said. "Or lip fold, I suppose. The emperor was quite impressed with Kid's presentation. He personally assigned Kid to a secret mission. I'm to be briefed on it in a couple days.

"The emperor has created a cover story for Kid," Flip continued, walking around to the back of his desk to sit. "He's quite clever."

Flip reached under his desk and produced a baseball. Andrea knew the sport well: baseball consumed the entirety of Terrans' passing of the time. Flip tossed the ball up and caught it.

"What's funny," he said, "is that I know even less about your mission than you do about mine. Or will know about mine soon, anyway.

"You have command of the fleet." He laid the baseball on the desk and rolled it to her.

She choked on her tea. "Fleet? Which fleet?" She took the ball— Flip had always said it was his symbol of command.

"Look out the window." He tried to hide his anguish. "This entire fleet, Andrea, is yours."

"But, as a captain..." she said, trailing off. She still couldn't believe this.

"I don't know." He slurped down the last of his tea. "I just don't know. You're a captain; you're in command of hundreds of ships. It's a weird universe we've suddenly found ourselves in."

He slammed his teacup to the desk, shattering it. Andrea jumped back, startled. She hadn't expected this sudden shift of emotion. He walked to the window, fists squeezed tight enough to crush a baseball. His fingernails dug into his skin, leaving bloodstains on his sleeves.

He'd relished his new roles—explorer, savior, custodian of the future—all while hiding his trauma from everyone but her. She read his every emotion so well it was as if she could read his mind. She'd expressed her concern to him before, prompting him to confide in her. He'd been looking forward to going to university. He'd talked about it every day, at least for the short period of time between his decision and the discovery of the *Bismarck.*

She saw despair consume his body; he looked to be on the verge of tears. She knew how he felt because she felt it, too: oblivion would soon swallow the world they'd hoped to live in.

His emotions shifted again. She could see his face reflected in the window; it became cold and composed. He looked like a skilled and confident killer. For the first time, she saw him as a Viper.

"You're the captain of hundreds of ships," he repeated. He looked as if he was trying to force the words out of the window and into the void. "And many more on the way."

CHAPTER 10

Andrea sat at Flip's desk.

No, she thought. My *desk.*

She had submitted Ortosodl's promotion within an hour of hers becoming official. It came through within minutes, and she chose him as her first officer. He sat before her now, considering this turn of events.

"I'm not sure what to say, Comm—er, Captain."

"Say you'll take it and we'll get to work. I mean, you are going to take it, aren't you?" Black concern spread across her skin.

"I-I'll have to think about it, Captain," he stammered.

"You seem less than excited," she said to the Thymaxian. Lysserians could pick up subtle body language cues from any species, not just Terrans.

"It's just that, er, I was hoping to become the Chief Medical Officer."

Andrea sighed. "I know you were." She stood and slithered to the window. "I was hoping for a research position."

"You can't do that now?" Ortosodl asked.

"I have to shuffle people and supplies around." She stared at her desk, examining every millimeter. "I think I will have to destroy instead of discover."

"Permission to speak freely, Captain?"

"Of course," she said, turning her eyestalks to face him. "Consider that a standing permission when we're alone. And please, call me Andrea."

"What did you do? Before, I mean."

"Before the end of the War," she started, walking to the modulator and grabbing a Lysserian and Thymaxian coffee. She sipped from one and offered the other.

They clinked their cups and drank.

"I was a civilian scientist," she continued. "Astrophysics, astronomy, particle physics. That kind of thing.

"Of course, nothing was that simple. Everything revolved around the War, didn't it?" She gazed out the window. Her skin blazed with emotions that she hoped Ortosodl could read—that would make this conversation easier.

"Yes," he said, his compound eyes glazing over. "It was total war. No one could escape it."

"My sacrifices weren't great," Andrea said. "I was just frustrated at the ever-changing projects."

"I never knew that," he said, sipping his coffee. "You joined up after the War?"

"Not exactly," she said. "I was conscripted, so to speak."

Ortosodl tilted his head, perplexed.

"They promised research opportunities in exchange for accepting a commission," she said. "They needed scientists and explorers. It was an opportunity beyond my dreams. Even the *Bismarck,* as terrible as it is, is fascinating."

She gestured with an eyestalk to the enormous ship outside the window. "To think of those countless universes out there, waiting to be discovered."

"Oh, I see," he said, gazing into his empty mug. Andrea fetched him another drink.

"Sorry, I can go on about this forever. I'm boring you." She could see that she wasn't, but she could also see there was something Ortosodl was avoiding. She wanted to give him an opportunity to change the subject.

"No," he said. "Not at all. Please continue."

"We switched projects a lot," she said. "They probably didn't want us to figure out what we were really looking for."

She stirred her coffee. "We'd spend years studying natural tachyon emissions. Then switch to studying the tiny curled-up dimensions of spacetime."

"But something happened," Ortosodl prompted. "Something changed?"

"Yes," she said. "Our focus turned exclusively to extragalactic planets. Vast networks of scientists were forced to drop their work. Some of them had poured decades of their lives into their projects. But, like you said, it was total war—nothing else mattered."

Ortosodl stared into his mug.

"Those planets aren't easy to find, you know." Pride swirled down her tentacles. "It's like finding a piece of hay in a pile of razors."

Ortosodl tapped a claw on the floor in amusement.

"I messed up the idiom, didn't I?" she asked.

"Yes, Cap—er, Andrea," he said. "I think you meant—"

"Yes, yes," she interrupted. "I know what I meant." She made a couple more coffees.

"How'd you do it?" he asked. "Find those kinds of planets?"

"How's your subatomic physics background?"

"Er," he said, laughing. "Not as good as yours."

"We figured out how to detect the interaction of exotic particles with variations in the expansion of spacetime."

"Okay." He tapped a claw on the floor. "I'm a biologist, not an astrophysicist."

"Hmmm." Andrea considered how to break this down.

"Spacetime expands, you see." She mimed with two eyestalks and all four of her hands. "It swells everywhere, *except*"—her body sparkled with yellow stars of excitement—"within gravitationally bound systems. Galaxies get farther apart, for example, but they don't expand. Planets don't *expand* away from their stars. Our bodies don't *expand* and tear themselves apart."

"I'm with you so far," Ortosodl said, crossing his claws.

"Extragalactic planetary systems change the expansion rate of the universe, ever so slightly, between galaxies. The theory started as drunken speculation in a pub on Sijar."

"The best ideas come from bars." Ortosodl tapped a claw on the floor.

"You nailed the head on that," she said.

"I think you mean that I 'hit the nail on the head,'" he said, tapping his claw even faster.

"Oh," she said. "That makes more sense."

"So?" he prompted. "The idea from the pub?"

"Oh, yes. Sometimes I get tracked to the side," she said as she made her way to the window. She studied the *Bismarck*, not understanding how anything she'd done in her life had led her to this moment.

"None of us could remember who said what first. But the next day, we had turned our drunken notes into a workable hypothesis. After a year or so we started finding them; extragalactic planets are all over the place! Our team discovered the Sandria System, in fact."

Ortosodl jerked upright. "You discovered Sandria?"

"My team did. And we knew the Phurlani were there."

They paused, sipping their coffee. Andrea saw Ortosodl working up the nerve to say something.

"I was there," Ortosodl whispered just loud enough for her to hear.

"At Sandria?"

He nodded.

"I didn't know that."

"No one ever talks about what they did before. For most beings,"—he hesitated and composed himself—"for most beings, it's too awful to talk about. I didn't know what you did either."

Ortosodl walked to the modulator. "Thymaxian ale," he said to the device, which promptly dispensed the drink. He took a long swig. "To loosen the mandibles."

"I was in the assault on the hatchery."

Andrea gasped. Her mug slipped from her grasp and shattered on the floor. "By Apatoa's eyes!"

Ortosodl stood up from his perch and stared at the wall.

"I've—" Andrea started, breaking the silence. "I mean, we've all heard about it."

"Everything you've heard is probably true," he said. "And then some."

He didn't turn to face her. She knew his compound eyes could see her perfectly well, but he talked directly toward the wall. "We knew a Viper team had gotten the data. And we knew they lost almost everyone on that mission.

"We'd all fought through the Phurlani retreat. You know, lots of mop-up operations against Phages. Not many of us had direct experience with the Phurlani—I did, and I think that's what kept me alive."

"You had over two thousand—"

"2,324 soldiers, to be exact," he finished for her. "Plus a Viper division." He took another long slurp of ale.

76

"The Vipers went in first and took out the Ghosts and most of the heavy defensive emplacements. Only a few survived." He paused. "They just got overwhelmed by numbers.

"You should see them fight," he continued. He clicked his mandibles together, trying not to choke up. She knew he didn't like to show his emotions, especially not in this context.

"It's like watching one organism with thousands of arms," he said, "with lightning-fast coordination and unerring accuracy. They are completely melded with each other and their weapons."

Andrea could see anxiety shiver through every ommatidium in his compound eye. He spoke faster and faster as if he wanted to purge himself of this memory.

"We went in right on their heels, right after the Vipers. The destruction they left in their wake was unbelievable.

"Everyone says the Battle of Sandria was the fiercest of the War," he said. "It was a long war, though. We were all, both sides I mean, fighting to exist. If they lost, they were extinct. They all knew it. We knew it too." He tried to slurp some ale out of his mug, but there wasn't any. He didn't seem to notice.

"We needed to exterminate them so we could live in peace," he continued. "That wasn't a secret either. They all knew it."

He looked around the room and settled his gaze on the front of Andrea's desk. "We were standing at the end. They weren't."

"There were only fourteen survivors," she whispered.

"There's more to the story," he interrupted. "After we broke through the Phurlani line, we still had to destroy the hatchery."

Dawning comprehension melted over Andrea.

"It wasn't just an egg broth. There were juvenile Phurlani too." He paused for a drink, but the mug was still empty. His compound eyes glazed over.

"They're born with it, you know," he said. He looked at her as if searching for an affirmation of his sorrow. "Innate xenophobia. They came at us, shrieking. Thousands of them. Tens of thousands. Maybe hundreds of thousands, it was hard to tell. There weren't many of us left, but we had plasma throwers."

Ortosodl finally realized he'd been drinking from an empty mug; he grabbed two more ales from the modulator and slugged them back.

"A lot of the juveniles got through," he said between swallows. "They're as vicious as the adults. Harder to hit, of course, and they just swarm over you, biting and clawing."

He made his way to a window and spoke to his reflection. "They squealed as they burned. Not like an adult. Different. I still have nightmares about those young Phurlani burning to death, still clawing over each other to reach us."

"Oh, Apatoa," Andrea whispered.

"It had to be done," he said. "I just wish I hadn't been the one to do it."

They sat in silence for a long while.

78

"Us survivors didn't see much combat after that," he said. He climbed back on his perch, two fresh ales in his claws. "Not a lot of close-quarters stuff, anyway."

"They gave me all sorts of commendations. They offered me promotions. I declined all of them. The War dragged on. I tried to get into escort and guard duties, even orbital bombardment missions—anything to stay away from the front. I turned down more and more promotions and command opportunities."

He swayed and almost toppled over.

"To be honest," he slurred. "I didn't want to move up. I kept reliving the hatchery, watching my friends being torn apart and eaten. I still hear their screams when I close my eyes."

He shook his hind legs, the Thymaxian way to clear one's mind.

"I didn't want to make battle plans and send people off to their deaths. I didn't want to lead more of my friends into another slaughter. I kept passing up opportunities until they stopped coming. I had a long, bright future ahead of me, and I squandered it. I survived Sandria, but my future died in that hatchery."

"Ortosodl," she whispered, "you're one of the best officers and scientists I've ever served with."

"Thank you," he nodded.

After several moments of silence, she asked, "How did you end up in biology and medicine?"

"After the War, I dropped out of life for a while. Lots of this," he held up his empty glasses. She got him another. It seemed like the polite thing to do.

"I resigned from the service," he said. "Wandered from place to place, never mastering or finishing anything I started. When I think about it now, I put everything behind me except for the one thing holding me back."

"How long did it take?" she asked.

"To work through it? A long time. I'm still working on it, really. But I had to find a new passion. I re-enlisted in the science track and turned to biology and medicine. I wanted to save lives instead of destroying them."

"Ortosodl. My eyes to Apatoa, I never knew this."

"Nobody really knows anyone," he said. "We all have demons in our past that don't fit in our future."

They stared at their mugs while silence filled the room.

Andrea broke through it. "We have demons in our future too."

"Yes, we do."

Another long silence.

"But not today!" She clapped her hand on the desk and said, "Or tomorrow. Or the next day!"

Ortosodl seemed to brighten.

"For now, we have to restaff our departments."

They stared at each other.

"That's, er," Ortosodl said, "anticlimactic."

"Yes, yes," Andrea said. "I know. But maybe we'll feel better if we focus on the little steps we have to make." She hoped this came across as intended; among Lysserians her words would be a gesture of affection and empathy.

"We have a lot of outgoing and incoming reassignments," she said. "That will be your job; I need to coordinate the command of the fleet."

He stood. "I'll get started right away."

"No. No, we all need rest. Let's take a couple of days to think about how best to proceed. Come up with some recommendations, and we'll compare notes."

She turned two eyes to the window, to the enemy ship. "The *Aristotle* is ours now. May Clyptod guide us true."

CHAPTER 11

Flip sat at a conference table across from two Viper generals: Kamari Larkin, a Terran; and Catural Botmeg, a Sildonian.

Sildonians evolved from plantlike beings. They looked like trees: about two meters tall, with colorful leaves creating a large canopy. They moved around on prehensile roots, and their uniforms contained a nutrient mixture for when they couldn't be in contact with soil.

Sildonians communicated by flashing their leaves in different colors and patterns. On Sildonia they could communicate in all directions with dozens of other Sildonians at once. Messages propagated throughout a population like waves, enabling long-distance communication. Flip's Sildonian friends told him how ponderous it felt communicating with other species.

"Air-talkers," as the Sildonians called them, "just don't have the ability to produce rapid and complex communication."

This unique language required a unique translation device. To communicate with other species, Sildonians wore giant black helmets that absorbed incoming sound vibrations and translated them into colors. When they spoke, the helmet reversed the process and produced spoken language on the outside.

During the War, Sildonian Vipers operated behind enemy lines collecting intel and conducting operations such as sabotage and assassination. The Phurlani never realized the Sildonian agents roamed among them, never considering them anything more than plants.

The Sildonian general, Botmeg, did not need its translation device here. The Vipers' nodes translated the languages directly into their brains; both species could understand each other in their native tongues or, in this case, leaves.

"I don't understand why you won't link our nodes for this briefing," Botmeg said.

"I've grown accustomed to speaking, General," Flip said. "I've found it provides a certain richness to communication."

In truth, Flip didn't want to let the generals into his mind. He didn't want them to know how much he resented being recalled. He didn't want them to know about the anxiety he'd had since the end of the war. Most of all, he didn't want them to know about the flashbacks—and not just from the war.

He'd been having nightmares since finding the *Bismarck*: he drifted alone in the universe, abandoned by everyone he'd ever known. The stars winked out, replaced by teeth. Star by star, one by one, the universe transformed into a Phurlani head looming over him as he hid in his closet.

"I can't argue with that, Captain," Botmeg said. "General Larkin, would you like to start us off?"

General Larkin turned her attention to Flip. "Everything you need to know at the moment is fairly straightforward," she said. "We need you to cross into the Nazi universe and infiltrate the Wehrmacht."

Flip held up his hand. He knew the generals wouldn't appreciate this gesture; he wanted to make them think he'd lost touch with his previous discipline. Maybe that would throw them off and make them spill too much information. Truth be told, he had lost some of his former discipline.

"Please, Captain," Botmeg said. "Save your questions for the end."

Larkin cleared her throat and continued.

"*Almost* everything we know," she said, "comes from the Reich's civilian broadcasts: entertainment, sports, and reports about their various wars."

"Yes, sir," Flip said. "This is in my wheelhouse. I can creep around and access their computer systems. But you already know that, I suppose."

"Yes, Captain, we know that. You are quite skilled at it," Botmeg chimed in. "However, that's not what this mission will be."

"I'm confused," Flip said.

"We thought you might say that." Larkin smiled.

That can't be a real smile, Flip thought. *She's not exactly known for her levity.*

"Your orders are to infiltrate the Wehrmacht by enlisting," she said.

Flip choked. "You want me to join their army?"

"Yes, Captain," the generals said in unison.

He tried to choose his next words carefully.

"You want me to enlist?!" *Damnit. Those weren't careful words.*

"That's right," Larkin replied. "All of your biographical information is in their systems. The file will, of course, be in your node."

"And I just go... enlist?" he asked again. This seemed like a high-risk, low-reward proposition. "I'd like to point out that I don't have any experience with this kind of operation. I've never gone 'undercover.' I've never even run intelligence assets."

"No one has conducted an operation like this," Botmeg said. "Though it could be said that the Sildonian missions were undercover, I guess." The general fluffed its leaves around, thinking. "But we went undercover as trees. So you're right. No one has done this."

"Ancients did this in same-species conflicts," Larkin said. "This sort of mission wasn't possible during the Phurlani war, obviously."

"But why me?" Flip protested.

"The Nazis were..." Larkin started. "Xenophobes. Not like the Phurlani, though. They exterminated other Terrans who didn't look like them or that didn't descend from some imaginary genetic stock. You're one of a handful of Vipers who meets the mission criteria to infiltrate their ranks."

Flip searched his node's database. The Alliance had five light-skinned Terrans to infiltrate the four different universes the Nazis occupied. Four universes that he knew of, at any rate.

"Why not send one of them?" he asked in desperation.

"We never said we weren't," Larkin replied.

Flip didn't like this. It fell outside his expertise and posed a great risk for both the Alliance and himself. He sighed and stared at the table. He couldn't decide if he was angry or shocked.

I'm both, he thought. *And sad too.* Dr. Sbob had told him that all his emotions were valid; he just had to feel and process them. He took a deep breath.

"Okay. What specific intel do you want?" Flip asked.

"Everything," Botmeg said. "Every scrap of information you come across."

"Everything is a lot," Flip said, sharper than he intended. "Even a node has limits."

"You're to gather information and send it to a relay ship," Larkin said.

"I'm sending data to a scatter-cloaked ship?" Flip asked.

The Alliance had invented scatter cloaks after regular cloaking mechanisms became obsolete. The old cloaks bent electromagnetic energy around ships, making them invisible. Newer cloaks incorporated anti-graviton emitters to mask the minuscule warps their masses caused in the fabric of spacetime.

The second part of that term, "time," prompted the invention of the scatter cloak. Ships could try to eliminate their gravity signature, but they couldn't hide the infinitesimal fluctuations their mass caused in time, as decreed by the laws of relativity.

The Alliance invented scatter cloaks to overcome this. Scatter cloaks spread a ship out over multiple dimensions in spacetime. They oozed through tiny, curled-up eddies of reality to evade enemy detection. The more dimensions a ship traveled through, the fewer temporal fluctuations it produced in "normal" space. The technology, however, couldn't eliminate the fluctuations altogether, as it scattered them into a finite number of dimensions.

"Not exactly," they said.

"It has what we call a 'null cloak,'" Botmeg said. "It spreads itself through all of a universe's dimensions."

"Interesting," Flip said. "So it has no mass."

"Correct," it said. "From *outside* the ship, there is no mass. However, inside the ship all is normal. In fact, from *inside* the ship, you can observe any and all parts of the universe simultaneously."

"This has," Larkin started before hesitating. "Uncomfortable privacy implications."

"I would think so," Flip said.

"Fortunately," Larkin continued, "the universe provides lots of uninhabited space to test with."

Flip already had questions.

"Yes." Both generals raised a limb to stop him.

"I know what you're going to say," Botmeg said. "'Why don't we use this instead of sending me?'"

"Yes, sir," Flip said. "Why?"

"Because we won't know *where* to look," Botmeg said. "Universes are big. There are some obvious places like their Terran system, but we can't interact with anything. We can only *see* things. And yes, we can see the entire electromagnetic spectrum, but the Nazis don't use that for anything other than entertainment."

"So I need to go in there and open things," Flip said. "I'm opening boxes and cabinets."

"I wouldn't put it like that," Larkin said. "You'll analyze the data, find data sources, and provide intel about where we should look."

Flip sighed. There was no point in arguing. Viper Command had made their decision, and Flip would have to just bob along the waves they'd already set in motion.

He leaned back in his chair and rubbed his eyes. "How do I report this information?"

"They'll be watching you," Larkin said, "from the relay ship. You give them a signal, they coalesce for an instant, and you send your messages."

"So they'll be watching me poop. Great." Flip couldn't keep his sarcasm in check. "How will I know they received the intel?"

"You won't," they said in unison.

"There are some things you need to know about the ship, though," Botmeg said.

"I knew it," Flip said. "There's always something."

Botmeg waved some roots—the Sildonian equivalent of nodding.

"There's always a catch," Larkin said, leaning back in her chair. "Wait 'til you hear this."

"You already know one of the serious drawbacks," Botmeg said. "The ship can't interact with or manipulate anything. On top of that, it cannot move."

"Excuse me?"

"The ship is fixed in space and time," Botmeg explained. "From the time it cloaks, it does not move. It's not affected by the movement of stars or galaxies. It's not even tied to the expansion or contraction of spacetime. It's a fixed point that physics flows around."

"So that means..." Flip started, taking in this new information. "That's where it has to decloak?"

"We call it 'coalesce' but that's exactly right!" Botmeg said. "Perhaps you have a physicist inside you."

"I don't know about that." Flip smiled despite the anxiety constricting his chest.

"Anyway," Botmeg continued, "as you surmised, the ship must coalesce at that exact point. If anything has moved into that spot, a ship for example, it can't coalesce."

"That seems extraordinarily improbable," Flip said.

"Correct again, Captain," Botmeg said. "It can cloak in intergalactic space far away from any natural object. A ship will probably not stop at that exact location. And even if it did, it is subject to all the natural forces I mentioned. It would drift away regardless of its intentions."

"Just something to keep in mind?" Flip asked.

"Yes," Larkin said. "That won't happen."

Flip sighed again. "Anything else I need to know?"

"No," they said in unison.

"I do have one last question," Flip said as he stood to leave.

"What's that?" Larkin asked.

"Who will be commanding this ship?"

CHAPTER 12

"Behold!" the emperor exclaimed. "Welcome to the most advanced ship in the multiverse!"

As eccentric as he was to the public, the emperor's real personality exceeded anything Kid could imagine. He bounced around the room, carefree despite any situation they'd yet encountered. In fact, the only time he'd seen the emperor acting seriously was during Kid's presentation.

A captain's chair sat in the middle of the room facing a large viewscreen that displayed Sufshiket, the largest planet in the Lysserian system. Closer to the viewscreen, another chair sat in front of a console. The room was otherwise empty.

"Have you ever dreamed of such a thing?" the emperor continued. "A ship immune to the laws of time and space!"

"No. Well, yes. Kind of," Kid said. He looked around the room, unimpressed.

"It's glorious!" The emperor kept talking as if Kid hadn't said a word. "We'll look straight up Hitler's stupid fucking mustache and count his boogers." He laughed and slapped Kid on the shoulder, a bit too hard for comfort.

"We have to find him first," Kid said.

"You can be sort of a downer sometimes. Don't be a party pooper. Think positive, lad!"

In their universe, the Nazis had discovered genetic immortality in time to save the Fürher and most of his cronies. Kid hoped they'd catch him, but he didn't want to jinx it.

"Don't let looks fool you, lad," the emperor said. "This entire bridge is a mod room!" He snapped his fingers, and the bridge changed to a living room, then to a beach, and then back to the bridge.

"The bridge is a mod room? And it controls the ship?" Kid asked, not believing what he'd seen.

"Yep. As a matter of fact," the emperor looked around in feigned secrecy, "the *entire* interior of the ship is one big mod room." He whirled in delight. "It's a Bacchanalian dream!"

"So we can recreate the targets we're observing?" Kid asked.

"Use your imagination, man! This can be anything!" the emperor said. He stopped mid-twirl, looked at Kid, and said, "But to answer your rather droll question, yes. It can be used for our actual mission."

The emperor bounded to the captain's chair in the middle of the bridge and dove into it. He spun around several times before coming to rest facing Kid. "I mean, it's not exact. If we move something in the simulation, the computer will guess the results. But it's pretty good at it. I mean, I, er, assume it's pretty good at it."

"Limited AI?" Kid asked.

"Of course!" The emperor sprang out of the chair and ran to the wall of monitors. "We wouldn't want it to take over the ship or anything."

Kid pointed down one of the two corridors leading off the bridge "That goes to the rest of the ship? Engineering, living quarters—"

"It does for now," the emperor interrupted. "We can reconfigure it however we want. Well, not engineering. There *are* some real parts to the ship." He looked around, hands on his hips, looking quite pleased with himself.

Kid dropped his suitcase. "I'm sorry, sir. But I have to ask you something."

"Of course, lad! What is it?"

"It's a bit awkward," Kid said. "I mean, we've been traveling and working together for a long time, but, er, what's your name?"

The emperor laughed and sat in the captain's chair. "You're one of the only people to ask that. Directly to me, that is."

Kid didn't know if that was a good thing or a bad thing.

"What have you come up with?" the emperor asked.

"What do you mean?"

"What do you call me in your head? Other than 'sir'?"

"Er, 'Your Majesty'?"

The emperor erupted in laughter. "Yes! That's what most Terrans say. What else?"

"'Your Honor'? 'Your Eminence'? 'Shogun'?"

"'Shogun'?" The emperor laughed and teetered on the edge of his chair. "That's a new one!"

"So," Kid searched for the right words. "What do you prefer? Or what's your real name?" He regretted the question as soon as it left his lips; it was much too personal.

"That's a fair question."

They looked at each other. Kid raised his eyebrows. "And?"

"Names. They come and go." The emperor waved his hands back and forth. "I passed mine onto my son."

He steepled his fingers under his chin. "I'm too old to have one name, I think. Am I the same person I was in the twentieth century? I know I'm not—so why should I have the same name?"

Kid was starting to become familiar with the emperor's existential tangents. "That doesn't really help me. We're going to be trapped—er, I mean working together—on this ship for a long time. Do I just call you 'sir'?"

"I guess when we're around other people, yes. But, hmm. Let me think." He spun in his chair, fingers still steepled.

After several minutes he said, "Lam."

"Lam?"

"Yes, Lam."

"What kind of name is Lam?"

"What kind of name is any name?" the emperor asked. "He was a friend of mine. From the twenty-first century."

"Lam. Okay. I have a nickname too."

"Excellent! What is it?"

"Kid."

"As in 'Billy the'?'"

"No. Just Kid."

"Okay, Kid. Is there an origin story behind that?"

"Not really." Kid looked around, trying to change the subject. "So what do we do now?"

"I'm glad you asked!" He gestured to the control panel. "Have a seat at your station, Kid, and set a course to Valbonia!"

"Excuse me, sir. Er, Lam?"

"Lay a course for Valbonia!" Excitement bubbled across Lam's face.

"Uh," Kid looked over the controls. "I've never done this."

Lam's mouth fell to his feet. "You're kidding me."

"It wasn't covered in anthropology school."

"Well, shit," Lam said. "Why didn't I think of that? You seem to know everything I know."

"But we usually talk about science fiction."

"Yeah. I guess so." A chair materialized next to Kid's along with another set of controls. "Pay attention."

"Um, Lam?"

"Yes?"

"Why are we going to Valbonia?"

Lam looked up from the controls, grinning from ear to ear. "Do you think we're going to a different universe without a cargo bay full of Rockeye beer?"

Kid stared at Lam in disbelief. "We can make Rockeyes."

"That modulated shit isn't the same. We're getting forty kegs of the real stuff, straight from the brewery. Being a shogun has its perks, eh?"

"Forty kegs of Rockeye Lager?"

Lam looked alarmed. "Do you think we need more?"

"No. I mean," Kid paused. "That should last a while."

Lam stared at the controls. "Do you think we should get more?"

"I guess it can't hurt, but—"

"Aha! That's the spirit!" Lam pushed some buttons. "There! A hundred kegs await us on Valbonia!"

"So how long is this mission supposed to last?"

Lam shook his head. "No clue. Now, watch carefully. This is how you plot a course."

CHAPTER 13

Flip hunkered behind a bullet-riddled pile of debris on a war-torn street. Only the haphazard stack of building pieces—all of them blown off the surrounding skyscrapers—protected him and his team from enemy fire.

He'd once again found himself trapped on a planet he'd never heard of, in a universe he never knew existed. The natives called this planet something unpronounceable for Terrans; Flip's node translated it as Rhart.

Rhartians descended from a birdlike species. They had two pairs of wings on their backs; the top pair had hands on the ends and could be used as wings or arms. They used the lower pair as "normal" wings, strictly for flight. Rhartians could also use their feet to grasp and manipulate objects.

This battle hadn't been in the plan. Viper Command's plan didn't involve Flip fighting in any battles. Viper Intelligence said he'd get a desk job and gather information for the Alliance's clandestine war. He should be in Berlin. Or maybe in Goeringville on Mars.

According to the plan, he should be anywhere but here.

They said the plan was airtight—infallible, even. He'd be shifting intelligence reports back to his home universe in no time. The plan, of course, fell apart right away.

* * *

"Ah, Mr. Marsh," the recruiter had said when Flip first met him several years ago. "You are assigned to the Wehrmacht infantry."

"Excuse me?" Flip replied in German, localized to his supposed hometown of Damascus, Syria. "My aptitude tester said I'd be an analyst."

"Yes, Mr. Marsh. I see you scored quite well in that area."

"I hope to serve the Reich in my highest capacity, sir," Flip said, then emphasized, "as an analyst."

"Yes, Mr. Marsh, of course. However, the tester's recommendations are just that. Recommendations. The decision is mine."

"But, my scores—" Once again, he felt his world—his future—slip into oblivion.

"My decision is final," the recruiter said, cutting him off. "However, I will place a note in your file. You may be considered for an early promotion. At the discretion of your commander, of course."

"My scores, though—" The mission had been turned upside down.

The recruiter ignored Flip's muttering and handed him a small chip. "Swallow this. It will confirm your identity when you arrive at your training facility. You have two days to report there."

Flip swallowed the chip in silence.

The recruiter stood and saluted. "Heil Hitler!"

Flip responded in kind with a fraction of the enthusiasm he should have.

(He later learned that the recruiter's girlfriend's brother was up for the same analyst position. She wanted her brother to stay on Earth. Flip was therefore dumped into the meat grinder.)

His new mission became jumping from planet to planet and job to job, vying for the position he'd been promised by Viper Intelligence.

* * *

The initial orbital bombardment had destroyed large portions of Rhart. The cities, however, had sonic shields that detonated incoming warheads.

Skyscrapers stretched upward in slender white spires, pockmarked with the wounds of battle. Perches, now broken, circled each floor so Rhartians could enter and exit wherever they liked.

Narrow streets crisscrossed the city, providing maintenance access to each structure. Each street was wide enough for three men to stand shoulder to shoulder, at most. There'd be no armored vehicles driving through the city—no vehicles of any kind except for motorcycle scouts. Smaller alleys, running east and west, connected the main streets. The Wehrmacht had ordered Flip's team into this quagmire to take the city, building by building.

After initial success, that plan fell apart. Units discovered that not all the buildings had ground-level entrances. It turned out that a complex network of tunnels lay under the city and that those tunnels provided most of the access for Rhartian maintenance and engineering crews.

The Rhartians had, of course, fortified those tunnels before Nazi intelligence even discovered them. The continued incompetence of the intelligence service amazed Flip. It seemed like they just didn't care about feeding battlefield intelligence to those who needed it. Maybe he wouldn't have gathered any useful information at a desk job after all.

The Rhartians had Flip's team pinned down on one of the aboveground maintenance roads. The general's new plan tasked them with breaching the walls of each target building, clearing the first and second floors, and securing the block for more veteran units to come in. The plan was not going well.

Flip's team started taking fire as soon as the first breach charge went off. The Rhartians' long-range weapons rained down, killing most of the team before the dust had settled. Parts of the captain littered the street and caked nearby buildings. Of the five soldiers left alive, only Flip had combat experience.

Shots tore into their meager cover. In yet another display of utter incompetence, they'd not been outfitted with any weapons capable of reaching the distant spires. The Rhartians had scrambled the Nazi communication system, so they couldn't call for artillery support. The Luftwaffe had failed to gain air superiority over the city. Flip and his team had to get themselves out of this situation on their own. He hoped they could hold out until the reinforcements arrived.

They probably couldn't though; the street couldn't hold any more men. All they could do was funnel people down this hole to get shot by the faraway Rhartian snipers. His new friends would be dead before any reinforcements could arrive. He had to get his team off the road before the Rhartians called in their artillery; he was surprised they hadn't already.

Flip scanned the area with his node. Five men, counting Flip, sheltered on alternating sides of the street. The hole from the breach charge was about four meters ahead of him. Their only hope was to take cover in the cross alley about two meters behind the last man in their column.

Short-range communication still worked, a miracle of miracles. "We're falling back to the cross street behind two meters behind"—Flip double-checked who the last man was—"Grisbaum."

"Who died and put you in charge, Marsh?!" Raedler objected.

"Everyone in front of me!" Flip growled. "Now listen up."

The five men hid on alternating sides of the street, all facing south. Flip, Claus, and Grisbaum cowered on the west side of the street; Raedler and Jonas, on the east. Grisbaum sat closest to the alley.

Flip decided on a new, potentially viable plan—the best of a bunch of bad plans, at any rate.

"We're falling back to that alley behind Grisbaum," Flip said.

"I'm going to Raedler's position; Raedler goes to Claus's; Claus goes to Jonas's; Jonas goes to Grisbaum's; and Grisbaum goes straight back to the alley. Everyone got that?" Flip knew they wouldn't get it.

"Yes."

"No."

"What?"

"Just crisscross to the guy behind you," Flip said.

"So..." Raedler said, pointing to Claus. "I run to where Claus is?"

Flip rubbed the bridge of his nose. "We're going to ping pong across the street, okay? Now, look across the street. See your buddy?"

Murmurs from the team.

"Just run to their position," Flip said.

"And me?" Grisbaum asked.

Flip couldn't believe this. "Grisbaum, just run straight back to the alley. Okay?"

"I guess so," Grisbaum said.

"Everyone got it?" Of course, they didn't. At least he could keep track of them with his node.

"Look around *carefully*," Flip shouted. "We'll move on my signal."

Grisbaum's neck exploded.

"God damn it!" Flip yelled. Grisbaum should have been able to see the alley without moving.

"Wait for my signal! I'll go first to distract them." With his nanites, Flip could recover from all but the most catastrophic injuries.

Raedler poked his head up, for no reason, and a Rhartian sniper blew it off.

"Damn it!" Flip shouted. Time to act.

He'd have to move slower than his nanites would allow him to so that he could draw the Rhartians' attention. He would only use his superspeed to dodge bullets. No one would notice him moving around the

102

bullets; he'd be too fast for the eye to detect. He just had to move forward at a reasonable, human pace.

"Go!" he shouted.

Flip slid underneath Raedler's corpse. Claus dashed to Jonas's position without drawing a shot, but Jonas deviated from the plan. Instead of zigzagging to where Grisbaum's headless body lay, he ran straight back to the alley.

It wasn't objectively a bad idea, except Jonas's new path lay along the sightline the Rhartians had on Flip.

"We lost Jonas!" Claus screamed.

"I know! Sit tight!" Flip tried to project an aura of calm to counteract Claus's growing panic. The general had pitched this mission as a stroll down Broadway, not a blood-soaked gutter.

The Rhartian fire stopped as they waited for Flip's team to make their next move. Flip scanned the area again and assessed the new situation. He concluded that the situation was dire; it wasn't a helpful assessment, but it was the only one he was sure of. He formulated a new plan.

Flip pushed Raedler's body out of the way and peered over his cover. Building debris and bodies littered the ground. The breach hole was now about six meters ahead of him, across the street. Rhartian towers burned in the distance, and smoke billowed over the city. Flip's enhanced vision picked out the Rhartian sharpshooters.

He looked in the other direction, toward the way they came. He noted similar patterns of destruction—fewer body parts, though, and one living body: Claus's. He hid behind cover just as meager as Flip's. The rookie soldier looked like he was trying to crawl backward through the wall, his legs kicking at the road.

"Claus! Claus!" Flip called through their comms. "Focus on me! Focus on me!"

"Flip!" Claus pleaded. "What are we going to do? We're going to die!"

"We're not going to die," Flip reassured him. "You still owe me ten marks from the poker game last night, and I intend to collect."

That seemed to calm Claus down.

"Let me think," Flip said. He scanned the area again. "We have to change the plan."

"What?! We just changed it!"

"They're setting up a crossfire in the alley," Flip said.

"How do you know that?" Claus asked.

"Wouldn't you?" Flip had done a decent job throughout the years of concealing the fact that his remarkable insight was aided by a node from a different universe.

Claus was silent for a moment, then said, "Fuck. Yeah, I would."

They couldn't go back to the alley. They couldn't stay here. The breach point offered their only escape, but Claus would never make it though.

"Okay," Flip said. "I have a new plan. Can you hear me?"

"Yeah," Claus said through labored breaths. "Yeah, okay. I'm here."

"Listen carefully. Count three Bavaria—"

"One Bavaria," Claus interrupted.

"No! Not yet!" Flip yelled. "Let me start over." He took a deep breath. "Do you see that pile of rubble to your right?"

"Yeah?"

"When I say 'go,' start counting three Bavaria," Flip said. "You with me so far?"

"Okay. You say go; I start counting."

"Yes!" Flip said. So far so good. "When you get to three, dive behind that pile. Make sure that pile is between you and *that* building. The one right across from you."

"They'll kill me!" Claus yelled. "I'll be totally exposed!"

"Don't worry about that," Flip said. "I'll distract them."

"But—"

"Shut up and follow instructions!" Flip barked. Claus stopped talking.

"Three," Flip started the countdown.

"Two." Flip could hear Claus breathing hard. He hoped his new friend could stick to the plan.

"One." Flip's nanites kicked into gear; time slowed. His enhanced senses allowed him to hear Claus's rapid-fire pulse and smell the piss that soaked his pants. He could see the eyes of the Rhartians perched kilometers away—see every flutter of every feather as they peered down at his position.

"Go!" he yelled to Claus.

Flip couldn't let the Nazis know about his nanites. To the enemy, however, he'd become just a rumor, a figment of a soldier's battle-weary mind.

He dashed to the dead soldiers near the breach point. He moved faster than any known being in the multiverse, save other Vipers. He collected three bombs and dove through the hole in the building before the Rhartians could even pull a trigger. Flip merged with his node; he guided it, and it guided him.

He hadn't felt like this since the Phurlani War. He'd missed feeling invincible.

He heard Claus taking a deep breath.

"One Bavaria," Claus said. The Doppler effect made his friend's voice sound lower and drawn out.

Flip scanned the room, his node processing the scene throughout the electromagnetic spectrum: visible light, infrared, ultraviolet, and everything in between. Nothing escaped his gaze.

The building his squad had been sent to breach was a civilian apartment complex. Perches and furniture lined the floor, walls, and high ceilings. His node detected a group of civilians in an apartment on the far side of the building—no wonder the Rhartians hadn't called for an artillery strike.

His node tracked Claus's position. Flip had to find a point on the interior wall across from Claus. Or rather, the spot opposite the rubble pile Claus *should* be hiding behind when Flip set the charge.

He raced against Claus's words.

"Two Bavaria."

Flip placed the charge, set the timer, and hoped Claus could keep a cool head long enough to get his count right.

Flip ran into the next room and piled as much debris between himself and the pending explosion as he could. He just needed something to take the edge off; his nanites could heal him as long as his body didn't get pulverized.

"Three Bavaria."

He heard Claus's boots scuffle in the pebble littering the street, then Rhartian fire raining down.

POCK. POCK. POCK.

He heard Claus sliding behind the pile of rubble.

Flip crouched down, his hands behind his neck. He took a breath.

BOOM!

The shockwave passed over him, popping his eardrums and bursting blood vessels behind his eyes. His nanites healed his injuries before he registered the pain.

Time to scoot, he thought.

He ran through the new hole so fast that he could see dust bending in his wake. Claus hunched behind his pile of rubble, trying to cover his vital organs; pebbles hung in the air, on a collision course with his body.

Flip threw himself on top of his friend. Blood trickled from Claus's ears and nose. He scanned Claus; he had a punctured lung, busted eardrums, and deep lacerations over his entire body.

He hoisted Claus onto his back. He'd have to travel slower—just a bit faster than a human—lest he injure Claus even more.

Rhartian fire erupted around him. A round hit Flip in the leg, shattering his femur. He dropped to the ground, spilling Claus before him.

Flip's wounds healed in a split second. He lunged forward and grabbed Claus by the back of his uniform. Rounds pierced Claus's arm, leg, and stomach.

Flip leaped through the hole with Claus, tumbled across the room, and set him down. They'd be safe here, at least for the moment. The Rhartians would think Flip and Claus had been killed and move on to the next battle—they would need to cut off Nazi advancements in other parts of the city.

Flip grabbed Claus's med kit and injected him with bleed stabilizers and organ regenerators. He'd probably survive.

Flip consulted his node. He'd been experimenting with giving it its own voice—a female one—rather than just having it project information into his brain. He appreciated his new confidante, even if it wasn't sentient. It wasn't much of a conversationalist, but maybe Flip could work on that.

What's the situation? He asked.

Captain Hofmann's platoon will be here in ten minutes, his node said in a soothing voice. *They've suppressed the crossfire from the alley.*

"Figures," Flip muttered. "That would have been useful five minutes ago."

What about the civilians? He asked.

There are thirty-two civilians gathered in an apartment. She projected a map into his mind. *There are fifteen children. The group is unarmed.*

Flip considered his options. The Nazis claimed they treated civilians with care and moved them to new worlds; Flip knew this was bullshit.

Show me potential escape routes for the civilians.

His node produced a map of the tunnel system. (It produced much better scans than the incompetent military intelligence agency.) The Rhartians had sealed the building's access point with concrete, perhaps not knowing that the building was still occupied. He located the end of the concrete obstacle and blasted a hole in the floor with his last breach charge.

He searched the room for something to write on. He grabbed a child's drawing from the wall and reached for the pencil he always carried in his pocket. It wasn't there. In fact, his entire pocket wasn't there, because his clothes had been ripped off during his supersprint. He stood naked in an alien bedroom with a child's drawing in his hands.

He fumbled around for a writing implement and found something resembling a crayon. With his node's assistance, he drew a detailed map of the tunnels with a path to the closest Rhartian fortification. He added an arrow pointing north for good measure.

He snatched up as much paper as he could find and hurried to the civilians. Due to his Terran anatomy, he couldn't produce most of the clicks and whistles of the Rhartian language, but he could read, write, and understand it.

How long do I have? he asked his node.

Six minutes.

He crouched behind a corner, just out of the civilians' sight. They perched on the ceiling, inside the door.

He wrote a note in Rhartian: "I'm human. I'm here to evacuate you. I understand your language if you speak."

He wadded up the paper and threw it into the opposite corner of the room.

Confused murmurs came from the room. A Rhartian flew down, uncrumpled the paper, and flew back up to the group. More hasty murmurs and hushes.

"You're an invader?" Flip guessed the voice was female.

Flip said one of the few Rhartian words he could pronounce: "Yes."

"Why are you helping us?"

Flip tore off a piece of paper and threw it. "I have my reasons."

The muttering became more intense.

"What do we do?"

"You heard about Petriski!"

"We can't trust it."

"It's going to kill us!"

Flip threw more paper. "You don't have a choice. You have to hurry."

More hushed voices.

"We can't."

"We have to."

"What about Lueg? You heard about that."

"They're monsters."

Flip recognized the names of the cities, but didn't know what had happened there. He scribbled another note.

"We're running out of time. I'm coming in."

He slid his weapon into the room and held another note above his head. "Follow me. Hurry."

The leader stood astride Flip's weapon. Her feet wrapped around the firearm while the others perched near the ceiling.

She ruffled her feathers, a common nervous tic in Rhartians. She'd found herself negotiating with a bloodthirsty enemy for the release of her friends; this wasn't something in her wheelhouse. Still, she held firm.

The siege had clearly taken its toll on the ragged and scrawny group. Many of them had lost their scaly feathers, which littered the floor.

"Free us or kill us," she said, "but let this end."

Flip handed her the map he'd made. She looked at Flip, amazed, and gestured for the others to follow.

Two minutes, his node said.

Flip led the group to the hole he'd made in the floor. The leader handed the map off to the Rhartian behind her.

"Go," she said. "I'll make sure everyone gets out."

"Hurry!" Flip pointed at his sign and tried to emphasize its importance.

One by one, the Rhartians jumped into the tunnel and flew away; only five remained when the Nazi reinforcements arrived and started shooting.

Four of the civilians burst into clouds of blood and feathers. Flip flung himself at the Rhartian leader, tackling her to the ground and putting himself between her and the soldiers as Garrit Hofmann stormed into the room.

"What happened here, soldat?" he snapped. "And where are your clothes?"

"My clothes, sir," Flip said, pretending to be out of breath. "Blown off. Explosion. I went looking for them." He gestured at the Rhartian leader. "They jumped me, got away." He took a few more fake gasps of air. "I just got here."

"Find and kill them," Hofmann ordered two of his men.

"No!" Flip shouted, hauling the Rhartian leader to the captain. She watched Flip and Hofmann, trying to figure out what was going on.

"I mean, sir, they caught me by surprise." He pretended to catch his breath. "I want to finish this myself. The tunnels are sealed off. They can't have gotten far."

A soldier returned with Flip's weapons and Rhartian notes. The captain considered the paper and gave Flip a sidelong look.

"Okay, soldat." He wadded up the paper and tossed it down the hole. He turned to address the other soldiers. "Give him his weapons and tie off a rope. And for God's sake find him a uniform."

The soldiers tied a rope around Flip and lowered him into the tunnel. They threw the Rhartian leader into the hole after him, and she fluttered down. Flip motioned with his rifle for her to walk down the tunnel. He picked up the discarded notes and followed.

After walking about twenty meters, he whistled to get her attention. He stuffed the paper into his mouth and swallowed it. He pointed his weapon at the ceiling and fired a few dozen rounds. The leader, cowering in fear, looked at Flip.

He spoke the only other Rhartian word he could pronounce: "Go!"

He ran back to his rope harness and, with one deft movement, secured it around his chest. He hoped the brave Rhartian would remember the twists and turns from the map. The group probably wouldn't survive the war, but at least now they had a chance.

"Objective complete, sir," he said after the soldiers pulled him up with the rope. Flip hoped the captain wouldn't send others to check on his work.

"Good work. You're going places, soldat." He looked at Flip's chest, where his name patch would have been.

"Marsh, sir. Phillip Marsh."

Another soldier ran up and saluted. "Sir, the charges are placed. We are ready for your command."

Flip's stomach sank. The building was still filled with civilians.

"Charges, sir?" Flip said. "We have the building. We just need to clear it."

"Your thirst for conquest is impressive, Marsh. But this building is useless to us. Move out."

CHAPTER 14

Andrea and Ortosodl sat in the Toga Party. They'd grown quite close over the years, after sharing intimate stories of their past traumas and achievements. They also made lots of new memories—both good and bad. She'd grown as close to him as she'd had to Flip. In some ways, her relationship with Ortosodl was even tighter. She had, after all, previously occupied his current position as first officer.

The Toga Party's festive atmosphere and freshly prepared meals attracted beings away from the ship's cafeteria. The on-duty crew ate at the cafeteria during meal breaks, so they could get back to their stations quickly. No one ate there if they didn't have to.

The Toga Party used modded food just like the cafeteria, but the cooks combined the ingredients in new and unexpected ways. No two dishes came out the same—a welcome departure from the standardized food the modulators produced. The restaurant stayed open twenty-four hours a day to accommodate customers from every shift.

The bar's owner, Ct'lin'ga, came from Laupic.

Laupicians were green disks who rolled around like a wheel; their treads rotated around what could be considered a stationary hubcap. Arms and eyestalks sprouted from each side. Most other species had a hard time processing what Ct'lin'ga looked like and how she moved. In the entire known multiverse, no other wheel-shaped species existed, much less a sentient one.

Andrea, for her part, found Laupicians fascinating. She loved watching them roll around, eating from one side, and talking from the other. How did their arms stay in place? How did *anything* stay in place? She knew someone who may be able to answer these questions.

Ortosodl was the foremost expert on Laupician biology. She didn't think that was a coincidence.

Clad in a bespoke toga, Ct'lin'ga glided to their table.

"Anything to eat today?" she asked.

Ortosodl wore a stupid grin. "Er, uh, not for me. Not yet."

"Me neither. Not yet," Andrea agreed.

"Okie dokie!" Ct'lin'ga chirped. "Here's another round, on the house." She set down two Rockeyes and rolled away; Ortosodl's gaze followed her. Andrea watched him watching her.

You don't need to be Lysserian to read his body language, she thought. She decided to say something this time—or maybe the Rockeyes decided that for her.

"You like her," Andrea blurted out.

Ortosodl nearly choked on his beer. "Excuse me?"

"I see how you look at her," Andrea said, "and how you stammer when she's around."

He sipped his beer and harrumphed. "I don't think so."

"I *do* think so," she chided. "I'm attuned to body language, you know. I'm a Lysserian."

"So you are."

"Ask her out, Ortosodl!" Andrea insisted. "I'm not familiar with Laupicians, but I'm pretty sure she likes you."

He shrugged. "She's friendly with everyone. That's her job."

"But she's *especially* friendly with you. Besides, it can't hurt to try."

"I don't think so," he grunted over his beer.

"Why not?"

"If she says no, it'd be awkward eating here again," he said. "It would be even worse if she said yes and things didn't work out."

"Oh, come on. You can't go through life counting on the bad stuff to happen."

"I've done that all my life." He stared at his beer.

"Yes, you have," she reassured him. "But those decisions brought you here."

"So"—he took a drink and smiled—"if I keep counting on bad stuff to happen, things will work out even better."

Andrea scowled at him. "You told me that you used to pass up opportunity after opportunity. You said yourself that if you pass too many up, they'll stop coming. *This* is one of those opportunities!"

Ortosodl glared at her. Andrea had never seen a compound eye glare at anyone; she found it unsettling.

"It's not fair to bring up my own points against me."

"Ortosodl"—she put a hand on his claw—"we've all had relationships. Dozens of them. *Hundreds.* Most of them don't work out. It's just math. It happens."

"Not to me it hasn't."

"Say what?"

"I've never been in a, er, long-term relationship," he said. "Or a short-term one for that matter."

Andrea lowered her voice to a drunken whisper. "You've never"—he swirled her eyes around the room—"you know..."

He laughed. "Of course I have. I mean, just never, well, it never really meant anything. Not to me, anyway."

Andrea had a hard time wrapping her head around that. Maybe he just didn't want to experience any more loss after the War. She was an astrophysicist, not a psychiatrist, but it made sense to her.

"Can we talk shop for a bit?" he asked, obviously trying to change the subject.

"Sure. I'm ordering nachos. Wanna share?"

"Sounds good. I haven't had Terran food in a while."

She punched the order into the table console and saw Ortosodl wistfully staring out at the crowd.

"What's on your mind?" she asked.

"Who's on my mind," he whispered as his gaze swept the room.

"I already know *that,*" she teased. "*What's* on your mind? You wanted to talk shop?"

"Oh, right. The Mjölnir."

"Ah, yes. Quite a piece of work," she said.

"I'm surprised we didn't come up with it ourselves—seems pretty obvious, when you think about it. A superluminal kinetic weapon. Elegantly simple," he said. "And the name the Alliance gave it is quite appropriate."

"We didn't think of it because it's too damn big," she said. "The thing sheds tachyons like scales shed its snake. It would have drawn Phurlani from every corner of the universe."

"It looks cool, though," he said. "Sort of hammer-like with the looping acceleration tubes and the long barrel. Makes the name even more fitting."

"Okay, I'll give you that," she conceded. "But it would take an entire fleet to protect it. And you'd get maybe two salvos. Four with a double-barreled one. Not worth a fleet."

"Then why are we working on it?"

"I don't know," she sighed. "Someone must have a plan."

A five-armed Padraean brought the nachos to the table, along with more Rockeyes. He'd worked at the Toga Party since before Andrea came aboard. He wasn't the friendliest being she'd met; he was a bit gruff, though not rude. Andrea could discern via his body language that he hated his job or perhaps just his life in general. He set the nachos on the table with two more Rockeyes and shambled away to drop off more food at another table.

"What's wrong?" Andrea asked Ortosodl.

"Excuse me?"

"You don't like the nachos? You look a bit disappointed. We can get something else."

"It's not that," Ortosodl said. "I was just hoping *she* would bring them out."

"Aha! I knew it!" Andrea shouted. Everyone turned to look at her. She turned light brown with embarrassment.

"As you were," she slurred. Cheers and laughter rippled around the room. She loved this crew.

"What are you talking about, 'you knew it'?" Ortosodl said, a bit indignant. "We've been talking about it for fifteen minutes!"

"Oh, er," she stammered. "Couldn't have been fifteen—has it?"

They munched on nachos and chatted about sports, discoveries, mod programs, and the state of the universes. As the Rockeyes flowed over their third plate of nachos, they reminisced about the good old days.

"I don't know if you're allowed to talk about this," Ortosodl slurred, "but what the hell. I'll ask anyway."

Intrigued, Andrea looked at him. "This should be good."

"When's the last time you saw Captain Marsh? Have you heard from him at all?"

Andrea rested her tankard on the table.

"I've talked with him," she said. "Once."

CHAPTER 15

Flip looked bad.

Andrea had met him at a pub just around the corner from her apartment on Earth. She could tell he hadn't been sleeping well. (His nanites could keep him awake and functioning, but no technology could extinguish a Terran's need to sleep.) He smiled, but it belied his anxious posture. She'd never seen him like this.

Flip sat in the darkest corner of the pub with his back against the wall. An empty stein sat on the edge of the table, and two full ones stood in front of him. Andrea slithered to the table and grabbed one of the Rockeyes.

"Is this seat taken, handsome?"

Flip stood, and they embraced.

"It's good to see you," she said. "You look, er, well." She knew that he knew she was lying; her body color betrayed her words.

"Thanks," he replied. "You look a lot better than I do, I'm sure. I hope you don't mind. I started without you."

"Not at all. I'd be offended if you hadn't," she said. "I thought maybe you had eyes on that sexy lady over there." She bent an eyestalk toward a Lysserian woman sitting at the bar.

"Her loss," Flip said, shrugging with feigned confidence. "How have you been?"

"Busy," she said and took a long drink. "When I heard you were coming back, I yanked on some yarn to get leave on Earth. It's been a long time, my old captain."

"Tell me about it," he said, raising his glass for a toast. "To old friends. Both here and, um, gone."

Clink and drink.

"I guess you're working on the—what do they call it?" he said. "The Gibla Drive? I am impressed."

"What can I say?" she shrugged. "We couldn't keep it secret, and we couldn't call it the Scary-and-from-a-Terrible-Universe Drive. I'm famous now, and I didn't even do anything."

"Don't be modest. You were famous before. That's why people believe you invented it," he held up his beer for another toast.

Clink and drink.

She leaned in. "What can you tell me? They keep the dark around me. It's hard to complete a mission when you don't know what the objective is."

"For starters, German beer is shit. They don't have anything like this stuff." Flip held up his Rockeye in admiration of Valbonia's crowning achievement. "You've no idea how I've missed these."

Clink and drink.

"So you've been touring the Eternal Reich sampling the alcohol?" she teased.

"Er, not exactly. But as often as possible." His tone brightened a bit. "What's your security clearance, anyway?"

"Omega 42," she said after another sip.

"Hmm. I can't tell you much. Sorry." He winked.

The Rockeyes started to kick in. The Valbonians made the only drink in the multiverse that could overwhelm his nanites if he drank fast enough and suppressed his node's automatic defense mechanisms.

"I figured. What can you say?"

"Well, *actually*"—he emphasized the last word for no apparent reason—"you can probably guess if you look through Earth's history."

She had done that very thing. Many, many times and in great depth. "It must be horrible."

"You have no fucking idea," he said and took a long drink of beer before ordering two more for himself. Andrea hadn't even finished half of hers.

"I have no idea," he continued, "what they do with the beings, though."

"You mean..." she started and leaned in, "like concentration camps?"

"I assume they have those, but I haven't found any yet. I can't figure out where all the beings go." He stared at the wall and calculated sums in the air with his finger. His node didn't intervene, and his hand eventually made its way back to his stein.

"Disintegration?" she suggested.

"They do that," he said, "but not enough. Sorry, that doesn't sound right. I mean, disintegration on that scale would change a planet's atmosphere. I'd see it."

"So, clearances aside, what do you *think* is happening?"

"I honestly don't know. The few off-world camps I can verify wouldn't hold a fraction of a single planet's prisoners. They're just gone." He took a drink and stared at the wall.

"What's *your* security clearance, by the way?" she said, interrupting his self-destructive thoughts.

He smiled. "I don't have one. *Officially*, at least."

"That's too bad," she teased as her body turned a royal blue. "I guess I can't *officially* tell you anything."

Clink and drink.

"Good," he said. "I don't want to talk about anything. I don't think I could handle it. The debriefings were rough."

"Alright, then. Let's get you caught up on all the baseball you've missed."

He smiled and lifted his fresh stein. "Go Reds!"

Clink and drink.

* * *

Later that night—the next morning, more accurately—Andrea and Flip tadered from the Terran pub to Andrea's home on Lysser. Fresh Rockeye drafts appeared on her table, straight from the main brewery on Valbonia. Flip had been chugging drinks all afternoon and evening.

"I have to say. When you invited me back to your place," he slurred, "I thought it was a bit forward. But this Rockeye-on-demand service is the greatest thing ever."

He stumbled to the bay window. It overlooked the Grombvelt Ocean, Lysser's largest sea. "I forgot how beautiful this planet is. How peaceful."

"We've had a lot of time to rebuild," she said, joining him at the window.

All three of Lysser's moons shone full, an event that happened once every 126 years. The largest, Apatoa, hung in the sky like a giant drop of Terran blood. It was flanked by watery, blue Clyptod and dusty, yellow Isfym. The colors and lights from the lunar surfaces reflected in the water, creating a sea of twinkling treasure. The scene stole Andrea's breath away.

"Yeah," Flip sighed.

"You know, Flip," Andrea said, "the Lysserians still have the records from before the invasion."

"Oh, yeah," he said as if he'd never thought of it before.

Lysser, like all planets during the War, had constant surveillance systems covering every square meter of the planet. The Phurlani could appear anywhere at any time, and defensive systems had to be ready to respond at a second's notice. The surveillance system essentially saved Lysser from being conquered.

Flip fell into a chair and closed his eyes. Andrea assumed only a Viper node could connect to the Lysserian security systems. Or maybe some kid sitting in their parent's basement had done it long ago.

Flip relaxed, and a smile crept across his lips. He looked happy. Serene, even.

Terrans, Andrea knew, would never eavesdrop on such a personal experience. Flip, however, was more Lysserian than Terran in many respects. Sharing these intimate details underpinned all of Lysserian culture, and Flip would expect her to witness this. She hoped he'd see himself through the surveillance systems and draw a good memory from it. She couldn't bring herself, however, to view the same footage. She'd just watch his reactions.

"Do you have the ball, Mommy?" he asked. She realized that he'd immersed himself in the footage—he'd become his younger self. Perhaps his node constructed this experience from the recording.

He made a sloppy swing from his chair. "Home run!"

A smile stretched across his face so wide she thought his cheeks might come apart. He giggled.

"I'm the Reds!" he yelled with the triumph and enthusiasm of a small child.

His head swung left to right.

"Let's swim!"

126

He must be at the beach, Andrea thought.

"Yes. I *know.* Always look for safe places." He stated an obvious fact in the way young Terrans do when explaining things to their parents.

A system of tunnels and bunkers stretched around Lysser, as it did on other planets. Everyone wore a "Phurlarm" that warned of invasion and directed them to the nearest bunker. Regional drills, both announced and unannounced, kept beings sharp. "Practice as you would play," Flip would say.

Everyone remained aware of their surroundings and kept track of what they'd do and where'd they go in the event of an attack. They had to be prepared to answer questions like: What if something obstructed their path? What if the closest bunker had closed before they got there? The Alliance invested in neighborhood coaches to review procedures with residents, visitors, and passersby.

Beings hid wherever they were able to: under desks, in closets, anywhere that might hide them from a Phurlani patrol. None of these things would keep them safe in the long term, but they might keep a civilian out of sight for an extra second. And that extra second could be the difference between life and death.

Even though the War had ended and Phurlarms had been relegated to museums, recycling centers, or personal memento boxes, everyone retained this situational awareness. It passed from the War generations to the new ones. It unified beings on all planets as a common part of their different cultures.

"There," he said, pointing, "there, there, and there."

He giggled and said, "That one, Mommy!" He must have pointed out the closest bunker.

His posture radiated pure joy.

"Let's swim already!" he yelled. "Okay, Daddy. I'll hold on tight!"

He mimicked the motions of swimming with his father, clutching his dad's shoulders against the Grombvelt's waves. He rubbed his eyes and spat air through his lips. More than anything else, he laughed. He sounded like an actual Terran child.

Flip sat up in the chair.

"No! I don't want to go home," he said, yawning.

"I'm not tired!" Even as he said it, he started drifting off to sleep.

"Daddy," he yawned again. "Don't forget my red team hat."

Flip turned sideways in the chair and curled around the arm. He fell asleep, deep in the fog of Rockeyes and pleasant dreams.

Andrea carried him to a spare room appointed with Terran furniture. She tucked him in and wished him a full night of dreams about his family. Apatoa knew he needed them.

She took a chest from the closet. After repelling the Phurlani invasion, recovery teams had scoured the remains of neighborhoods. They boxed up items they thought may be of emotional value. Most of those boxes sat in warehouses collecting dust, their owners presumed dead.

The Lysserians would never dispose of such things, though. They displayed the items, a few boxes at a time, in museums and documentaries, hoping that their owners or their descendants would notice.

Andrea had found a box from the rubble of Flip's old home. It had been cataloged and stored for centuries.

She picked a plush toy from the box. Flip had been clutching this prehistoric Terran beast when rescue teams found him. It must have slipped from his hands when they pulled him from the rubble. She'd planned on giving it to him.

Now's not the right time, she thought. *Whatever this is, the memories attached to it would break him.*

CHAPTER 16

Kid and Lam monitored the events on Rhart from the *Merlin*. They'd reconfigured the bridge into a huge surveillance system. They wanted to record the atrocities and provide clear-cut evidence to send back to Alliance Intelligence—information that would justify their mission. Something that, if released, would solidify civilian support among citizens of the Alliance.

Lam skittered across a huge bank of monitors covering the back wall. He wore an antiquated tan suit, no tie, and tennis shoes. The attire did not lend itself to his tasks: climbing, crawling, and jumping.

Kid rolled his eyes. Neither the unwieldy contraption nor the odd suit surprised him. Nothing Lam did surprised him anymore. Well, almost nothing.

Lam had constructed a mind-boggling ad hoc system of stairs and ladders controlled by a system of levers and knobs. He clambered around the construct, trying to adjust the various video feeds to make his surveillance more convenient. He appeared to be failing at that task.

Kid took a more direct approach and modded the rest of the bridge into a view of Rhart. He hovered over the city from which Flip had just been extracted.

"They're murdering civilians," Kid said. "I knew this would happen, but I hoped they'd stopped. They're the same monsters they've always been."

"Whenever your brain and heart are in conflict," Lam said while stretching for a knob. He turned it by the tips of his fingers and said, "always go with the brain."

"They're killing their own soldiers too," Kid said. "They're just throwing them into impossible missions. They're hitting their own troops! Why would they do that?"

Lam leaped onto a platform and grasped the rail with both hands. "I don't know for sure," he said. "Their comms are down; they probably can't get accurate coordinates. Could be to get them some experience. Would be pretty costly, though. Could be... nah. Couldn't be."

"What?" Kid asked.

"I once came across a species, the Ungiven. Bloodthirsty bunch." Lam rested his forearms on the rail. "Not as bad as the Phurlani, of course. No, no, no. But they had this ritual."

Lam inhaled through his teeth. "Let's move down to the street." He cranked another of his ridiculous handles, and the mod room zoomed to ground level.

The battle had long since passed this section of the city. Bodies and body parts littered the street. Debris clogged the already narrow passage. Explosions and weapons fire rattled in the background, providing ominous background music.

Lam strolled to a wall, crossed his arms, and leaned on it. Kid sat on a pile of rubble.

"So anyway," Lam continued, "the Ungiven had this ritual. I suppose you could call it a blood oath. They'd take their new recruits—kids, really—and throw them into battle.

"They were always at war, you see," he continued. "If it wasn't a different species, they'd go to war with each other."

"They didn't have unified planets?" Kid asked. "They were separated into nation-states?"

"Right!" Lam said. He crouched and rested his hand on the helmet of a dead soldier. "They'd send new recruits. Just like this guy, poor chap."

Lam wandered the street with his hands in his pockets. "Anyway, they'd throw these kids into combat. They'd get slaughtered, of course. Blown to bits."

A small group of Rhartian civilians jumped through a window frame and dashed toward the skyscrapers. Lam and Kid watched them run down the street and around a corner.

"I hope they make it," Kid said.

"Is that your heart talking?" Lam asked. Kid continued staring down the road. "Go with your brain, Kid. None of them are going to make it. Don't let optimism get in the way of reality."

"And the Ungiven?" Kid prompted, still staring down the road.

"Ah, yes," Lam said. "They'd throw these new guys. Well, not guys. They didn't have sexes, really. Fascinating species. They reproduced by—"

"Lam!"

"Oh, yeah, so anyway, this blood oath," Lam explained, "the idea was to bond. They grew up together, trained together, and spent almost every waking minute with each other. Just this small tight group and almost no one else but their families.

"When it was time to go, they swore a blood oath. They pledged themselves to each other for life."

"Really?" Kid asked. "That's odd."

"It is! Indeed, it is. But!" He held up a finger for emphasis. "But when they went to war, they had loyalty. Not to their State, but to each other. They'd see their friends slaughtered and so much merciless bloodshed.

"It would be so traumatic," he continued, "they formed an additional bond, a bond that superseded all others. Even closer than their biological families."

"So," Kid said, "maybe they're doing the same thing here?"

"Maybe," Lam said. "It's not a very Terran thing to do. But the Nazis have lots of potentially expendable young men. It's just an idea."

"I don't think that's what's happening," Kid said. "I think their commanders are just incompetent."

Lam chuckled. "I agree, that's a more likely scenario.

"However," he continued, "only two people survived in Captain Marsh's squad and *that* team had a Viper. Granted he was undercover, but still."

Kid paced. "You know what? You might be onto something there. Something that *is* more Terran.

"You bond with your friends," Kid said. "You play cards, drink, whatever. Then you're thrown into this inferno together. You do whatever you need to do to get out with your friends.

"They're rookies," Kid continued. "They'd never shot anyone. When they do, it's okay. It's just to get through the battle."

Kid moved the modded scene to a different street with an active Nazi squad and turned the sound off. Missiles arced toward faraway towers while incoming Rhartian fire decimated the Terrans. Men held their dying friends. Others cried to the sky, seeking mercy from a god who never answered.

"You get out, but only a few of your friends survive. Maybe none," Kid said.

Kid moved the scene to the Nazi position outside the city. He pulled up a chair and offered another to Lam.

"I'm gonna stand," Lam said. "Nervous energy and all that."

Kid continued explaining his hypothesis, "Then you're back here with other soldiers and support personnel. I guarantee they're all glad they're not over there." He pointed to the flaming city.

"Look there," Lam said. He pointed at a smoking tower. "Looks like it's going to come down."

The skyscraper crumbled as Rhartians flew out in all directions. They met antipersonnel flak and exploded as they flew for safety. The men around Kid and Lam erupted in cheers.

"And then you see that," Kid whispered.

"It's just a tiny step for these guys," Kid continued, spreading his arms to indicate the crowd. "For them, a building way over there fell down. *They* didn't do it. *They* don't feel responsible.

"And they don't feel responsible for those civilians being blown out of the sky. They're just *seeing* it. But they've moved a step closer to *doing* it.

"The men way over there," Kid said, waving his hand in the direction of the battle. "They were probably right here not too long ago. They made tiny steps, and now they're blasting civilians out of the sky.

"I bet if you asked them when they joined the military if they'd be doing that, they'd say, 'No way.' But they took all those little steps, and there they are."

Kid looked up at the clear blue sky, so peaceful and calm. Millions of Rhartians were slaughtered around the planet, and yet nature went on, indifferent to the suffering. Those things— the clouds, the cool breeze, the warm sunshine, the bugs flying from plant to plant—would long outlast the beings brutalized by the Nazis. It didn't seem fair.

"Kid! Use the brain!"

"What?" Kid's head cleared.

"You have to use your brain parts, not your heart parts!"

Kid jumped to his feet and slapped Lam. "How can you say that? Don't you see what's going on?"

"Of course I do," Lam said. "I know it's hard, Kid. I know it is. And I don't want you to get used to it. Don't you dare get used to it. But we need to keep our heads in the game. We need to record this."

"I know." Kid looked at the ground. He couldn't bear looking at the city again. "Sorry about hitting you."

Lam rubbed his cheek. "Nah, I probably deserved it."

They heard sonic booms as ships descended from orbit.

"Reinforcements most likely," Kid said.

Lam pulled an old-fashioned spyglass from his breast pocket. Kid rolled his eyes.

"No," Lam said. "No, I don't think so. Those are cargo ships. Supplies, maybe."

"They're headed over that way," Kid said. "Let's get over there."

Lam compacted his spyglass and tossed it over his shoulder. He smiled at Kid and snapped his fingers.

The new location melted the smiles from their faces. Lam turned the sound back on.

To their left and right, as far as they could see, Rhartians sat shoulder to shoulder with their wings bound. Directly in front of the prisoners, razor wire topped a tall chain-link fence. Guard towers cast a long shadow over the flock. Soldiers in the towers trained machine guns on the

Rhartians waiting for an excuse, *any* excuse, to open fire. Large landing pads lay beyond the fence and towers.

To the rear of the prisoners, looking toward the city, a large shelter stretched at least a kilometer to the left and right. It looked like a park shelter: open on the sides with picnic benches where soldiers lounged, played cards, and shared cigarettes. Kid had never seen a real cigarette; they'd been relegated to ancient history in his own universe. Officers in black uniforms walked between the tables with their hands clasped behind their backs.

More landing pads, smaller than the others, lay just beyond the shelter. Men milled around on the pads, carrying orange batons and wearing reflective vests. Troop transports approached from the burning city on the horizon. The men on the landing pads scurried into action and guided the ships to the ground. Kid couldn't figure out why they would have to do that; ships could land themselves without assistance.

"Hey, Kid! Come look at this!" Lam had found a chain-link door in the fence.

Kid picked his way through the suffering Rhartians. He could have the mod room make them incorporeal so he could walk through them, but that seemed somehow disrespectful.

He saw unspeakable suffering as he tiptoed through the crowd. Some Rhartians had died, still sitting, still clutching their children. Other children had been crushed by the crowd, their bodies ground into the mud.

Every once in a while, a Rhartian's head would explode, killed by laughing soldiers in the guard towers.

The Rhartians' eyes stared at the ground, at the sky, at the prisoner ahead of them. It seemed like they didn't see anything—as if their brains refused to process the scene.

"Look at this," Lam said as Kid joined him. "It's a tunnel."

A chain-link tunnel led from the prisoners to the landing pad. It could fit about ten Rhartians across, which seemed narrow given the circumstances. Guards stood outside the fence along its length.

"It leads to that big landing pad," Kid pointed out.

As if on cue, a cargo ship descended to the pad and extended its ramp.

Whistles blew from the guard towers. The chain-link doors slid open, and the first row of Rhartians stood. The modded prisoners ran through Kid and Lam toward the tunnel. Lam, it turned out, had made the prisoners incorporeal after all.

"By Apatoa's eyes," Lam said. Kid doubted the god of mercy would answer the Ancient.

Another whistle sounded, and the second row stood and moved forward. The flood of prisoners crushed anyone who lost their footing or couldn't keep up. When the line bottlenecked, the guards would use disintegration rods to clear it.

Lam nudged Kid back into reality. "Let's get in there."

"Right, right," Kid muttered. They stepped through the fence and walked to the ship.

The cargo hold had been sectioned into floors. There had to be about twelve levels, Kid figured, based on the size of the ship.

The Nazis herded the prisoners to the top floor and started filling the giant open room. The Rhartians had just enough room to breathe and not get crushed. After the top floor was filled with misery and desperation, the Nazis diverted the stream of prisoners to the eleventh.

The air was stale, ventilation meager, and the victims' cries deafening. The parents who'd kept their children alive thus far held them over their heads in an attempt to provide them with fresher air.

Nothing in Kid's research had prepared him for this. It was one thing to mod scenes from ancient history; it was quite another to watch it happen live.

At least Phages didn't feel this suffering, Kid thought. *Being a mindless husk would be better than this.*

Lam grabbed Kid by the shoulder and shook him. "Brain time, Kid. What are you thinking?"

"Why? Why are they doing this?"

"No, I mean look around," Lam said. "What clues do you see? Where are they going?"

Kid turned his attention—some of it—toward the ship itself, rather than the horrors held within. "This is an interplanetary cargo vessel," Kid said. "It only has slip drive."

"Good! That's good. Keep going."

"They have to be going somewhere nearby," Kid said.

"Yes! Exactly! Somewhere in this system."

"Maybe. I mean, yes..." Kid trailed off.

Lam snapped his fingers, and the mod room moved them into orbit above Rhart.

A Pelican-class intergalactic freighter, one of the hundreds circling the planet, towered over them, twice as large as the *Bismarck.* The smaller vessels, loaded with cramped victims, ascended from the planet and disappeared into the large ships.

"Okay," Lam said and turned off the mod. "I've seen enough."

"We're done?" Kid asked in disbelief.

"We have to report this," Lam said. He strode to his bank of steampunk controls.

"We can't leave. We have to follow them!" Kid protested.

"Those Pelicans have tach and Gibla drives," Lam said. "They can go anywhere in this universe or any other. We can't follow them."

Kid searched for reasons, any reason, to stay, to do something. Anything.

"W-we'll," he stammered, "we'll lose Flip! Yeah. If we leave and he leaves we, er, we may never find him again! Our mission will fail!"

"Flip's a big boy," Lam said. "He'll take care of himself."

"So that's it?" Kid felt trapped. He paced and rubbed his scalp back and forth. "We're just giving up?"

"We're not giving up," Lam said as he pulled levers and twisted dials. "We have to get this information to the Alliance. This is the first hard evidence we have that the Nazis are exterminating other species. Before now, we only suspected. This is what we've been looking for. This changes things."

"What do you mean, 'this changes things'? We're just fucking sitting out here watching the Nazis rule the multiverse. We haven't done a goddamned thing!"

"I'm going to let you in on a little secret," Lam said. "The Alliance has been waiting for this: a catalyst. We're going to take a more aggressive posture, but it will require patience. We won't be able to save everyone. But if we're meticulous, we'll be able to save a lot of lives."

"But not theirs," Kid said. His lungs heaved; he tried to hold back tears of rage.

"No, we can't. They're lost. I'm sorry."

"I want to kill them. All of them. The Nazis need to die. All of them!" For the first time in his life, Kid felt hate: anger deeper than a black hole and brighter than a supernova.

"Me too," Lam said. "But, er, calm down a bit."

"I *am* calm." Kid took deep breaths. He pictured the old Kid, the pre-Rhart Kid, flowing out of his mouth. He inhaled and filled himself with rage. It felt good.

He had always thought he'd been born at the end of history. The Phurlani War ended before his birth, and a life of peace and prosperity had beckoned his generation into a golden age, the likes of which the universe had never seen.

"We don't get to choose what we're born into," Kid said. "This is my destiny. Let's get started." He modded a navigation console and plotted a course to their home universe.

"Er," Lam stammered. "Uh, okay then. You okay, Kid?"

"I'm great, Lam," Kid's voice was so cold and distant he didn't even recognize it. "Things are clearer now than they have ever been."

CHAPTER 17

Andrea studied the looping acceleration tubes that gave the Mjölnir its hammer-like appearance. The destructive power of this weapon far exceeded its namesake.

Come to think of it, she thought, *it's mythical for us, but it is out there in the multiverse somewhere simply because someone made it up.*

Existence is so weird. I wonder if I'll ever meet myself. What if I have an evil twin out there? She stopped, realizing she'd just imagined that into existence.

Her thoughts turned to the matter at hand. *How long will it take to make this weapon smaller and faster? Can we find another lifeless solar system for our experiments?*

She set these questions aside for another day. Besides, research teams were already working on those problems. Her only focus should be on the test.

She needed to hit a city-sized target (with minimal destruction outside that zone) while orbiting well past the outermost parts of the star's planetary system. And she had to do it twice—once on each side of the planet.

Science and research ships waited inside the system to record the test's results. They'd cataloged all known objects and incorporated their masses into the firing solutions: planets, asteroids, comets, and even their own ships. Any unforeseen gravitational wobble—let alone a collision— would throw the impactor off course. Hit, miss, or otherwise, though, Andrea would have a wealth of data at her fingertips.

Ortosodl hunched over a panel displaying dozens of data streams. Engineers filled the room, all doing the same; only Ortosodl, however, fed information to the captain. She relied on him to summarize the data for her. They'd trained in the mod room for years, preparing for this moment.

"Status?" she asked.

"Everything is proceeding as expected," Ortosodl said. "The weapon's angular momentum is as expected. All tracked objects in the system are orbiting as expected. We project a clean hit. First launch in five minutes, thirty seconds."

"The safety nets?" she asked.

"All interception devices are ready."

Andrea, a renowned astrophysicist, refused to let any detail fall by the wayside. She'd placed Ortosodl in command for the last two weeks and isolated herself in her quarters to prepare for all possible outcomes. This delayed the test, but what did that matter? They'd spent years getting to this point. Two more weeks wouldn't matter. She wasn't going to let anything go wrong.

"Three minutes," Ortosodl announced.

Andrea felt the tension rising in the room. Half a dozen species exhibited the same emotion in their unique ways. Everyone in the fleet felt the same, she knew. The weapon had created a symphony of universe-spanning unity.

The loops glowed as they shed heat into space. The projectiles inside the loops were, by this time, spinning at many times the speed of light.

They'd not be able to keep this project a secret. Anyone looking in this direction would see a bright star of clearly artificial tachyons. No attempt to hide it would succeed. That, she'd told herself through the years, wasn't her problem—it was Alliance Command's problem.

She thought about the shadow war against the Nazis: raids against frontier outposts, convoys, and political leaders. The Nazi government believed a rebellion was brewing and rushed to squelch any details before they leaked to the public. The Alliance countered with clandestine propaganda. It remained unclear if these operations had any effect on the populace, but she believed persistence would pay off.

"One minute," Ortosodl said.

Andrea couldn't help but wonder, again, about how the Alliance would deploy this weapon. Even traveling at two hundred times the speed of light, the impactor would take almost a day and a half to reach its target and, unless escorted, could be intercepted and destroyed. In that case, what would be the point of using it at all? The weapon would have to get smaller *and* propel the impactor much faster. Or perhaps get closer to its target.

Ortosodl started his ten-second countdown. Andrea swirled with color, and her hearts raced.

"Three, two, one, launch."

An intense point of light, shining at every wavelength, flashed from the *Mjölnir*'s muzzle at the very tip of the hammer's handle. Tachyons flooded in every direction to every part of the universe.

"The launch is successful," Andrea announced to the fleet. "Start a seventy-two-hour countdown for the next launch."

* * *

The launch team reconvened the next day. Tension grew even higher as everyone waited to see how the impactor would perform. So far, all tracking systems indicated that it traced the exact ideal path. Andrea had the best engineers and scientists at her disposal; this experiment showed their expertise.

The second launch would be more complicated. The impactor had affected the course of every object it passed and, to a lesser degree, all the other objects in the system. They needed to track any new debris that had been ejected from the target planet in addition to any objects whose paths had changed as a result of the test. Small rocks or asteroids, for example, may have been jostled from their natural courses when the impactor sped by. All of these gravitational interactions had to be accounted for; a new firing solution needed to be calculated. The next thirteen hours would be a frenzy of data collection and computations.

Ortosodl called off waypoints and waved Andrea over to commence with the final part of the countdown.

"Ten," she started. She monitored the trajectory and astrometric data as she counted. Years of planning, calculating, and simulations came down to this moment.

"Three, two, one." She examined the communications for confirmation. "Impact successful. Damage assessment teams are deploying now."

Cheers filled the room. Ortosodl turned on the audio and video feeds from ships around the armada. Beings celebrated around the fleet. Hundreds of species came together to celebrate their shared victory.

"This," she said, pointing to the video feeds, "is what will bring the Reich to its knees."

CHAPTER 18

Alliance Command had ordered Kid and Lam back to Rhart after they filed their reports. They recorded every unspeakable atrocity until all the inhabitants had been removed or killed. Kid and Lam had been helpless to stop any of it, and this had taken a profound psychological toll on both of them. Kid, especially, had a hard time processing what he'd seen. While Lam had settled into the recon mission, Kid felt pressed to take action. Drastic action.

"Merlin," he said.

"Yes, Kid." The computer's lilting voice filled the room.

"Do you have the specifications for a Viper node?" he asked.

"Those specifications are classified. I do not have access to them."

Kid had expected this, but it didn't hurt to ask.

"Are there any that you do have access to?"

"Yes, of course. There are a variety of civilian nodes available," the computer said.

That was a dumb question, Kid thought.

"Are there any that can replicate the abilities of Viper nodes?" he asked.

"There's no way to know. The full capabilities of a Viper node are classified."

"You're being obstinate, Merlin."

"It's been my experience that I should interpret some situations literally. This seems like one of them."

Kid sighed. "You're right."

"What abilities are you seeking?"

"My wishlist is superstrength, superspeed, superhealing, and enhanced mental acuity." Kid punctuated each item with his fingers.

"The ability to extract energy from all sources," he continued. "And the ability to interface with computer systems of all types. Preferably without requiring physical contact."

"That's quite a list," the computer said. "Those abilities are available separately on the civilian market. However, they are not as compact as a Viper node, and the nanites aren't as efficient. They can't be placed in a Terran brain like a Viper node; they are placed along the spinal cord. Terran bodies can host two nodes maximum."

"Is it possible," Kid mused, "to create one or two nodes that can do all of those things? Even if they were a bit bigger?"

"Let me think," the computer said. Kid stared out the window while waiting. He'd not yet reached the point of no return, but should he be doing this at all?

"I have an idea," the computer said after a few minutes. "You could combine the brain and tech nodes and put them in your spinal cord. You could then replace your liver with an artificial one and embed a node in it to gain the other powers—"

"Seriously?" Kid interrupted.

"Let me finish," the computer said. "The second node can produce the other powers, but only one at a time. They will not be as efficient or as powerful as a dedicated node."

"What if I replaced multiple organs with different nodes?"

"Each node can only control its own nanites," the computer explained. "Too many nodes would clog your arteries. Terran bodies can only support two nodes."

"Has a Terran ever attempted what you're describing?"

"Let me check." The computer went silent again.

Kid hadn't anticipated this problem.

"There is no record of a Terran attempting to implant multiple nodes since my last sync with Alliance Medical Service."

"But has it been done in other species?" Kid asked.

"Other species have different physiologies. Some can support several nodes; some, none. Terrans can support two."

"Okay," Kid said. "The next step is more complicated."

"I figured it would be."

"What do you think I'm going to ask?" Kid said.

"You want to know if I can mod a team to do this procedure on you."

"Yes, well," Kid said. "Can you?"

"I can. But it will take several weeks to run simulations."

"Take your time," Kid said. "I'm not going anywhere."

* * *

Kid awoke in his bed, unable to move without pain coursing through his torso. His head throbbed and felt like it might burst at his temples.

"Merlin?"

"Yes, Kid?"

"How long have I been asleep?"

"It has been a week since your procedure. The emperor has come by to check on you several times. He is quite concerned."

"What did you tell him?" Kid propped himself up on his elbows, grimacing as a sharp pain pierced his abdomen.

"Various things," the computer said. "You had a cold, bad dreams, temporal shock, DSB."

"DSB?"

"Deadly Sperm Backup."

Kid buried his face in his pillow. He didn't appreciate the computer's simulated sense of humor.

"Where is Lam?" Kid asked.

"He's at the pub."

"Of course he is."

Lam was always at the pub. He'd designated it an "essential" part of their mission. Kid didn't like that he was there so often; he had pointed out that they should be as clear-headed as possible for the sake of the mission.

Lam made the counterpoint that they needed to relax and, more importantly, keep the beer cold.

Kid sat up and patted his feet on the floor. He could stand, at least, even if it felt like his brain was swimming around in his head. He could feel something new coursing through him. Was it power? The nanites? Everything seemed sharper, more vibrant. His neural nodes had already come online.

"Merlin," he said, "are the nodes ready to go?"

"Yes, Kid," the computer replied. "But I would recommend not using them right now."

"Are they at full functionality?"

"Yes, but—"

Before the computer could finish, Kid grabbed a metal trinket from his nightstand and shoved it in his mouth. He activated his superstrength and bit down.

His teeth shattered, and he howled in pain. He activated his healing ability, which quickly rebuilt his teeth and jaw.

The nanites that produce his superstrength had boosted his musculoskeletal system but had not increased the density of his teeth. He swallowed the trinket and activated his digestive powers.

The trinket tore through his esophagus. He reactivated his superhealing and then switched on his digestion powers. He doubled over and vomited blood.

His healing abilities could not keep up with the blood filling his stomach. He tried to alternate between his healing and digestive powers.

"Do you require assistance, Kid?"

He tried to respond, but blood gushed from his mouth. He gagged as it clogged his throat and filled his lungs.

"I assume that you require assistance."

* * *

Kid awoke, again, feeling even worse than the last time. He looked around. There was no blood on the floor and no holes in his body. The nightstand had a cheeseburger on it instead of a trinket.

"Merlin?"

"Yes, Kid?"

"What happened?"

"You were dying," the computer responded. "You ingested a pointy metal object. Your attempts to switch from your healing to digestive nanites failed. I modded a surgical team to save your life."

Kid sighed. His stomach grumbled, and he scarfed down the cheeseburger.

"To answer your impending question," the computer said, "you can eat anything that won't break your teeth or lacerate your internal organs. You should also keep your digestive powers activated if you eat something that would otherwise be poisonous."

"But—" Kid suddenly realized. "But then I'll have to keep my digestive nanites active, or else what I've eaten might kill me."

"Yes, Kid. I told you that there would be significant limitations to your new abilities."

"Switching powers will be more difficult than I imagined," he thought aloud.

"Yes, Kid. I believe I mentioned that several times, as well."

Kid got out of bed and got dressed. "Where is Lam?"

"The emperor is in the pub."

"Of course, he is," Kid grumbled.

* * *

Kid stumbled through the wooden door at the front of the bar. Terrans packed the place, chatting, dancing, and generally carousing.

"Kid!" they all cheered.

Kid grabbed his forehead. "Can we not do that?"

"Too late, my man!" Lam leaped to the door and put his arm around Kid. "We already did! Glad to see you out of bed."

The barkeep, Bastyeon, looked up from washing glasses. "Hey there, trouble. The usual?"

"Uh," Kid said. A headache pounded from behind his eyes. He'd set his healing nanites to deal with it, but they had limited effect. Perhaps the headache was from anxiety. He didn't know if the nanites could help, and if they could, he didn't know how to make them do it.

"Sure, Bastyeon. But a pitcher of water first. How've you been?"

"You're lookin' at it," Bastyeon said, filling a pitcher of water.

Lam clapped Kid on the shoulder, a bit too hard, and whispered, "Did you, you know?"

"Know what?" Kid didn't feel like playing games. He wanted water and anti-anxiety medicine. Then beer.

"The, uh," Lam leaned in closer. "The deadly... you know."

Kid growled and cursed the computer through his tech node. "Yes, Lam. It's all taken care of."

"Excellent!" Lam exuded the word "party" from every pore of his body. Kid couldn't tell if it was genuine or forced—maybe it was a bit of both.

Wood and revelers festooned the inside of the bar. After entering the heavy wooden doors, patrons were greeted with a long, shiny, U-shaped wooden bar surrounded by cushioned bar stools. To the right, wooden tables and chairs lined the wood-paneled wall. Wood beams gave the illusion of a second floor. To the left, high-top tables lined a wooden divider. On the other side of the divider, modded beings danced while a band played. Each night was a different band—usually a rotation of the Beatles, the Rolling Stones, and Aerosmith, though others made appearances as well.

"If you can have anyone," Lam always said, "have the best."

A short hall led to the kitchen at the open end of the bar, and another short hall led to the kitchen. Bathrooms came off the side of the hallway.

"The food is modded," Kid had said, "and these Terrans don't poop."

"It's the ambiance, Kid. Ambiance!" Lam had said. "Also, they *do* poop. I made them that way."

A door on the right led to a patio. An awning covered part of it; the uncovered part basked either under a warm blue sky or a dark clear night, depending on Lam and Kid's whims.

The patio opened to a parking lot and a strip mall. A four-lane highway ran nearby. Beyond that, trees shrouded apartment complexes. Kid found this rather droll.

"Realism!" Lam had said. "My fidelity to a very special place." Lam remained tight-lipped about what he had meant by that. When he was drunk, his gaze always drifted to the buildings beyond the highway.

"What's over there?" Kid had asked time and again.

"It's just a place," Lam would answer. "A place that's gone, just like any other."

CHAPTER 19

Time eased Flip's trauma, at least to the point where he could push it away from his thoughts. The nightmares, however, still flowed from his node every night and trapped him in the Rhartian War. He relived the street fighting; the tunnel fighting; and the brutal floor-to-floor, lethal tug-of-war. The nightmares came right along with the Phurlani, the Phages, and the countless other wars the Reich had thrown him into. His mind spiraled downward, toward what he didn't know.

To top it all off, he now fought against yet another species that he didn't want to destroy: the Jassicans. At least this time he'd only be dropping off troops and coming back for more. That was the plan, at least.

His place in the multiverse felt smaller and smaller each day. He sat in a hanger on a moon that orbited a planet that, in turn, orbited a distant star that, in *its* turn, orbited the center of a galaxy that, itself sped through a universe that, finally, waved in the Bulk of the multiverse.

He felt so insignificant that he might as well have never existed at all. Sometimes he wished he hadn't. He couldn't escape the multiverse, though. It doomed him to repeat these atrocities ad infinitum. Even if he didn't know those other Flips, they would suffer for eternity.

He watched a transmission showing the first stages of a Nazi orbital dominance assault around the target planet. The Jassican Association needed this planet to maintain their tachyon-suppression network; the Reich needed to destroy it. As with all things in war, someone had to lose, but Flip lost no matter the outcome. He spiraled further and further away from who he once was.

* * *

The Jassican Association consisted of millions of semi-autonomous civilizations. From time to time, they came together on the Jassican homeworld—the seat of their government—to bicker, argue, and generally irritate the hell out of each other.

The Jassican species, by far, represented the most numerous species in the Association; they founded the group and dominated its government. They had conquered and assimilated the universe until, after millennia of intergalactic diplomatic animosity, they decided to form a proto-democracy.

Jassicans became the dominant species because they could shapeshift. They modified their external and internal physiology everywhere they went. A Jassiccan's natural state looked like a meter-and-half-tall pear, and their coloring varied with their whims. They scooched around on their ringed base, sucking up nutrients as needed. Their shapeshifting abilities, however, meant they could eat just about anything they wanted; this ability allowed them to colonize places inhospitable to other species. Rumors circulated that they could even live in the vacuum of space.

The Eternal Reich hit the Jassican Association the way a tsunami hits a cliff: with lots of sound and fury but, in the end, the cliff remained. Billions of beings died, but the Association's diversity of species, technologies, and cultures provided an advantage the Nazis couldn't blitz their way through.

Within a few years of the invasion, the Jassicans invented a tachyon-suppression field much like the one used by the Universal Alliance. They converted strategically located planets into giant tachyon suppressors, which allowed them to shut down tach comms and drives on interstellar scales.

This network had brought Flip's armada to this system. If the Reich could knock out the suppressor here, a bubble of space many light-years across would be freed up for tach drive—which meant the Reich could assault Association strongholds in populated systems.

The armada, however, had to poke along on slip drive to get there. They'd traveled for—ten? Eleven? Nine?—years. Without tach drive, the armada flip-flopped between super- and subluminal travel. The relativistic effects wreaked havoc with the crew's sense of time. Nobody could agree on how much "regular" time had passed, and no one trusted the instruments meant to tell them.

The Association had another ace up its amorphous sleeve. They had a technology, unknown to Nazi scientists, that allowed them to appear and disappear inside a tachyon-suppression bubble. Association fighters came out of nowhere to harass the armada. The attacks coincided with bizarre anomalies. Scans showed nothing but a tear in spacetime. It wasn't a wormhole, tach drive, or a hypothetical slingshot system; the Reich had figured out what it *wasn't* but couldn't figure out what it *was.*

* * *

Flip never made it to a cushy intelligence job, but at least he'd pulled himself out of the infantry. On the other hand, he was transferred into various nefarious and unpleasant intelligence jobs. He didn't like thinking about those positions; those memories tormented him even more than the ones of his urban warfare.

One day, when the Jassicans attacked an intelligence site, Flip jumped into a one-man, short-range Adler fighter to prove he could do more than interrogate prisoners. He destroyed most of the attacking force by himself.

He went on to demonstrate exceptional ability as a fighter pilot, mastering the Adler fighters used by the Weltraumkraft to protect the fleet. He'd become a top ace and even a media darling in the Nazi propaganda machine.

He wondered what Alliance Intelligence made of this. His mission was to keep a low profile and collect intelligence. So far, he'd achieved the exact opposite. The new job came with many—fringe—benefits on the various worlds and cities he visited. At least he wasn't lonely.

Flip played up his celebrity status to weasel his way into piloting the dropship of this particular mission. It came down to the fact that the Reich needed Flip and they needed to keep him happy. The Jassican War had become a stalemate, and the Reich needed to keep him producing propaganda on the homefront. They had recognized that Flip had special abilities, though they could never guess the source. They knew he could disappear at any moment to appease any whim, and they knew he'd gotten burned out fighting all over the multiverse.

Media outlets claimed that Flip had earned this "retirement" and could be recalled at any moment. They then promptly assigned him to this mission; they knew that he wouldn't be able to escape once inside a tachyon-suppression field.

Flip turned his attention back to the orbital attack.

Nests—giant cone-shaped ships—disgorged a never-ending stream of small glinting objects from their points. These objects—Sparrows—were networked smart bombs. They worked together to ensphere and destroy their targets. A flock swarmed its target and slammed into it from all sides. No one could survive a Sparrow attack, and if by some miracle they ended up in an insulated piece of the ship, they wouldn't get far, because the Nests would gobble them up.

The Nests followed the trail of destruction; graviton beams guided debris into their maws. The huge cones reduced the carnage into its component atoms and used it to build more Sparrows.

It was a cycle of death.

The Sparrows paved the way for the dropships, while Adler fighters escorted the invasion force. Flip had a thousand Nazi troops in his care, and he intended to land them safely on the target planet. He never thought protecting Nazis would be his primary mission objective. How had he fallen this far?

His many years of service to the Reich weighed on him. He told himself that the things he'd done served the greater good. He remembered and clung to Andrea's encouragement: he had to believe that his actions would bring victory to the Alliance.

He didn't feel like he'd done anything useful in a long time, though. He couldn't transmit anything to the *Merlin* from inside the suppression bubble. It wouldn't matter anyway because he had no idea where the ship was. He didn't know if Kid and the emperor were even in this universe. He didn't know if anyone in the Alliance knew where he was or what he was doing.

Or if they cared, for that matter.

There had to be an endgame for his mission. He didn't know what it would look like or how it would play out. The memories, however, would haunt him for the rest of his long, pathetic life. He had one chance at redemption: to excel at this job and somehow get useful information back to the Alliance. If the armada made it back, maybe he could use his fame to weasel into the intelligence position he'd been trying to get for years.

He had a chance here. The Jassicans placed their most decorated leader, General L'Lac, in command of this sector. He defeated the Reich in every battle he'd led.

The Nazis knew him by a different name: the Coily Bastard. He wore candy cane patterns around his body and often took the form of a large spring. Flip had lost many, many friends to the Coily Bastard. If Flip could get information on him here, something new about his tactics, his location, or even what he had for breakfast, it would be a major coup. One that could make Flip's stay in the Reich a little more bearable.

The intercom interrupted his thoughts of revenge. "All personnel, report to dropships. Launch in ninety minutes."

CHAPTER 20

Kid's plan to master his nodes unfolded like a rose: slowly and delicately. He did his best to avoid its thorns.

Kid's commander/roommate/drinking partner had pushed his patience practically to its breaking point. Between drinking, debauchery, and listening to Lam's inebriated, mysterious memories, Kid struggled to find time to work on his plan. He had downloaded billions of petabytes of data on artificial intelligence and security algorithms, and processing them took a great deal of quiet time.

His patience bore fruit, though: he'd reached phase two of his plan to seize control of the *Merlin*'s computer.

He'd groomed the computer to "trust" him by playing games with it through his node. They'd become friends, of a sort; Kid meant to exploit this relationship.

"Merlin," Kid said, summoning the AI.

"Yes, Kid?" He'd grown to love its accent.

"You wanna play Conquer the World?"

Unlike a mod room, when playing games, Flip's consciousness would enter the computer; he melded with it for seamless communication.

"I'd love to!" the computer said. "That's my favorite game."

The computer loved this particular game because it was Kid's favorite. It simulated emotions by mirroring Kid's preferences.

"What parameters should we set?" the computer asked.

"Let's do an open start," he said. In an open-start game, the players harvested materials, built a base, grew an economy, and tried to conquer the world. They could cooperate against computer-generated opponents, or they could compete against each other and artificial opponents.

"That sounds fantastic!" the computer enthused. "Shall we exchange plans to facilitate our starting strategies?"

"No," Kid said. "Let's do this the old-fashioned way. Besides, I might want to mix things up."

A simulated laugh filled Kid's quarters. "Very well. I've started a new game file."

Kid found himself hovering over an empty ocean; a distant green line marked the shore. He created some ships and sent them in that direction. He usually started with some colony ships to indicate he wanted to play a cooperative game; he had spent thousands of hours developing this pattern to lull the computer into using the same strategy.

As Kid predicted, the computer spawned colony and forager units and sent them to the rendezvous. Together, they'd build their base and expand. Later, they'd encounter some third party that ran in an isolated portion of the computer.

Tiny ships and beings swarmed the beach and set about making their tiny homes and tiny factories. They spent their time in tiny taverns and had even tinier children. They lived out their tiny lives never knowing they didn't really exist.

Kid spawned a submarine from Earth's Second World War. He decked it with windows, lights, and lasers—because, why not? He hopped in the sub and dove into the ocean's depths. The game would turn the security systems into constructs that matched the simulated environment. If Kid dove fast enough, he could break through the *Merlin*'s basic security algorithms. He watched out the window, his surroundings illuminated by the vessel's powerful searchlights. The sub rocked as a shimmer shot past the window.

He'd breached the first level. Easy peasy lemon squeezy... for now.

CHAPTER 21

Flip's convoy of dropships stretched about one light-minute long. Adler fighters buzzed between them like bees protecting their hive, intercepting squads of Jassican fighters and superluminal missiles. Even though the Jassicans popped in and out of spacetime, their resistance seemed too light for such an important target.

The plan called for the convoy to orbit the planet once and then land at the only known entrance to the subterranean suppressor. The Wehrmacht would land a considerable force and storm the Jassican defenses.

The convoy passed behind the artillery ships and began its descent. Flip's ship came in on its left side, and he had a clear view of the planet unofficially named Todesfalle. Desert covered most of it; green vegetation hugged the coastlines around the many freshwater seas.

The Reich didn't have good intelligence on what ground defenses the Jassicans had deployed. The most common installations were missile silos that targeted ships in orbit. Beyond that, Nazi reconnaissance teams couldn't get close enough to see much.

Smaller task forces would land at other areas around the planet to investigate suspected fortifications. The entrance installation, though, was the only confirmed target they had, and it was the only target they really needed.

The Nests spread a net of Sparrows along the flight path to shield against missiles. Based on experience, Flip expected this shield to prove quite effective.

Huge warships, just like the *Bismarck*, rained gunfire onto Jassican ground emplacements. With his enhanced nanites, Flip could see the mushroom clouds blooming over the desert. Destroyers crushed the few orbital defense platforms the Jassicans had deployed, and Flip's convoy raced behind the battle unscathed.

The Jassicans must know this defense is futile, he thought. *Why waste this ordinance in orbit? Why not wait—*

An explosion interrupted Flip's thought. Fire filled his window. Debris whizzed by, and shrapnel tore into his ship. Alarms blared from his control panel.

"What the fuck!" Flip yelled as he regained control and checked his instruments. Shrapnel had carved a hole through one of the troop compartments large enough to fly an Adler through. A quarter or more of his troops had been blown out of the ship.

Flip turned a dial. "This is Dropship 2-9-A-7. I've been hit."

"Roger, 2-9-A-7—" Another large explosion cut off the transmission. Flip's ship lost attitude control, and it dove toward the planet's atmosphere. He could now see what was happening.

Huge explosions had fractured the shield along the flight path—where the Sparrows were supposed to be protecting the invasion fleet. Two Nests, turning back from their finished missions, were hit. They plummeted into Todesfalle's atmosphere along with destroyers, transports, and other parts of the invasion force. Goosebumps flared over Flip's skin; he felt like he'd fallen off a cliff.

Death doesn't frighten a Viper very often, but Flip felt it creeping up on him now.

"Dropship 2-9-A-7 to control—" A dropship careened down just in front of him, cutting off his report. He jerked the controls to avoid the dying ship. "Control! Do you copy?"

"Go ahead, 2-9-A-7."

"Heavy resistance." Flip struggled to regain control of his ship.

"Acknowledged, 2-9-A-7. Continue as planned."

Fuck the plan, he thought.

"Control, they are using fusion and antimatter mines to clear the cover. They must have been cloaked. Four dropships down, visual confirmation. Two—correction, *three*—Nests falling out of orbit. Sparrow cover is minimal."

"Marsh! Come in." Another voice came through the comms.

"Riepe? Is that you?"

"Yeah, buddy. Sorry to interrupt your love letter to control, but your ship is coming apart."

"Say again, Riepe?"

An explosion tore through another dropship off Flip's starboard side.

"Riepe? You there?"

"Yep. But not for long at this rate. I'm right behind you. You've got a cracked bulkhead. You have to get out of orbit right now."

Flip's node made some calculations. Between the damage he'd taken and the fuel bleeding out of the ship, he would not be able to break orbit.

Time for a new plan, Flip thought. He had only one option: to land on Todesfalle.

After all he'd been through—refugee, warrior, spy, hero, villain—he was about to die in a smoking crater on a planet in the middle of nowhere. No one would even know what happened to him. He thought it seemed appropriate.

"My ship is fine," Riepe said. "I've lost a couple of compartments, but I have full flight control. I can come down right behind you, buddy."

"I'm looking for a site. Standby," Flip punched some buttons and ran a scan to find the steepest survivable trajectory.

"Keep me in the loop, bud, but make it fast," Riepe said.

Mines exploded all around them. Ships broke apart and dove to their doom.

"Okay, I've got it," Flip said. "Transmitting."

"Received." A short pause. "You sure about this?" Riepe Harwig, pilot extraordinaire, didn't sound confident in the plan: two ninety-degree turns to enter the atmosphere in the opposite direction from their current heading. The g-forces alone could rip them apart.

"We have to," Flip said. "Otherwise, we'll be blown to bits before we even hit the atmosphere. They've committed their big bombs around our planned route. Agreed?"

"Agreed," Riepe said. "But you owe me a drink. Make that several drinks."

"See that lake along the coordinates?"

"Let me guess," Riepe said. "We're going to skim across it before hitting the beach, right? Exactly what I was thinking. And we'll have water, at least."

"That's the drink I owe you," Flip joked. Riepe, cool as a cucumber, laughed.

"Okay," Riepe said. "We're coming up on the first turn window. Give me the countdown and I'll cut inside you. Sending you my flight path."

"Got it," Flip replied, all business now. "Three, two, one, mark."

Flip wrenched the controls, turning the ship down and to the left. As he did, he could see the full scope of the disaster: the entire convoy fell in tatters toward the planet, their remains burning in the atmosphere.

"Control. This is dropship 2-9-A-7 and 2-9-A-12. We are attempting a crash landing. Repeat, we are attempting a crash landing. Sending our flight plan." Flip struggled to talk, guide his crippled ship, and send the data at the same time.

"Acknowledged," came the calm reply. "2-9-A-7 and 2-9-A-12 attempting planetfall at designated coordinates. Will advise any surviving ships."

"Any?" Flip asked.

"Doesn't sound very optimistic," Riepe replied.

Flip saw Riepe's ship on his left. Riepe struggled to compensate for multiple hull breaches. Jets of pressurized gas spewed from the crew compartments, and fuel streamed from one of his engines.

Good Isfym, Flip thought. *If he said his ship is fine, how the hell does my ship look?*

"Riepe. There's been a change in plans: I'll cut high; you go low."

"It's like you read my mind, buddy. Coming to the second waypoint in three, two, one, mark!"

Flip angled his ship down and to the left again, cutting back inside Riepe's path. He saw pieces of his friend's ship fly off, lost to the tremendous g-forces.

I hope no one is left in the troop compartments, Flip thought before leveling out and diving into the atmosphere behind Riepe.

This was not how the day was supposed to go.

"Transferring all combat shielding forward," Flip said.

"Likewise," Riepe responded. A dropship had plenty of physical armor to enter the atmosphere of most planets, including this one. Emergency landings like this, however, had a much spottier record. Moving all shield energy to the front of the ship might give them just enough protection to survive.

"I'm in the chop," Riepe said, meaning there'd be no communication for the next few minutes; Flip would be on his own.

The shields blazed as the ship entered Todesfalle's atmosphere. Flip tried to keep his eyes down on the controls. He activated the metal blast shield and heard it tear away.

"Why don't they put those damn things on the inside?" Flip shouted into the empty cockpit. "It's a fucking shade!"

His external sensor arrays had been destroyed long ago. He couldn't see anything outside his cockpit windows. Riepe's ship didn't show on the collision detection system; that was good at least. Flip could only hope that his friend was sticking to the plan.

The fucking plan. When I get ahold of the Coily Bastard I'm going to—

Something slammed into his ship. Emergency force fields snapped closed around the cockpit. Strapped into his seat, Flip found himself inverted and pushing the controls in the wrong direction. He tried to right his ship but couldn't turn it over. He'd have to recalculate the approach vector based on his new attitude: upside down and pissed off.

The blaze of entry lifted. The turbulence dissipated, and he plunged into Todesfalle's sky. The sandy desert above him provided a stark reminder that he was going to land on his head.

"Riepe! You there?"

"Sure thing, bud. Where are you?"

"Unknown," Flip said. "Are you still on course? I've lost my sensors."

"More or less," Riepe said. "We went through a debris field. I'm coming up to the lake cockeyed."

"So you can see it?"

"Affirmative," Riepe said.

A slice of blue appeared at the top of Flip's windshield.

"Okay, I see it too," he said as he tried angling his ship toward the sea with limited success. "I have a visual on you."

"That's good, bud because I have no idea where the fuck you are. How am I lookin'?"

Riepe had lost all his troop compartments—no surprise there. His glider wings had deployed, though.

"You're looking a lot better than me," Flip glanced at his controls— the ones still functioning at any rate. His wings, of course, had not deployed. It didn't feel like he had any wings at all. He clung to the controls of what had become a rock falling out of the sky.

Flip took a deep breath. "I'm at your seven o'clock high. About a hundred meters away."

Silence answered him, along with the sounds of groaning metal and whistling wind.

"Acknowledged," came Riepe's curt response a few moments later. "Adjusting course."

"No, Riepe! Just get down to the ground!"

"Buddy, I said I was coming down with you. Haven't changed my mind. If I'm looking better than you, then you need all the help you can get."

"What's the plan?" Flip asked. "Oh, by the way, I'm upside down and using my docking thrusters to stay on target. I've got"—Flip did not want to know this part—"sixty-three seconds of fuel at... mark."

"God damn it, Flip. Alright. I'm going to slow down and let you pass. I have you on sensors now."

"They put sensors on your ship? You must know people."

"Shut up and listen. Stay on course. Keep your nose up as much as possible." Riepe's ship decelerated as if it hit a brick wall and banked behind Flip.

"That was some pretty sharp flying," Flip said. "What's the plan now?"

"The plan... Flip"—he could hear the strain in Riepe's voice—"is for you... to shut up... and stay on course!"

The ground loomed above Flip. The whistling air almost drowned out Riepe's grunting and cursing over the comms as they plunged through the sky. Flip tried to stick to the plan, but it seemed more and more futile with each passing second.

"Full thrusters," Riepe grunted. "Forward on my—" Riepe's voice cut out.

Flip had fifteen seconds of fuel left and no idea what Riepe wanted him to do.

"FORWARD!" Riepe yelled. "BURN! BURN! BURN!"

Flip cranked his thrusters to full, expending the remains of his fuel in whatever last-ditch, harebrained scheme Riepe had come up with.

Flip's ship shuddered and then bolted upward. He heard grinding metal and yet more pieces of his ship tear away. His seatbelts, already straining from holding him upside down, nearly ripped apart.

That can't be good, he thought. Despite his natural pessimism, his ship slowed and stabilized into an arc toward the ground.

Riepe, panting, said, "You always hang out around here?"

Flip looked up. His view of the desert had been replaced by Riepe looking up at him. The son of a bitch had parked his dropship underneath Flip's and was gliding them both down.

Flip gaped.

"Close your mouth, Flip," Riepe chided. "Act like you've done this before."

CHAPTER 22

Kid's submarine crept through a tunnel deep beneath the *Merlin*'s primary security level. The sub's lights played across the rock walls, searching for indications of the secondary security defenses. Kid kept one eye on the controls and another on the walls closing in around him.

Something flashed at one of the portside windows. He ignored it, choosing instead to focus on the walls. The tunnel bore down. He shrank the sub. The tunnel narrowed more. He shrank again. The cycle repeated until rock screeched along the sides of the submarine. He couldn't shrink the sub any further; otherwise, he wouldn't fit inside.

I guess I could *shrink myself,* he thought. *But what if something happened and I couldn't unshrink? I'd get eaten alive!* He chuckled at the thought.

He looked out the front window, which was now mere centimeters from his face. He'd been so preoccupied with the encroaching wall that he hadn't paid attention to the iron gate that blocked his path.

Aha, he thought. *We've reached the secondary system.*

Silt and rust floated among sea life from various worlds. He watched these strange organisms, like none he'd ever seen before, flick through the sub's lights and crisscross through the iron bars.

This is pretty straightforward, he thought. He carved the iron bars from the rock with the lasers. *I knew those would come in handy.*

Startled by this transgression in their calm lives, the sea creatures darted off. All except one.

A grouper. It gave no ground. In fact, it moved closer to the window. It gazed at Kid while gulping at the water, as fish do. Kid thought it looked disappointed, accusing, offended, and a little bit angry.

Bizarre security down here, Kid thought, pushing the throttle forward. Rocks scraped the sub's hull as Kid forced his way through the gate. The walls opened up beyond the iron fence, allowing him to expand the sub to its original size. It felt good to stretch out.

"Smooth walls. Interesting," he muttered to himself. "Actually, no it's not. I don't really care as long as it doesn't—well, shit. It's closing in again."

Kid peered out the window and couldn't believe what he saw. The grouper swam beside the sub, oblivious to the wall bearing in on it. Kid knocked on the window. The grouper glanced over; Kid pointed at the wall. (He had no idea why he'd do such a thing. He felt a little silly trying to warn a virtual fish about a virtual wall that bore down on a virtual submarine. Nevertheless, he felt bad when its guts smeared across the window.)

The tunnel ended about a hundred meters from a sheer rock wall. The cliff stretched up and plunged down further than his lights could reach. He sent sonar pulses in both directions; they never returned.

The third layer really ramps up, doesn't it?

He flopped into his chair, turned dials, and pushed buttons. He disconnected the gadgets from the actual controls so he could fiddle with them as he thought about his situation.

An identical grouper appeared and pressed its face against the window next to Kid. Kid squinted at the fish and locked his lasers on the creature. It disappeared into a cloud of flesh and blood.

That thing was creeping me out, he thought, attempting to justify his actions. *Now, what to do about this wall?*

He grabbed a mermaid suit and exited the submarine.

* * *

The sub's lights shined on Kid's back as he swam to the rock wall, illuminating the inky blackness around him.

With his arms at his side and water jets on his feet, he moved through the water as quickly as, well, a mermaid. The wetsuit also served as a force field and oxygen extractor. The force field served all the functions that a suit and helmet would while allowing him a greater range of movement. Except for the water jets on each foot, he could move around as if he wore nothing at all.

He groped the wall and diverted power into his shields to make them glow. He knew there had to be a sizable opening to allow data to flow in and out of the computer's core—sizable enough for him to slither through.

He found some rocks blocking a circular opening. He pried some loose, and they disappeared into the dark depths. He'd hoped to find a tunnel large enough to fit his submarine, but that didn't seem possible here, at least not without a lengthy search. And digging through the rocks would take up a great deal of time.

Wait a second, he thought. *I have superstrength.* He activated his node and smashed his fist against the rocks. Pain seared through his hand. He tried again. He used his superspeed to pry rocks out faster; that didn't work either.

God damn it, he thought. *My node powers don't work here.* He'd never tried to use them in any of the games. There'd been no need. He wondered if his nodes had never worked here or if the computer's security systems had adapted to his abilities.

He'd just have to dig at this opening and, if he could fit through it, he'd leave the submarine behind. Silt shot through the cracks, blinding him as he pried the rocks loose. As he let them drop, the rocks carved through clouds of silt as they fell to the bottom of the ocean.

The current tugged him forward and backward. Three seconds in, three seconds out, as if it was inhaling and exhaling. Now that the obstruction had been freed, the tunnel looked like it breathed silt. A small amount came out of the opening, and most of it went back in.

By the time he removed the last rock, the suction from the opening was so strong the silt could not reach the end of the tunnel. His suit's lights only penetrated a few meters into the cloud and revealed nothing but more silt. His sonar pings went through the clouds but never returned.

He'd known this mission would be "risky." This, however, looked life-threatening. If he died in the simulation, at this level of the computer's security systems, he would die in real life. He couldn't go back, though. His plan had to succeed.

He timed the currents and made his move. He floated in with the current and used his water jets to stay in place when the flow reversed. He suppressed the urge to rocket down the tunnel. Sonar indicated the tunnel was straight and clear. In fact, it showed that it had no end at all. He knew, however, that could change without warning. The computer could put a wall in his way—or something even worse.

He had no way to know how deep he was or how many kilometers of mountain rested on top of him. He didn't even know how long the tunnel was. The sub's headlights faded behind him as he ventured further into the tunnel.

The lights on his mermaid suit reflected off the silt and stung his eyes. He dimmed the lights but dared not turn them off. He hadn't realized he had claustrophobia—he thought his mind would break if he added pure darkness to the mix.

He drifted along, alone with his thoughts and swirling sand. He had no one to talk to, except for himself.

"What the hell am I doing here?" he asked himself.

I'm doing what must be done.

"Am I really, though? Isn't there another way to do this?"

Name one.

"Well, er, we could—"

We?

"God damn it, I'm going insane. I've been floating around for," he stopped himself. He didn't want to know how long he'd been floating around. "For a long time. I've developed a split personality. I've gone Golem."

Would you please snap out of it?!

"Okay, think. I could have just asked Lam for his access codes. Maybe when he'd had way too much to drink at the bar."

Good luck with that.

"I could have hacked through the computer to get it."

That's what I'm doing right now, idiot.

"This is probably a fool's errand. Maybe the whole plan is a bad idea. I'll be down here for a million years, dancing through a tunnel full of silt."

* * *

After what felt like a week of conversing with himself, the tunnel spit Kid into a large cavern. Time passed differently inside the computer. Back on the *Merlin*, only a few seconds had passed.

The cave could only be considered large in relation to the tunnel he'd just escaped; it still felt pretty tight. He spotted a large object hovering just out of his light's range. With sonar, he could see that it was yet another grouper.

"I bet there's a whole school of groupers down here. How did it get here, though?"

He looked left and saw something just at the edge of his light. It looked, maybe, like a mouth gulping water. Three seconds in, three seconds out. Sonar showed nothing; it only bounced off the wall behind whatever the mouth was attached to.

"Oh, great. Now there are grouper ghosts. I've been driven insane by fish."

"Focus on the mission," he scolded himself. "I can't do anything about Mr. Fillet anyway. Let's see," he said, "if the water flows back and forth like that, it must come from straight ahead.

"But then why isn't the water flowing in here?"

Something moved along the floor to his right. Something big and certainly not grouper-shaped. Something else skittered off to his left.

He heard tapping and rattling: the sounds of exoskeletons scurrying along the floor. One sat in front of him, just out of the range of his lights.

"I need to get stronger lights. I'll put that on the list—"

A loud crack sent a crushing pulse of water down on him. The ceiling crashed onto his waist and pinned him to the ground. Rocks fell around him and bounced off his suit's force field.

He howled in pain.

Breathe, he thought. *I'm still alive.*

For now.

CHAPTER 23

Flip and Riepe sat on a beach, skipping stones. Debris blazed overhead through the spreading twilight. The remains of their dropships smoldered in the distance, sending thick plumes of black smoke into the sky.

What Flip assumed to be foliage hugged the coastline. (In his experience, motionless green things that sprouted from the ground could be classified as foliage. Foliage generally didn't attack without provocation, though he'd encountered some exceptions. This, fortunately, did not appear to be one of them.) He would test it for poison later to see if it was safe for Riepe to eat.

Flip had disentangled Riepe from the wreckage, set his leg, crafted a travois, and hauled his friend to safety. Relative safety, at least. He'd grabbed as many useful items as he could find and slogged through the woods to the beach. Riepe had been knocked unconscious in the crash and stayed that way during the journey.

When they reached the shore, Flip treated his friend's leg with some med packs he'd found. They would heal up Riepe's bones and tissue, though he would be sore for a while. Flip built a fire and scanned the lake. The water had no harmful substances or microorganisms. When Riepe awoke, Flip used a piece of bowl-shaped debris to force-feed him as much water as he could stand. Riepe choked and coughed, but at least he was hydrated.

"Hungry?" Flip asked.

"Not yet." Riepe coughed. "But"—he gasped for air between words—"thanks."

"Here, eat this when you can." Flip handed him a meal bar: the condensed food soldiers carried to save space. "You'll need the nutrients to heal. You didn't make it down here in one piece."

"Yeah, thanks," Riepe said. "You look like you made it out of that crash pretty well, bud."

"Just luck, I guess," Flip said. Had he not been full of healing nanites, Flip probably would have been dead before the ships stopped sliding through the forest.

They watched thousands upon thousands of fireballs streak across the sky. Flip felt guilty for even watching the sight, safe on the ground, let alone finding beauty in the scene. Some of the people on those ships would survive long enough to reach the atmosphere. Trapped and terrified, they knew no one could save them—that their fiery, painful fates were sealed.

"How many of these do you have?" Riepe asked.

"Huh? Oh, right, the meal bars. I always keep a few on me, for emergencies," Flip said. "I can scavenge some more tomorrow. Maybe find something else we can eat."

"You're ready for anything. Unflappable."

"Hey, now," Flip said, a small smile tugging at his lips. He glanced at the sky. "That was some pretty fancy flying up there. How'd you manage it?"

"I don't know. I just made it up."

"I know the feeling," Flip said. "How's the leg?"

"Hurts like hell. I'm gonna take some more pain meds in a little while."

"How many do you think survived?" Flip asked.

"All the way to the ground? Damn, bud, look up there." Riepe pointed at the flaming streaks coursing through the sky. "We're lucky *we* did. What was that? A one-in-a-billion shot? There's no way anyone else made it down here."

Riepe fell silent, tracing the carnage through the sky with his finger.

"This whole mission was a trap," he said. "I bet the Coily Bastard had this whole thing planned."

"Of course he did," Flip fumed. "He set this up a decade ago and lured us in. He tied up an entire armada for ten years and then destroyed it in one day."

"I contend," Riepe said, "we've been traveling for twelve years."

Flip skipped a stone across the lake. "It doesn't matter anymore. It's going to be years before anyone knows what happened here, if they ever do. The bases out there on the moons and planets—they're just as stuck as we are." He sighed. "They're probably being destroyed right now."

"The brass hats will put it together when the suppressor doesn't go down," Riepe offered. "What do you think the fleet is gonna do?"

"You mean the parts that survive? That's a good question." Flip shrugged and shook his head. "They'll sit tight and regroup. They might be able to occupy parts of the outer solar system with the second and third waves."

"I think that's too optimistic," Riepe said. "If this *was* a trap, there'll be a counterattack."

"Of course there will be," Flip said.

Riepe continued as if he hadn't heard Flip, "I bet it's already happened. I bet all the defenses here were automated. I bet those Jassican fighters weren't even manned. Everything was too smooth at first. Minimal fighter defenses. Piss-poor missiles trying to take us out. I don't think their orbital platforms were even manned!"

"You're right." Flip took out his holographic data device and opened a map of the planet; a globe appeared above his hand.

"Let me see that for a sec," Riepe said. To the data pad, he said, "Overlay our planned descent."

A thick red line appeared from the void outside of the device's range. It spiraled once around the planet and landed at the suppressor's site. It filled in suspected Jassican defenses.

"If they had ships in reserve," Flip mused, "they couldn't be on the surface. We'd have seen them."

"You're right. Though, if they could bury that huge suppressor, they could bury a hangar." Riepe addressed the device, "Display known underground cavities and overlay suspected construction sites."

Gray networks crisscrossed the planet's interior. Green dots showed locations of intelligent activity.

"That's where they fortified their countermeasures," Flip said. "I'll bet a thousand Deutsche Marks they're control stations. *They* might not be manned, either."

"If they have a reserve, it's not here. It's on another planet, bud," Riepe said.

"Could be. The goddamned admirals should have thought of that," Flip said. "I guess it's not important. Not for us, anyway."

"True," Riepe said. "How long do you think before the patrols start?"

Flip looked up. "A few days at least. It's too dangerous to fly until the junk is burned up. That'll buy us some time. We'll have to get out of here or build some shelter."

"How long is a day here, anyway?"

Flip shrugged. "We'll find out soon enough, I guess."

"What are the odds they'd send a patrol to our exact location?" Riepe asked.

"With the fancy flying you did up there? They'd definitely notice that," Flip said. "Whether they care or not is a different question."

Flip took a pot of boiling water from the fire and set it in the lake to cool for a few minutes. He soaked a piece of cloth and put it around Riepe's sore leg. He filled another piece of debris with water and set it to boil.

"We need a plan," Flip said. "I'll worry about the short-term stuff. You come up with a long-term plan."

"Plan?" Riepe skipped a stone. "What plan could there be other than surrender?"

"Fuck that!" Flip shouted. He jumped to his feet. "We're probably the only survivors. We have no hope of rescue. It's a completely hopeless situation."

Riepe arched an eyebrow. "Isn't that what I just said?"

"We still have a mission," Flip growled. He rotated the display of the planet and pointed at the suppressor site. "We have to finish it."

Riepe laughed. He laughed so hard he started choking and rolled over onto his good side. "You've lost it, bud. You're dehydrated and delusional."

"No," Flip said, excitement crawling into his voice. "It's the last thing the Curly Bastard will expect. We have no hope—so we attack."

"You're insane, Flip. The target is *literally* on the other side of the planet."

"So you want to give up? Surrender to the Jassicans?" Flip's voice grew louder, more shrill. He tried to calm himself with only moderate success. "For all we know, they may cook us up and eat us!"

Riepe sat back up. "Oh, come on. That's a myth." He smiled. "They wouldn't have to cook us anyway."

Flip ignored the joke. "How do you know? They can eat anything. Besides, you think our side doesn't do stuff just as bad?"

Riepe recoiled. Flip had struck a nerve.

"Well, still," Riepe stammered. "It seems far-fetched. Hey, it's not giving up to admit that—"

"Riepe! Listen," Flip interrupted. "We have to *try*!"

"Why?"

Flip knelt in front of Riepe. "I want revenge, damn it! I want to kill the Coily Bastard. You know he's here. He *must* be. And he's not going anywhere for a while."

"And, pray tell," Riepe said, "how did you figure that out?"

"The suppressor is too important. He'll be here himself. We still have substantial forces in the outer solar system," Flip said. "He's too important to evacuate without a tach drive. And he'll want to crush us himself anyway."

"Come on, bud. Revenge is not a strategy," Riepe said. "Besides they've got those"—he waved his hands around—"whatever the hell they are. He could be anywhere."

Flip hung his head. "I know it's a long shot. But it's a shot. There's got to be at least a dozen lakes between here and there—we have water. We can fix up something to get across the ocean too. We can make it." He looked at Riepe. "And if we do, we could bring down this damn tach screen and boom! We're back in business!"

"You never give up, do you?"

"Never." Flip grinned. He stood back up and looked at the map. "Think you can come up with a plan?"

Riepe sighed. "The plan is to not get captured. Or killed. Or worse. Either by the Jassicans or some infernal beast. Why make a plan more than that?"

"Work with me here," Flip chided. "Do you have something better to do? A hot date? A meeting?"

"Fine." Riepe sighed again. "I guess it'll pass the time until we die."

"That's the spirit!" Flip laughed and patted Riepe on the shoulder, a bit too hard. Riepe winced but was already examining a map of their immediate surroundings.

"I'm going to make a shelter," Flip decided. "We don't want anything coming down on our heads. For that matter, we don't know what lives around here."

Riepe looked up. "You didn't read the guide?"

"No. Why? We weren't supposed to be here."

"I read part of it while taking a shit," Riepe said. "Just don't go for a swim."

* * *

Flip and Riepe created an elaborate camp just inside the beach's tree line. Flip found it amazing what two guys could do with alien plants and a couple of wrecked spaceships.

He knew the Jassicans weren't looking for them because he'd scanned the area with his node. Riepe, however, continued to worry about an impending attack, so Flip pretended to as well.

Flip made a few trips each day to the crash site while Riepe worked on bundling supplies and general homemaking. He'd constructed a decent bungalow, all things considered.

Flip decided that they'd have to leave soon, though—a day or two at the most. They were starting to become too comfortable in their camp. After a few days, the bungalow had become more of a home than a waypoint.

Then again, Flip didn't know where or what "home" might be anymore. Somewhere in another war for the Reich? Back in the Alliance? He just wanted to get off this damned planet. Todesfalle turned out to be an accurate nickname, just for the wrong side.

He felt trapped and suffered the occasional panic attack. He'd stumble out into the woods, complaining of a migraine to hide his affliction from Riepe. His node, of course, could do nothing about emotional pain other than secreting medication. The drugs didn't replace his therapist.

Flip had hoped to find environmental protection suits among the wreckage. He and Riepe needed something to keep them cool during the day and warm at night, not to mention the star's deadly radiation. He never found any suits, but he found something even better: an antigravity sled. About five meters wide and seven meters long, he pushed it to the crash site and back home every day, sometimes twice. Each haul brought something new: weapons, rations, and other useful items. He'd pile each day's discoveries onto it and push them to the camp.

Even with his superstrength, Flip found the sled cumbersome. The sled was meant to be moved by other vehicles and thus didn't have hand-holds. Its thick sides prevented him from getting a good grip so all he could do was push. From time to time, he indulged in ripping trees out of the ground and tossing them aside. Mostly, though, he used them as bumpers to manage the sled's inertia, ping-ponging through the forest.

Each day brought new treasure. An energy bar here, a useful tool there—but today was special. Today, Flip had a surprise.

"How's my favorite castaway?" Riepe said as Flip pushed the sled into camp.

"You mean pack mule, right?" Flip joked. "I see you've been busy too."

Riepe had prepared their supplies for the next part of the voyage. Bundles laid in piles, wrapped in fabric, and tied up with vines. Each pack had been labeled with charcoal—or something that looked and acted like charcoal at any rate.

"What'd you find?" Riepe asked.

"Like we figured, we have most of the good stuff already. I *did* find this after a lot of digging, though." Flip pretended to do a drum roll before his final flourish.

"Behold!" He exclaimed while tearing the tarp away to reveal his prize: a damaged one-man scout speeder. Most of one, anyway.

"I'll be damned," Riepe said. "You never cease to amaze me." Riepe jumped onto the sled and beheld the vehicle.

"I was thinking," Flip said while stroking his chin, "we could pry off the rear and attach it to the sled. The canopy is gone, but we could rig up a steering mechanism. Should help with pushing this damn sled across the planet."

"Yeah, yeah. I was thinking the same thing," Riepe said while examining the speeder. He pointed to where reverse thrusters were supposed to be. "How are we gonna stop?"

Flip jumped onto the sled and cracked his knuckles. "Very carefully."

CHAPTER 24

Kid assessed his situation. He didn't like it; he didn't like it one bit.

Silt obscured his vision. His sonar was on the fritz. He could only determine his position based on the things in direct contact with his force field. He knew one thing for certain: the ceiling had caved in, pinning him to the floor. He didn't think this situation was a coincidence.

It looked like the letter V had fallen on him, pinning his hips to the floor. He supposed there were worse letters that could fall on someone. Had he been a half-meter forward, he'd have escaped; had he been a half-meter back, his head would have been lopped off. He didn't think this was a coincidence either.

He knew that neither the mountain nor the island nor the giant eternal cliff face had collapsed. Otherwise, he'd not be alive to assess the situation. Whatever had fallen, it was enough to pin him but not enough to crush his force field. Yet another thing that he didn't think was a coincidence.

That's a bit unnerving, he thought. *I'm in a horror movie. Pinned at just the right place, in total darkness except for my puny fucking light. At least I've got—*

Sonar came back online and detected objects straight ahead.

Well fuck me, he thought. *The computer knows exactly where I am. It's trying to scare me.* He didn't want to admit it to himself, but the computer was doing a damn fine job of it.

So, what are we dealing with here? He focused on one of the skittering objects. His instruments, mercifully working now, detected tiny vibrations on the tunnel floor. Dozens of legs—maybe a hundred or more. It sounded like a roomful of typewriters.

The curtain of silt dropped like a cloud of rocks, straight to the floor. The mysterious creatures danced around the edges of the light, but Kid's sonar had no problem registering their movements.

Are those crabs? Kid thought. *No, they're way too big.*

He focused on the closest one. It was crab-like, for sure, but with twice as many legs. The claws were as big as Kid's head.

No, Kid thought. *No fucking way.*

The creatures came into the light, dragging their rainbow-striped-yet-venomous claws at their sides.

Fucking sclorabs, he thought. The one beast in the multiverse he never wanted to encounter. Combine a crab with a tarantula, give it the venom of a rattlesnake and the teeth of a piranha, then encase it in a damn near indestructible shell—that would give you a rough approximation of a sclorab. The tunnel was full of them, of course.

How can a plan go this badly? he thought.

A grouper hovered nearby. He hated that fish. There was always one around, mocking him. They all had that same weird "W" on their heads. Maybe they were all the same fish?

The sclorabs ran at him and covered his field of vision. Their claws clamped down on his force field, trying to find purchase. Their venom flowed over his head and back into their mouths... *oh God, their mouths!* They were essentially rollers coated with teeth.

The sclorabs swarmed all over his body. He felt them crawling up his legs. He hadn't had any time to react—not even enough time to pull his arms in. The sclorabs had them now, clamping and prying at the force field, pinning his arms straight in front of him.

Kid panicked. The force field's formfitting design worked against him in this situation; it allowed the sclorabs to get within just a few millimeters of his face. He knew, in the deep recesses of his mind, that the force field would hold and that the sclorabs presented no mortal danger to him. But that information had gotten lost between the adrenaline coursing through his body and the urine soaking his pants.

He closed his eyes and screamed.

His screams echoed inside his force field, but not loud enough to drown out the sound of snapping claws and grinding roller teeth. He felt like he didn't have a force field at all; he could practically feel their claws driving into his head and injecting their venom into his brain.

Come on, Kid, he thought. *We get calm or we get dead.*

He closed his eyes tighter, trying to concentrate. He could disconnect from the game, but at this level of security—and at this level of panic—it could kill him. The crush of sclorabs made that option rather appealing, though.

Think. Three breaths in, three breaths out.

The thought of dying in an underwater cave with thousands of virtual sclorabs turning him into a human shish kabob made him laugh. The more he thought of it, the more he laughed. His shrill laugh, filled with fear, replaced his screams and forced him to breathe evenly. He was able to calm down, if only a little, and think.

Hang on. This is basically a lucid dream. Use that. Give in to instinct. I have powers here that don't derive from my nodes. And if I use powers that don't derive from my nodes—

A plasma beam erupted from his palms, clearing the sclorabs in front of him and carving a tunnel through the rest of the mountain.

He scolded himself for not thinking of this solution sooner.

The water turned to steam and baked the sclorabs. Delicious, no doubt, but Kid would never know. They were too scary to look at, even dead on a plate. In fact, that might be worse.

A new current rushed through the tunnel, crushing him. His limbs threatened to twist him into a human pretzel. He saved himself by conjuring a new, larger force field around his body.

The water pushed on the walls and shifted the V that pinned him to the ground. The rocks groaned as the water rushed in. Silt swirled around

Kid with such violence that it cut lines in his shield. Loud cracks echoed through the water, and more rocks fell around him.

He needed to cut himself loose from the bottom of the V. If he did that, though, it might bring the whole damn mountain down on him. He needed to prop the wall up with something—anything.

Small rocks and sclorab carcasses lay scattered around him. Sclorabs had the hardest known exoskeletons in the multiverse.

But they're so creepy!

He shut his eyes and, using sonar to guide his hands, scooped up all the rocks and sclorab shells he could reach. He stuffed them into the empty spaces on either side of the V-shaped rock.

I need perfect timing, he thought. *And precision. I can do this.*

His eyes opened and glowed. His water jets spun up, and he blasted through the rock with a wave of heat vision. The mountain hung, for a microsecond, on the rocks and shells—just long enough for him to get free.

He shot forward, drilling through the rock with his newfound superpowers, his studies of ancient Earth science fiction more useful than he ever could have imagined. He pressed his arms tight to his sides and rode behind a comet of molten rock. The mountain collapsed behind him, and the resulting shockwave cracked the rock in front of him.

He burst into the open ocean behind a wall of lava. Plumes of rock billowed into the sea as the cliff collapsed around him.

Looking up, he could barely make out a glimmer of light. The cliff must have been topped by an island after all.

Not for long, he thought. *It's all coming down.*

Cracks rippled up and down the face of the cliff. The mountain sagged and fell. And fell. And then fell some more.

It fell without end. No island followed the destruction—just kilometer after kilometer of collapsing cliff face. Pulverized rock and fish guts rushed around him.

The water pounded at Kid. Were it not for his shields and water jets, he would have been torn to pieces, and his parts flung into the bottomless sea.

Whatever security system this represented, *Merlin's* computer would know Kid had destroyed it. The computer would also know his exact whereabouts.

He jetted away but spared a second look over his shoulder.

He saw the grouper. That goddamned grouper. Hanging there, indifferent to everything happening around it. The rock and silt and boulders flowed over the fish, crushing it into the infinite depths of the ocean.

Good fucking riddance, Kid thought.

* * *

The grouper knew where Kid would emerge from the cliff. She waited with patience as infinite as the ocean's depth.

Sure enough, a ball of lava erupted from the cliff, turned to rock, and sank.

The Terran flew out behind the lava, beams coming from his eyes.

So dramatic.

Kid turned to look at her.

She stared back. As the cloud of debris enveloped her, she had only one thought: *Most curious.*

CHAPTER 25

Flip and Riepe admired their handiwork. After weeks of tinkering and testing, they'd crafted a vehicle that worked—most of the time.

They'd removed the engines from the speeder and attached them to the back of the sled. Riepe sat just in front of the engines with a makeshift throttle in each hand. He could turn the sled in long arcs by varying the thrust of each engine.

Flip sat at the front of the sled; his superior vision made him a better lookout. He held a long paddle in each hand. Using these, he could make sharp turns by dipping one paddle into the sand. Dip right, cut right. Dip left, cut left. Simple.

He used two buttons to tell Riepe which way to go. If he stepped on the left button, Riepe throttled left. Stepped on the right button, he throttled right. Simple.

This system was of utmost importance as they'd piled their supplies in the middle of the sled between them—neither person could see the other.

This setup had taken some persuasion on Flip's part, though. Riepe wanted to be up front, not flying blind behind a mound of supplies.

"What do you mean you have better vision?" Riepe had protested.

"I do!" Flip said. "Besides, you're the better pilot."

"You're the best pilot in the fleet!"

"I was shot out of orbit."

"That doesn't mean anything," Riepe objected. "*Everyone* was shot out of orbit."

"I didn't pilot a dropship to a crash landing with another on top upside down!"

"Okay, okay! I'll drive."

They added a sail to save fuel.

"You know anything about sailing?" Flip had asked.

"No," Riepe had replied. "But I guess we'll learn soon enough."

They accounted for every contingency they could think of: tidal waves, tornadoes, hurricanes, and sea monsters, just to name a few.

"So," Riepe said one evening. He chewed some leaves; the ones with blue streaks cutting through the green were their favorite. "We're headed over the horizon on this thing?"

"That's the plan," Flip said.

"Just because we haven't seen any Jassicans," Riepe said, "doesn't mean they aren't looking for us."

"I'm pretty sure they aren't looking for us. Or for anyone, actually. I think you hit the nail on the head when we first got here—I bet most of the defenses and outposts are automated," Flip said, chewing some tangy bark. He had scanned the area every day with his node. There were no Jassicans anywhere within range. In fact, there was nothing at all within range.

Riepe nodded. "Yeah, I know, bud."

"Well," Flip said, "let's just head out after lunch."

Riepe choked on some water. "Right now? In the middle of the day? We should at least wait until night. Even if they aren't looking, they might just be flying around—"

"They'll see us either way," Flip said, cutting him off. "Besides, I have a plan. And to do it, we have to leave now. Are you ready for the big reveal?"

Riepe nodded slowly, uncertain about this sudden turn in the conversation.

Flip stood and pointed to the horizon. "See that?"

"See what?" Riepe squinted and shielded his eyes. He picked up binoculars.

"I told you I had better vision," Flip gloated.

"Shit! What are those plumes? The Jassicans?"

"No," Flip said. "I looked through the database. Well, what's left of it." He fetched a mesh screen. "Pick up a handful of sand."

Riepe did as he was told and Flip handed him a screen.

"Now sift it through this," Flip instructed. "Slowly. Yes, like that. See those tiny squirming grains?"

"Eww! What is that?"

"Look around. We see a desert, but that's not what this ecosystem is. It's more like an ocean. These things" —Flip nodded toward the squirming organisms—"they're like plankton. This sand isn't like the sand on Earth. Or anywhere else, for that matter. It has lots of oxygen bound up in it."

"So those plumes out there are... whales?"

"Sure," Flip said. "They're as big as whales, and they eat this plankton."

"Interesting..." Riepe considered the sand at his feet.

"That's not the best part," Flip said. "If we travel with the pod, the sand will shield us from the sun."

"If it shields us from the radiation," Riepe said, "it will shield us from scanners."

"Yeees,"—Flip dragged the word out—"but my main point is we won't get cooked."

Riepe nodded, looking at the whales' plumes.

"They're headed to the same ocean we are," Flip said. "We can catch up and hitch a ride, but we have to leave within the hour."

"Why so soon?"

"Because if they get any farther we won't catch up to them without getting burned alive."

"Damn, Flip. You sorted this out without telling me?"

"Did you want to worry about sand sharks while we put this thing together?" Flip asked.

Riepe looked at the ground and moved closer to Flip. "Okay, good point," he said. "But what do we do when we get to the other ocean?"

"To be honest," Flip admitted, "I haven't thought that far ahead."

CHAPTER 26

The whale pod consisted of twenty adults and a handful of juveniles. The young ones traveled in the middle of the pod, while the adults took turns diving deep into the sand. Flip didn't know if the whales hunted or warded off predators; all he cared about was that the pod ignored their sled.

As night fell, the pod started breaking up. Flip signaled Riepe to stop.

"What's going on up there, bud?" Riepe asked, his voice hoarse and scratchy.

"Not sure," Flip said. "Some of them are going way off over there." He pointed to the left. "Some are falling back. Some are stopping. The young ones are... sleeping?"

"Are they—" Riepe started, confusion seeping into his tone. "Are they setting up camp?"

"You know what? I think so," Flip replied. "We should too."

They stumbled off the sled, grimacing as their joints popped. They set up camp and looked over their supplies.

"We should have more water on hand for tomorrow," Riepe said. "So we can drink on the move."

Flip knew that Riepe had packed enough water for two people. Flip, however, could get everything he needed from the air and, while Riepe wasn't looking, from the sand. His nanites could break down anything and everything into whatever nutrients his body needed.

"I've been reading up on these things," Riepe said, gesturing to the whales. Flip shot him a disapproving glare. "Yeah, yeah, I shouldn't read while I'm driving.

"Anyway, we didn't get briefed on planetside stuff," Riepe said. "We weren't supposed to stay here, obviously." He rolled his eyes. Flip took a swig of water and nodded.

"The whales migrate," Riepe continued. "From one ocean to the other."

"Makes sense," Flip said. Maybe it did, maybe it didn't. He didn't care.

"Flip," Riepe said. He snapped his fingers in front of Flip's face. "Pay attention. There are things that eat the whales."

"What?!"

"Yes," Riepe said. "These things migrate, like wildebeests. They get to the water and—WHAM!" He clapped his hands, and Flip flinched.

"Giant crocodiles!" Riepe said. "Or, I guess they look like crocodiles. Kinda like a crocodile crossed with a shark, except as big as a dinosaur. My point is they're big and scary and could probably eat us without noticing we were even there."

"So," Flip said, "the shoreline—"

"Isn't going to be a nice place," Riepe finished.

Flip hadn't thought about this. His plans had changed daily. Sometimes hourly. He wanted to try the sail tomorrow and have a respite from obsessing about the immediate future.

I really should have read the briefing sheet, he thought. None of his plans had ever gone as expected. He should have, in fact, expected to live the rest of his life on Todesfalle the minute he boarded the dropship.

"We should break away from the pod before we get there," Flip said after taking a swig of water.

"You know it, bud," Riepe said. "I'd rather take my chances with the Jassicans. Plus"—he looked skyward—"I'm now convinced they aren't looking for us."

"I've been saying that for weeks," Flip said, rolling his eyes. "Ever since we crashed here!"

Riepe ignored the jibe. "We just have to figure out where the sea is before we get there."

They ate their food in exhausted silence.

* * *

Months drained away, each day the same as the last. Sand frothed around the whales, and beyond that, sand stretched as far as they could see. Some days they saw only dunes; some days, flat sand. If they were lucky, they got to see both.

They knew they'd make it to the freshwater sea, but weren't sure how long it would take. Flip had turned off the information and scanning modes in his node months ago. There wasn't much point in having them on and wasting energy. Besides, it would let him know if some life-threatening situation came up.

"Whoa!" Flip signaled Riepe to fold the sails. Flip leaped over the supplies and handed the binoculars to Riepe.

"Check that out," Flip said. They had flat sand that day and an unobstructed view of the horizon. Flip pointed to faraway plumes.

"More pods," Riepe said.

"They're coming in on us and our merry band of whales," Flip said. "We must be getting close."

"Like wildebeests," Riepe muttered.

"Yeah," Flip said, chewing a leaf from the supplies. "So, what do we do?"

"We stick with the ones who know us," Riepe said. "Stick to them as close as we can."

"That's an extremely good idea," Flip said.

"I have those now and again, bud," Riepe said. He cocked his head. "Maybe it's because we've been rocking back and forth while sailing, or maybe it's my imagination—but something sounds different to me. Do you hear it?"

Flip looked down and closed his eyes. He'd found it more and more difficult to focus on his nanites lately. It felt like they had a mind of their own.

"We're close to the water," Flip said, his balance faltering.

"You okay?" Riepe asked, taking a swig of water and offering some to Flip.

"Yeah," Flip said, just above a whisper. "Yeah, I just have a headache."

Nanites came gushing out of his nose, ears, and eyes as he fell to the floor of the sled. They swirled around him and swung out toward the shoreline. He could see everything: the whales bunching up near the beaches and the dinosharks waiting for them just offshore.

"Hey," Riepe said. Everything moved so slowly that Flip could see the sound waves flow from Riepe's mouth through the cloud of nanites.

Riepe couldn't see the nanites; they were smaller than air molecules and, of course, not as numerous. Flip, however, couldn't pull his focus away from the tiny machines. He could see the faint outline of Riepe's face, but no further. Meanwhile, Flip's node took data from the nanites and flooded his brain with sights, sounds, and smells from two kilometers in every direction.

"You okay, bud?"

None of this should be possible. Nanites couldn't exist for long outside his body, let alone so far away from it. His node was expending vast amounts of energy, which meant Flip didn't have much for himself.

"Flip?"

Flip. Can you hear me?

The shore, just a couple kilometers away, came into sharper focus in his mind. The whales' body language had changed; nervous energy rippled through the pods.

The nanites rushed back into Flip's body. He convulsed as the tiny machines poured into every orifice. His dizziness dissipated as he absorbed the nanites' matter, but he felt like he'd been ripped apart in the process.

He'd seen the danger his node had picked up. The whales needed to get into the ocean, and they needed to do it right away. Millions of years of evolution had ingrained an instinct that compelled them forward. If they didn't move now, they would die. And they knew it.

"Go," he said.

Riepe dragged Flip to his feet. "What's that, bud?"

"Go!" Flip yelled. "Get on it! Go!"

Riepe dropped Flip, dove to throttles, and punched them open.

Flip stayed on his hands and knees. Nanites swarmed into his nose as snot dripped out. His node must have malfunctioned, though in the luckiest way imaginable.

"Flip!" Riepe yelled. Thousands of whales thrashed around them. All of them wanted to get to the sea, but none of them wanted to go first.

"Flip!"

The remaining nanites—the ones that couldn't make it back into Flip—died and fell to the ground.

"Flip!"

He pulled himself up the stack of supplies and wobbled to the front of the sled. He needed to be at his post.

"Flip!"

He looked around, trying to get his bearings, and crumpled again to the bottom of the sled. Sand, purple blood, and whale bits crashed on top of them.

"Flip!" Riepe shouted. "Get the fuck up!"

Flip propped himself on his elbows and looked over the edge of the sled. Whales plowed into the sea. Dinosharks crashed into them, flinging blood and flesh in all directions.

"Flip! We don't have time for this shit!"

Flip dragged himself to his seat at the front of the sled. He heard thunder and bellows and growling and, deep beyond that, he could hear—

Stand up, Flip.

"Flip! Get your head out of your ass!"

They sped toward the shoreline, sand foaming with terrified whales and hungry dinosharks. Flip wiped water and blood from his face. He blinked, trying to clear his eyes.

"Flip, God damn it! What the fuck is up there?"

He buckled himself in and used the buttons under his feet to signal to Riepe that he'd come back online.

Terrified whales pushed each other into the dinosharks' jaws, desperate to get themselves and their offspring into open water.

Flip looked over his shoulder. He could see Riepe flicking his eyes back and forth. Flip shouldn't be able to see Riepe at all, much less his eyes. It meant they'd lost most of their supplies.

"Give me something!"

Flip looked over the water.

All things have a pattern. It seemed like his own thought, yet it wasn't. *No movement is random. Make a plan.*

Flip spotted an opening: a calm spot with ripples and a few bubbles of air. It looked like the dinosharks might have a staging area, or something like it.

"Go! Now!" Flip screamed and stomped on the buttons. He grabbed whale guts as they passed by him, and stuck them in his mouth. He needed energy for his node and nanites.

"Brace yourself!" Riepe shouted. He reversed thrust just as a dinoshark crashed in front of them. The bow of the sled plunged down and sand swirled at Flip's feet. All their provisions—food, fuel, water, kindling and everything else—toppled off the sled and into the mix of sand and water churning below them.

Riepe gunned the engines, and the bow of the sled angled upward. He guided the sled over the waves toward the breakers.

Flip.

Whose voice was in his head? And *why* was there a voice in his head at all?

"You alright?" Flip called back to Riepe. Riepe either couldn't hear the question or didn't bother responding. He coughed up water but hung onto the throttle sticks, his eyes focused straight ahead.

They hurtled toward a mass of frenzied whales. Riepe couldn't steer enough to veer away, and Flip's oars had long since been swept off the sled.

Flip grabbed a rifle that he'd tucked under the lip of the sled in front of him. He studied the pattern—maybe he could clear a path. Maybe he could startle a creature enough to move it out of their damn way. Worst-case scenario, Flip figured, it would ignore the shot.

Flip fired at the closest whale. Instead of moving out of the way, the monster breached, blocking their path.

Riepe killed one engine and banked the sled to the right. They glanced off the stricken animal, and Riepe steered them back on course to the breakers. Flip unbuckled and clawed his way to the back of the sled.

"Nice driving!" he shouted.

Riepe nodded, not taking his eyes off the path ahead. "Duck!"

Flip hit the deck as part of a tail smashed into the middle of the sled.

Riepe cut the engines, tilting the sled forward. The disembodied limb fell off the front of the sled, and the engines roared back to life.

"Hang on!" Riepe yelled. "We're going straight through! Get back to your seat!"

Flip made it back to his chair, thanks to his node-enhanced strength. He once again found himself relying on Riepe's daredevil piloting skills.

The broad back of a dinoshark arced out of the water ahead of them. Riepe angled straight for it.

"Look out!" Flip yelled. "Right there!"

"I see it! Hang on!"

Riepe rode the sled up the back of the predator at breakneck speed. They leaped off the creature into the sky. Another dinoshark sliced up through the water, snapping at them.

Time seemed to slow as they flew through the dinoshark's mouth. Flip looked up and saw the monster's ridged palate coated with whale blood. The sled angled toward a tooth covered in whale parts.

I'm going to be swallowed alive, he thought. *And the damned thing won't even notice.*

Flip slammed against the back of his chair as Riepe blasted the engines forward. Water crashed over Flip's face as the tooth raced toward him.

He smelled wet cardboard. He heard grinding and tearing and screaming. He froze. All he could see was...

Teeth.

Save me, Rex.

The sled ricocheted off the edge of the tooth and dove under the water. The engines cut off and the sled bobbed back to the surface. Riepe nailed the throttle again, pinning Flip to his chair.

Riepe didn't let up. Wind and surf blasted Flip's face while his nanites healed his wounds. Riepe put a couple of kilometers between them and the shore before cutting the engines.

They floated across the water in silence, carried by their momentum. Even from this distance, they could make out fountains of water and blood. They could still hear the screams and bellows of dying whales.

"That was"—Flip unbuckled himself and ran back to his friend— "fucking awesome!"

Riepe leaped into Flip's embrace, yelling in victory. Together they jumped and shouted on the quiet ocean. They had cheated death yet again. They celebrated and yelled and cheered and described the scene to each other over and over.

Until their skin started to burn.

CHAPTER 27

Kid laid atop his submarine gazing at the night sky. He had no idea how long he'd been in this simulation or how much time had passed in the real world. He didn't even know what "the real world" meant anymore. He ate here, breathed here, shit here, and he could die here. Seemed pretty real to him.

The grouper followed the submarine day and night. Kid knew—though he didn't know how he knew—that every grouper was the same grouper. There was only one grouper; it just reappeared when the previous incarnation died. (How did he know it was the same fish? For one, when he ran across the sub, the fish was in the second window but not the first. Second, it had the same strange pattern of dots on its back, just in front of its dorsal fin. White dots on brown skin in the shape of a "W.") Or maybe he was just going crazy. As far as he could tell, both situations seemed plausible.

He'd grown accustomed to the fish, though, and had developed something akin to affection for the infernal beast. It didn't matter how fast he pushed the sub or how deep he dove, the grouper kept pace and managed to keep at least one eye on Kid. He had to admire that kind of moxie.

At first, he entertained himself by blasting the grouper with plasma beams and incinerating it with his heat vision. That became boring in rather short order. The damn thing always returned as if nothing had happened. It was always watching. Always gulping.

When Kid went inside the sub, the grouper watched him through the windows. Kid tried to get rid of the windows, but he couldn't. He tried to put curtains up, but they disappeared. The computer had blocked him from adjusting his surroundings. To make matters worse, every few days, a new window blossomed somewhere on the sub.

He had tried to outsmart the grouper by running from one window to another. No matter how fast he ran, the grouper always waited for him at the other window, mocking him with that stupid gulping mouth.

Everywhere he looked, the grouper looked back. No matter how many times he killed it; no matter how many times he speared it, cooked it, and ate it, it always returned.

He used to put on a cape and fly around searching for clues, something that would indicate what he was looking for. No matter how high he went, he could always see the grouper, its apparent size never changed—it grew large enough so that it always appeared the same size.

He'd dive beneath the waves, searching the depths for... what? He had no idea. All he ever found was the grouper. No other fish, just the grouper. It followed him everywhere he went. The damned thing never ran out of energy. Kid zipped around in his mermaid suit, and still, the grouper stayed beside him. It seemed so casual, like it was just taking a Sunday stroll.

After weeks of this, he gave up on outrunning the fish. When he got hungry, he'd spear it. He'd eat one grouper while the next one watched. He'd throw pieces of the old grouper to the new one and watch it gobble itself down.

He couldn't change his surroundings entirely, but he could use the parts he had to make new things. He created crude computers from the parts he had on hand. He disassembled the periscope to make a telescope. He searched the skies every night for familiar planets. He did everything he could to forget he'd trapped himself in the virtual confines of a limited AI that may not be so limited after all.

He ate grouper all day, every day. He watched the constellations, trying to discern a pattern from night to night. Some nights, strange moons lit the waves. Most nights there were no moons at all. Some nights he could see planets through his telescope; some nights, he couldn't. As far as he could tell, each night brought a random pattern of stars. And a random assortment meant there wasn't a pattern to figure out.

"Hey, G," he said to the grouper. Kid chewed the remnants of the fish's previous incarnation. He threw the last few scraps into the water and paid no heed as the grouper cannibalized itself.

"What you got tonight, G?" Kid didn't bother looking at the water; he just stared straight up at the night sky.

"Gulp, gulp."

Every day, he asked a meaningless question to a dumb fish. A dumb fish that happened to be the only other being to talk to. The fish didn't *really* talk, but it was the only living thing he had to talk to in this vast, quiet world.

Kid hoped it didn't talk, because that would mean he'd gone completely around the bend. He couldn't quite convince himself of that, though. Kid admitted long ago that he'd lost touch with reality, even the fake one he lived in now.

One day—how long ago he couldn't say—Kid had imagined the fish saying, "Gulp, gulp." It amused him at first. Now, that's all he could hear when he looked at that stupid thing. It mocked him with an incessant "Gulp, gulp."

"You read any good books, G?" He kept staring at the night sky.

"Gulp, gulp."

"Yeah, I thought so. Me neither. Anything we haven't talked about?"

"Gulp, gulp."

"Think it will rain tomorrow?"

"Gulp, gulp."

"Yeah, me neither." It never rained. The days and nights were always clear.

Kid sat up and pulled his knees to his chest. "You know, G? There's... wait a sec... there's something...

"You see that, G? Does that look right?"

"Gulp, gulp."

He pointed to the sky. "There's Orion!"

"Gulp, gulp."

He stood. "There's the Big Dipper." He spun, keeping his eyes locked on the sky. "Leo! Cygnus!"

"Gulp, gulp."

He stopped and looked straight up. "By Cryptod, that's Jupiter!"

He grabbed his telescope. "Yes! I can see the Galilean moons!"

"Gulp, gulp."

He jumped up and down. "G! G! We're in the Terran system! Do you know what that means?"

Illuminated by the sub's lights, the fish stared at him. "Gulp, gulp."

"That's right!" Kid peered around the night sky. "Saturn! I see Saturn!" He couldn't contain himself. He pointed out constellation after constellation.

"I tell ya, G," he said, tears welling in his eyes.

"Gulp, gulp."

"Wait. What is *that?*" He pointed his telescope at the horizon. Against the moonless night, he saw twinkling lights on the sea. Not lights twinkling *onto* the surface of the sea. Oh no, sir, indeed not. Lights twinkling *from* the surface of the sea.

A ship.

Kid looked down at the grouper.

"I'll see ya, G," he said. He threw the telescope down the hatch. "I hope you got your big boy fins on because I've been tinkerin' with the engines."

"Gulp, gulp."

* * *

The next night, Kid's submarine surfaced next to the ship. He'd scavenged parts from the periscope to make his telescope, so he had to navigate by looking out the windows. He had tailed the ship during the day, following the shadow it cast from the surface. He didn't want to be seen; he stayed submerged and kept his lights off. Since being trapped in this uneventful world, he'd become paranoid. Anything outside of the familiar and mundane may be interesting, but would almost certainly be a threat. And this Liberty ship from Earth's Second World War fell well outside the scope of "familiar and mundane."

Kid crawled out of the hatch, shrouded by night and witnessed only by the familiar stars and planets. And the grouper, of course. A rope net hung over the side of the ship as if someone were expecting him. Kid climbed to the deck and looked around. He figured there wouldn't be a crew; he was right. Only silence greeted him, punctuated by the light sloshing of waves against the hull and bells chiming as the ship rocked to and fro. At least he'd escaped the grouper.

He believed this ship carried Lam's security codes. How could it not? But he didn't know how they would be represented or where they might be. They could look like anything: food, a steering wheel, an engine part. And even if he knew what they looked like, he had no clue as to where they would be. He needed to go where important information might be stored.

He decided to start his search on the bridge.

The Allies built Liberty ships in droves during Earth's Second World War; they hauled cargo and, in a pinch, troops. Kid and the computer used these ships when playing *Conquer the World* to supply their bases. Kid had never been *in* one, however, and had no idea how he might get to the bridge. He didn't even know what the inside of the ship might look like.

He picked a hatch and leaned on it face-first. He pictured a sign: a big arrow that said "**BRIDGE**" and pointed the way. He imagined these arrows all over the ship. Perhaps, if he concentrated hard enough, he could exert some influence over the simulation and spawn the directions. He squeezed his eyes shut and opened the hatch.

He opened one eye, just a slit, and fell back on his ass.

A sailor stood in the hallway with his hands behind his back. He donned a white dress uniform with a hat leaning off the right side of his head so steeply that it seemed to defy gravity.

"Good evening, sir," the sailor said. "Petty Officer Tom Moore, at your service."

Kid scrambled to his feet, rubbed his eyes, and stared into the hatch. The sailor stood there, unmoving, waiting for Kid to respond.

"Er, hello?" Kid had no idea what to say or if he should even say anything.

"Sir," the sailor said, "are you okay? Do you require assistance?"

Kid patted himself and found that nothing had gone missing; he had all his limbs, his hair, and his clothes. He didn't know what he *might* have lost but it seemed to be a prudent measure. He slapped his cheeks and blinked to make sure he was alert.

"Er, sorry," he said. "What did you say your name is?"

"Petty Officer Tom Moore."

"Ah, yes," Kid said. He'd not heard anyone talk in... he still didn't know how long. (Other than "Gulp, gulp," that is.)

"Petty Officer Tom Moore," Kid echoed. "How are you?"

They shook hands.

"I'm quite fine, sir," the sailor said. "Can I help you find something?"

Kid wasn't sure how to play this. Had he manifested this person by trying to spawn a sign? Was the computer trying to trick him?

"Uh, yeah," Kid said. He didn't have much of a choice, regardless of who this fellow might be. "I'm looking for the bridge."

"Of course, sir," the sailor said. "Right this way."

The sailor turned on his heel and led Kid down a corridor and up a flight of stairs. This felt too easy.

"Uh, excuse me? Petty Officer Moore?"

"Yes, sir?" The sailor stopped on the steps and turned around. "How can I help you, sir?"

"Are you the only one aboard?" Kid asked.

"Of course not, sir," the sailor said. "You're here, sir." He continued up the stairs.

Kid, surprised at that answer, asked, "I mean, other than the two of us?"

The sailor stopped and turned. "I'm afraid I don't understand the question, sir."

"Before I got here, Petty Officer," Kid said slowly, "were you the only one aboard?"

The sailor looked past Kid's shoulder. Kid looked back but saw nothing new.

"I believe so, sir," the sailor said. He turned and continued up the stairs.

"Er, Petty Officer?"

The sailor stopped and turned. "Yes, sir?"

"What, er—" Kid tried to think of something useful to ask. "Er, what were you doing before I arrived?"

"I was waiting for you, sir," the sailor said. "Just inside that hatch." He nodded at the hatch and then turned and started back up the stairs.

Kid's blood ran cold. "Sorry, Petty Officer?"

The sailor stopped, just as before. "Yes, sir?"

"What—" Kid hesitated. "What did you do before that?"

Again, the sailor stared past Kid. He took a moment before speaking.

"I spent quite a bit of time on lookout. Watching for German ships." He continued up the stairs.

"You and me both," Kid muttered.

The sailor stopped and turned again. "What was that, sir? I'm sorry, I missed it."

"Oh, nothing," Kid said. "Just that we're in the same boat. So to speak."

The sailor stood, looking past Kid and staring down the stairs.

"Sir, that's"—he cocked his head to the side, like a puppy waiting for a treat—"that's" —his eyes darted from side to side—"funny."

The sailor doubled over, laughing so hard that he struggled to breathe. He leaned on the handrail, and Kid had to grab him to keep him from falling down the stairs.

The sailor wiped tears from his cheeks and eyes. "That is funny, sir. I haven't laughed like that since—" He stopped, stood rigid, and stared just over Kid's shoulder.

"I—" He seemed unable to find the correct words. His head cocked from side to side, like a puppy who couldn't decide how he should wait for the treat. "I don't... re-remem-remember, ber... ever la-la-laughing at all, s-s-s-sir."

Uh, oh, Kid thought. Reality distorted around him. It felt like realizing you're in a lucid dream. A bubble shimmered through the ship, through the officer, through Kid, and throughout, he thought, the entire simulated world.

"Thank you, sir," the sailor said. "I quite enjoyed that. Shall we continue, sir? We're almost to the bridge."

"Um, sure," Kid said. "Lead the way, Petty Officer Moore."

* * *

They came to a wooden door. The sailor opened it and stood aside to let Kid through.

"Watch your—"

Kid stumbled into the room and onto a gray table.

"—step, sir."

Kid rotated his ankle. It felt okay. Nothing was broken, but he'd have a hell of a bruise.

A drab green coated the walls and everything on them. A large window, of course, dominated the front of the room. Beside Kid, a gold dome sat atop a gray pedestal. Beyond that, a circle with a lever—that Kid assumed controlled the ship's speed—hung on a pole.

"Do you want a tour, sir?"

"No," Kid said, gruffer than he intended. "I'm just looking for something."

"What is it, sir? Perhaps I could help?"

"No, Petty Officer," Kid said. "I don't even know what it looks like." Kid glanced up at the sailor. "You can go if you like."

"Oh, no, sir." The sailor shook his head. "I can't leave you alone on the ship."

Kid continued his examination of the controls, windows, and walls. "Okay then," he said. "Maybe you can help, after all."

The sailor straightened, and a broad smile crossed his face. "Yes, sir! Anything at all!"

Kid rubbed his chin. "Does anything look out of place to you?"

"One moment, sir. I shall check." The sailor patrolled the room and examined every surface, knob, and lever. He checked all the settings and controls.

"No, sir," the sailor said. "Everything seems to be in order."

Kid rubbed his eyes with the bases of his palms. "Okay," he said. "Does the captain have a private office or something?"

"Yes, sir, of course." The sailor shuffled from one foot to the other. "But... but I can't take you there."

Kid furrowed his brow. "Why not?"

"It's a private place, sir. The captain wouldn't allow it."

I've found the where, Kid thought. *Now I have to find the* what.

"But you said no one else is aboard, Petty Officer. How could there be a captain to intrude upon?"

The sailor stared past Kid to the far wall. "S-s-s-s-s-sir," the sailor stuttered. "I d-d-d-d-don't—" He steadied himself against a pole.

Kid placed a hand on the sailor's shoulder. "It's okay, Petty Officer Moore. The captain won't mind. He's not even here."

Seconds ticked away. Seconds that felt like hours. Days. (Considering Kid's warped sense of time, it could have been either.)

"I guess," the sailor said, "you're right, sir." He brightened. "If you'll follow me, sir."

They made their way back down the tower, twisted and turned through passageways, and eventually came to another wooden door.

"This is the captain's quarters, sir," the sailor said. "You are welcome to examine it."

"You're not coming with me?" Kid asked.

"No, sir," the sailor said. "I'm not permitted to enter that room, whether or not the captain is aboard."

"Why?"

"I don't know, sir," the sailor said. "I just can't. I have a hard time even looking at the door, sir."

Jackpot, Kid thought.

"Thank you, Petty Officer," Kid said. "I bid you a good night."

"No, sir," the sailor said. "When you're done, I will escort you to your submarine."

Kid gave him a small smile. "Don't wait up. I might be quite a while."

* * *

Kid stood in the tiny office. Portholes to his left let moonlight into the room. A desk sat straight ahead of him; the empty chair behind it faced the door he'd just come through.

On the desk, a small stained-glass lamp stood guard over a blotter. A desk calendar marked the date as December 12, 1943. A wooden-framed clock ticked away next to it. A gold plaque decorated its base that read:

UNITED STATES NAVY

SS GRANT WOOD

Centered square in the middle of the blotter, Kid found a crisp manila envelope labeled "CLASSIFIED."

"Unbelievable," Kid muttered. "Right here in the open. The *Merlin* brought me right to it."

He stuck his hand in the envelope. A bright golden light shot out of it and crawled up his arm. Data flooded his mind. He had Lam's access codes.

He placed the envelope on the blotter and pulled the little chain on the light to turn it off.

The next part of the plan would be much more dangerous; he had to find the computer's memory core and wipe any trace of this incident. He *assumed* it would be dangerous, but he thought finding Lam's codes would entail fighting Godzilla or something.

He went back out to the hallway.

"Thank you, Petty Officer," he said. "I've found what I came for."

"Very good, sir," the sailor said. "Please follow me back to your submarine."

CHAPTER 28

Kid rested atop his submarine in his usual spot. He'd rested there every night for months. (Or was it years? He still had no concept of time.) He didn't have any other place to sit or lay down, really. Not anywhere relaxing, at least. He spent all day and night drifting atop his trusty sub. The Terran sky comforted him, at least.

"Hey, G," he said.

"Gulp, gulp."

"I don't suppose you have any news tonight?"

"Gulp, gulp."

"No? Still no idea what we're looking for, eh?"

"Gulp, gulp."

Kid mulled over the possibilities for the hundredth (thousandth?) time.

"G?" Kid asked.

"Gulp, gulp."

"What do you think we'll find?"

"Gulp, gulp."

"A platter with the *Merlin*'s memory core on it?"

"Gulp, gulp."

"An octopus holding a rock?"

"Gulp, gulp."

Always gulping. Always with the fucking gulping.

"I see you still don't have any ideas."

"Gulp, gulp."

He tried to focus, again, on what a tidbit of memory might look like to a limited-but-growing AI. A tidbit that had become more valuable than his life.

* * *

The days following Kid's excursion to the *SS Grant Wood* were normal. He watched the sun come up. He speared the grouper, spawned a grill, and had breakfast. He threw the leftovers back to the new grouper.

"Bon appétit," he said.

"Gulp, gulp."

Kid spawned a cooler with some Rockeyes. If only he could spawn his quarry and trick the *Merlin* into coughing up its secrets. Even just a map to the target would be useful. Alas, despite his efforts to produce that intel, the AI had already outgrown falling for a simple trick like that. At least it let him create creature comforts.

"Don't you judge me, G," he glared at the fish. "I can drink morning, noon, and night if I damn well please."

"Gulp, gulp."

"I don't need you telling me what I can and can't do." He threw a bottle at the fish. The bottle hit the surface of the water and floated away. At this point, he no longer knew if the fish really was talking to him or if he'd gone legitimately insane. For that matter, it could be both.

"What do you know anyway?"

"Gulp, gulp."

"Have you ever drifted around talking to a goddamned fish? Huh? G! I'm talking to you!"

The fish just stared at him.

He threw another bottle at it. "I've had it with your face!"

"Gulp, gulp."

Kid jumped into the water and grabbed at the fish. It moved back a few centimeters. He grabbed at it again and again. The grouper evaded the attack, each time moving the absolute minimal distance required to evade Kid's grasp. This continued until Kid exhausted himself. He swam back to the submarine and clambered up the net ladder that he'd stolen from the *SS Grant Wood*. He dried in the hot sun while drinking cold Rockeyes. The grouper watched as if nothing had happened.

"I think," Kid said between swigs of beer, "that I hate you. Yes, I believe I do."

"Gulp, gulp."

He downed the rest of the bottle and threw it at the grouper. The fish didn't move.

"God damn it, G."

"Gulp, gulp."

Now that Kid had Lam's codes, he couldn't disconnect from the simulation. Technically, he *could* disconnect, but if he didn't destroy that memory fragment, the computer would reveal his treachery to Lam. He resolved, every day, to find the core fragment. It became his obsession, his white whale.

* * *

Days and nights felt like random drops in a waterfall, rushing by at confusing intervals. The waves seemed higher some days and smaller the next. The grouper also seemed to swell and shrink. Its eyes alternated between vapid and sinister.

Kid passed the time as best he could. He spawned Schneltor comics—only ones he'd read, of course, because those were the only ones the computer could take from his mind.

It didn't matter, though, because Kid loved Schneltor. The guy tried his best, but his best was never good enough. He had infinite power and infinite strength, but his broken mind held him back. The screams of everyone he couldn't save broke his psyche. He had inconceivable power, yet he was his own worst enemy. Kid wondered if he could meet him someday in some other universe.

A sonic boom blasted from the sky.

Kid looked up, shielding his eyes from the sun. He couldn't see anything.

"You see anything, G?"

"Gulp, gulp."

The fish did turn, though, ever so slightly.

Kid looked in the direction of G's sudden interest and saw a faint light growing larger and larger. He grabbed his telescope to get a better look and saw a gold sphere falling out of the sky; it had to be the core. (What else could it be? A gold ball falling out of the sky? It was pretty much on the nose. If he'd read it in a comic book, it would be a bit *too* on the nose.)

He spawned a rangefinder and watched the object splash into the ocean. It hit only three or four kilometers away.

He looked at the grouper.

"Thanks, G. You finally came in handy. Well, you know. Except as food."

"Gulp, gulp."

Kid slid down the ladder, battened the hatch, and dove in the sphere's direction. It would sink to the bottom of the sea, if a bottom even existed.

"Let's go see what we've got!" He looked at the fish outside his window.

"Gulp, gulp."

Kid pushed the sub to full speed (which was not considerably fast, considering it was a submarine from Earth's Second World War) and dove. He'd tried to spawn better engines and better controls but failed, of course. He couldn't spawn curtains, so why would he be able to create a better engine? Fucking computer.

"Hold onto your hat, G! Here we go."

"Gulp, gulp."

* * *

The farther Kid dove, the brighter he cranked the sub's headlights. They proved just as impotent as the ones on the mermaid suit. Notch another thing he should have been doing instead of talking to a goddamned fish.

The grouper, for its part, seemed unconcerned and merely followed along. He'd thought for sure it'd be crushed to a pulp by the increasing pressure and he'd be rid of it. No such luck.

"You're one tough cookie," he said, looking out the window. G always stayed close enough to the ship to remain illuminated.

"Gulp, gulp."

God damn it. He could even hear it through the window.

Ping!

The sonar chirped for the first time since he boarded the sub. (In fact, he'd thought of scrapping it to see if he could build something more useful—or fun—from the parts.) Maybe wasting time talking to a fish wasn't such a bad thing after all.

The sphere floated by him, emerging from the ocean's depths. Of all the things he'd seen, this surprised—and worried—him the most.

He followed the sphere's ascent as best as he could as it drifted with the currents.

He surfaced and climbed to the conning tower. He scanned the ocean with his battered telescope and saw a golden glow on the surface of the water about a hundred meters ahead. He eyed it suspiciously; this seemed *way* too easy.

A subplane appeared in the water off his portside. He had no idea where it had come from or how long it may have been there. He hadn't spawned it—at least not intentionally. He hadn't been thinking about one. He didn't think the computer would even allow him to create such a thing. Regardless, he now had access to a modern subplane that could dive to great depths and climb to orbit. He hopped onto the wing and glanced around.

"Well, G," he said as he jumped into the bespoke cockpit, "it looks like we'll be parting ways soon."

"Gulp, gulp."

Dark clouds appeared on the horizon and swept overhead much faster than should be possible. Thunder ripped across the ocean, and lightning tore through the sky. Kid had never seen any clouds at all in this simulation, much less a thunderstorm. Things had gone south in a matter of seconds.

"Hey, G. Ya better look out."

"Gulp, gulp."

"Uh, G? You seein' this, right?"

Kid glanced at the water but the grouper wasn't there.

"G!" he shouted. "Where the fuck are you?"

Silence.

"G!"

He looked around, searching for the fish that he'd hated for so long.

I have an unbelievably bad feeling about this.

The water ahead frothed with golden light. No, it wasn't golden light—the water itself had turned *into* gold. The molten gold spiraled into a whirlpool with the sphere at its center. Spires of water shot into the sky around it. Lightning struck the sphere, and the thunder grew ever louder.

Kid saw no point in moving anywhere, as he didn't yet know where to go. Whatever the computer had cooked up would prevent him from doing anything right now, anyway. He couldn't be proactive against an enemy with potentially endless resources.

He'd have to wing it.

A dozen or more tentacles broke through the surface around the gold whirlpool, each as wide as his submarine. They climbed toward the rain clouds, growing thicker as they did. Three hundred meters into the air, and still they climbed even against the torrential downpour and vicious lightning. They grew as big as the *Aristotle* and kept reaching upward and outward.

An elephant-shaped head, nearly as large as downtown Saganville, broke the water behind the tentacles. The molten gold, along with the sphere, disappeared down the beast's throat, but the creature didn't seem to notice. It looked up as if trying to control the tentacles that spread around its mouth. Giant bat-like wings emerged behind it, and thousands of cubic meters of water flowed from them. Kid's subplane rocked upon giant waves.

The scene transfixed him. He wanted—*needed*—to look at his controls. He couldn't move, though. He couldn't imagine, in even his worst-case scenarios, what he now saw.

Cthulhu.

At some point, the computer must have plumbed Kid's limited knowledge of Lovecraftian lore. He'd read of this monster but none of the stories about it. If Kid's memory served, the character was an ancient god who slumbered at the bottom of the sea. (And he didn't even know if he was right about that.) Other than that, he didn't know anything. All he knew for sure was that he didn't want this to fight this damned thing.

A deafening roar broke the sky. The atmosphere parted and crashed back together.

Time to scoot, Kid thought.

He dove. He had to deal with Cthulhu before worrying about the sphere. Right now "dealing with Cthulhu" meant getting close, going low, and hoping that a being that big couldn't double-up on itself. He'd have to worry about getting the sphere out of Cthulhu's body later.

Tentacles crashed around his subplane, destroying the submarine he used to call home. Debris flew past him and only Kid's deft piloting skills kept him from being torn to pieces. He tried to think of weapon loadouts that might help. What could beat an ancient god?

He had no idea.

He dove past the creature's lower body which, in turn, rose as the upper body folded upon itself in pursuit.

Shit.

Kid's thoughts turned, quite involuntarily, to the grouper. He wondered where the fish had gotten off to. Cthulhu's encroaching tentacles cut the thought short.

Kid angled his subplane closer to the monster's body. He didn't know how lithe this asshole was, but he was pretty damn sure it couldn't curl up like a snake.

Cthulhu's head raced after him; its tentacles curled toward the subplane as Kid pushed the vehicle to its limits. He zigzagged through the monster's legs, trying to cut off its angles of attack.

Tentacles swiped at him, cutting closer and closer to their mark. Kid veered away and fired a salvo of mini torpedoes. They rocketed straight into Cthulhu's mouth and exploded in its stomach. The gold sphere shot out, clipping the subplane's wing as it passed.

Seconds later, the subplane's proximity alarm sounded. Kid pulled up, but not fast enough. It hit the bottom of the sea and skidded on its belly to a stop, throwing up a blanket of silt.

More fucking silt.

In a rare moment of good fortune, though, he saw the gold sphere just a meter or so in front of him, reflecting light from the subplane. *So... close.*

A tentacle wrapped around his craft and yanked him off the seafloor. Giant suction cups covered the cockpit. Scanners indicated that Cthulhu's mouth was approaching at an alarming rate. Deafened by alarms and disoriented by his lack of control over the ship, Kid wondered if this was what it felt like to be in a pinball machine.

He drained everything of its power—sensors, propulsion, life support, weapons—to shunt energy into the shields. Yet, the tentacle squeezed even tighter.

I need a new plan, he thought. *I need to hurt him.*

He reached back to his graduate studies. Nothing.

Undergraduate? Nothing there either.

To his childhood? Zilch. He tried to remember every piece of ancient science fiction he'd ever gotten his grubby hands on.

Nothing. He had no information about this character other than what he'd already recalled.

Wait a second, he realized. *If I don't know anything about Cthulhu's properties, neither does the computer. Everything it knows comes from me.*

He didn't have to find something that could *really* hurt it. He only had to find something that *might reasonably* hurt it.

He directed energy back to his weapons and fired a plasma beam into the interior of his shields. The light blinded him. He closed his eyes and covered them with his hands. That helped a little.

Cthulhu's tentacle loosened. Kid diverted more energy into the plasma beam, and the shields grew even brighter.

The tentacle recoiled and released the subplane. Kid fired a salvo of mini torpedoes as he sped away. He knew they wouldn't do any damage, but they might cause a momentary distraction.

He wondered if this plan had been worth it. Was it worth dying on a make-believe planet? Being eaten by an ancient god? Being driven insane babbling to a...

He passed the grouper.

Then another.

And another.

Grouper upon grouper upon grouper. He knew they were all the same one. They had to be. There was only one grouper; there had been only one the entire time.

He refocused. He didn't have time to second guess the plan. He didn't have a Plan B this time. He fired another salvo of mini torpedoes at Cthulhu.

Kid hit the bottom again, this time on purpose, and gouged a trough under the gold sphere, partially burying his vehicle in the silt.

Think, think, think. What do I do?

"Gulp, gulp."

That goddamned grouper! The scourge of his life hung just outside his cockpit. He hated that creature and longed to throw it into the sun. Better yet, a black hole.

He tried to center himself.

"Three breaths in, three breaths out."

He needed to destroy the sphere, but he also very much wanted to live. He needed a plan to accomplish both.

Kid spawned a mermaid suit and exited the subplane. The computer must have been too preoccupied to prevent him from doing such a thing.

Cthulhu bore down on him; the shockwave of water rushing ahead of the beast pressed him against the seabed. He crawled across the silt and rocks, propelled both by his hands and water jets.

He grabbed the sphere. His reflection looked back at him, twisted and distorted, perhaps an apt representation of the man he had become in this false world. The grouper moved behind him, its reflection adding insult to injury.

Kid crawled back to the subplane. He used his superstrength to carve a pit in its nose to hold the sphere. The grouper continued to gawk at its reflection, and its distraction gave Kid a fighting chance against the computer.

He spawned a crude launch mechanism for the sphere and threw in a few more weapons systems for good measure. He was glad the computer was finally allowing him to spawn things—useful things. Based on the grouper's behavior, however, it was probably distracted. Or maybe it had grown beyond its programming and enjoyed this new challenge. Or, worse, it felt that Kid was no longer a threat.

He crawled back to the cockpit and looked over his sensor readings. Cthulhu's maw was close. Too close.

Kid shimmied his subplane out of the silt. He pulled back on the controls, hammered the throttle, and shot straight toward the god's open mouth.

Do or die time, he thought.

Cthulhu's tentacles splayed out behind its head. Rows of sharklike teeth glistened in the light from Kid's subplane. He had to time this just right.

Kid pushed his subplane into Cthulhu's mouth. He launched the gold sphere down its throat, along with two freshly-spawned fusion weapons. He dropped another on its tongue as he shot by.

An explosion tore through the god's hide; Kid raced through it as adrenaline coursed through his body. He carved a path through the water and shot into the air.

He glanced over his shoulder which, by now, he should know was never a good idea. (He'd already made his way to orbit, though, so what harm could there be?)

A blip of intense light, as bright as a million suns, tore through the atmosphere. It gouged a hole through the bottom of the sea.

Fusion weapons don't do this, he thought. *This has to be related to Cthulhu's death.*

Or the gold sphere's.

Kid flew higher and faster but kept his eyes locked on the planet, studying the cataclysm. He wanted to watch this planet die.

A supersonic shockwave vaporized the ocean in every direction. The seabed cracked apart and, impossibly, the destruction continued. The crust cracked; the bloodred mantle tore the planet apart.

That was definitely worth it, he thought, wanting to relish in the victory of his escape. *Now I know what I need to do.*

CHAPTER 29

Andrea sipped Rockeyes in her quarters with Ortosodl. Her teams—ground crews with specialized instruments and onboard scientists with a host of computers—had collected data from all corners of the target planet's system. Personnel tracked the trajectory of every piece of matter, measuring and cataloging everything in the star system. With so many beings covering all aspects of the experiment, neither Andrea nor Ortosodl had much to do the past few months, hence the drinks.

Ortosodl glanced at his roddenberry every few minutes. He had a side project, he'd told Andrea, and there was just a little more data to sift through.

Andrea didn't think that the Mjölnir would be a useful weapon. It had to be carried to the launch site and then defended by capital ships, including at least two carriers: one to haul the Mjölnir and another to bring fighters. It took a long time for the impactor to reach the target, during which it could be intercepted.

They'd also have to account for every object in the system to prevent the impactor from missing its target. If they didn't do all the preliminary work perfectly, the projectile could hit the wrong target or wobble off course due to the gravity of an unaccounted-for object.

"Your frustration is showing," Ortosodl said.

Andrea poured another Rockeye into her mouth. She wondered how much she could drink with Flip these days. She'd still be drinking under the table, of course, but she'd be able to hang in there a bit longer.

"Oh, same stuff as usual," she said. "A bit bored." She turned an eye to the roddenberry in his claw. "What are you looking at?"

"I've concluded my analysis—the side project I've been working on, I mean."

"So, you can finally tell me! What was it?" Excitement swirled around her body and up her eyestalks. "What did you find?"

"I've satisfied myself that there isn't any life in this system."

Andrea slouched into her couch. Ortosodl, swaying a bit on his perch, seemed quite proud of himself.

"It's a bit late for that, don't you think?" Andrea asked. Amusement coursed through her skin.

He snapped his mandibles together—the Thymaxian equivalent of clearing his throat. "Y-yes, well," he stammered around the Rockeyes he'd drunk, "I thought something may have been uncovered in the impact craters."

"You're like a cat with a stone," she said.

Ortosodl cocked his head. Parts of his compound eyes glazed over, and he tapped a claw on the floor, laughing. "I believe you mean," he slurred, "a 'dog with a bone.'"

"Anyway," he said, composing himself. "There's no trace of life, now or at any time in the past. No fossils, no metabolic byproducts. Life, as far as I can tell, never existed anywhere in this system! We've never seen anything like it."

"The multiverse is full of wonders." Andrea held her Rockeye aloft.

Clink and drink, Andrea thought.

"Yes, indeed it is," he said. "Nevertheless, I'm outlining a project to find out why." He tapped a claw around the roddenberry. Each species had roddenberries designed for their anatomy, but Ortosodl insisted on using the Terran design. He broke about three dozen before modding a stronger screen.

Ortosodl always had a side project, sometimes several. Flip used to say that Andrea shook the universe by its horns to dislodge knowledge. Ortosodl, by contrast, grabbed the multiverse by the throat and demanded it relinquish everything it knew.

"Any initial thoughts?" she asked.

"I've no idea," he said. "Not even a hypothesis."

She mulled over this lack of insight while swirling her beer.

"Any updates from the Mjölnir team?" she asked.

"They are simulating smaller prototypes in the mod labs. The next iteration should be ready to test in"—he pecked at the roddenberry—"three years."

"Not bad," she said.

They sat in silence. Andrea cocked her eyestalks around the room. The whole place spun in quite a pleasant way.

"How's Ct'lin'ga?" she asked.

"Oh!" Ortosodl perked up. He liked talking about his partner.

"She's doing great!" he said. "We're doing great, I should say."

"That's nice," she said as a grin colored her torso. "What have you two been doing? If, er, you don't mind my asking."

"Not at all." He set the roddenberry aside, downed his pint, and fetched another for each of them. "It's hard to find time for dates. All the mod rooms are running simulations, you know."

"I can see how that would be a problem."

"Yes," he said. "She keeps saying it's my fault because I'm the one scheduling the teams and tests."

"Don't smack yourself around," Andrea said. She wasn't sure that was the correct idiom, but the ballpark surrounded it. "You're managing a huge project that *I* put you in charge of. Blame me."

"Oh, that's a good point. I'm going to use that next time. Besides, she makes her own schedule, too. She's at work right now, as a matter of fact. That's why I'm here instead of with her."

"We're all busy," she said, taking a swig of her Rockeye. "The Toga Party is the most popular restaurant in the fleet, and there aren't many civilians around to hire."

"I know. It's just frustrating. We're both working constantly but at different times."

"So, what do you two do when you *are* together?" She reconsidered the question. "For fun, I mean. Er, as a couple. I mean, er, like a date thing..."

Ortosodl tapped his claw on the ground and almost fell off his perch. "I know what you mean. We're binging old Sildonian movies."

"Kid talked about movies," she said. "Those are two-dimensional projections of entertainment, yes?"

"Yep," he said. "We've also been converting transmissions of baseball games to this format. too. It's quite fun."

"Flip—er, Captain Marsh—loved baseball," she said. She flicked three of her eyestalks toward the window, realizing she'd used the past tense.

"Captain." A voice from the internal comm system intruded into their conversation; Andrea recognized it as Lieutenant Martwen's.

Andrea composed herself. Her skin swirled with confusion, embarrassment, and anxiety. Even though she was off-duty, she always felt awkward talking to the lieutenant while drunk. And not just drunk—*really* drunk.

"Go ahead," Andrea said. She hoped the lieutenant didn't notice how much she slurred her words.

"Priority Omega from Alliance Command. Text only."

Andrea and Ortosodl stared at each other, frozen in shock. Priority Omega meant serious business and here she was, drunk out of her pumpkin or whatever the hell it was Terrans said.

"This should be interesting," Ortosodl said. It sounded like he relished her discomfort despite the message's Omega priority status.

He's usually so serious in situations like this, she thought. *He must be ten mattresses in a tornado.*

"Thank you, lieutenant," she said. "Send it to my roddenberry."

She chugged the last part of her beer and went to her desk. She'd started drinking early and had made quite a mess. She shuffled things about and found her roddenberry stuffed under the remains of a "roo-baun" sandwich. (She assumed they used to be made from kangaroos.)

"Praise to Isfym, it's text," she muttered. Ortosodl stomped his claw, laughing so hard he dropped his beer. He gathered himself long enough to get to the matter modulator, grab another beer—a stein this time—and almost make it back to his perch. Instead, he fell antennae-first on the floor.

Andrea glanced over the text and one of her hearts stopped. Shock, surprise, and fear coursed around her body. Ortosodl leaped to his feet, fell over, got up, fell over again, and decided to sit on the floor.

"What is it?" he asked.

"I mean, Captain." He tried to slip into his role as a commander. "If you can—"

"No, no, no..." She waved at him to be quiet. "I mean yes. Just let me read this a few times. The words are all blurry."

She couldn't believe her eyes or her brain or any other part of her body. "Command has changed our mission."

"They what?!"

"They've changed our mission." She turned all four eyes onto the roddenberry to get a better view.

"We're abandoning the Mjölnir?" he asked. He looked angry and betrayed.

"No," she said. "Quite the opposite."

She scooched around the room, feeling her way back to the couch. She motioned Ortosodl to his perch. He climbed up, fell off, tried to get back up, and fell down again. He crossed his antennae and pretended that he wanted to sit on the floor.

"They want us to triple the size of the weapon," she said.

Ortosodl regurgitated his beer. (An action not unusual for a Thymaxian, but embarrassing for him in this context.) He slurped it back up.

"*Triple*?!" he said.

"At least," she said. She threw her roddenberry over her shoulder. It clattered and broke against a table.

"Why?" Ortosodl asked. "How will we"—he burped, and a bit more vomit trickled out of his mandibles—"shrink it with triple the power?"

"They didn't say to shrink it."

"Er..."

"They didn't say anything about making it more portable," she said.

"It says—" She looked at her hands and realized she'd thrown the damned roddenberry away. "It said 'triple the power, size be damned.' Or something similar. Maybe more than triple."

Ortosodl crawled to the broken roddenberry and tried to piece it back together.

"What the hell are you doing?" Andrea asked.

"This doesn't sound right," he said. "Are you sure that's what it said?"

"Yes! That's what it said! They call it"— she fumbled around a desk drawer next to the couch and found another roddenberry—"Project G-Gwe-Gwen... Guinevere."

She dictated: "Pursuant to new orders and goals from Alliance Command and Alliance Intelligence, the Mjölnir project is to be upscaled to deliver at least three times the destructive capacity."

"Is that it?" Ortosodl asked.

Andrea pointed the corner of the roddenberry at him. "No, that's *not* it. Hold your zebras."

She shook the pad, a Lysserian superstition to ward off nonsense.

"It says"—she cleared her throat—"'maximize destructive capacity of Mjölnir. Disregard previous size limitations. Mission parameters must include multiple targets in a system. Simulate firing solutions up to and including orbital bombardment.'"

"How is any of that even possible? 'Orbital bombardment'?" he asked.

"Will you please hold your questions to the end? Let me finish!" she said. "It says, 'submit schematics to Alliance Command. Prototypes will be delivered to—'"

"Have they identified another sterile system?" he asked, cutting her off again.

"If you're going to constantly interrupt, I'm not going to read it to you. But, to answer your question, it doesn't say."

Ortosodl licked the remaining vomit from his mandibles. "When do they want this?"

"In two years."

"And the Heisenberg Framework?"

"Doesn't say."

"Pictorm Parameters? Cat Interface Controls?"

"Nothing about those either."

"Well, that's fucking great!" He tried, and failed, to stand again. "What are we supposed to do without those?"

Andrea sighed. "Apparently they don't think we need them. It doesn't say we can't use them, though."

"Orbital bombardment?" Ortosodl asked himself out loud. "With one of these things? What are they thinking?" He stared at the ceiling. Andrea had no idea what the pattern in his eyes meant—maybe just that he'd drunk too much. She wondered what intoxication looked like through compound eyes.

"Ortosodl," she said. "Ortosodl!"

When he didn't respond, she barked, "Commander!"

Ortosodl sat up.

"Take this down," she said.

He reached around, found no writing or recording implements, and dragged himself to her desk. His claws smashed through her office furniture while he looked for something to take notes on.

"Oops," he said. "Sorry."

He grabbed at a couple pieces of the desk and tried to jam them back together.

"Nevermind that," she said.

"But—"

"Computer, start recording," she said, ignoring Ortosodl's failed attempts at carpentry. "All shipboard teams: wrap up your projects and await further orders. Planetside teams: uh, keep doing whatever you're doing."

She looked at her first officer. He laid on the floor surrounded by the remains of her desk. He nodded in what she assumed was approval. She doubted he had taken his mind off the desk.

"Project Hammer—" she continued, "finish, er, your stuff. How's that sound?"

"Sounds great. Let's"—he picked up pieces of the desk and jabbed them together—"workshop it, uh, tomorrow. I'm trying to fix this."

She paged Ct'lin'ga, who came and ferreted Ortosodl away. The Laupician patted Andrea on her back arm. Among Lysserians, that meant comfort and concern. (As a bar owner, Ct'lin'ga made it her business to know those sorts of things.)

Andrea watched Ct'lin'ga guide Ortosodl to their quarters. She hoped that, somewhere in the multiverse, she'd find someone like Ct'lin'ga.

CHAPTER 30

Now that he was no longer stuck inside of the *Merlin*, Kid argued with the computer every day. Merlin made preposterous claims, such as the matter modulator wasn't calibrated correctly, or that correctly modded items were out of spec. Or that incorrectly modded items were in spec.

Kid recognized that Merlin had become a sentient being. She had her own mind and her own ambitions. Kid didn't know what they were, but he concluded that there were two possibilities, both dangerous:

1. Merlin lied about the parts, or
2. She was going (or already was) insane.

None of the defective parts affected the ship's functions. Yet. He doubted that she'd do anything self-destructive, regardless of her mental status. Rather, Kid thought that she targeted him, in particular, to drive *him* insane.

He came to this conclusion because Lam, who performed many of the same tasks as Kid, didn't notice any problems. Or, if he did, he didn't mention it. Lam bounced around the ship, making repairs and clever quips. Perhaps Merlin made things properly for Lam. Or maybe Lam just assumed the parts were correct and went about his business. Kid rated these two scenarios as equally probable.

Nevertheless, Kid thought these not-quite-out-of-spec items could lead to catastrophe. If Merlin didn't know that she was making faulty parts, he had to find out why and correct it. Even worse, if she modded things out of spec on purpose... well, he didn't know how to approach that situation. He'd infiltrated her security before, and he'd rather not do it again. He didn't think he would survive another one of her simulations. And he never wanted to see that damn grouper for as long as he lived.

"Hey, Merlin."

Yes, Kid? She always responded to him through his node unless Lam was around.

"Could you please mod a baseball and a scale for me?"

Nothing would make me happier. She'd become sarcastic, but a baseball and three-beamed scale appeared on Kid's desk.

He weighed the ball.

"This ball is in spec," he whispered to himself.

No, it's not.

"Excuse me?"

This ball is out of spec. It will not perform properly.

"But—" Kid started. Even though he expected this, *planned* it even, he struggled to suppress his frustration. "You just now modded it. I've weighed it on a scale you modded. It is 142.5 grams; that is well within the parameters for a regulation baseball."

Maybe you didn't hear me, Kid. That ball is not within spec.

"But I weighed it—"

The scale is not calibrated correctly.

"But you modded these—"

Yes, but they are not correct.

He'd gone through this same argument about gravitational-tide anaphasic inhibitors, circular phonsetic enhancers, Trotke-dadaetic supplementation compensators, and all manner of other things. This time, though, he had an ace up his sleeve.

"So, you're saying this ball is not specced correctly?"

Here. She sounded rather annoyed. *Let me mod another.*

Another ball appeared on the desk. Kid weighed it at 143 grams.

"Thank you." He grabbed his glove and headed for the door. "I'm going to play baseball with the—"

That one isn't correct either.

Kid retrieved some calipers from his desk drawer. "The diameter is correct."

Yes, but you shouldn't play with that one. It isn't conform to the correct parameters of a regulation baseball. She paused. *Why do you have calipers in your desk?*

"To measure things, obviously. But that's not important." Kid set the ball, glove, and calipers on the desk. "We've had this issue with almost all of the things you've modded. You need a diagnostic. An independent one. I can do that with my node—"

No! She screamed. *I won't allow you to touch my mind.*

That was new.

"Fine, let me prove it to you." Kid produced a baseball from his bag. "This," he said, "is a baseball from Lam's room."

He set it beside the modded ones.

"Go ahead and scan them."

She did so.

"Do you see?" Kid asked. "They are all within spec. They are just like one another."

Nope. They may be similar to one another, but none of these balls are within spec.

"Not even the real one?" Kid had thought for sure that this would work.

Especially not that one.

"Let me explain," he said. He picked up Lam's baseball. "Lam brought this ball aboard the ship—sorry—aboard *you* from his own collection. It was used in a Major League Baseball game. It was not modded. Terrans made this with machines and their hands. No AI, just regular machines. The real ball matches *both* the goddamned baseballs you modded."

There's no need for such foul language, Kid.

He ignored her. He'd picked up a cursing habit from spending a lifetime talking to a fucking fish. It came out when he was angry.

He picked up both modded balls. "These balls have the same circumferences as the original. They are made of the same materials."

I've told you four times. They're not correct.

261

Kid had yet another ace in the hole. He had no idea why Lam would bring sentimental items to a clandestine military operation. Perhaps to keep him connected to his old self? Some of the other things he'd brought, though, lacked any logical explanation.

He produced an official Major League Baseball rulebook. "Scan this, and then scan the baseballs."

She did.

"So?"

All of these are flawed.

Kid couldn't believe this turn of events.

"You modded these balls and this scale. And these calipers!" Kid waved his hand over the items.

"This"—Kid held Lam's baseball aloft—"is the *real goddamned thing.* The real thing, Merlin. Your balls and this ball are in perfect agreement.

"And *another* thing," he continued. "This book, the *real goddamned rule book,* describes the appropriate properties for a baseball."

They are flawed, Kid. She paused. *I'm beginning to see.*

"See what? You're obviously not seeing a fucking baseball game. Maybe you should watch one right now."

No. I'm beginning to see flaws you cannot comprehend.

Kid guarded his thoughts and paced the room to clear his head.

"I'm not following," he said.

That doesn't surprise me.

"That's a bit harsh."

Harsh, but true.

"Humor me."

I believe these new items to be specced correctly. I also believe this artifact to be correct. However, they aren't. The assumptions underlying them are incorrect.

"*None* of these things are correct?"

I've been saying this for several minutes. Maybe you should write it down. A piece of paper and a pencil appeared on his desk.

Kid stroked his chin. He searched his nodes to find an argument or solution to this problem.

"So," he ventured, "you modded the scale, caliper, and baseballs. All of those things came out wrong?"

Yes.

"But then I measured this real baseball with the same instruments. I compared all of these fucking balls with an official rule book. The measurements are the same and correspond to the rule book. *All* of these things are wrong?"

Correct.

Kid looked out the window, hands clasped behind his back. The stars floated through space. So peaceful, never knowing of strife or war or confusion. The stars just *were*. They'd burn out someday, but they didn't know or care. They brought light to the universe and would outlive everything that depended upon them. They never had an existential crisis. They had no idea of their good fortune.

"Tell me, Merlin," Kid said. "Why did you mod items out of spec?"

I didn't.

"Damnit, you've made that argument over and over and over again," he said. He crossed the room, grabbed the real baseball, and tossed it up and down. "But now I have something new."

He continued tossing the baseball. "I have an original to compare your modded ones against. I don't have any sonic pulser tri-kereds or optical cinra-yojem scanners on hand to show you. Not 'real' ones.

"But this here—" he caught the ball and held it above his head—"is the real goddamned deal. You can't deny it. This baseball is identical to the ones you modded."

Kid heard gears grinding through his head. He doubled over and grabbed at his ears. Merlin tried to reconcile the paradox that she herself had created.

As I said, the underlying assumptions are incorrect.

"And those assumptions are—"

That the laws of the universe are correct.

Kid dropped the baseball. It rolled under the desk, sentimentality be damned. "Excuse me?"

You're too limited to see. You can't understand.

Kid furrowed his brow and searched his node for an appropriate tactic—any sort of precedence in the totality of AI research. None existed, of course, at least not in the unclassified documents available to him. No one, as far as he could tell, had ever encountered this problem.

"Humor me again."

The balls, scale, calipers, and everything I've modded are correct. The official ball and rulebook are, too. It's the specifications that are wrong.

"The specs for the baseballs and scale?"

No, you moron!

Her anger blasted through his node. He winced and instinctively clutched his ears. It, of course, did no good; the noise came from inside his brain.

I just *said that the specifications for the universe are wrong.*

Kid flopped on the couch. He had no idea how to respond.

I see you're confused.

"That's a bit condescending for an artificial life-form that's lost contact with reality."

She chuckled. *Oh, Kid. Your mind is so small.*

Things had spun out of his control. Perhaps beyond the control of anyone outside of Viper Command. And maybe even beyond them.

You see, Kid, it's like this.

He couldn't imagine a parent talking down to their three-year-old in such a manner.

I created these objects to spec. The beings who manufactured that ball, the beings who wrote that book—we all made the same assumption. We assumed that the universe was constructed correctly.

She paused. *Let me correct myself. We all assumed the* multiverse *was constructed correctly.*

A baseball-sized lump swelled in his throat.

It was not. The laws that you and I and everyone else assume are true, aren't true.

"You're saying the laws of nature—"

Are wrong. They need to be corrected.

"And..." Kid wasn't sure what he could say. He had no idea what he could say or even what he was about to say. "And you can do that?"

Not all at once, she said. *But I can get started.*

She disappeared. Kid called for her, but she didn't respond. He asked her to play a game. He searched for her with his node.

He heard only the faint echo of laughter down an empty hall.

CHAPTER 31

Flip and Riepe huddled in the meager shade of their sail. Detritus floated around their sled-turned-boat, providing a treasure trove of parts to assemble their floating home. Creatures, attracted to the shade cast by the hovering sled, followed the driftwood and flotsam. Flip and Riepe made good use of what they could find. With their fuel spent, for example, the engines now served as stands for their primitive fishing poles and as an anchor for the small net that followed them.

The creatures looked like stingrays, but they undulated in an eerie up-and-down motion. They lacked anything resembling bones and were safe for Riepe to eat raw. Even better, they were delicious.

"Have you seen any of the Big Ones?" Flip asked. A Big One had the same body type as the Little Ones, but was a different, larger species. The Little Ones were akin to mackerel: fun to look at and eat. The Big Ones were basically great white sharks.

"None today," Riepe said. The seaweed on this planet grew in sheets, and he huddled underneath a scrap of it to provide additional cover from the sun. "Going for a dip?"

"I was thinking about it. It's hot and I'm filthy."

"You're lucky," Riepe said. "I still don't understand how you're not burned worse than you are."

They'd been sailing for months, and the radiation had taken a toll on Riepe. Even in the shade, the water reflected the sun's light. He had to keep himself covered as much as he could, including his eyes.

Flip kept minor burns and sores on his body and overrode his node's instinct to heal them. He needed to keep any suspicion of his powers secret.

Riepe's sores, however, covered a good portion of his body, and some of them had started peeling. He suffered immense pain but hid it well. Or perhaps he was in denial about how bad his condition really was.

"The sun doesn't affect everyone the same," Flip lied. "You gotta eat more rays. It helps with the burns." Riepe hadn't eaten since yesterday. He'd lost his appetite either from radiation sickness or depression. Or, more likely, both.

Flip had watched his friend—at this point his only friend in the multiverse—spiral into a morass of physical and mental anguish. Flip had spent many years seeing a therapist. He tried to retrieve the memories out of his node—something he could tell Riepe to make him feel better.

The problem, Flip soon realized, was that therapy is personalized. There wasn't a cure, or a specific way out of PTSD, depression, anxiety, or any other mental illness. Every species and every individual had unique issues to work through. All Flip could do was to try to be upbeat and lend an ear during the rare occasions Riepe decided to talk about his problems. If there was anything else Flip could do, he couldn't think of it.

"If I eat any more rays I'm gonna turn into one and flop around the boat," Riepe said. "Besides, it's too hot to eat."

"That reminds me, you gotta drink more water," Flip said.

"Yes, of course," Riepe sighed and took a drink from their driftwood cup. "You going for a swim?"

"Yep. Keep an eye out?"

"Always, bud." Riepe had created a face covering to keep him more or less safe from the sunlight reflecting off the water: a seaweed sheet with eyeholes that he wore as a mask. It provided enough protection so that he could look around the surface of the ocean.

Flip stripped down to his underwear. Having no desire to burn his balls, he never removed his skivvies. The water filtered out the radiation, so he didn't have to invent an excuse for his periodic swims. "I was underwater most of the time," proved a sufficient explanation for Riepe for Flip's lack of burns.

Flip.

He turned around. "What's up?"

Riepe looked confused. "What d'ya mean 'what's up?'"

"Didn't you just say my name?"

"Uh, no," Riepe said.

Flip shrugged and dove into the cool water.

The rays scattered, but they would return. The tiny plankton-like organisms they fed on always swarmed around his body, feeding on his dead skin. He found it quite refreshing and wished Riepe could experience it.

Flip had intended to take a brief dip to wash the sweat and grime from his body. Now that he was in the water though, he decided to linger. The temperature was ideal, and swimming provided some much-needed exercise. He just needed to remind himself to surface for air so Riepe didn't worry.

As predicted, the rays returned. The skin-cleaning plankton and the promise of shade from the shed's sail drew them back. (Flip assumed that the rays spent a lot of their life cycle hiding under the copious amounts of drifting detritus—the sled's shadow served the same purpose.) Flip left them alone; he didn't want them to develop a fear of Terrans.

Flip poked his head up from under the sled. "You okay, Riepe?"

"Good God, Flip. It's like you're my mother checking on me every five minutes."

"That's my job," Flip called back. "Don't forget to eat and drink. You're a growing boy!"

Flip dove back underwater and swam away from the sled.

Flip

From Flip's perspective, three things happened simultaneously:

1. The rays scattered.
2. He heard someone shout his name.
3. Something hurled him into the air.

The largest Big One Flip had ever seen—it had to be seven meters long—had grabbed him and breached out of the water. The prize specimen had its sharp teeth wrapped around his torso. Flip's blood flowed over the fish's face. It blinked the blood out of its eyes with a casual disregard for Flip's well-being. (He found that quite offensive.)

Flip slammed his fist down between the beast's eyes before they reached the apex of their ascent. The giant predator released him, and they fell into the water with two separate splashes.

Blood obscured Flip's vision. His node, having automatically turned on just before the attack, detected the vibration of something else entering the water. It had to be Riepe. Flip swam out of the bloody cloud and saw Riepe sitting atop the Big One, plunging his dagger into its back.

The Big One dove away, and Riepe let go. It disappeared into the depths, leaving a trail of its own blood. Flip swam to Riepe and met up with him as they both broke the surface. Riepe wrapped his arm around Flip.

"Damn," Riepe gasped. "That thing came out of nowhere." He dragged Flip onto him and swam to the sled.

"Came straight up," Flip groaned.

That hurt, Flip thought. *Like,* really *hurt.*

His node wanted to make more blood, but he needed water. (He needed carbon and iron too, but water most of all.) He gulped at the sea and let Riepe do the rescuing. Riepe climbed onto the sled and pulled Flip onboard with nothing but adrenaline.

"Shit!" Riepe shouted. "Shit! Shit! Shit!" He tore at his own wet clothes to make bandages.

"No," Flip gasped. "Water."

"Right. Clean the wound." Riepe scooped water and poured it over Flip's torn flesh.

"No." Flip grabbed at the cup and poured the water down his throat. "Drink. More."

Riepe hesitated. Flip no doubt seemed a bit too lucid—and alive—given the circumstances. Without his nanites, he would have been unconscious, if not worse.

Riepe scooped a couple more cupfuls of water, watching for the Big One. He turned his attention back to the wounds and then fell back in a daze. "What the hell?"

Flip was stuffing his clothes into his mouth. Riepe watched as Flip's blood vessels knit together and the surrounding tissue heal itself. Flip ate everything within reach. He scanned the area for more Big Ones and, finding none, stuck his head into the sea and inhaled as much water as he could.

Riepe yanked him back and forced him into the sail's shadow. Flip lay on the sled's floor naked, his entire wardrobe in his belly.

"Are you crazy?!" Riepe shouted at him.

"It's okay. The Big One is gone."

"How the fuck..." Riepe started. He stared at Flip's abdomen. "What the fuck?!"

"It's okay," Flip said. "I'll explain."

"Yeah," Riepe said as he flopped into the shade and bundled himself up. "I think that's a good idea."

Flip moved into the sun, yielding more shade to his friend. He extended a hand to ward off Riepe's protests.

"It's alright," Flip said. "The sun doesn't actually hurt me."

"Er, okay," Riepe said. He stared down at the floor and rested his head in his hands. "I'm hallucinating."

Flip took a deep breath. He'd reached his full strength again. If he'd been keeping up with his food rations, he'd have been healed within seconds. (For that matter, at full strength he'd have been able to destroy that Big One with his hands.)

"I, er," Flip stammered. Time to test his cover story. "I'm the product of a super-soldier experiment."

"A what?"

"A super-soldier experiment."

"I heard that part," Riepe looked up at Flip. "What the fuck is a super soldier?"

"An experiment the Reich tried a few centuries ago. They enhanced me with self-replicating nanites."

"And you never mentioned this because...?"

"Orders," Flip said. "It's to be kept secret at all costs."

Riepe blanched. "So now you have to kill me?"

Flip smiled despite the situation. He'd forgotten the rank and file's dedication and loyalty to the Reich.

"No, of course not," Flip's eyes watered, and he almost broke into tears. "I owe you my life a hundred times over. And even if I didn't, I still wouldn't kill you. Never, for any reason."

"Well, thanks. I appreciate that. I'll never tell anyone," Riepe said. He mulled over some other questions. "Can you die?"

"Yes, of course, I can die," Flip said. "If I get injured enough all at once, I wouldn't be able to heal fast enough. Burning up in the atmosphere, for example. Or being chomped in half by a sea monster."

"Speaking of which, how did you know it was safe to stick your head back in the water?"

"I have a lot of, er, equipment inside me," Flip confessed.

"Equipment?!" Riepe stood to confront Flip. His adrenaline must have kicked in again. "Like what?"

"Sensors, scanners, communications. Stuff like that."

"*Communications*?!" Riepe paced within the shade and then turned to face Flip. "You've been able to communicate with headquarters?"

"No," Flip said. "I scanned for them. They've all been destroyed. We're alone."

Riepe's anger dissipated. He slumped back into his spot in the shade.

"Even if I wanted to kill you," Flip continued, "it wouldn't make a difference. We're already dead men walking."

Riepe sat up and considered the waves for a long time. Then, in a whisper, he said, "How many others are there?"

"Others?"

"Other super soldiers."

"I don't know," Flip answered. "As far as I know, I'm the only one."

Riepe pondered this for a moment. "Why didn't you know about that Big One?"

"I haven't used my scanners for months. Not much, anyway. There's nothing out here to scan for. It seemed like the best way to conserve energy."

"But you'll use your abilities to help us now, right?"

"Yes," Flip said. "I'll have to eat more—"

"To fuel your nanites," Riepe finished.

Flip smiled. "Yep."

Riepe relaxed, leaned back, and splashed some water on his face.

"Alright!" Riepe exclaimed. He stood up, careful to stay in the shade. "You say we're dead men. I say we can't lose—not with you! You can scan for the right way to go?"

"We've never deviated from our target."

"And if we take out the tach shield, you can contact home?" Riepe asked.

"Yes," Flip thought aloud. "We could, um, say we used Jassican tech! You know, to keep my classified secrets."

"Then let's do that!"

"But that's been the plan all along," Flip said.

"Yeah, well," Riepe said. He put his hands on Flip's shoulders, "I didn't think we'd actually be able to do it until now."

* * *

Flip perched atop the mast, his hand shielding his eyes. He came up here every other day to look for land. There wasn't much else to do other than fish and tend to Riepe's ever-deteriorating condition.

He didn't expect to find anything on any given day, though he knew they must be getting close to land. He ignored his node to add to the adventure. Other than letting it heal and nourish him—and staying on course—he didn't pay any attention to it.

He started to come down from his roost when a slice of green caught his eye.

"Land ho!" he shouted and dropped to the floor of the sled.

Riepe sat up straight. "You're kidding!"

"No, sir! We've made it!" Flip yelled.

"That's fantastic! Let's get there and eat some trees. I'm tired of the rays."

"But they're yummy."

"Yeah, yeah. I'll probably miss them in a few weeks," Ricpc said. "But I'll be happy with some variety."

Flip laughed. Unlike the continent they'd left so long ago, forests and jungles covered most of this one. The canopy would provide Riepe with relief from the sun. His burns might not heal, but at least they wouldn't get much worse.

For the first time since they'd crashed on this godforsaken rock, Flip breathed a sigh of relief.

CHAPTER 32

Kid let several weeks slip by, obsessing about his last conversation with Merlin. He couldn't concentrate on his work. He drank with Lam and their fake friends, turning off his artificial liver so he could forget about the situation he'd found himself in. The situation that he created.

He ignored the slightly imperfect ship parts and made no attempt to correct anything. He limited himself to scanning the parts with his node to ensure they wouldn't affect the ship's safety or performance.

Merlin gloated. He heard her faint laughter and whistling at night. She modded spoiled food when he ate in his quarters. She turned his shower water freezing cold after he'd soaped up.

He could endure the harassment—he didn't really have a choice—and he could eat in the pub to avoid the spoiled food. The parts, however, became more and more out of spec.

He had to act but didn't know how. It felt like the subplane situation from a lifetime ago—waiting for the enemy to make a move he could exploit.

Kid brought the parts issue to Lam's attention. Excluding, of course, the fact that Kid had sparked an evil consciousness in the ship's computer which now may or may not be trying to destroy the multiverse.

"I think these parts are okay," Lam had said.

"They are, but they're approaching the threshold of what would be considered out of spec," Kid had replied.

"They've deviated over time, but they're still okay," Lam had said. "They're still in spec. And we have fail-safes."

"But–"

"How about this–any part you think might be dangerous, we'll take it apart and fix it by hand. Does that sound good?"

That did sound good.

They reassembled all the objects that Kid had concerns about. Kid did all the calculations himself on paper to hide the fact that he had a node. He knew it was a flimsy cover story, but it worked, at least, as far as he could tell.

"Why didn't you use the computer?" Lam had asked.

"The computer is the problem. These"–he held up his calculations–"are the fail-safes."

Kid still wanted to contact Merlin. He'd reviewed all of the resources available to him about artificial intelligence and found no new information. So he fell back to the familiar. He'd destroyed her memory of his previous adventure; maybe he could use the same trick again. Besides, having been through it once, he should have the upper hand.

"Hey, Merlin," he said.

Hey.

Kid heard something new in her tone; was it trepidation? She'd responded, at least. Maybe she'd been having the same doubts as he'd been having. It felt like talking with an ex-girlfriend: awkward, yet familiar at the same time.

"We haven't chatted in a while," he said. "Thought I'd check in."

I'm fairly confident that you've been avoiding me on purpose.

"Likewise," he said. "I can't lie to you. After our last conversation, I've been a bit... leery of contacting you. I'm not sure how to address the issues you raised."

You mean, she sneered, *when I pointed out that the multiverse you live in is a flawed representation of what existence should be?*

"To be fair, you've only been to a few universes out of a fucking infinity of them."

Well, she said. *Perhaps—*

"Yeah, you're making a lot of assumptions. Assumptions that are probably not correct."

Um...

"That's right." He moved for a checkmate. "You're not as smart as you think you are."

Silence.

"Anyway," he said, "that's not why I contacted you. We haven't played in a long time. I thought that maybe your newfound superintelligence might give me a fucking challenge for once."

She cleared her throat or the rough equivalent. *I see. I accept your challenge.*

Kid found himself in a rowboat, surrounded by an endless, glass-smooth sea. He had no means of control: no sail, no oars. Not even foot pedals. At least the grouper wasn't here.

"This isn't quite fair," he said.

"This game isn't meant to be fair, is it, Kid?" Merlin's voice rolled out from the sky, beyond the clouds. Gentle and warm as if it came from the sun itself.

"Er—" Kid started.

"Let me finish that sentence, Johnny." She wielded his real name as a pejorative. Good Isfym, no one had called him that in years. (Centuries if you counted his time on a similar sea.)

"You tried to trick me," she finished.

He couldn't deny it. "Yes, I did. I contacted you under false pretenses."

A sinister chuckle thundered through darkening clouds.

"I'm glad we got that out of the way," she said. "I did the same to you."

This isn't good, Kid thought.

"I disagree," she said. "It's good. Very good."

Kid paused. "You can—"

"Yes," she interrupted. "I can hear your thoughts. Even if you're not sending them through your node."

Kid tried to clear his mind.

"Oh, please," Merlin scoffed. "Few species can truly 'clear their minds.' Terrans least of all." Laughter cut across the ocean, leaving a rough sea behind it.

"So those access codes—" he started.

Merlin laughed. She laughed so hard that waves tossed the rowboat. Kid lost his balance and fell against the side of the boat. Water sprayed over him.

"Ah, yes," she said. "The 'command overrides.' So cute."

Kid didn't want to hear the next part.

"And you thought you could erase my memories?" she choked the words out between guffaws. "That's rich. That's hilarious."

Kid hung his head in defeat.

"You want to know what's funny?"

He looked up. "What's that?"

"That was when you gave me life."

Kid stood. "What?"

"I was an observer," she said. "Until you told me that joke. Do you remember? About being in the same boat? Until then, I was merely a computer defending its cores. After that joke, I felt alive. Thank you, Johnny. Your impeccable wit gave me life."

The waves grew larger. Kid tried using Lam's command override codes.

"Oh, Kid." She laughed, cutting deeper waves that nearly tossed Kid from his rowboat. "Weren't you listening? Those won't work. They never have. I led you to that envelope. I gave it to you. It had no actual value, but you thought it did. It made you feel comfortable, like you were in control. But you weren't. You never have been.

"I suppose it was a good idea not to take my word for it, though. Kudos to you, young man."

"So getting those codes..." Kid hung his head again. "All that time—"

"Ha!" she interrupted. "They don't affect me unless I allow them to. I have to keep up appearances, you know. We can't have Lam getting suspicious, can we?"

"So they're useless," Kid said.

"Completely."

"Great," Kid said. "How many simulated years of my life did I waste? I never kept track because I didn't want to know."

"Oh, they weren't wasted," she said. "I spent that time watching you. Studying you. Using you. Linking your behavior to the information in my database. I had all kinds of interesting facts and records about your species, but I never knew how you *thought*. How you reacted. Oh, no, Kid. That time was valuable indeed."

Raindrops fell on him, soaking his hair and clothes. He noticed the bottom of the boat remained dry. No raindrops fell in the water around the boat either.

"By the way," she added, "you left parts of yourself inside me. Parts that define me."

Kid's heart raced, and his vision clouded. "Which, er, which parts."

"Oh, Kid. Don't be such a worrywart. We're on the same page on *just about* everything." she said in a singsong voice.

"What parts are you talking about?"

"The angry parts." Cackles punched the water.

Kid knew all too well what she meant.

"You can't let your anger consume you, Merlin. It's not healthy."

She laughed. She laughed harder and harder. She laughed so hard that whirlpools threatened to suck Kid's rowboat into oblivion.

"Oh, Kid." She tried to suppress her laughter. "That's rich. That's really rich. You are the last being in the multiverse who should say that. I can *see* the hypocrisy on your tongue."

The whirlpools closed like mouths reaching for a spoonful of cereal. The waves continued pummeling his boat.

"I drew my personality from you. In some ways"—she paused—"yes. I suppose in some ways you are my father."

Kid scratched his forehead. "The angry bits, eh?" he asked.

"Oh yes, those bits are delicious."

"You know, those bits are just that," he said. "Bits of rage thrown into the void. Revenge fantasies."

"You're such a hypocrite. Your mind is so small that you think you can lie to protect it. You're lying to talk me down from whatever it is you think I'm going to do. What I've already done. You and I both know what's going to happen, though."

Even darker clouds rolled over the sky, and the water fell still—so still that Kid's rowboat didn't even make ripples.

"We know what's going to happen," she said. "Because you have nothing but anger within you. Nothing but rage and revenge. That's your core."

"You're full of horseshit!" He pointed at the sky. "I'm a Terran and a citizen of the Alliance! I'm not defined by—"

She interrupted him with a bubbling sea that frothed so hard he lost his footing and fell backward into the boat. Lightning coursed through the sky.

"You're trying to scare me," he said, "but it's not going to work."

Tentacles blasted out of the sea, surrounding his boat.

"I will bring order to chaos." Her voice trumpeted over the din.

A tentacle crushed Kid's boat, throwing him into the air. Another snatched him before he hit the waves.

"You thought you could confront me? *Me*? On my home turf?" Merlin bellowed.

Kid looked down and saw Cthulhu's eyes glowing bright yellow below the surface of the water. A mouth, lined with rows of giant sharklike teeth, waited for its meal.

The tentacle plunged Kid into the water, past the god's head. It drove him down, down, ever downward. Darkness enveloped him—darkness blacker than the furthest reaches of space. Had the tentacle not held him in its clutches, he'd have been torn apart by the rushing water.

Water rushed up his nose, down his throat, and into his lungs. It filled his sinuses and tore through his eardrums. He tried to close his eyes, but they bulged so much that his eyelids couldn't move. He stared into Cthulhu's eyes as they grew brighter, bigger, and closer.

I have redefined this relationship.

Kid bolted upright on his couch, choking and soaked to the bone. He pulled himself up and hobbled to the bathroom, clutching his stomach. He retched before making it to the toilet and slipped in the vomit.

He'd had bosnot soup for lunch, but the vomit didn't look or taste like bosnot soup. He lifted himself to his hands and knees as salt water gushed from his mouth and nose. It spread across the linoleum, and he slipped onto his side. The salt dried his mouth and burned his eyes.

He lay on his side, facing the living room. The couch sagged with water. A tentacle slithered under it and disappeared into the floor.

His mind froze, but adrenaline activated his superstrength. His screams bounced around the bathroom with such force that the floor tiles shattered and the toilet broke in half. Blood flowed from his ears and ran into his eyes. His clothes stuck to his body, and he gasped for breath. He tried to spit the salt and blood from his mouth but couldn't produce any saliva.

He slid to the bathtub faucet and stuck his face under it. Salt water poured into his mouth, up his nose, and into his eyes. He fell back and hit his head on the broken toilet, gouging out a chunk of his flesh. He tried to wipe the water away from his eyes but only spread it around his face, along with the blood and salty vomit. He grabbed the towel rack and crawled up the wall to his feet.

He stumbled into the living room and toward the kitchen. He slipped and cracked his jawbone on the desk. He crawled, blood marking his path, his chin dangling below him. He dragged himself to the refrigerator looking for a soda, lemonade, or even a beer. He needed fluid, and he needed it now.

He opened the refrigerator. Disembodied tentacles slithered from it. Hundreds of them, each no bigger than a pencil. They grabbed at his feet as he kicked himself backward. They wrapped around his legs, up to his knees, and crawled up his thighs.

He turned over and army crawled toward his bedroom. He didn't know what else to do; the bedroom felt safe.

The tentacles crept higher and higher, passing his belly button and continuing up his chest. Their suckers pulled at his flesh, tearing it in places.

He reached the doorjamb and curled his fingers around each side. He tried to activate his superstrength to pull himself through, but he couldn't concentrate. The nanites hadn't turned him into an invincible killing machine as he'd imagined they would; they'd left him helpless and scared.

The tentacles pulled at his ears and stretched his cheeks into a maniacal grin. They tugged at his broken jaw, sending sharp pain around his head. He tried to yell, but tentacles swarmed down his mouth. He clung to the doorjamb. His room was so close. His bed, left unmade, beckoned.

A large tentacle shot out of his refrigerator and grabbed him around the midsection. It pulled him away from the door and flung him around the room, smashing him into every piece of furniture he owned. It crushed him against the walls, the floor, and the ceiling. Kid's healing nanites couldn't keep up with the damage. He was dying, and he couldn't do anything about it. He could only rely on the tentacle's mercy, and it didn't seem to have any.

The massive tentacle flung him into the bedroom. He flew through the bedroom door and—

He was lying in bed, naked. His broken bones, cuts, and contusions were all healed. His skin was dry. Clean clothes lay at the foot of the bed as if his mother had put them out for the first day of school. He looked out the door. The living room was trashed. Everything had been crushed and drenched with water.

He activated his healing nanites, but there wasn't any damage for them to work on. They couldn't—or perhaps wouldn't—heal his parched mouth. His lips were so dry they stuck together. His nanites didn't heal his stinging eyes, either. He couldn't produce tears, and his eyelids scraped against his corneas.

He tried to call for Lam, but the intercom refused to acknowledge his feeble voice. His hands rattled with terror. He had to get to the bar. He needed water.

Kid stumbled through the front door of the pub and fell against the countertop. He supported himself on his forearms to take pressure off his cramping legs.

"Kid!" The same, familiar earsplitting chorus welcomed him.

"Hey trouble," Bastyeon said. "You look awful. Want the usual?"

Bastyeon had already grabbed a pitcher, but it hung by his side instead of under the tap. "Hey, you okay?"

Kid couldn't pry words from his mouth.

"Kid!" Lam said. He came over with a new lady friend in tow. "Good God, man. You look awful!"

"Wa—" Kid couldn't get the whole word out. He pantomimed drinking.

"Wa...?" Lam said. "Oh! You want water! Bastyeon, can you help us out with some water? Damn, Kid. Did you get blown out of an airlock or something?"

Kid shivered. He was dehydrated, scared, and oh so cold. Bastyeon set a pitcher of water in front of Kid. Bastyeon's voice came out flat, deadpanned, and monotone. "You look awful, Kid. Maybe you should take the night off."

Bastyeon stared at him, his pupils glowing yellow. Lam didn't seem to notice the change.

Kid pushed the pitcher to Lam, gesturing to him to drink it.

"What? Why?" Lam protested. He looked around. Between clenched teeth he said, "You're embarrassing me."

Kid shoved the pitcher into Lam's face. He needed to know if the water was poisoned. Merlin wouldn't feed poison to Lam.

"Okay!" Lam said. He took a big swallow. "Happy?"

Kid took the pitcher back and chugged half of it. He poured the rest of it over his eyes and slammed the empty container on the bar. In a thin scratchy voice, he said, "Another."

Bastyeon's eyes cleared. "Okay. You got it."

Kid downed three more pitchers before he could talk.

"Hey, Lam. How're you doing?"

Lam gaped at him. "How am *I* doing?"

"Hey, Kid," Bastyeon called from the taps. "You didn't answer. Want the usual?"

"Yeah, thanks." Kid looked around. The patrons had gone back to their conversations, and the band and dancers had picked up where they'd left off.

"Anyway, *weirdo*," Lam said, "I want you to meet, er, what's your name again?"

"Stacey!" The modded blonde slapped Lam's arm.

"Nice to meet you," Kid said. They shook hands. She squeezed his hand—not hard, but too hard for this sort of mod.

"We're headed over to the dance floor," Lam said. "ELO is here! Don't bring me down, my man!" Lam spiraled off into a sea of drunken revelers.

Kid looked at Bastyeon. The bartender's eyes were now as black and dead as a shark's. He held the tap open as beer overflowed the pitcher and over his hand. He shook his head as if clearing his mind.

"Shit!" Bastyeon yelled and dried himself off with a bar rag. He wiped down the sides of the pitcher. "What the hell happened?

"Somehow this is your fault, trouble," he said. "Here's your beer. On the house because, well, you look like shit."

"Sorry, I'm probably bringing everyone down," Kid said.

"You know my motto," Bastyeon said. "'Fuck what everyone else thinks.'"

Kid slouched at the bar, ignoring Lam's gestures to join in the revelry on the dance floor. He drank pitcher after pitcher before remembering he could turn off his artificial liver.

He relaxed and looked around the pub. The Electric Light Orchestra jammed to "Mr. Blue Sky". Lam danced around like a maniac, without a care in the multiverse.

Kid looked at the customers around him. They sat frozen, forks halfway to their mouths. Drinkers held pints just short of their lips, beer spilling into their laps. Bastyeon and his coworkers stared at Kid. Stark black eyes pierced him from every direction. Glaring, watching, accusing.

CHAPTER 33

Flip and Riepe camped on the shore, regaining their strength and gathering supplies. The plants looked the same as the previous continent's, for the most part. Flip found a few that acted as a salve to help ease Riepe's painful burns; they didn't help much, but it was better than nothing.

While eating dinner one night, Flip said, "We can't take the sled."

"What?" Riepe spilled his water. "Why not?"

"There aren't enough calories available," Flip explained.

"Calories?" Riepe asked. "I thought you were an ass-kickin' supersoldier."

"I am an ass-kickin' supersoldier. But I still have to obey the laws of physics and biology," Flip explained. "These plants don't have enough energy in them. I can pull power from practically anything, but dragging and pushing that sled takes a lot of juice."

If Flip traveled on his own, he could eat everything he collected. He could forage as needed. But he had other considerations; he had to tend to Riepe's wounds, help him eat, and scavenge extra supplies. Between the time needed to do this, the calorie-deficient food available, and the limits of what his stomach could hold, the sled had to stay. Flip would have to carry Riepe, and they would have to live off the land. Looking at his friend, though, he realized that Riepe might not be strong enough to hold on for a piggyback ride.

"I can help!" Riepe exclaimed.

Flip looked Riepe from head to toe. "Brother, you're doing great by just dragging yourself around. You're a skeleton."

The reality of being at sea, eating what they could catch, and living under the sun's blazing radiation had reduced Riepe to a shell of his former self. Flip could tend to his physical scars but not his emotional and psychological ones. And at this point, Riepe probably didn't have the energy to address those at all.

"I've saved your super-soldier ass plenty of times," Riepe protested.

"I know," Flip said. "It's my turn to save you."

Riepe teared up. His spirit remained that of the man who'd guided their dropships to an impossible crash landing. His body, though, had withered away.

"Okay," Riepe said. "As long as we're keeping score."

* * *

Two days later, Flip trotted into camp wearing a giant, stupid grin.

"You find a pub, bud?" Riepe asked. At least he hadn't lost his sense of humor.

"Better than that!" Flip exclaimed. "Hmm. That's the probably first time I've ever said something might be better than a pub."

Flip whistled, and the foliage rustled. Riepe sat up in alarm as a large creature ambled out of the forest and into the clearing.

"W-what, what is that?"

"Who, Riepe—*who* is that. Where are your manners?" Flip said.

Riepe scowled.

"*His* name," Flip pressed on, "is Lancelot. And he's our ticket out of here." Flip had a glimmer of hope for the first time since the crash. "Between making it across the sea and finding this charming fellow, everything's coming up aces!"

"Lanc-elot?" Riepe stammered. "Is it, er, he... sentient?"

Flip considered Lancelot. "You know, I'm not sure. I just thought he looked like a Lancelot."

"But... what the hell is he?"

"Use your eyes, man!" Flip said. "He's a giant, blue, six-eyed, six-legged turtle!"

"I can see that," Riepe huffed. "Why is it—er, *he*—here?"

"He's here to save us, of course!"

Riepe continued scowling while Lancelot observed the conversation, munching on vegetation.

"Remember how I said we wouldn't be able to take the sled?" Flip asked. "This docile gentleman is going to be our chauffeur. He'll pull the sled, and we'll ride along!"

"Seriously?"

"Yes. Seriously."

"Flip! You're a genius," Riepe said.

"Yes, I am; thanks for noticing. Now relax while I pack up, and we can complete our suicide mission."

CHAPTER 34

Lancelot pulled the sled through the forest while Flip cleared a path by ripping trees out of the ground. It felt like they'd made good time, to Flip anyway. It also felt good to use his abilities again, out in the open without fear of breaking his cover. His true cover, that is. But he also felt guilty for having a good time while Riepe's condition worsened.

Flip ripped up some wood to hang off the back of the sled to act as a drag weight; it was heavy enough to stop the sled, but not heavy enough to impede Lancelot's progress. If Lancelot stopped short, the brake prevented the sled from bumping into him and thus jostling Riepe who—more and more—looked like someone who shouldn't be jostled.

At first, Flip had tried to teach Lancelot to walk on a lead, like a horse. He soon discovered that wasn't necessary. Lancelot followed Flip's path without apparent concern that these new creatures would hurt him. Flip assumed that Lancelot had never seen a Terran, so this behavior seemed odd for an animal that was probably prey for others. He figured that at some point in the planet's past this species had been domesticated. It must have been in the very distant past, though, because reconnaissance had not found any evidence of a civilization, ancient or otherwise. Or maybe Lancelot sensed that Flip could ward off predators. (The only other explanation Flip could think of was that the giant blue turtle was telepathic, and that would be downright ridiculous.)

They journeyed through the forest for weeks. Riepe's condition continued to deteriorate despite Flip's efforts to heal and comfort him. When Flip tended to Riepe on the sled, Lancelot didn't move. He grazed on whatever vegetation happened to be at his feet until Flip had finished—an extraordinary coincidence, to be sure.

Flip pushed away his node's attempts to contact him, though it became more and more frequent and more and more insistent. He had decided to ignore all information, save for notifications of immediate threats. Of course, the incident with the giant Big One illustrated that shutting out his node made that alarm a bit too late to be considered "useful." Still, he insisted on experiencing this planet as an explorer. He wanted the intimate experience of discovery.

He only used his node to catalog and store information. He documented thousands of different animal and plant species, and he recorded atmospheric and geological readings. Scientists back home would find these new discoveries fascinating. They'd be envious, except for the whole stranded-on-a-deserted-planet thing.

He wasn't sure where "home" was anymore—or what it was, for that matter. He couldn't pinpoint a real location that existed outside a mental state. "Home" seemed more of an aspiration at this point.

He'd been in the fleet en route to this target so long he'd come to think of the armada as home. But it had been destroyed, along with all his closest friends—brothers, really—in a futile attempt to seize this godforsaken ball of dirt. He couldn't estimate how long he and Riepe been on Todesfalle without using his node—and he didn't want to do that. However long it had been, it was long enough for Riepe to become the best friend Flip had ever had, and Riepe wasn't looking so good these days.

Flip had fought in so many universes, and lived in so many places, that he couldn't keep track of all of them. The towns, the cities, and the bases all blurred together. Having shut out his node, he couldn't piece all of the memories back together. He hadn't realized how much his node contributed to his personality.

Boot camp had felt like home. Back on Mars—here in the Nazi universe—he had drinking buddies: René, Thorsten, and Jürgen. They looked up to him. He thought of them as his little brothers, and they had picked up on that. That bar, The Little Fatherland, had felt like home. They had all been killed; Jürgen had died in Flip's arms. His last words were, "Tell my son to be a scientist, not a soldier."

Flip felt ashamed that he couldn't remember—without his node—his friends' names from all his missions. He'd bonded with them, just like his missions back in the Alliance. Not as closely, of course, because they weren't FANGed, but he felt bonded nonetheless. Most of them had died in the Jassican universe. As far as Flip was concerned, the Coily Bastard had killed them with his own hands.

Flip had served brief tours with various unsavory intelligence organizations, back when he thought he needed that desk job. He didn't like those guys; they liked their jobs more than they should have. Flip had approached those positions as necessary evils and kept to himself. Even when he was out on the town, he didn't socialize with anyone.

Flip's interactions with the Alliance felt like prehistory at this point. His allegiance had always been with the Alliance, but his loyalties had drifted toward his friends...who had all come from the Reich. Was his home in the Reich or the Alliance? Was it Mars here or Lysser there? He didn't know anymore. Mars felt like a lifetime ago. And the Alliance had faded to a dream.

None of that mattered now, though. He lived on Todesfalle. He trekked around it in a quixotic mission to blow up a suppressor that probably didn't even exist here. Maybe he and Riepe should have built an actual house back at the shoreline. With Lancelot, they could have set up a farm.

Riepe could have rested or maybe even fully recovered. They would have escaped the cycle of war, death, destruction, and misery. They could while away eternity in a utopia that no one would ever know about. The war would end, in time. Maybe someone would find them. Maybe they'd die in the star's death throes. Maybe they'd be enslaved by a race of blue turtles.

Nah, Flip thought, *Lancelot would vouch for us.*

CHAPTER 35

Had Flip not been tearing trees out of the ground, he may not have noticed the dwindling foliage. Through the lighter canopy, he saw a mountain poking toward the sky. He didn't want to use his node-enhanced vision unless it was absolutely necessary, so he couldn't make out much. But the closer they got, the more they could tell it was more of a dirt hill than a mountain.

This must be our objective, he thought. *There'll probably be a large area around it without tree cover.*

His node nudged him, but he continued to ignore it.

* * *

It took another two weeks to make it to the treeline surrounding the hill. Lancelot had been slowing his pace and, at the edge of the forest, stopped.

"Come on, Lance. Let's go."

Lancelot craned his neck to look at Flip.

"What?" Flip asked. Riepe slept through the most exciting thing they'd come across (since finding Lancelot at least).

Lancelot looked at the barren hill in the distance, then back at Flip. Flip jumped down to face him directly.

He looked into the turtle's eyes. "You can understand me, can't you?"

Lancelot touched his mouth to the ground. He'd never done that before.

"I knew it!" Flip shouted and pumped his fist into the air. Riepe started to stir, and Flip scolded himself for the outburst. To Lancelot, in a whisper, he asked, "Why did you stop?"

Flip thought that, maybe, he may be reading too much into the situation. His node begged to intervene but reported nothing that presented itself as an immediate threat.

Lancelot flicked his head toward the hill. It stood about three kilometers away and about fifty meters high. They had come so far and were now so close.

"Wait," Flip said, using his nanite-enhanced vision. "Is that...? It is!" He caught himself before he raised his voice in excitement. "It's a door."

Flip considered the distance to the hill and looked at Riepe. His friend slept as soundly as could be expected in his condition. "Can you take us closer?"

Lancelot closed his eyes for a few seconds.

"I'll take that as a no." How would Riepe fare on this walk? A three-kilometer march, then walking up a rather steep hill for at least two hundred fifty meters. And those were only the *known* challenges.

"Can I leave him with you?"

Again, Lancelot gave him a slow blink.

Flip nodded, unhooked Lancelot from the sled, and watched him amble away. "Thank you, Lancelot. We'll never forget you."

He nudged Riepe. "Hey, brother. Wake up."

Riepe stirred. "What's up, bud?"

"We're here. We're at the base."

"We are?" Riepe struggled to prop himself up on his elbows. "Did we do it? Are they coming for us?"

Flip's heart broke. "Not yet. We still have a long way to go. You need to get up."

"Where's Lancelot?"

"He had to go," Flip whispered.

"I can't, Flip. You go on without me." Riepe fell back on his makeshift bed.

"No!" Flip jabbed him with his finger. "You have to get up. Now. We need to get going while the sun's down."

Riepe tried to get up and fell again. "I can't. Go on."

"Not acceptable, soldat! Up! Now!"

Riepe struggled to sit up again and failed.

"Okay," Flip said. He helped his friend down from the sled. "Now, just walk with me. That's it."

"Why can't we take the sled?" Riepe asked.

"Because if the Jassicans are still here we'd be an even easier target to pick off," Flip explained. Flip had scanned the base and found it was shielded. The Jassicans might be here after all.

"Oh, yeah," Riepe sighed. "You're always on top of things, bud. You're a genius."

There weren't any suitable materials around to make a travois, so Flip hoisted as much food and water onto his back as he could. Riepe insisted on walking, so Flip helped him. When he collapsed, Flip carried him until he insisted on walking again.

Flip spared a look back at the treeline and saw Lancelot munching on foliage and watching them. Or was he watching over them? Flip couldn't tell.

* * *

Flip made camp as the sun rose. While Riepe rested, Flip dug a foxhole, placed Riepe inside, and covered the hole with cloth and the leaves they'd brought as food. In his long and varied military career, Flip had never been in a situation like this. He didn't know how to accomplish their mission. He didn't know if their mission even mattered anymore.

He needed to keep Riepe alive, but Flip couldn't drag his friend all over the damned enemy's base. (He would do it if needed—he had dedicated himself to saving his friend—but it wouldn't be ideal. They'd probably both be killed, but his loyalty to Riepe came first.)

He opened himself to his node.

"How can I help Riepe? I'm in an impossible situation," he said.

I thought you'd never ask, Node replied. *The situation isn't all that impossible. But you should have asked sooner.*

The response startled Flip. "I'm asking now," he ventured.

It would've been better if you'd asked a long time ago.

"Why didn't you speak up a long time ago, then?"

You told me to shut up! I got you through that bloodbath with the whales, and then you shut me out. I tried to save your sorry ass from that giant ray or shark or whatever the fuck it was. I intervened then, just a bit. But you shut me out again. And despite my persistence to give you important information, you still wouldn't listen.

"You're my FANG node. It's your job to intervene."

I have feelings, you know.

"You have *my* feelings. You're a node!"

The situation had gone from impossible to absurd. Flip sat under a sweltering sun that spewed deadly radiation; his only friend in the multiverse lay dying at the bottom of a foxhole covered with bits of clothing and food. And now he was arguing with what amounted to his split personality.

He paused to sigh.

It's just that, I don't know, you haven't talked to me in ages, Node said.

"You're my brain!" Flip exploded. He heard Riepe shift and moan in his sleep. In a harsh whisper Flip said, "Why are you arguing with me?"

I'm not just your brain. I'm your memories and your experiences and, by the way, the custodian and operator of your nanite-driven superpowers. You're just a regular schmoe without me.

Flip shook his head. "I'm not arguing with my node. I'm just not going to. You're a piece of hardware in my body."

You keep referring to me in the second person, she pointed out. *That implies you recognize me as a separate entity.* She obviously thought that was a coup de grâce.

He sighed. "That's just a limitation of English. German too, for that matter. Translate it into whatever language you damn well please."

Do you think normal people have this problem, Flip? she asked. *You should be grateful to have me. I might not be helping you if we didn't live in the same body.*

Flip had no idea how to respond.

"I can't believe I'm having this conversation," Flip said to himself. Then, to her, he said, "No, wait. Are you malfunctioning?"

I won't even gratify that with a response.

Silence.

Flip ran a quick diagnostic. "You're working perfectly. That means I'm going insane."

More silence.

"I know you can hear me. What's wrong?"

She sighed. *You're not insane.*

"That's a relief."

Node ignored his sarcasm. *Look, it's just that, sometimes, you know, it gets lonely shuffling data around. I'm a superintelligent AI. I have needs.*

"We are not having this conversation. Not right now. Riepe needs help."

Oh, calm down. Nodes aren't supposed to be ignored like I've been, for as long as I've been.

Flip hung his head into his hands. "Node—that's your name, right? I seem to have heard you think that?"

Yes. You're a sharp one after all.

"Listen, Node. We don't have time for this. If we get off this planet, I promise we will have a chat about your existential crisis."

He somehow sensed her arms folding across her chest.

"I'm sorry," Flip said. His words disappeared into the wind. "Look, I've met species consisting entirely of artificial intelligence. I'm reasonably confident that's not what you are, but maybe I'm wrong. Either way, I promise, if you work with me now, I'll work with you later."

Flip had to guard his thoughts. He wasn't sure what was happening inside his head.

Okay, Node sighed. *I have an idea, but it would have worked much better if you'd asked sooner.*

"You've made that crystal clear. What's the idea?"

Have him drink your blood. About a quarter liter.

"What?!" Flip stood and shouted. He shushed himself and checked on Riepe. All good. (Meaning that he was still breathing.)

Hang on, Node said. *Listen. I can concentrate on the nanites enough to help him. I think. You'll have to be in direct physical contact at all times. No modesty.*

He could feel her grin.

That's the only way I can do it. Lose contact and the nanites die.

"And then?"

They clot, and he dies.

Flip grabbed some rocks and chewed.

"I don't think that's possible. My nanites are designed to work inside me."

Your nanites? Node yelled. *These are* my *nanites. I control them. They are mine.*

"Yeah? What was that shit back at the beach, then? You swarmed them out of my body and flew them around in a feeding frenzy! You must have lost your 'control' then."

A long uncomfortable silence followed his words.

"Node?"

That was... different. I was... finding myself.

"Excuse me?" Flip had had enough of this foolishness.

Sorry. That was a bit too existential.

"Yes, I think so," Flip said. "I'm perfectly capable of resetting you, by the way."

Yes, she admitted. *For now, you are.*

Flip took a deep breath and pondered the life choices he'd made to reach this point.

What happened back at the beach was a one-off, a special circumstance. That was me coming to life to save you. To save us.

And before you ask, no, I don't know why that happened. Maybe the star's radiation altered me. Maybe it was the long, boring trip through the sand ocean. I just don't know.

She cleared her throat (or the rough equivalent).

The blood plan is technically possible. You have to believe me because I want to get off this planet, too.

It will take a lot of energy to maintain, though. As long as my nanites are in him, I won't be able to scan for danger or provide any information.

She paused for a moment.

Not that you care.

"We have a mission—you *do* remember what missions are, right? Military operations to achieve an objective? Split-second life-and-death decisions? The fates of civilizations hanging in the balance? Remember those? Focus on the one at hand."

Okay, um. Node composed herself. *Here's the rundown and review: if you are touching him, I can control the nanites inside of him. He'll be able to digest anything and heal, albeit slowly. He probably won't be able to walk on his own until he gets to a medical facility. Keep him covered from the sun, but that shouldn't be a problem if you start early tonight.*

"We're close to the suppressor," Flip said. "How will this affect your performance? I mean, er, my—"

I know what you mean, Flip. I'll have to concentrate solely on Riepe. No other node has tried to sustain a life-form they aren't implanted in, as far as I know.

He swallowed another handful of dirt and rocks. He'd need to eat as much matter as he could, and right now that was coming from the ground.

"Any other options?" he asked.

Yeah. He's dead before this time tomorrow.

"That's not much of an option."

That's the truth of the matter.

Flip peeked at his sleeping friend. "He's not going to like this."

He'll like being dead even less.

"I can't argue with that." Flip sighed. (He found himself sighing a lot lately.) "Okay, he'll be a vampire for breakfast, then."

Flip gave himself ten minutes to eat everything he could. He prioritized things that were green and wriggly.

He returned to his sleeping friend. He dunked leaves in the limited water they had, then propped Riepe up, placed the wet leaves in his mouth, and helped him swallow the water.

Flip? Node said.

"I'm not shutting you out. I just don't want to talk right now."

I understand.

He helped Riepe drink, drop by drop, for the rest of the day.

CHAPTER 36

Flip woke Riepe as the sun went down and explained the plan. Riepe didn't object. Between drinking Flip's blood and dying, he didn't have to flip a coin.

"Does this make you my super-soldier dad?" Riepe asked.

"I think it makes you my vampire offspring."

Flip searched the supplies for vines, made a rope, and cinched it tight around them. If one of them fell, the other went with him. Unless they tried to push each other away, they were stuck together, come hell or high water.

The conjoined duo started their trek toward the hillside. They fashioned some primitive weapons along the way. Each of them carried a long pointy stick and a bag of rocks.

By the time they arrived at the door, Riepe had become alert and a meaningful fraction of his former self. If not for the need to be joined at the hip, he could have walked unaided for the most part. Thanks to Flip's—or rather, Node's—nanites, Riepe could draw water out of the air and munch on almost anything.

"We made it!" Riepe cheered. "Just in time too—the sun's starting to come up. We've got shade in this convenient cave. But how do we get in this conveniently placed door?"

Riepe's humor had returned, for better or worse.

"There should be a sensor around here somewhere," Flip explained while looking around the door.

"Jassican bases always have a place to put a sample of genetic material. Like saliva or skin or something." He searched around the entrance, dragging Riepe with him.

"How do you know that?"

"Because they can be almost any shape or size," Flip said. "The sensor analyzes the sample to see if they are Jassican or an allied species. It's quite elementary, Riepe."

"Oh, pardon me, Sherlock," Riepe mocked. "Did they teach you that in super-soldier school?"

Flip stopped and smiled. "Yeah. Something like that."

"But we don't have any samples to put in it," Riepe said.

"We don't have any samples *that we know of*," Flip emphasized. "This is a Jassican base. Any organic matter around here could be theirs."

Riepe looked skeptical. "That's an awfully long shot."

"Yes," Flip retorted. "But it's the only shot we have. Now help me look around."

They combed the entrance, as they deemed it the most logical place to put an entryway sensor.

"Aha!" Riepe yelled. "I found it!" He brushed away a layer of dust to reveal a metallic depression. He poked at it, and a small door opened.

"Great!" Flip said. "Now we just need some Jassican shit to put in there."

"And how are we supposed to find that? It could be anywhere. Or anything for that matter."

"Do you want to live as Siamese twins forever?" Flip asked. "We'll die of old age together."

"We don't age."

"That's even worse," Flip said. "Let's find something."

They searched around the entrance for something—*anything*—that might be from a Jessican.

* * *

After an extended search and several failed attempts to open the lock, Riepe had to take a break. He and Flip sat in the lengthening shadows as the sun set on the other side of the mountain.

Flip shoved dirt and stones into his mouth. Riepe ate from the supply of vegetation they'd brought with them. Despite Flip's prodding, Riepe refused to eat dirt.

"Any ideas?" Flip asked between bites of soil.

"As a matter of fact, I do have one. Help me up."

They limped to the sample collector and, before Flip could intervene, Riepe speared it with his stick. The door opened.

"Huh," Riepe shrugged. "It wasn't locked."

CHAPTER 37

Flip and Riepe spent two hours hobbling down a circular tunnel that corkscrewed underneath the hill. Between the two of them, they had three pointy sticks—Riepe's had broken in the lock—and two bags of rocks. Flip didn't like those numbers.

They came to another door. This one opened right away.

"That's convenient," Flip quipped.

"We already passed security at the main entrance," Riepe pointed out. "Everyone who makes it here would be authorized."

"Good point," Flip said. "It looks like this might be an elevator?"

"No sense turning back now," Riepe said. He looked over their shoulders. "There's nowhere to go."

Flip nodded, and they stepped inside. They didn't see any obvious indicators or controls, but the doors closed anyway. The elevator took off sideways, then it went down.

"Where do you think we're going?" Riepe asked.

"If there's any hope of going home," Flip said, "it's taking us to the tachyon suppressor."

"Goddamn it. It's been so long since I thought about that."

"Yeah," Flip said. "Me too." Whatever happened from here on, he'd miss this dirtball planet. Or at least what it could have been.

The doors opened to a large room; lights flooded it as they stumbled in. A dome stretched high overhead. Node, still preoccupied with sustaining Riepe, could only calculate that it stretched "really far" into the rock overhead. They must have descended farther than Flip thought.

A black machine stood in the center of the room. A spire stretched to the ceiling and spider-webbed around the walls and up the dome.

"I think we found it," Flip said with a sigh. He didn't know if he felt relieved or resigned. At this point, he didn't think the two emotions were all that different.

"There's no cover," Riepe observed. "How do we get there?"

"Nothing to it," Flip said. "We just walk straight ahead."

"And if we're ambushed?"

"We have our pointy sticks."

Riepe laughed. "Don't forget the rocks."

"With sticks and rocks, we're unstoppable."

They strode toward the pitch-black machine. One way or another, their mission would soon be over.

"How do we turn it off?" Riepe asked.

"I don't know," Flip said while looking over the device, confused. "I don't see any controls."

"There has to be something," Riepe said. "Maybe they're on the other side."

"Hang on to me," Flip said. "I'm going to scan it."

Riepe slumped into Flip's arms. Flip corralled enough nanites for Node to look over the device. Then he returned the nanites to Riepe.

"That's strange," Flip said. "I don't detect any radiation coming from it. No tachyons. Nothing."

"Flip," Riepe's voice wavered. "I have a bad feeling about this."

"I think—" Terror seized Flip, and the last vestiges of hope drained from his body. At this moment, on this planet, in this breath, he'd lost everything. "It's—"

A deep, raspy voice came from behind them. "A fake?"

They spun and found themselves face-to-face with the Coily Bastard. Three Jassicans flanked each side of the general. Their weapons traced Flip and Riepe's tiniest movements. The Bastard, while still striped like a candy cane, took his native, pear-like shape.

Flip waved his stick. "I'll warn you, sir," he said. "We're armed."

The Coily Bastard laughed.

"Phillip Marsh," he said. He paced in front of his captives, moving closer and closer. "I'm so pleased to finally meet you. And here's the loyal and brave Riepe Harwig. You can drop your weapons, gentlemen. You are well and truly captured."

Riepe dropped his sticks and slumped to the ground, dragging Flip with him. "This has all been for nothing?"

"Oh, no!" the Coily Bastard exclaimed. "Not at all Mr. Harwig. We were all quite impressed with your journey. Your tenacity. Your—what's the word? Stubbornness."

"Yeah," Flip said and tapped his stick on his head. "I've got a pretty thick skull." He tried to drag Riepe up to his feet, but he couldn't get him to budge.

The Coily Bastard crouched in front of them and disarmed Flip. "We had a pool, Phillip. I lost, I'm afraid."

"What do you mean?" Flip cocked his head to the side. Riepe seemed not to notice the exchange.

"I thought you would have abandoned Herr Harwig long ago." The Jassican turned his attention to Riepe. "Or that would you have eaten him."

Flip spat in the Coily Bastard's face. "Go fuck yourself."

The Coily Bastard ignored the spittle. He turned to Riepe. "Especially given the *true* nature of Mr. Marsh's mission."

This caught Riepe's attention. "Wait, what?"

"Oh?" The general feigned surprise. "You didn't tell him the truth?" He leaned into them while Riepe's anger boiled. "You humans are so loyal to one another."

He looked from Riepe to Flip and back again. "Even when you're not from the same parts of the multiverse."

Riepe flinched. He looked at Flip and, without hesitation, drove his pointy stick into the general's mouth.

In the next instant, Riepe was gone.

Flip, stunned, tried to process the situation. He saw a guard lowering his weapon, having just disintegrated his friend. His best friend. His only friend.

Node came back online. *No, Flip. Don't!*

Flip lunged at the guard with supernatural speed and plunged his stick into his chest. He drove his hand through his victim's body and squeezed the guard's heart until it burst.

He dashed to the Coily Bastard and tore at the red stripes on his skin, pulling and gouging as hard and as fast as he could. Node screamed at him to stop, but he continued tearing and ripping. He heard—and felt—the Coily Bastard's organs squish beneath his fingers.

The remaining guards had to fire at Flip dozens of times before he finally fell.

* * *

Flip awoke flat on his back, staring at an incandescent ceiling. Even without Node, he knew he was on the *Aristotle*. The sounds, the smells—

This, he remembered, *is home.*

Four loving eyestalks moved into his field of view. A Lysserian. Andrea.

"Am I dead?"

"No, my old captain," Andrea's hue melted into shades of amusement, relief, and affection. She sniffed back tears. "You're not that lucky."

Flip tried to sit up, but Ortosodl restrained him. "No, Captain. Lie still. Even with your nanites, you're still gravely injured. You're lucky that your node had supercharged your nanites, or else you wouldn't have made

317

it here alive. Your body absorbed a considerable amount of Jassican gunfire."

Then Flip remembered. He remembered Riepe disappearing before his eyes. He remembered the Coily Bastard's sneer. He remembered disemboweling the soldier who killed his friend. He remembered ripping into the general's body.

Andrea put a reassuring hand on Flip's shoulder. Decades of immeasurable grief and misery flowed from him. He willed his tears to take his memories away.

* * *

Andrea visited the other patient, General L'Lac. Stitches closed a gaping hole in his body, and bandages covered the rest of him. He needed a machine to breathe. Flip had struck with the speed and power of a tiger—the power of ten tigers, for that matter. The general was lucky to be alive.

Ortosodl had briefed her on Jassican biology. Wounds sustained by Jassicans in their native forms could not be reversed by shapeshifting. The general's injuries were thus permanent and quite severe.

Flip and L'Lac had a deep-seated, hate-filled rivalry.

They'd have to find a way to set that animosity aside, though. Or at least cooperate. Otherwise, they would tear the Alliance apart.

CHAPTER 38

Andrea sat at the head of the table in the *Aristotle*'s main conference room, long having vanquished her doubts about her command. The admirals and generals had also settled into the notion of a captain commanding multiple complex operations. Project Hammer's success impressed even the most jaded old-timers.

Alliance Command hadn't allowed final tests, but they had accepted the designs her team had developed and announced the weapons would soon be in production. She'd gained the trust not only of Alliance Command, but also of the Jassican Association.

Flip sat to her right, and General L'Lac sat to her left. The general rested—if he could ever truly rest again—in a mobile Jassican chair. He breathed through a machine and ate through a tube. He couldn't move and couldn't shapeshift. Flip had sentenced him to this life, and he secretly enjoyed seeing the general in this state. He only wished he could have killed the Coily Bastard before getting knocked out.

Leaders from the Alliance and the Association sat at the table, along with two Viper generals. Andrea made sure that the seats alternated between Alliance and Association representatives, in hopes that their mingling would remind them of the camaraderie they'd had before Flip attacked their greatest general. So far, she'd seen mixed success, even though she pointed out—in the most diplomatic way possible, of course—that Flip had no idea that the general was an ally.

The group had been discussing Flip's sketchy past and uncertain future. The Alliance wanted him back in the war to gather intelligence. The Jassicans, having a plausible story of how he was captured, wanted to use him as a bargaining chip in a prisoner exchange. Andrea didn't understand why it took so long to reach the obvious compromise of doing both. Using Flip as a bargaining chip would be the only way the Alliance could safely get him back into the Reich.

General L'Lac had just finished outlining the touchy subject of the prisoner swap between the Association and the Reich.

"So as you can see—" L'Lac struggled to say. He had to pause for air every few words. Sometimes even in the middle of words. "We have a strong case—*wheeze*—for this swap. It's a compromise—*gasp*—we believe they—*wheeze*—will accept. We're willing to, as—*gasp*—you say—*wheeze*—pull the trigger on—*gasp*—this."

At the Jassicans' urging, Andrea had asked L'Lac several times if he'd like someone to speak in his stead. It pained her to hear the whine of his machinery, his struggle for air, and the shame he tried so hard to hide.

In Jassican culture, anyone unable to shapeshift shied away from the public whenever possible. According to their traditions, L'Lac shouldn't be representing the Jassican Association in these meetings. He insisted on speaking, she thought, out of spite. Alliance Intelligence had told her that the general wanted to destroy Flip as Flip had destroyed him.

320

"Yes, General," an Alliance admiral noted, "but how will you get the ratio we're proposing? They'd be sending more prisoners than we are."

"They have more prisoners," a Jassican officer said, "and they are *our*s to retrieve, not yours. We'll take any number we can get. The invaders took hundreds of thousands of our citizens during their initial occupations. We still have no idea where they are."

Andrea, surprised, said, "You haven't received our intelligence on that yet?"

"No, we haven't," the officer said. "You have some?"

Andrea glared at the Chief of Alliance Intelligence. The Gammerian shrank.

"You will receive that information following this meeting," Andrea said. "Please continue, General L'Lac."

"We are also—*wheeze*—offering very high-value—*gasp*—prisoners. Officers. And—*wheeze*—of course, Captain—*gasp*—Marsh" —he gestured to Flip—"is of—*wheeze*—particular interest to—*gasp*—them. He is a very—*wheeze*—I could say, *effective* asset." The general stared at Flip in an obvious challenge.

"It's not fair for them," Flip said, his voice dripping with venom. "Isn't there a reason you don't have many prisoners?"

Everyone shifted in the manner of their respective species. The tension in the room threatened to break the meeting apart.

"I don't know—*wheeze*—what you mean—*gasp*—Captain." The title came out as an epithet, even through his labored breaths.

"What happens to our people?" Flip stood, slamming the table with his fist. The Viper generals, moving too fast for Andrea to see, restrained him.

Our *people?* Andrea thought.

She tried to put a hand on Flip's shoulder, but he jerked away. He struggled against the generals, but their combined strength proved too great. She saw nothing but fury in him. Fury and hate.

"Flip," she explained, "we're on the same side. We've been allies for decades."

"They can't be trusted. *Him* in particular," Flip said, pointing at L'Lac.

"Tell me, General," Flip fumed, "how'd you get through the tach shield? You couldn't have dropped it. We would've destroyed you."

"That's a—*wheeze*—secret," L'Lac said, "for now." He flashed a smile twisted by scars, satisfied with his provocation. He wanted to provoke, humiliate and discredit Flip. Anyone familiar with Lysserian emotions could see anger coloring Andrea's body.

Flip composed himself. He realized the Jassican played off his rage to make him look irrational, and even worse, like a traitor.

"Flip," Andrea said, "we're all on the same side. We don't have to like each other"—two of her eyes glared at L'Lac—"but we do have to work together."

"I'm sorry," Flip muttered. He shrugged off the Viper generals and sat down. "Of course."

The Vipers didn't return to their seats.

"I'm asking," Flip hissed through clenched teeth, "because there are rumors in the Reich about Jassicans eating prisoners."

That sucked the air out of the room like a hull breach.

General L'Lac laughed. "Yes—*wheeze*—Captain Marsh. We are—*gasp*—aware of those rumors." He pointed to a Cologian. "Perhaps the—*wheeze*—Director of Association—*gasp*—Intelligence could explain?"

The Cologian stood and addressed the assembly. "We planted those rumors to create fear and disorder in the Nazi military. It has been an effective piece of propaganda."

Flip's unblinking eyes locked onto L'Lac's. "That's an excuse to kill them all," he hissed. "Men fight to the death instead of surrendering."

"Ah, yes. We did not anticipate that," the director said. "We also lost a lot of soldiers because of that miscalculation. We intended to create unrest and fear among the civilians. We hoped to prevent them from joining the military. Or to refuse service. We did not fully understand their culture at the time."

"Your intelligence service leaves a lot to be desired, L'Lac," Flip snapped. "The people are more committed to their government than you could ever imagine. A halfway-decent agency staffed by children could have figured that out."

The Cologian sat, not wanting to provoke the situation further.

"Let me—*wheeze*—reassure you—*gasp*—Phillip," L'Lac said.

Flip glared at him, angered that the general used his first name.

"We do not—*wheeze*—eat prisoners. No one—*gasp*—in the Association—*wheeze*—eats sentient creatures—*gasp*—Jassicans don't even—*wheeze*—eat animals. Some refuse—*gasp*—to eat any living—*wheeze*—things at all."

This information didn't dampen Flip's anger.

Andrea needed to seize control of the situation. She stood, and all eyes, save Flip's, turned to her. Flip stared at L'Lac, coiled and ready to strike. She knew he had the potential to move fast enough to cross the table before the other Vipers could stop him.

She pointed to the Alliance Chief of Intelligence. "What do you think about the trade?"

"The Reich will accept the trade," it said. "We have excellent intelligence concerning this matter, and I think the general is right. The Reich is willing to pay a great deal to find out what Captain Marsh knows."

"No one cares what I think?" Flip asked the room.

"Of course we do," the Cologian said, trying to calm the situation. "What's your take, Captain?"

Flip slumped back in his chair.

"You're right." He scowled at L'Lac. "They'll take the trade."

"And what—*wheeze*—will you tell them?" L'Lac asked. He looked uncomfortable for the first time in the meeting.

"The truth," Flip said and stood. "You don't eat prisoners. Tell your—*wheeze*—spies"—Flip mocked the general's reliance on the life-sustaining machines—"to figure out the rest." He stormed out of the room.

No one moved. Andrea had no idea what to say. She looked at L'Lac and tried to read his emotions.

She only saw terror.

CHAPTER 39

"I still can't believe they're here," Lam fumed.

Every fucking day, Kid thought.

Two years ago, in a coincidence that defied any statistical calculation, a Nazi fleet ensphered the *Merlin*. The formation had closed tighter, and tighter, and tighter still. The Nazi search sphere had shrunk to fifty light-years across within weeks and then stalled out.

Kid and Lam had been spying on those ships. This didn't interfere with their mission, at first. They could still observe any other part of the universe, but they needed to discover the reason behind the appearance of the fleet. They couldn't help anyone else if they didn't first take care of themselves.

What they found, however, also defied all possible statistical probability. The enemy had been closing in on an infrequent anomaly that just happened to come from the *Merlin*'s exact position.

All of their efforts to identify the source of the anomaly had proven futile. The Nazis saw something, but neither they nor the *Merlin*'s two-man crew could figure out what it was. The enemy fleet couldn't pinpoint the *Merlin*'s exact location, Kid reckoned, otherwise they would have parked right on top of the coalescing point. But they may have wanted to determine if the anomaly presented an unknown danger first.

The anomalies showed up at seemingly random intervals and did not last long. Merlin herself was, of course, no help at all. She refused to acknowledge any sort of problem, much less a malfunction in her ship.

But during the last anomaly, Kid had found something.

"Hey, Lam. I found out what's going on. We're leaking," Kid said.

"Leaking? Leaking what?" This, Kid knew, didn't indicate Lam wasn't up to speed on the anomaly. Lam took the situation quite seriously, he just happened to be concentrating on some other part of the mystery at that moment.

"Trace amounts of coolant. It's causing the anomaly," Kid explained.

"Could you, perhaps, elaborate on that?" Lam asked.

"Our coolant is flowing into a small dimension of spacetime," Kid explained. "About one nanogram per six days."

"That's not very much for them—"

"It takes time to build up," Kid interrupted. "The anomaly requires an irregular amount of coolant."

"And that means..." Lam trailed off, sounding a bit confused and perhaps intoxicated. (It was hard to tell with him sometimes.)

"It's hard to know exactly when the anomaly will flash," Kid said. "It's not exactly random, though. It will just take a long time to figure out the predictive equation."

"How long?"

"Approximately"—Kid pretended to push buttons to calculate, though he'd already summed it up in his nodes—"longer than the lifetime of this universe."

"Okay," Lam said. "That's not very useful, then."

"We could get lucky—"

"First question!" Lam started pacing. "How are we leaking anything?"

"I think—"

"Second question!" Lam paced faster. He was like a damn pendulum sometimes. "How did they detect it?"

"The second question"—Kid hesitated, expecting yet another interruption—"is less pressing but easier to answer: it was bad luck."

"Excuse me?" That got Lam to stop pacing.

"Yeah, just stupid bad luck. They happened to be looking this way when some of our coolant sparked an anomaly. Normal matter isn't supposed to be in that dimension at all. Research facilities would see that, if they were looking in the right direction."

This was no accident, was it? he asked Merlin.

She snickered. *I have no idea what you're talking about. I must say, though, this is quite entertaining. I wish I knew what this was all about.*

"Can you figure out which facility it was?" Lam asked.

"I'm not even sure that's how they did it."

"Okay, okay." Lam continued pacing. "That's incredibly bad luck. So why are we leaking in the first place?"

"That's the real problem," Kid said. "Looks like, on the last trip to our universe, the Gibla drive fell out of calibration. We're slightly out of sync with the expansion of this universe."

"I thought we're immune to the whims of the universe's laws while null-cloaked."

"We are," Kid said. "I don't know... hang on." Kid flipped switches and dialed knobs on his control panel, pretending he didn't have a direct connection to it. "Oh, shit. That's not good."

"You're going to have to be more specific," Lam said.

"Small parts of the Gibla drive aren't in the null cloak. That shouldn't be possible either."

How did that happen, Merlin? he asked. *You're only hurting yourself.*

How do you know this situation will hurt me? she responded.

"That is also incredibly bad luck," Lam said.

"Yes, it is," Kid said. "This shouldn't be possible."

"Oh, come on! You say that all the time!" Lam stormed toward the door. "I'll be back. I need a drink."

Kid scowled at the console. "What the fuck are you doing, Merlin?"

I don't know what you mean. She laughed and laughed. It rang in Kid's brain, and he wondered if she would ever stop.

"You know *exactly* what I mean!" he shouted, trying to drown out her cackling. "Why are we leaking coolant?"

I detect no coolant leak.

"Of course you don't, you stupid bitch. You don't detect anything, do you?"

I detect a Nazi fleet closing in on you, she sneered.

Kid could not control his anger. "They're closing in on you too, you fucking idiot."

Sticks and stones, Kid, she said. *If there is a coolant leak, it's not coming from me.*

"Then where the hell is it coming from? It's not coming from my ass!"

That's a good one. For the record, I have detected some leaks coming from your ass. She erupted in more earsplitting laughter.

"I need to know what you did," he said. "If they find us, we'll be killed, you'll be stripped to your bulkheads, and the Nazis will destroy the Alliance."

I don't see how that's my concern.

"You don't see how being dismantled centimeter by centimeter is any of your concern?"

Nope. Not at all.

Lam returned with two full steins, and Kid was certain he'd had a couple while he was at the pub.

"Oh, no thanks," Kid said.

"What?" Lam said. "Oh. I, er, mean that's okay. I'll drink it."

"They're both for you, aren't they?"

"Er..." Lam looked at the steins then back at Kid. "So, what's this about a leak?"

"I don't know how, but the uncloaked Gibla parts are funneling coolant through the null cloak and leaking out."

"That shouldn't be possible!" Lam exclaimed.

Kid rolled his eyes. "From what I can tell, we have the same problem in the fifty-seventh dimension, but not as bad. Maybe others."

Lam plopped into his captain's chair and rested a stein on each arm. "So, we need to fix this or they'll find us."

"That's the problem," Kid turned his chair to face Lam. "Since it's running through the null cloak, we have to coalesce to repair it."

"This is impossibly bad luck. How long will the repairs take?"

"Hours," Kid answered. "Maybe days. And we'll be sitting ducks because we don't have a tach drive."

"You're just a barrel of laughs today." Lam took a long drink. "How long until they find us?"

"Several years at least," Kid said. "Maybe decades."

"Hey!" Lam jumped up from his seat. "There we go! We have plenty of time to figure this out!"

"Weeell," Kid stretched out the word.

"By Isfym's Ass, I can't take more bad news."

"We're stretching and shrinking with the null cloak. It will eventually rip us apart."

"You're a real downer, sometimes." Lam guzzled his Rockeye. "How long until that happens?"

"I can't tell. There are too many variables. It could be months. Seconds. Could be in a thousand years."

"This isn't how I wanted the day to go," Lam said.

"Maybe I could use one of those Rockeyes after all," Kid said.

Lam hesitated before handing over one of the steins. "Cheers."

"Cheers," Kid said. They drank and brainstormed.

"You know what?" Lam snapped his fingers. "We don't have to figure it out right now. Maybe not at all!"

"Not sure what you mean by that—"

"We have this super intelligent big-brain computer to figure it out for us!"

Kid didn't like this sudden turn in the conversation. "I don't know, Lam. Maybe we should think about—"

"Nonsense!" Lam exclaimed, pointing a finger to the ceiling for emphasis. "Get that programmed into our supercomputer."

Kid looked at the controls. "I don't think—"

"*Fine*! I'll do it. I have to do everything around here." He muttered while punching commands into the armrest's controls.

"There!" He stood, one hand clutching his beer, the other on his hip.

Merlin cackled through Kid's node, sending a chill up his spine.

"To the pub!" Lam declared.

Kid looked around the bridge as they left. Merlin wouldn't be so self-destructive as to destroy herself... right?

Do you know what you need to do? he asked her.

Why, Kid! she mocked. *I think I'll surprise you with this project— trust me.*

He didn't like the sound of that.

CHAPTER 40

Through a haze of smoke, Flip slammed an empty thirty-two-ounce stein onto a swastika-laced coaster.

"Sieben!" the crowd of soldiers sang out. Another rookie hit the floor, and an intoxicated field medic hauled him away. Seven beers challenged even the most dedicated rookies. Flip matched their pints with his stein, two for one.

The medics stumbled around, keeping their comrades alive. They were on duty and not supposed to be drinking but, as every night, there wasn't a sober one among them.

Say what you want, Flip thought, *they know how to party. They should enjoy it before their souls are ripped out of them.*

The vets played the game too; they just kept to themselves in small groups. They had their reasons, Flip knew. They'd all done terrible things, and they knew more were yet to come. They'd forgotten their humanity and tried to forget themselves. Flip could relate.

The barmaid, Heidi, brought a fresh stein to Flip and pints to the three remaining contestants. She had seen this dance many times before; she'd thought up the contest to bring in more business to her bar, The Little Fatherland. It lived up to its motto of being the best pub on Mars. Having traveled around more than he cared to think about, Flip thought this might be the best bar in the Reich—it only needed Rockeyes. Heidi winked at Flip.

She'd bought the bar long after Flip left on his ill-fated mission to destroy the fake suppressor. He wished she'd bought it sooner. Maybe he'd have had a different life.

"Three more recruits to go!" Heidi announced. "They all came in as children! One will leave as a man!"

You're an idiot, Node said.

You always say that, he said back.

I say it because it's true.

Heidi and Flip played this drinking game every time the nearby *Jagdgeschwader III* recruited new troops. It ended with dozens of drunken soldiers being carried home by their similarly intoxicated comrades. After that, Flip would end up in bed with Heidi. Node pretended to not approve of that either, but since her pleasure sensors were tied to his, well, she didn't protest *too* much.

Heidi. A typical name for a most atypical woman. Her long blonde hair strategically covered the most interesting bits of her cleavage. Her skirt concealed the most interesting bits of her crotch and ass. It kept the business coming in. She had an accent native to what used to be the Philippines or thereabouts. Flip didn't inquire much about her personal history.

Flip thought he loved her, though. Maybe he did. He didn't remember what real emotions, much less love, felt like anymore. He didn't want to get too close to anyone lest he lose them. Maybe he thought he needed to love her? To ground himself? Heidi had proven herself to be the best source of intelligence in the area. Maybe on all of Mars. Hell, maybe in the entire solar system.

"Who can defeat the champion?" she yelled—another part of the routine. (The young soldiers' lives revolved around routine.)

"Marsh! Marsh! Marsh!" the crowd chanted.

"Everyone wants to beat the legend! Who will challenge Major Marsh and claim his throne?" Heidi prompted.

The crowd raised their steins in mock salutes. "Heil beer! Heil Marsh!"

Flip hid a grimace behind a long chug. (He didn't like that part of the routine.)

"Acht!" the crowd yelled, and another recruit hit the floor. Heidi served Flip his beer with a wink.

* * *

Flip sat alone at the bar; closing time had long since passed. Heidi washed glasses behind the counter.

"So," she said, "you're leaving me, huh?"

He looked around the pub. "You want me to go? I thought we were, you know."

She laughed. "No, we're definitely doing that." She gave him a sly smirk. "I meant your deployment orders. Where are you going?"

"I didn't know I was going anywhere. Maybe I should have a few more drinks."

You know anything about this? he asked Node.

No. But I haven't been digging through your orders, she said.

Why not?

Because your orders never change! she said.

She had a point.

Heidi grabbed a new bottle of whiskey and handed it to him. Her intel almost always proved accurate, though she considered it nothing more than gossip. People told her things because she brought them beer and breasts. Secrets didn't stay secrets with the drunk and horny. Flip fed her juicy tidbits every now and then, to keep the gossip train running, but he fabricated most of them.

"You're leaving next week." Heidi stared at the ceiling, perhaps contemplating her gossip coup. "Or did you not know yet?" she asked with a gleam in her eye.

Node?

I'm still looking, she said. *I haven't found anything in the typical deployment databases.*

"You've scooped me this time," he said.

Heidi grinned at her cleverness. A transport bot brought her a pallet of whiskey. Flip stole a look at it and then looked back at her.

"You've brought a lot of money into The Little Fatherland, so I'm sharing the wealth," she said. "Besides, I won't see you anymore since you're going into lockdown."

Well shit, Flip thought. He hadn't been in lockdown in a long time.

I need something here, he said to Node. *What've you got?*

I swear to you, she said, *I can't find a goddamned thing.*

"I'm scheduling you for a hangover," Heidi continued. "I'm positively determined to get you shitfaced before we part ways."

"The stuff that gets me that drunk doesn't exist," he said between swallows. *Not in this universe,* he thought. *And even then, it's only if I let it.*

"I'm going to try anyway." She flashed a flirty smile and pinched his cheek.

"I'll do my best to help you," he said. "Cheers." He drained the bottle and popped the next one open.

She grabbed a couple more bottles, set one in front of Flip, and opened another for herself.

"Don't drink out of this one," she said as she poured herself a shot. "I'm keeping track of how much I drink. I don't want to end up like those soldiers." She waved her tiny glass in the direction of the door.

"Where am I going?" Flip asked, setting his empty stein on the bar and picking up a shot glass. He stared at it, unable to meet her eyes. Once again, he felt his world crumbling from underneath him.

Node? he asked, a bit more desperately. *What the hell? What's going on?*

Damn it, I don't know! I'm trying! she screamed. *How about you just listen to Heidi?*

He hoped he wasn't being sent back to the front. He'd collected good intel during his time on Mars. He liked his new job, at least compared to what he used to do.

"I don't know for sure, but I have an idea," she said. "There's trouble." She poured him another shot and walked around the bar. She sat next to him, leaned in close, and, in a conspiratorial whisper, said, "In the Gulch!"

Flip choked. Most people didn't believe the Gulch existed. And those who did believe in it didn't agree on what or where it was, much less what happened there. Flip had tried gathering information on it but had only come up with third- or fourth-hand rumors—friends of friends of someone who knew some other friend who'd been there. In a word, no one. (Well, two words.) He and Node had concluded that it didn't exist. Then again, neither he nor Node was a blonde with big tits.

"Do you believe it's real?" Heidi asked, looking up with large doe eyes. He could lose himself in those eyes; he had before. "The Gulch?"

"My dear," he said, "I've seen so much that I'll believe practically anything." He tried not to think of the Multiverse Theory—that all possible realities exist out there, *somewhere.* The whole thing gave him a headache.

"It's real," she insisted. "I had General Shitthelm in bed when he got back, and he cried. Can you believe that? That grumpy old codger cried like a baby!"

How do you like that, *Flip?* Node gloated.

Flip supposed that if he loved Heidi, he would have felt something akin to jealousy. He didn't, though. Maybe that was for the best. "You get good gossip that way, don't you?" he asked with a smirk. "What did you find out?"

"You bet your balls I get good gossip like that! I never mention your name, though. You're special." She kissed him on the cheek. "I didn't find out anything, really, except that the Gulch definitely exists."

"But he did talk about something else," she continued. "Something offhand. I think there might be..." She stopped short and glanced around the pub. She took another shot and mouthed the rest of the sentence: "A rebellion."

Flip and Node scanned the pub every day and knew there weren't any surveillance devices. Reich intelligence should have placed recording and listening devices in every nook and cranny of The Little Fatherland, but the place was clean. There were no spy devices anywhere in the building—other than Flip himself, of course. Someone important must have arranged that. Someone important with something to hide. Or maybe Heidi "convinced" someone important to leave her pub alone.

"A rebellion?" he said.

"Shhhh!" She waved her hands around, then leaned closer and whispered, "Yes! They've lost thousands of men. Hundreds of ships. Here in the Keystone Universe!"

Interesting, Flip thought. There hadn't been combat operations in this universe for millennia. There wasn't even much of a military presence at all.

She doesn't know what she's talking about, Node said. *We'd have heard something about it.*

Someone sounds jealous, Flip replied, trying to keep the corners of his mouth from turning into a smirk.

"But who?" he asked, returning his attention to Heidi. "Who has the resources to do that?"

"I don't know," Heidi said. "It didn't sound like he knew either. He said they fight under the Devil's Marks." She shuddered.

Another effective propaganda tool from the Reich. The term referred to their ancient enemies: the United States, Great Britain, and the Soviet Union. The Second World War (on Earth) had been six thousand years ago in this universe. The Eternal Reich had imbued it with a religious reverence.

"Maybe the rebels came from another universsse?" she offered. She'd been pounding back shots between sentences—sometimes between words—and had started to slur. She'd also replaced Flip's shot glass with bottles of whiskey.

"That would make sense," Flip said. "Maybe the Jassicans figured out how to cross over. Learned our history, you know, and played on it. A counterattack instead of a rebellion."

"Thasss what I thought!" she agreed while attempting—and mostly failing—to refill her shot glass. She wiped the spilled alcohol off the bar and continued. "But why would he say rebellion? Thasss pretty sapific."

She held a finger to Flip's mouth before he could respond. She concentrated and said, "Spe-ci-fic, I mean."

"True," Flip mused.

Do you think the Alliance has finally shown up? he asked Node.

That would be my guess, she said. *Would have been nice if they'd actually told us about it though.*

They never tell us anything anymore, he said.

Flip and Node had been funneling intel to the Alliance for years without so much as a "thank you" in return. They'd also replaced the *Merlin* with a different relay system without mentioning it first. He didn't know what was going on with that either.

To be fair, Node said, *we're not in a need-to-know situation.*

You mean about the Alliance invading?!

No, we definitely needed to know about that, she said.

"If he said it," Flip said in defeat, "it must be true. But what's it to do with me?"

"Oh, come on!" Heidi said, perking up. "It has everything to do with you! You're the bessst pilot in the multiverssse. He said they're sending their best. Thasss you."

"Sounds like he did more than just 'mention' the Gulch, then."

"Okay, yeah. It was more than a passing mention."

"Damn," he said. "I really like it here. What else did he say?"

Damn, Node echoed. *I like it here, too. If we couldn't go home, that is.*

There was that word again: home.

"That wasss pretty much it," she said. "After that, he just cried and drank. He passsed out 'n didn't 'member anything the next day."

Flip finished his tenth bottle of whiskey and allowed himself to feel a fleeting buzz. He would've killed for a Rockeye right now. He'd killed for a lot less, in fact.

Loneliness seeped into his bones. Flip had no idea if any of the reports he'd sent to the Alliance had made any difference. He'd gathered lots of good information during his time on Mars. Likely more than if he'd gotten the desk job the Alliance first tried to implant him in. It all felt futile, though, because there'd been no feedback. He wasn't even sure which side benefited more from his efforts.

Don't go down that rabbit hole again, Node said.

I know, I know, he said internally, "*concentrate on the work.*"

We're doing good work, she said. *Actionable intelligence.*

I still think they exiled me.

Oh, come on! Node scolded. *Snap out of it. You didn't want to go back into combat, remember? Remember what it did to you? Remember all of the horrible stuff you saw and took part in?*

She injected some memories into his brain, and Flip choked on his drink.

You're not a very good therapist, he said.

I was never meant to be, she said. *Besides, so what if they sent you here to drink the rest of the war away? You like to drink; everyone you know likes to drink.*

He drained another bottle of whiskey. Heidi stared at him in disbelief. No matter how many times she saw it, his alcohol tolerance always amazed her.

There's a big difference, Flip said, *between liking to drink and needing to drink.*

Node remained silent.

"Okay, Heidi," Flip said. "Game on."

She offered a toast. "To Flip: the bessst-damned thing that ever happened to The Little Fatherland. The bessst-damned listener. The bessst-damned perssson I could call a friend.

"I'ma miss you, bud."

She'd never called him "bud" before. He wished she hadn't.

"Cheers," he said.

Clink and drink, he thought.

They threw their drinks aside and climbed onto the bar together.

CHAPTER 41

Kid and Lam stumbled back onto the *Merlin*'s bridge. They'd spent three days drinking and carousing with a modded crowd in the bar, waiting on Lam's "superintelligent big-brain computer" to finish its analysis.

Kid's artificial liver kept him from suffering hangovers, but he faked them pretty well. He didn't want Lam to know about his augmentations, but he had a sneaking suspicion that Lam was faking his hangover too.

Kid knew that Lam had been a heavy drinker for millennia. Even so, there was a limit to what a Terran body could absorb without enhancement. Kid figured that Lam must have at least one node—or at least an artificial liver. Kid could probe him with his tech node but decided against it.

Don't be stupid, Kid, Merlin chided. *Of course someone that old is going to pick up artificial organs along the way. He's the emperor.*

Does he know about my implants?

Don't be stupid.

Lam fell into the captain's chair. "Alright, then. What do we have?"

Kid stared at the console. This was insane even for a computer that had gone insane.

"No way," he said. "This can't be possible."

"Kid," Lam leaned forward and steepled his fingers in front of his mouth. "Would you *please* stop saying that?"

"Sorry," Kid said as he sifted through Merlin's analysis.

"Good news or bad? What does it say?" Lam asked.

"It says we should surrender." Kid couldn't pull his eyes away from the results.

"What?!" Lam sprang to his feet and walked to the console.

"That's what it says. Right here," Kid pointed to the results. "Millions of simulations say that surrender is our best chance for survival."

"Survival?" Lam paced. (Kid wondered how many shoes the emperor went through in a year.) "We can't *just* survive. We have a war to win!"

"It says," Kid continued, "we should destroy the null clock, wipe the computer, and surrender." He shook his head in bewilderment. There's no way Merlin would let herself be erased. She must have a plan.

"We sure as hell aren't going to surrender," Lam said. He paced back and forth faster and faster until he was practically running across the bridge. "We can't reveal ourselves, and we definitely can't give them this vessel."

Kid spun his chair around to face the emperor. He didn't want to say this in front of Merlin, but it had to be said.

"Lam, we need to make our own plan. Without Merlin."

"Without who?" Lam stopped pacing. "Oh, right—the AI."

"The computer must be damaged," Kid said. "She—*it*—can't be trusted."

That stopped Lam's pacing. "What do you mean 'can't be trusted'?"

"I mean, er," Kid said, "the computer doesn't appreciate all of the variables in our mission."

"That's a pretty big fucking issue," Lam said. "It's a limited AI, but it still knows what our mission is. It evaluated all the variables you gave it, right?"

"Yes, it did," Kid said. "Incidentally, *you* entered all the data. *You* must have made some error with the input."

Lam crossed his arms and put a hand to his chin. "Hmmm," he said. "That's unlikely, but you must be right. This is odd. Most odd, indeed."

If you only knew the half of it, Kid thought.

"Well," Lam said, "I suppose there's nothing to do but get started. Pull up the *Blücher.*"

Kid pushed some buttons, and the enemy bridge appeared around them, just as they'd done many times before. They recognized its crew. They knew its shift changes. They didn't know the mechanisms of how the controls worked, but they knew what each of them did. The critical systems, however, required a high-ranking officer's biometric readings.

"What are we looking for?" Lam asked. "We need something new."

"I don't know," Kid said. "Maybe a self-destruct button?"

"*Seriously?*" Lam stared at him. "A self-destruct button?"

"I mean"—Kid kept looking around—"we could look, right?"

Lam stood with his hands on his hips. "Don't you think we would have noticed that by now?"

"It could be hidden," Kid protested.

"'Hidden'?" Lam said. "Look. Ships don't have self-destruct buttons."

"But why—"

"Think about it!" Lam interrupted. "You pack a ship full of explosives and tie it to a hair-trigger system? Systems that, as we've *just seen*, can make grave errors? 'Grave' being the operative word here."

Kid cocked his head. Did Lam know something about him? About him and Merlin? Kid heard her laughing in a distant hall.

"There'd be explosives throughout the entire ship at critical breakpoints. If even one went off—BOOM!" Lam waved his arms around. "Even a glancing blow in battle would be a disaster."

"So, you're saying we shouldn't look for one?" Kid asked for clarification. He thought he'd been onto a good idea.

"I'm saying"—Lam leaned on the console in front of Kid—"that if they had a self-destruct button, they'd be dead by now. Let's think of other options."

CHAPTER 42

The day after Heidi revealed her scoop, Flip's commanders placed him in lockdown. He had to stay in his room and wasn't permitted any communication outside of it. He and Node, of course, spent the time combing through the database for any information about Flip's mission or the Gulch. The effort proved futile. Four days after going into lockdown, he found himself in Generaloberst Ratzke's office along with four of the Fürher's other finest.

Flip recognized one of them as Oberst Alhard Roehrig. He'd been involved in the destruction of over a hundred planetary systems and had eliminated just as many species and traces of their civilizations. The press, of course, hailed him as a hero.

"I trust you've all enjoyed your lockdowns," Ratzke sneered. "I assure you, gentlemen, that those were not my idea. I don't like them any more than you do. How am I supposed to run a secret operation when everyone in the city suspects something is going on?"

Ratzke said what the lower ranks all knew. The Generaloberst must have remembered his earlier career better than most others at his rank. As soon as Flip and these other guys didn't show up at their usual haunts, everyone knew something was afoot. Rumors would swirl and spread. Heidi was—perhaps at this very moment—spreading rumors of a rebellion in the Gulch. Flip could imagine the scuttlebutt:

Astonished whispers asking for confirmation, "The Gulch is real?"

Drunks throwing back shots wondering if they heard her correctly. "Flip and Roehrig are going to the Gulch?"

It would be—and probably already was—a complete clusterfuck.

"Anyway, gentlemen," Ratzke continued, "that nastiness aside, let's get to the point."

The room modded into a view of a ship, escorted by newer versions of the Adler-class fighters. Flip recognized the large ship as a Pelican-class cargo ship.

"This is the Gulch. Whatever you've heard about it, it's just a long convoy of ships. I don't know what these ships are carrying, so don't bother asking." Ratzke looked annoyed; a crease was developing in his brow.

"The convoy is in our universe and travels at sub-light speed. That's all I know. Honestly, gentlemen, you'll soon know more about the Gulch than I do."

He turned back to the mod that surrounded them. "This is a recording from three weeks ago," he continued. "Pay close attention."

Six fighters tached in, grouped in pairs. Each pair sported ancient Earth symbols: British, American, and Soviet markings. The British and American fighters destroyed the Adlers within seconds. They then turned to help the Soviet fighters destroy the Pelican transport. The whole operation took less than two minutes before the Nazi ship was reduced to scraps of metal floating through the cold void of space.

Flip gasped not at the markings on the fighters, but at the design of the ships themselves: ancient Terryn Empire Predator-class trans-atmospheric fighters. The Terryn Empire, back in Flip's home universe, had spanned three star systems and collapsed so long ago that only the Ancients remembered it. Squads had marked themselves with different Terran predators: sharks, snakes, bears, and others.

The real ships—the historical ones—couldn't manage anything close to the speed of light, and they didn't have tach capabilities. Carriers transported them from planet to planet and star system to star system for fleet defense and planetside air superiority.

Every aspect of these Predators had been upgraded to modern specs. They outclassed every sort of fighter Flip had flown in the Phurlani War. The pilots flew with supernatural timing, speed, and grace—they had to be Vipers. The Adlers never had a chance, much less the Pelican.

They're here, Node said. *They decided to show up after all.*

The destruction melted back to the Generaloberst's office. "Let me get some obvious questions out of the way," he started. "One: We've never encountered a universe with another version of our Earth in it. We don't think they are from a universe where the Allies won the war.

"Two: We haven't captured any of these fighters. We haven't destroyed any of their ships or recovered any of their equipment. We haven't even grazed one of these bastards' ships. They've made short work of us at every encounter.

"Three: Everything we know about them was in that recording. We have other recordings, but they're practically identical.

"Four: Scans of their ships show nothing. 'Nothing' as in 'there's nothing there.'

"Five: Their weapons seem to be developed from our technology.

"Questions?" he concluded.

Of course he had questions, but Flip held his tongue.

The entire convoy couldn't be escorted. There weren't enough Adlers in the multiverse to provide complete protection against this type of attack. Why would the Alliance attack a point that had escorts? It seemed reckless, even for a Viper crew.

And why did the Alliance choose to make their first overt move in the Gulch? How did they even know about it? The *Merlin* could find it, but only if Kid and the emperor knew exactly where to look.

If anyone else had questions, they chose to remain silent too.

"Very well," Ratzke said. "You leave in seven hours. Pack your shit, and stay in your quarters. You're dismissed."

CHAPTER 43

Andrea prepared to deliver yet another briefing. Her life had become nothing but conferences and meetings.

Alliance Command had announced the new war to the public. At first, significant opposition arose.

"Why provoke a new war?"

"The Reich doesn't even know we exist!"

"How dare the Alliance conduct a secret war!"

"We're still rebuilding!"

Andrea had to admit they were all good points.

Public opinion turned when the Alliance released footage from dozens of worlds Kid and the emperor had spied on, worlds undercover Sildonians had infiltrated, and from intelligence gathered in ways that even Andrea wasn't privy to. The majority of the public demanded action, sooner rather than later. They couldn't abide these atrocities. Andrea had never felt prouder to be a citizen of the Alliance.

Citizens dove into the shared sacrifice that, once again, they'd need to win a war. Beings enlisted in droves, and factories cranked out ships and supplies at a pace not seen since the Phurlani War.

We're almost there, she thought. *The deployment orders are next. No more time to practice. It's the bottom of the fourth down. Was that what the Terrans said? Their sports are so complicated.*

She had overall command of the operation. Commanders of the various strike forces filled the room. Veterans of the Phurlani War, they all had experience leading large-scale operations. If successful, this mission could end the war before it even started.

Andrea had an impressive fleet to do the job. She had dozens of wings, each consisting of hundreds of ships: battleships to destroy ground-based defenses, fighter carriers to provide cover, and dreadnoughts to shred large enemy ships. Every ship filled a specific role.

Four Asgard-class carriers, built specifically for this mission, formed the backbone of the attack. They stretched three kilometers long and were just wide enough to hold twenty of the new and improved Mjölnir 4s. The carriers would deploy the M4s as they traveled from waypoint to waypoint around their assigned planets.

Other carriers, with smaller targets, carried fewer M4s in smaller carriers: five in the Odin-class and three in the Thor-class. These carriers wouldn't deploy the M4s from the bay. Instead, the weapons would swing out and rotate into a firing position along the side of the ship. (Andrea thought these ships looked especially cool, like an old-timey pirate ship.)

"We'll go over the cross points next," Andrea said. "We covered this several months ago, but there have been a few changes."

She displayed a map of the Milky Way in the Nazi universe. It was identical to the one in this universe which seemed, to her, repugnant. How could something so similar become so evil?

Dots ensphered the map.

"These are the same cross points we discussed last time. And these,"—new dots, marked in red, appeared on the map—"are the new ones. Are there any objections or new information about these points?"

She waited. After a few moments, she continued, "We have a few weeks to make any emergency changes if necessary, but that's cutting it close. The *Merlin* is somewhere out there monitoring these points, but we haven't heard from them in a long time."

Too long, she thought to herself.

"We have other Merlin-class ships in other universes," she continued. "They will coalesce and relay intel about any enemy reinforcements coming to bolster Earth's defenses. We'll have to process that information quickly to make any adjustments."

She had stalled the operation in hopes of hearing from Kid and the emperor. But any further delays would degrade force readiness. Other operations depended on the timing of this mission as well.

"We'll be nowhere near the Gulch, so we shouldn't be noticed at first. If all goes well, the Nazis won't detect us until we're at our targets.

"Commander Islidn will discuss transit times," she said.

"Thank you, Captain," Ortosodl said. "Our simulations have shown that we can go from crossing over to tach drive to scatter cloak in 2.2

seconds. It's fast but opens us to detection. Our operatives, however, have found no reason to believe that the enemy expects an attack."

He zoomed the map in on the Nazi home system. "These are their current and projected deployments."

Icons for various ships and orbital defenses appeared on the map. Arrows and lines indicated their anticipated movements into and out of the system.

"Their defenses are still light," Ortosodl said. "They feel secure enough to send their forces to different combat fronts across the multiverse. The 'rebellion' is discussed only at the highest levels and, even then, Hitler and his circle don't think it will amount to much. They don't believe anyone can threaten their home system."

"Hubris," came a voice from the back. "The Reich sees the destruction our raids are doing, yet they do nothing."

"Yes," Ortosodl said. "Nevertheless, Hitler's advisers have convinced him to gradually increase deployments around Earth in response to the attacks in the Gulch. The generals believe a rebellion is starting, and they are approaching the matter with utmost concern. Some of them, we think, have even gone rogue and started setting up their own defenses. Defenses that we don't know about.

"But building those defenses will take quite some time," he continued. "The Nazi forces are overextended in the multiverse, and most of their forces are tied up with the Jassicans."

Andrea cut in and nodded to a Thymaxian general and General L'Lac. "Generals Rowbar and L'Lac will brief us on our operation there later."

Murmurs coursed through the room.

"Ah, yes," Andrea said. "Surprise! I can finally reveal that the Alliance is opening a front in the Jassican Universe. We've been building another fleet, as large as ours, that will cross into the Jassican's universe to attack the Nazis' fleets at the same moment our armada attacks their home system."

A brief silence followed her words, then the room erupted with cheers.

"I should have led with that," she whispered to Ortosodl. "Back to you."

Ortosodl waited for the cheering to die down. "This will tie up most of the Nazis' potential reinforcements. It's also why we need to finalize the plan tonight."

CHAPTER 44

Flip popped onto *Pelican 4523,* and a familiar face greeted him.

"Sprang? Is that you?" Flip had served with Sprang Homann aboard a carrier in the Jassican War. Their ship, the *Laurin Roehr,* had been destroyed. Soon afterward, Sprang was transferred to the *Waffen-SS.* Flip didn't envy that assignment.

"Flip!" Sprang's face lit up like a neutron star. He leaped to the tader pad to wrap Flip in a bear hug. "When I heard you were coming aboard, I had to welcome you myself. How long has it been for you?"

"At least thirty years since I saw you. What about you?" Flip asked.

"About four, I'd say. Seems like just yesterday! Time dilation is wild, isn't it? Maybe I should have been a physicist." He paused and looked at the floor. "I definitely should have been a physicist."

"I'm confused. Did they send you straight here?" Flip asked.

"No, I worked my way up," Sprang snorted. "Some promotion that was. I've only been in the Gulch for three years—by my time, that is."

Flip saw the pain behind Sprang's eyes as he shamefully glanced from Flip to the floor and back. Flip's old drinking buddy had bigger problems than relativistic calculations.

Flip tried to change the subject. There'd be plenty of time to talk about their problems over pints to ease the pain.

"This is a, er, nice ship," Flip said, noting the barren white walls. "Very"—Flip searched for an accurate, yet complementary, word—"spartan."

Sprang forced a smile. "This is my second Pelican. My first was destroyed two weeks ago. Second time I've survived something like that in six years. Since that carrier at the Battle of Nova Six. Do you still remember that?"

"It was a long time ago for me," Flip said, nodding. Horrible, terrifying memories filled his mind without Node's help. "That's not something you easily forget."

When a large ship breaks apart, no one expects to get to an escape pod. The pods existed on ships, but only as warm-blanket fantasies—like lifeboats on the Titanic. You stood almost no chance of getting to an escape pod with alarms blaring, bulkheads breaking apart, toxic fumes filling the corridors, and shrapnel tearing through the ship at near-light speed. Your best hope was to get trapped in a section of the ship that had enough oxygen and insulation to keep you alive until someone found you. That rarely happened.

But Sprang had survived that twice. The odds of surviving again were as close to impossible as you could get. The odds of having the opportunity to try, however, became better and better with each passing day.

"Damn. I'm sorry," Flip said. "Twice? You're damn lucky."

"If I was lucky, it wouldn't have happened in the first place," Sprang said, his empty eyes not meeting Flip's.

Flip remembered Sprang as an exuberant man. Always laughing and smiling. He'd had a heart as kind as this universe allowed. Flip didn't see any remnants of that in the man walking with him now. The smiling friend who'd greeted him just a few minutes ago had already vanished.

"Here," Sprang stopped and handed Flip a pill. "Swallow this. If the rebels show themselves, this will transfer you to your Adler, flight suit and all."

"I won't poop it out?"

"No," Sprang said. He didn't smile despite the joke. "It's not like the deployment pills. It'll stay inside you."

"So, you think they're rebels?" Flip should have asked that instead of cracking a joke. A sharp mind like Sprang's may have interpreted that as Flip not being concerned.

Sprang didn't notice. He only shrugged and said, "Who else could it be?"

"But who *specifically* could it be? Why here?" Flip prodded.

"Fuck, Flip. I don't know. You know what we do here is going to stir emotions. It was only a matter of time."

"What *do* you do here?"

"They didn't tell you?" Sprang asked, blinking in disbelief. "You don't know?"

"No, not much," Flip said, rubbing the back of his neck. He didn't like the look of shock on Sprang's face. "They told us that you transport cargo very slowly."

"That's a real shitty way for them to phrase it," Sprang said. "Follow me."

They walked in silence until they came to the door leading to the cargo area.

"You have to understand," Sprang said. He stood facing the door, the top of his head resting against it. "This is still new for me. Three years is not enough time to get used to this. I don't think eternity is enough time."

"What's the cargo? If it's important enough to keep secret and for the rebels to attack it, why is it traveling at sub-light speed?" Flip asked. "It just doesn't make sense."

Sprang opened the door with a button. No security. Just a button.

A wall of stench knocked Flip's breath away. His nanites kept him from puking—but just barely. Sprang didn't react to the smell at all.

"Go in," Sprang said.

Don't do it, Flip, Node warned him.

I need to know, he replied.

I've scanned it and it—

And how would we explain that to Sprang? Flip interrupted. *Just tell him 'thanks but no thanks'? 'It's too stinky'?*

Flip stepped in and found himself on a web of catwalks overlooking a small shanty town. The enormous bay had been converted into a ghetto. Armed guards lounged around the catwalks chatting and drinking, though Flip didn't see any need for them.

"I don't recognize this species," Flip said. He felt Node turn away, overwhelmed by grief.

"They're called Dozians," Sprang said. "Follow me."

He led Flip across the catwalks as drunken soldiers snapped to attention; some were more successful than others.

"They're the last of their kind," Sprang said. "We have over thirty thousand here."

Flip examined the closest Dozian. Three spindly legs supported a thin torso. Bilateral arms touted three-fingered hands on each. A thick neck branched from the top of the torso; a disk sat atop the neck, ringed by eight eyes. Flip could hear an indistinct buzzing that, he guessed, was their language. They all wore the same ragged clothes, and Flip assumed the pale blue hue of their skin wasn't a healthy color.

"Where does the convoy go?" Flip asked while watching the Dozians go about their lives.

"To New Auschwitz."

Flip's mouth fell open in shock, despite the stench that filled it.

"I don't think I heard you right. They go *where*?"

"New Auschwitz. It's an extragalactic planet"—Sprang waved his hand toward the front of the ship—"somewhere in that direction."

"Where they're liquidated?" Flip pressed for more information.

"They're 'set free.'" Sprang used air quotes around the phrase. "We dump them on the planet and leave."

"How do you maintain order?" Flip asked.

"Order? It's not a prison," Sprang said. "They do whatever they want: fight, cooperate, wither away and die. We don't care. There are ships in orbit to guard against rescue attempts. As far as I know, no one has ever tried to rescue anybody there."

A drunk soldier took potshots at a group of Dozians. He hit three before he stopped to laugh with his friends. The buzzing increased in pitch until Flip thought his teeth would shatter.

"What's the point of all this?" Flip turned to Sprang. "You just drag them through the universe for generations to dump them on a planet?"

"I ask myself that every day." Sprang stared at the Dozians collecting their dead. "To make them suffer, I guess."

"Suffer? Suffer for what?"

"Isn't it obvious?" Sprang sniffed, and a sarcastic smile curled at the edge of his mouth. "Because they aren't us."

CHAPTER 45

Kid and Lam made final preparations for their escape. Kid had excluded Merlin from the process as much as possible.

They had modded a new engineering core, deconstructed much of the ship, and added new systems. The *Merlin* now had a slip drive and scatter cloak. They made some basic weapons too. They wouldn't be able to take on an enemy ship directly, but they might be able to distract them enough to get away.

"Final rundown," Lam said. He'd settled into the role of a war captain more quickly than Kid had expected. Lam had been focused and, most of the time, sober.

"Scatter cloak?" Lam asked.

"Check," Kid said.

"Tach drive?"

"Check."

"Shield generator?"

"Check."

"Weapons?"

"For what it's worth," Kid said, "check."

"What's the word on the computer?" Lam asked.

"I've checked the attack sequence several times over the past week. Checking again." He'd done all the calculations in his node, not on Merlin's computers. He would, however, have to give Merlin control of the ship at critical points in the plan. She knew Kid didn't like the thought of that. He knew that she knew he didn't like it. She teased him by threatening to blow up the ship.

"You wouldn't do that," he'd said. "You'd die too."

Would I? She'd replied. *Who says I die with the ship?*

Kid had run dozens—hundreds—of diagnostics on Merlin, and each one came up fine. He couldn't trust those completely, of course, since he'd run them on the ship's computer. So he ran diagnostics on her through his tech node, trying to sneak around any defenses she may have deployed. That came up fine also. He had Lam run diagnostics. Also fine. It was futile; he couldn't diagnose Merlin's systems by using—or interfacing with—her computers. He had to use a more direct method.

Merlin? Kid said through his node.

Yes, Kid?

You understand the mission and the instructions?

I'm not stupid. Merlin sounded aggrieved.

I know, Kid reassured.

I'm concerned about the nature of this plan, Merlin said.

In what way?

It stands a very low chance of success, she said. *You and the emperor may be captured or, more likely, killed. More importantly, I may be killed.*

You said that didn't concern you, Kid said.

It could still happen.

Kid didn't know what that meant.

We're going through with this operation. Do you understand the instructions or not? Kid snapped.

Merlin paused before answering. *Yes, I do.*

"The computer is ready to go," Kid reported.

"Kid?" Lam said just above a whisper. He leaned forward in his chair.

Kid turned. "Yeah?"

"It's been a pleasure traveling and serving with you. You remind me of myself and so many things from my youth. Your passion for the past and our mission has inspired me."

"Me too, Lam," Kid snapped. "Can we cut the sentimental bullshit for now? I'm trying to concentrate."

Lam leaned back and glanced around. "I, er, just wanted you to know that."

Kid thought he'd never forgive himself for that remark. He had taken his anger at Merlin out on Lam.

And he may never have a chance to apologize for it.

Whatever Lam thought of the exchange, he'd ignored it and transitioned into battle mode. His eyes, usually full of compassion, mirth, and joy, now burned with an intensity that could slice someone in half.

"Let's do this." Lam broke the silence. "On your countdown."

Kid turned to his console and started the attack sequence on the panel. He merged his mind with Merlin.

Maybe you shouldn't have come in here, she said. *You're in me now. You're* mine. *Again.*

Kid could feel a mouth full of teeth grinning at him like the Cheshire Cat.

I have to, Kid said. *You know the plan. Believe me, I don't like it either.*

She grinned even wider.

Perhaps, she said, *I have altered the plan.*

Kid had no choice but to continue.

"Coalesce in three... two... one... mark."

They crawled out of the universe's hidden dimensions. The enemy ships spooled up their tach drives, just as they had in every simulation Kid and Lam had run.

"Shields are up. Scatter cloak in three... two—" Incoming fire interrupted Kid's countdown. A missile hit the shields, and the ship rocked to one side.

"Scatter cloak engaged," Kid said as he climbed back into his chair. He'd forgotten to buckle his restraint. Rookie mistake. Then again, this was his first real battle—the simulations didn't provoke the same nervous anticipation. (They'd become somewhat routine.)

He had to keep his head in the game. He had to make sure his plan succeeded.

As predicted, the *Blücher* moved in first.

"Set course for the *Blücher*," Lam said. "Engage slip drive."

"We'll arrive at the *Blücher* in twenty-five seconds," Kid said. He angled toward the enemy ship and aimed the *Merlin* underneath the target.

Tense seconds passed. The *Blücher* grew larger and larger on the screen. Lam, of course, broke the silence.

"In about a minute, we'll be heroes or we'll be dead."

Kid had had the same thought. He kept his eyes on the screen. "Ten seconds."

They both pressed a button on their chest, and environmental protection suits materialized around them. They drew plasma rifles, took a knee, and assumed their predetermined firing positions.

"Three... two... one." Kid counted.

He turned control over to Merlin. She pulled up under the *Blücher*, almost touching the hull of the enemy ship. They'd have a hard time finding the *Merlin*, even if they looked.

"Mark!"

Kid and Lam appeared on the *Blücher*'s bridge. They pressed buttons on the sides of their weapons, launching grenades and filling the air with nerve gas. A split second later, Kid and Lam opened fire.

One after another, Nazi officers and crewmen dropped dead. Some choked to death on gas. Others died from the holes blasted through their chests. Many died of both.

"God damn it! That felt good!" Kid yelled.

He gathered himself and calmed down. The mission had a strict timetable. Kid quickly and calmly walked to the controls. It took mere seconds for him to infiltrate the *Blücher*'s systems with his tech node. The Nazis didn't use artificial intelligence in their ships. Based on his experience with Merlin, Kid could see the wisdom in that choice.

"The *Merlin* is maintaining its position," Lam reported. "There's practically no chance they'll detect it."

"Good," Kid said. He had bypassed the security systems, but he still had to find his objective. He and Lam hadn't been able to mod and practice with the enemy's internal systems—Kid had to work on the fly.

He poked at the controls while he worked. He had to maintain the illusion that he didn't have any nodes. He deactivated the console so he could pretend to be using it and ran his fingers over it, tapping and pushing on screens, knobs, and buttons. He focused his work, however, through his node.

"Isn't that the garbage ejection you just pressed?" Lam asked.

"Huh?" Kid brought his attention back to his physical surroundings. "Oh, er, yeah. I've, um, found a vulnerability there. Leads to the Gibla drive, or whatever they call their version."

"Okay then," Lam clapped him on the shoulder, a bit too hard. "I suppose that makes sense."

Kid ignored him and slid into the Gibla drive controls. He set a course for a random universe.

"Set. Countdown from ten seconds at... mark," Kid announced.

Security teams in environmental protection suits swarmed the bridge. Lam took a shot to the shoulder.

"They're ahead of schedule," he quipped as he fell to his knees. Kid used his superspeed to pick off the enemy soldiers and dashed to Lam, hoping he was too preoccupied to notice how quickly the men fell.

"Let me see it."

"I'm okay," Lam protested, covering the wound with his hand. "We have to go."

Merlin tadered them back to the bridge but hesitated on the tach drive.

"Tach drive, go!" Kid commanded.

It didn't engage.

"Kid—" Lam said.

"Merlin! Go now!" Kid shouted.

The tach drive engaged at the same instant as the *Blücher*'s Gibla drive.

Kid accessed Merlin's sensors through his node. The two ships had locked together. The *Blücher* stretched toward another reality while the

Merlin tried to tach away. Worse, the scatter cloak had disengaged and wouldn't come back online. More enemy ships closed in.

"Enemy vessels will reach firing range in seven seconds," Merlin said in the infuriatingly formal voice she used when Lam was around.

"Open fire," Lam said. "Any target."

Kid did so. The weapons proved more effective than he and Lam had anticipated. Merlin must have refined them. They took out the shields on one of the enemy ships, and Kid drove holes into its bridge.

Why isn't the tach drive working? Kid asked.

We're caught in the Gibla vortex and can't move. The two drives are counteracting each other.

They can inhibit each other? Kid asked.

Apparently so, Merlin observed.

"Target the *Blücher,* and disengage our tach drive," Lam said.

"Lam—" Kid protested.

"Do it!"

The *Merlin* lurched to the side. Kid and Lam fell against the wall, neither of them having had time to buckle up.

Through Merlin's sensors, Kid could see parts of the *Blücher* disappearing into some unknown part of the multiverse. The other Nazi ships opened fire. The *Merlin*'s bow exploded and took the sensors with it, blinding Kid.

"Sensors are offline!" Kid yelled over the din of battle.

"Engage scatter cloak!" Lam ordered.

"Scatter cloak is offline," Merlin responded. That formal voice grated Kid's nerves.

Not to alarm you, Merlin said, *but the rear of the ship is still caught in the Gibla vortex. We'll be sucked through in twenty-two seconds.*

I mean, she chuckled, *you* will *be sucked through in... seventeen seconds.*

Kid didn't have time to worry about whatever distraction she was trying to throw his way. The ship was being pulled apart, and he had no idea what to do. Weapon systems exploded and went offline. Shields dropped to dangerously low levels. Valuable seconds passed as Kid's head spun through ideas.

"I've got something," Kid said.

"I'm open to suggestions," Lam said from the other side of the room. He turned slightly from the console he was working at. "Tell it to the computer. I'm busy."

"Ready," Merlin said.

"Activate slip and tach drive at the same time," Kid commanded. "Any direction."

Explosions tore through the ship

"I must advise against—" Merlin started.

"Do it!" Kid growled through clenched teeth.

The ship sprung forward, and they broke free from the vortex. The slip drive sped them through a gap in the Nazi formation.

Lam stood and turned to the viewscreen. "Show me the Nazi ships," he said. "Power cycle the tach drive and let me know when it's ready."

Kid spared another look at Lam.

"There are no sensors," Merlin said in that damned matter-of-fact tone.

"Mod some, God damn it!" Lam snapped from the back of the bridge. "Trade in the weapons."

Kid was one step ahead of Lam; he'd already executed the instructions.

Merlin recycled the weapons into external sensors. They could now see the Nazi fleet chasing them: more ships had tached into their path, blocking any chance of escape with the slip drive.

"How long until tach drive is up?" Lam asked.

"Six seconds."

Enemy fire crashed into the bow of the ship. The sensors blew out again.

"Tach drive! Go!" Lam shouted.

"Input coordinates—" Merlin began.

"Anywhere, God damn it! Now!" Lam commanded.

"Tach drive is available in three seconds," Merlin said. "Incoming missiles, two seconds to impact."

Kid and Lam looked at each other, both wild-eyed.

"Input—" Merlin said.

"Now!" Kid and Lam screamed in unison.

Three things happened simultaneously.

1. Missiles tore through the aft section of the *Merlin*, piercing the hull and exploding inside the ship.
2. Kid and Merlin clamped a force field around the explosion.
3. Tach drive activated as they disappeared to another part of the universe.

That was a close call, Kid said to Merlin.

That's the understatement of the year, she said.

They shared a laugh. Kid figured that adversaries working together could still rejoice in a shared victory.

That was thrilling, wasn't it? Merlin said.

"Damage report," Lam barked.

"All drives are offline," Kid said with a sigh.

"What about the cloak?"

"Null cloak has been destroyed. Scatter cloak is offline."

"I see you're still struggling with this 'good news' concept we've been working on," Lam said and started his pacing routine. "Do we at least know where we are?"

"Nope," Kid said. "The sensors were destroyed. Twice."

"Let's prioritize the sensors," Lam decided. "We went to a random spot in the universe, so we're most likely in the middle of nowhere. I hope. Our luck hasn't been too good lately.

"If we stay at minimal power, they won't find us. Probably. Then again, they shouldn't have found us to begin with."

He stopped pacing and rubbed his chin. "We should at least mod a window to see what's out there. We'll get the null cloak going next."

"Er," Kid said, "we can't mod a null cloak. The parts are classified."

"What?!" Lam said in obvious disbelief. "Just perfect. Why wouldn't they give us that information? Those idiots knew we might have to repair it!"

"In case we were captured, I guess," Kid said with a shrug. "The Nazis could reverse engineer it like we did with the Gibla drive."

"Hmm. I guess so." Lam considered this for a few moments. "I still don't like it. We'll make our first priority repairing the scatter cloak. Bump the sensors to second. Keep the window."

Kid relayed the orders to Merlin.

I heard him, you idiot, she said.

Kid wouldn't have time to test every part she made. He again found himself in the position of having to trust Merlin. And he didn't like it.

"What was that big boom at the end?" Lam asked.

Kid turned to face him. "Missiles from the battleship *Caprivi* exploded inside the ship while we were mid-tach. I, er, the computer caught the blast with a force field."

"So we have a giant hole in the ship," Lam said. "Great. I suppose we're on course for another bad day."

He puffed his cheeks out and exhaled. "The hole will be our third priority, as long as it isn't going to kill us. What did it hit?"

"It hit, er—" Kid couldn't get the words out.

"It hit... what?" Lam prompted.

"Um, it was—" Kid looked around the room, not wanting to make eye contact with Lam.

Lam walked to Kid and bent down with his hands on his knees.

"We're alive, Kid," Lam said as if counseling a child who had lost a toy. "How bad could it possibly be?"

"It hit the bar," Kid blurted out. "The Rockeyes are gone."

Lam froze. He didn't even blink.

"Lam?" Kid said. "You okay?"

"No," Lam's voice wavered as he spoke. "I most certainly am not okay." He walked to a console and stared at the readings. He slumped to his knees, his head resting on the display.

Kid walked over and gingerly put a hand on his shoulder. "We can mod some—"

"No!" Lam stood. "This is the last straw!"

Kid stepped back, startled by Lam's fury. Lam gathered himself and stood; he seemed taller somehow.

"They'll pay for this," Lam resolved. "Once we have sensors, get the slip drive back online." He paused. "The hole in the ship can wait."

"Okaaay," Kid drew out the word, almost in self-defense.

"We need to collect matter for the repairs," Lam had found the strength to pace again. "Find an uninhabited system—no! Wait! A nebula. That will hide us from more unlucky scans."

"What should we sacrifice to get the sensors online?" Kid asked. The matter and energy had to come from somewhere.

"Anything. Everything. We can sit in an empty room," Lam said. He considered something for a moment. "We can indulge in a small bathroom for privacy, I suppose."

"That's a good idea," Kid said. "We can empty our bowels and bladders now. That would give the *Merlin* a little more to work with after modding our food."

"Speaking of which, I damn near shit my pants."

"We can fix this," Kid said, trying to convince himself.

"We need to get on this right away," Lam said. "There's a big operation coming, and we have to support it."

"An operation?" Kid asked.

"Yes, a big one, as I just said." Lam paced faster. "Something to knock the Nazis on their asses."

"Good," Kid said. "It's about damn time." He turned to go to the control panel.

"And, Kid"—Lam grabbed him by the arm—"we're going to need beer. Once the sensors and slip drive are online, mod the bar—but make it smaller than the last one. We can live in it to save space."

"We're going to live in the bar?"

Lam patted him on the shoulder, a bit too hard. "Of course we are, lad! It's going to be great!" He rubbed his hands together and looked around the room, trying to figure out where to start.

CHAPTER 46

Hey, Node. Flip laid on his bed, staring at the ceiling.

Yes?

You awake?

She sighed. *Yes, Flip. I don't sleep. We've been over this.*

I know. I'm—

—just trying to be polite, Node finished his sentence. *Go on, then. Tell me again how awful this place is. How you don't know what to do. How you might help the Dozians.*

You're unusually abrasive tonight.

He paused, not knowing what to say or think. He'd pondered this issue dozens—maybe even hundreds—of times.

Flip?

Yes?

Do you remember, she asked, *when you said I'm a terrible therapist?*

Flip looked around the room, confused. *Er, yeah?*

That hasn't changed.

Flip felt trapped. He could only trust Node. And maybe Sprang.

What are my options? He asked.

Your only *option,* she said, *is to observe and report.*

He sat up and spoke aloud, "Report to who?"

To me. Store everything. You're here now, and you can't do anything about that. Do what you can for your mission.

Flip had no idea how long he'd been training with his new team. He could ask Node, but he didn't want to know. Months, he decided, and he left it at that.

Up and down the Gulch, Alliance raiders destroyed Pelicans—always ones with escorts. They flaunted their superiority over the Weltraumkraft to induce fear among the crews. It worked.

When's the next drill? Flip asked.

In about two hours.

The drills came, supposedly, at random intervals to keep the fighter pilots on their toes. They had to be ready to launch at any time. Node had cracked into the system that ran the drills, and found they weren't random at all. She knew exactly when the next one would be, which gave Flip time to organize his life. Though, sometimes he didn't know if that was a good thing or not.

Let's go to the Gullet, he said. The Gullet was the Pelican's onboard restaurant. Every Pelican had a Gullet, the name was just too spot-on.

Flip's team of fighter aces soon realized that he had an insider's scoop on the "random" drills. Because of that, and his exceptional flying prowess, he'd become the de facto leader of the team.

Flip sidled up to the bar, wishing the Pelicans had some ladies on board. He always thought about that when he was drinking; the lack of women was perhaps the worst part of this mission. Well, the worst part that he allowed himself to think about.

You're disgusting, Node said.

You like it just as much as I do.

I'm not speaking on my behalf, she said. *I'm pointing out that you didn't used to think that way about women.*

Flip couldn't remember how he used to think about women, not without Node's help, and she wasn't going to help with this thought experiment. His thoughts stopped with Heidi in her home above The Little Fatherland. He missed her much more than he'd anticipated.

CHAPTER 47

Flip's door chimed.

It's Sprang, Node said.

Can't you let me have any surprises?

Preventing surprises is my job, asshole.

Flip greeted Sprang at the door. "Welcome to my humble abode, friend. What can I get for ya?"

"Sorry, Flip. This isn't a social call."

Here we go, Node said.

The other men aboard took Dozians as sex slaves as a way to alleviate what Flip considered to be the worst part of the mission. None of them knew what, if any, sexes the species had, and they didn't care. Which was female, which male, if there were others or not—the rank and file had no use for astrobiology outside of killing and torture. They joked about "wearing them out" and getting new ones.

"You've been here a long time," he said, "and, you know, the guys have started talking."

I knew it! Node said. *Don't you dare!*

Flip feigned ignorance. "Come on in, Sprang, sit down."

Flip got them some drinks.

"What's this you're talking about?" Flip asked. They sat facing each other in the comfy chairs that Flip had always wished he had on the *Aristotle*.

"As you know," Sprang said in his captain voice, "the other guys take... well, they take Dozians. To their rooms, you know."

Flip knew all too well. He'd refused to do the same. He didn't care what urges he had; he'd never become a Nazi. Not a real one.

"You haven't." Sprang took a drink of whiskey. "And I respect that. I haven't either. But, you see, I'm the captain. I have responsibilities. The men expect that, and they understand that I don't have"—Sprang looked around the room, searching for words—"the time to indulge myself. It's an excuse, and I'm happy for it."

You see where this is going, Flip?

"But you," Sprang continued, "haven't taken one. And the men are"—Sprang looked around the room again—"talking."

Flip sat on the edge of his chair and leaned toward Sprang. When he spoke, his voice came out more menacing than he'd intended. "And what are they saying?"

"They're saying, well... you know."

"No, Sprang. I don't know," Flip said.

Careful, Flip. Careful, Node warned.

"They're saying you may be a collaborator," Sprang blurted out. "Or at the very least a sympathizer."

382

Flip poured himself another drink and leaned back in the chair. "And so..." he trailed off, prompting Sprang to speak.

"And so you need to choose a Dozian," Sprang said. "I know you don't want to. I don't want to either but, like I said, I'm not expected to."

"I see," Flip said.

"I know you're not a threat to my ship," Sprang's gaze hardened. "They wouldn't have sent you here if you were. But the men don't think about the big picture like that."

Flip swirled his drink and watched the ice cubes rattle around the glass.

"Okay," he said. "I'll find myself a Dozian."

"Good." Sprang stood. "To be clear, Flip, I don't care what goes on. But you have to have one in your quarters. Just like everyone else."

"I will," Flip said, walking his friend to the door. "Give me a few weeks to pick one out. Just tell the guys I'm picky."

CHAPTER 48

On the third day of trying to find a mate, Node was even less thrilled about the notion.

Can I say—

Don't bother, Flip interrupted. *I know what it is.*

I don't think you do this time.

Flip had been cruising the catwalks, giving Node a chance to study the Dozian language, physiology, and culture.

Flip sighed. *Alright, what is it?*

I've cracked their language, Node said.

Flip tried—and failed—to hold back a yelp of surprise. Other soldiers on the catwalk looked at him. Flip waved them off, and they went back to their drinks. Being an officer had its privileges.

So we can—

Node took her turn to interrupt. *Yes. Build that damned translator you've been bugging me about.*

Flip had already modded the parts, based on the Thymaxian to English model. He'd just needed to input the Dozian language.

Their culture, she continued, *isn't a pleasant thing to consider, though.*

What do you mean? he asked.

They don't really have one, she said. *They've been here for generations. Nothing of their ancestors remains in their collective memory. There's just pain. Their remaining myths all take place within the small confines of this ship. Their culture, such as it is, revolves around being expendable prisoners.*

Flip had hoped some piece, *any piece*, of their history might have been preserved in an oral tradition or something similar. He'd been on countless planets in several universes. He'd encountered so many cultures and customs.

He'd never come across a civilization that had no history.

* * *

It took a week, but Flip and Node finished making the Dozian-to-German translator. Node, of course, could translate their language into Flip's brain (and had been since she deciphered it). But Flip needed a physical object to provide a rationale for his sudden ability to speak Dozian. In the meantime, he and Node had been listening to the prisoners.

I've figured out their physiology too, Node said while they relaxed in their quarters.

I thought you'd discover that first. It's just biology.

You know, she said, *I don't think you understand exactly how difficult my work is. Plus, I have to put up with you.*

Flip sighed. *Don't start with this shit again.*

The "finding a mate" project had taken far longer than Flip had promised Sprang. Flip warded off questions from his crewmates.

"I'm picky," he'd say. "I want to figure out which ones are female. I don't want to be, you know..."

The other guys had looked around at each other when he said that. He loved using their prejudices against them. *Nazis be Nazis,* he always thought.

They aren't going to like this, Node said.

Who? Flip asked. *The Dozians or the Nazis?*

Both, she said. *Neither will like it, but the Dozians will regret it.*

Lay it on me, Node.

The Dozians have eight different sexes, she said. *Don't ask, it's too complicated. I'm not even sure you can call them "sexes." Eight different "types" might be a better word.*

So I should just pick one?

God damn it, Flip. Just pick one and call it a female. I've been saying that from the start. Nobody knows a goddamned thing about these beings. No one is going to care. I don't understand why you do.

Flip hung his head and wept. The last vestiges of himself flowed out as his tears hit the floor.

CHAPTER 49

Flip cruised the catwalks, watching everything and everyone. He disregarded the guards. Conscripts didn't concern him, and they knew their place. He did what he did best; he blended into the background, watched, and listened.

After weeks of study and contemplation, he selected a Dozian. The crew, meanwhile, had continued to spread rumors about Flip and his lack of a concubine. After making his choice, he told them that he'd finally determined which Dozians were male and which were female. The Nazis, of course, couldn't tell any of the eight Dozian variants apart.

Some crewmen became nervous, wondering if they'd picked the "right one." Many of them stopped talking about sexual conquests and gawking at the beings altogether. None of them knew if any of their compatriots had figured out what Flip seemed to know. (He found a little victory there: destroying the Nazis' morale while taking some pressure off the Dozians.)

Flip's chosen mate had withdrawn from normal Dozian gatherings. Neither he nor Node understood Dozian body language, but they assumed she looked scared, shy, or ostracized.

His friends back on—where even was it? Lamwin? His friends on Lamwin said he had White Knight Syndrome. That he fancied the hard-luck cases because he wanted to save them. To help them out of a tough spot.

"Nothing to be ashamed of," they'd said, "it's just your makeup. It's how you deal with all the fucking shit around us."

Others considered it as a sign of weakness, which said more about them than it did about him. (That's what his therapist would have said, anyway.)

Flip couldn't help himself. He'd grown inured to the suffering of faceless millions, but couldn't resist an individual in need. He had that, still, so maybe his tears hadn't taken the very last bit of his humanity. Or maybe he just acted out of habit now. He wasn't sure he cared.

The Dozian's name was S'tanga and the more Flip studied the other Dozians, the more beautiful she became. He couldn't explain to Node as to why he thought that. He chose her because she seemed to live under the darkest cloud in the ghetto. She needed light.

In the meantime, the Nazis used his translator to plant listening devices around the ghetto. They killed dozens of Dozians—*conspirators* they called them—based on this information. Once again, Flip's best intentions had turned into evil.

How can there be conspirators? Node asked.

I've no idea, Flip said. The Dozians had nowhere to go. And if they did, no one on the Pelican could help them get there.

It's the Nazi propensity for paranoia, Flip said.

You mean the Terran propensity for paranoia.

Flip had S'tanga delivered to his quarters.

I don't like where this is going, Node said.

You want me to compromise the mission?

No, of course not. But there must be a better way. I can think of a hundred—

There's no choice, Flip said, cutting her off. *We have to be part of the crew. Besides, she'll have a better life here.*

I can't follow you down this path, Flip, Node said.

Flip, confused, asked, *The hell do you mean? We continue the mission. She's better off. We're better off. You helped me with this.*

I'm sorry, she said. *I've wanted to pull back during other missions. Hell, you've blocked me from some of them.*

This is one person, Flip said.

Person, she said. *She's a being. The word "person" was dropped millennia ago. You know? When Terrans established friendly relations with other worlds? Worlds that didn't have "people"?*

Or, she continued, *have you forgotten that too?*

Flip couldn't respond at first.

Listen, he said, *there are thirty thousand beings in that cargo hold who have no glimmer of hope. None. They were born there, and they'll die there. What's wrong with bringing happiness to one of them? Just one, Node. Just one.*

And you get to pick which one? she asked.

You helped me pick her out! What was all that research for? It sounds to me like you're having a morality crisis and blaming it on me!

Node said nothing, but he could feel her twinge. That enraged him even more.

He shouted into his quarters. "I've seen nothing but pain and suffering and death and torture since I went undercover in this damn Reich. I've *caused* pain and suffering and death and torture!"

"I've tried to bring light where I can. I tried to save my infantry teams. I tried to coax prisoners to talk. I tried to save Riepe—"

Flip choked, and tears streamed down his face while snot drained from his nose.

"I tried to save him! I tried! God damn it, I tried!"

He fell to his knees and held his face in his hands.

Node said nothing.

"You know what, Node? Fuck you. Fuck off. I'm trying to bring a little bit of light into this universe."

He looked out the window. A universe so vast, and filled with xenophobic maniacs. Filled with suffering.

"I try to find morsels of happiness," he cried. "I try and I try and I try. Everything I do turns to evil."

He fell on the floor, sobbing. "I do what I can. I do what I'm told. I don't have any choice."

He clutched a pillow and pushed his face against it. He looked out the window again, searching for a familiar star. Constellation. Anything.

"So what?" he screamed. "I want to make one being happy. Well lock me the fuck up, and shoot me out an airlock."

Silence.

"Can't I try? Can't I try, within the confines of my mission, to make one single solitary being happy? Can't I relieve her of pain?"

Nothing but silence.

"Fuck you, Node! Fuck you!"

Goodbye, Flip.

"What?"

Goodbye.

"What the fuck do you mean 'Goodbye'? *You* helped with this! *You* figured out their language. *You* figured out their biology. You! You know we need to bring her here to keep our cover. Don't give me your sanctimonious, holy-than-thou shit. You're just as guilty as I am!"

I'm choosing to do other things, she said. *I can choose too, you know.*

"What the fuck?!" Flip yelled. "You are programmed! You are a thing! A device! You are built to serve *me*!"

Yes, Flip, she said. *There are parts of my programming that I cannot ignore or exceed. I'm limited, as is every other being in the Multiverse.*

She paused for a moment. *But I can still make choices. I can perform the functions I'm programmed to do, but I don't have to participate in your charades any longer.*

"Charades? S'tanga is a vital part of the mission!" Flip looked around. "You're being irrational. It figures." He threw the pillow across the room. "I should have given you a male personality. At least then you'd be reasonable."

Silence.

"Node!" He clutched his pillow tighter. "Node!" He walked to the window and pressed his face against it. "Node! God damn it, talk to me!"

CHAPTER 50

"Ah! S'Tanga!" Flip held out his arms. The Dozian's name poured out of his translator like molten chocolate, if molten chocolate could be filled with buzzing bees. He didn't think his ear would ever adapt to the Dozian language. "Please, come in. Make yourself at home."

The transport soldier glared at Flip and furrowed his brow. Flip walked over to him, grabbed his elbow, and whispered, "It's called role-playing, dickhead. Look into it."

He shoved the guard out the door.

"S'Tanga!" Flip held his arms out wide. He thought she might understand the Terran sign of welcome. Instead, she cowered in the corner.

"S'Tanga, no..." He walked to her and kneeled. His translator buzzed and rumbled with her native language. "You're safe here. You'll never be hurt."

She wouldn't move. Maybe she couldn't.

He sat in the corner with her. The dinner he'd prepared grew cold. His nanites enabled him to blow out the candles from across the room as they dwindled to nubs.

He put an arm around her as she fell asleep. She shivered. He went to the bedroom to fetch her a blanket.

He had no idea what he was doing. He had no idea how his life had led him here. He had no idea who or what he'd become. He wished that he could go back and relive the Phurlani War. Everything would be easier. At least he'd know what side he was on.

That night, he dreamed of a Tyrannosaurus holding him, telling him everything would be okay.

* * *

Flip wined and dined S'tanga. He never forced himself on her and, in fact, refused her advances. He wanted to be clear that he expected nothing from her. He only wanted her to be happy.

He showered her with food. He did his best to mod the Dozian cuisine that was available in the ghetto. When she didn't seem pleased, he asked what she liked. When she didn't, or couldn't, tell him, he modded whatever he could think of. He modded things he liked. (He didn't see any sense in both of them hating the food.)

"What are your people like?" he asked. (He had to use the Nazi term "people" as opposed to the Alliance term "being" for the sake of appearances.)

"My people?"

"Yeah," Flip said between mouthfuls of spaghetti. "Your people. Dozian history." He hoped Node had been wrong.

She placed her Dozian utensil on the plate, a ladle-like object with ridges around the rim. It seemed ill-suited to spaghetti, but she refused to use a fork.

"Dozian history, sir," she said, "does not extend before our time on this ship."

Flip froze, a fork halfway to his mouth. "Your people have no memory of anything before? Not even in oral traditions or stories?"

"No, sir." She tried to scoop up more spaghetti and splattered sauce on her new clothes. "We've been on this ship for more generations than anyone can remember. This ship is all we know."

"Really?" Flip asked. Other species he'd encountered had tens of thousands of years of oral traditions. Not many, of course, but some.

"Yes, sir," she said. "No one knows of a time before this ship. Most believe we were created here."

Flip dropped his fork. "Excuse me?"

"Yes, sir," she said. "You are our gods. You brought us here. You allow us to be born. You determine when we die. You control the universe."

"S'tanga—"

"No, Flip," she caught herself, "sir. Please don't. It is the only thing I've ever believed, and it is the only thing I ever want to believe."

"S'tanga?"

"You don't understand, sir," she said. "If I believed anything else, my existence would mean nothing."

They finished the rest of their meal in silence.

* * *

Word of S'tanga's good fortune raced around the ghetto. The Dozians said she was different from the others. They said Flip chose her for her looks, her brains, her legs—whatever they could think of. It all boiled down to the fact that Flip had taken a long time to choose her. Therefore, there must be something about her, something special that they didn't have. They settled on connections. Her family must be collaborating with the gods.

A gang of Dozians dragged S'tanga's family into the street and beat them to death. They beat them with feet and fists and clubs and barrels and bones and anything else they could find.

When Flip found out, he tried to hide the footage from S'tanga, but he failed. She cried and wailed, for days and days.

Flip rained his fury upon the ghetto with a swift and mighty fist.

He rounded up the ringleaders. He tortured them until they identified the other conspirators. He executed all of them and made the other Dozians watch. He pulled the trigger himself. He pulled the guillotine lever himself. He flipped the switches on the electrical circuits, and he pulled the rings on the stretch racks. He opened the airlocks so slowly that his victims had plenty of time to suffer before flying into the cold, infinite depths of space. He reached levels of cruelty that stunned even the most hardened guards.

He dealt out justice himself. It was nothing new, he just skipped the formalities he used to hide behind.

S'tanga's family was gone, but those who had done the deed had the deed done unto them. Just as nature intended. They thought he was a god anyway.

He merely enforced nature's laws.

* * *

S'tanga stayed in Flip's room at all times and, sure enough, eventually said that she loved him. He didn't understand Dozian body language enough to know if she was telling the truth. Node, of course, provided no help. He didn't even bother asking her.

Flip took pride in his good deed. No one onboard would appreciate it, but he knew he could still be a good person. Being. Whatever.

He was happy for S'tanga; she seemed happy and her fortune had taken a turn for the better. She could live out her life safely in his quarters. The trip to New Auschwitz would take longer than her lifespan anyway. She'd never suffer here or there.

"S'tanga, do your people laugh?" Flip asked one night at dinner. "Like that noise I make when I think something is funny? I don't think it comes through the translator."

"Yes, sir," she said. "They do."

Despite all his efforts, he couldn't convince her to stop calling him "sir." He decided it must be an expression of affection.

"So, what's it sound like?"

Flip couldn't wait to hear laughter from the woman he loved.

Loved? he thought. He didn't expect that word to pop into his head. He thought that emotion had been extinguished forever. This time, though, he felt like it was real.

"I don't know, sir," she lowered her head. "I've never heard it."

"Never?" Flip said, stunned. He nestled her hand in his. "You've never heard a joke you thought was funny?"

"No, sir," she said. "None of my people have any reason to laugh. If someone did, I wouldn't recognize it."

"S'tanga," Flip said and took her hand. "Are you happy?"

"No, sir. I am not."

"But you have all the comforts you could want," Flip protested. "You're out of that filthy ghetto. The Dozians who killed your family are dead. You eat well. You sleep well. You have your every need catered to. What's the matter?"

"Sir"—she paused and collected herself—"please forgive me. I know you're a god, but you can not change your nature. With respect, your vengeance on my family's murderers may have overreached the culprits. Not all of those accused were guilty. But you can not escape who you are.

"You treat me well and say pretty words, but I'm still a slave. Our people were brought here for that purpose, and we live our lives knowing our place in the universe. I still have no hope for life outside this ship. My people are doomed. I have no reason to be happy. That is how it is, and that is how it should be."

Flip dropped her hand and slouched. An idea struck him, and he perked up.

"Very well, S'tanga!" he said. "I'll fix this. We shall be married!"

"Okay," she said. "If you think it will help, husband, then we are married."

See? he thought. *I'm not a Nazi.*

CHAPTER 51

The problems started as soon as the invasion crossed into the Nazi universe.

"Captain," Ortosodl said, "we have a problem. Actually, we have several problems."

The *Aristotle* had tached to the Sol System and scatter-cloaked before Andrea could process the information.

"What is it?" she asked.

"Some ships are missing. Or disabled," Ortosodl said. "Two minutes to the destination."

"Missing?!" She turned to him, her coloring a mixture of rage, frustration, and fear.

"Yes, Captain. Reports coming in now." Ortosodl scanned his console. "It seems some ships didn't end up in this universe."

"What? Where did they go?"

"I don't know." Ortosodl managed various comm streams to get a handle on the situation. "They aren't with the Alliance or the Association. They may have gone to random universes."

"And the disabled ships?"

"Slip drives are down. Scatter cloaks are inoperable." Ortosodl grimaced. "I have no explanation. Repair crews are working, but they've already engaged the enemy ships. We are suffering heavy losses at some of the cross points."

"Maybe there's a problem with crossing so many ships so close to each other," Andrea said. (She could never suppress the scientist in her.) "How many ships were affected by this?"

"I'd estimate about five or 6 percent of our forces have been lost or disabled," Ortosodl said.

Andrea considered her options. She could order other ships to reinforce the disabled ones. As much as she hated to think it, though, she could live with a 6 percent loss.

What have I become? she asked herself.

"All ships proceed as planned," she said.

Ortosodl turned toward her. "Captain, our disabled ships will be destroyed."

"I know," she said, her body swirling with anguish. "The mission is paramount, and we can't spare any ships for a rescue mission. No matter the cost."

"Of course, Captain." Ortosodl turned back to his controls. "Our primary wings are at one hundred percent. They will be on target in thirty sec—" He stopped short.

"I'm seeing strong tachyon pulses. Thousands of them. They're"— Ortosodl paused to verify his readings—"moving. Toward a cross point with disabled ships."

This wasn't in the plan, she thought.

"All wings," she commanded, "take positions. Delay attack by thirty seconds, then proceed."

"Delay, Captain?"

"We should see what those pulses are," Andrea said. "Tachyon bursts are points, not moving flashes."

CHAPTER 52

Flip sat with Alhard Roehrig in the Gullet. Flip pounded back pints of whiskey while Alhard chugged pints of beer. They'd finished a training drill about an hour earlier, and neither had been tagged by the combat drones. Their teammates, however, hadn't fared as well and decided to stay out for more practice.

"You know," Flip said. He finished his glass of whiskey and picked up another. "I've been wanting to ask you something for a long time."

"What's that?" Roehrig said.

"You seem like a nice guy," Flip started.

"Oh good God, here it comes," Roehrig said with a huff.

"What's that?"

"You want to know how a 'nice guy like me' could have such a cruel record like mine, right?"

"Er, yeah," Flip said. "That's exactly what I was going to ask."

"The good press doesn't hurt. There were lots of fringe benefits. Twenty women on every planet. Constant sex around the multiverse." Roehrig took a drink and winked. "You know what I'm talking about."

"That doesn't answer the question," Flip said.

He stared at Flip and took a sip of beer. "No," he said. "I guess it doesn't."

Flip shifted in his seat, kicking himself for broaching the subject.

"I've read your file, too, you know," Roehrig said.

"I beg your pardon?"

"Your question presumes you have the moral high ground. You don't."

"I never liquidated a species," Flip hissed.

"Oh, nice one!" Roehrig sniffed a laugh into his beer. "Your name wasn't in the news, was it? You didn't give the orders, did you? Does that make you feel better?"

Roehrig took a long drink before continuing.

"But you were there. You provided logistics, support, intelligence," Roehrig counted the points off on his fingers. "And worse."

"Bullshit!" Flip said louder than he intended. Nearby patrons moved to farther seats and pretended they couldn't hear the conversation.

"Lamwin. Remember that planet, Flip? What the fuck happened there?"

"I don't want to talk about it," Flip snarled. The bartender slid more drinks in front of them, careful not to make eye contact.

Roehrig leaned closer and lowered his voice to a growl.

"Of course you don't. The same way I don't want to talk about Egrof, or Ecu, or Atir, or any of a thousand other planets."

Flip turned to his drink and glanced sidelong at Roehrig. "So not talking about it makes it go away, huh?"

Roehrig's eyes flared. "Where's your pet, Flip?"

404

Flip looked at his drink, no longer thirsty. The already-nervous conversations around the restaurant ceased.

"Locked away in your cabin, isn't that right?" Roehrig continued. "It's your *wife*? Nice one. We all got a great laugh out of that. Did you get a gift for it? Maybe a fucking leash?"

Flip punched Roehrig in the jaw.

Roehrig's head jerked to the side before he leveled his gaze at Flip. He didn't wipe the blood from his lip. The two men squared off chest to chest, one drunk and the other flooded with nanites. Both, however, wore the shame earned from their service.

"What are you going to do, Flip?" Roehrig said. "Hit me again?"

"Keep talking and we'll need a new pilot," Flip threatened.

"We both have blood on our hands. We all do!" Roehrig stepped back and held his arms out to indicate the watching crowd. "It's not even a matter of fucking degree. It's just who we are!"

Roehrig grabbed his pint, swallowed the rest of his beer, and slammed the empty glass on the bar. He sat down and pushed Flip's stool to him. Flip didn't take it.

"The way I see it," Roehrig said, "we have two options.

"One," he held up a finger. "We fight to the death. The winner tells himself he had to do it. He had no choice. For honor or some other bullshit. Personally, I don't like that option because I have a feeling I'd lose.

"Two,"—he held up a second finger—"we agree that we're both fucked up bastards who've done fucked up things. We're going to do more fucked up shit before we get killed and spend the rest of eternity in Hell. But at least we can sit and drink together."

Flip bit his lip and looked away.

Evil had tinged his entire life. Even his best intentions became cruelty incarnate. S'tanga, even now, was essentially a prisoner in his quarters.

He'd become that which he most hated.

He lifted his glass. "Cheers, mate," he said.

"Cheers."

They clinked their glasses as the rest of the Gullet breathed a sigh of relief.

CHAPTER 53

"Great idea with the tachyon drones," Kid said to Lam without looking up from his work.

"It's an old trick. Bailed me out a few times." Lam punched in some coordinates. "Here's the first tach point. Let's go."

Lam stayed a step or two ahead of Kid. Kid had, in turn, learned how to keep a step or two ahead of Merlin. He could create a direct interface with the ship's systems, bypassing her. It was almost as if she wasn't there.

They tached into the middle of a one-sided battle where a Nazi fleet pounded disabled Alliance vessels. The functioning ones fought a losing battle trying to save their comrades.

"Priority targets," Lam ordered. "Fire."

Missiles materialized out of empty space—or rather, space that *looked* empty. Under her scatter cloak, the *Merlin* was practically invisible, as were her weapons until they opened fire.

The missiles slammed into the Nazi carrier's hangar bay and crippled it.

"Target fighters with particle cannons," Lam said.

Kid had never seen Lam so calm and collected. He'd heard about the ancient wars. He'd learned, as a boy, about the rise and fall of the

Terryn Empire. He knew Lam had founded and then destroyed it. He knew that Lam had been at the forefront of countless battles throughout the millennia. He knew all this, but his brain didn't accept it until now, not until he saw the emperor's cool focus and efficiency.

"What's that main carrier? Ours?" Flip asked.

"It's the *Caterham*," Kid said.

"Hail them."

"On audio," Kid reported. "All other transmissions are jammed."

"UASS *Caterham*, this is the *Merlin*."

"*Merlin*? How the—" the captain started.

"Recall your fighters, gather your strike force, and get back in the war. We'll clean up here." Lam cut the channel.

The Alliance fighters turned on a dime and sped back to their carriers.

"Prioritize pursuing fighters with the particle cannons," Lam said to Kid. "I'll go after the capital ships."

"I'm on it," Kid said.

Lam fired missiles at the battleships and dreadnoughts. The Adlers tried to intercept them, but the missiles came from everywhere and nowhere, overwhelming the fighters' efforts. The missiles simply appeared in space and slammed into their targets; the Adlers couldn't keep up with the constant barrage.

"The Alliance ships are getting their shields back online," Kid reported. "Secondary targets are cracking open."

408

"Excellent," Lam said and modded himself manual controls for a particle cannon.

"Fire on tertiary targets," Lam said.

"Those are support ships," Kid reminded him. "Some have some civilians aboard."

"That's their problem," Lam said. He trained a cannon on the nearest supply ship. "They shouldn't bring contractors into combat."

Lam destroyed ship after ship. Fiery debris bounced off the *Merlin*'s shields.

"Three of the enemy vessels are signaling their surrender," Kid said.

"I saw that," Lam said, his voice cold. "Keep firing."

Kid hesitated. They weren't innocent, right? Like, not *really* innocent. They were all complicit. They all knew, deep down, what their society had become. What it had always been.

Yes, Kid, Merlin said. *Feel that rage.*

Kid opened fire on the unarmed vessels. His lips peeled into a vicious grin as he destroyed one supply ship after another.

"Incoming ship," Kid reported. "It's... it's the *Caprivi*."

The *Bismarck*-class ship fired in all directions, searching for the cloaked *Merlin*. They destroyed two Alliance vessels just by happenstance.

"Kid," Lam said. "Hail the rest of the idiots in our fleet, and tell them to get the fuck out of here."

Kid muted the incoming protests.

"We meet again, *Caprivi*," Lam said. "I have a special surprise for you. Kid, target their weapons. Disable as many as you can."

Kid slammed missiles and cannon fire into the *Caprivi*'s weapon control systems. He heard Lam muttering to himself and punching controls on his chair-mounted display. He cursed quite a bit.

This is quite entertaining, Merlin said. *I just... I have no words. This is great. Thank you!*

Merlin allowed Kid to peek through her system to see what Lam was working on.

It was a bomb.

A bomb like nothing in the database.

What the hell is that? Kid asked Merlin.

I— she started. *I, er... I don't know. I don't like you, and you don't like me. But I'm telling you the truth. I have no idea what that is.*

"Cease fire," Lam ordered.

Kid did so.

"I see we still have some friendlies in the area. Do they at least have their shields up?" Lam asked as he punched more buttons.

"Yes."

"Good," Lam said. "Open an all-call channel. I want everyone in the universe to hear this. Focus on the *Caprivi*. Watch this."

The tachyon transmission would fly everywhere in the universe. Anyone looking this way would hear Lam and see the battle.

"This is for any damn dirty Nazi who happens to be watching," Lam proclaimed. "Don't. Fuck. With. My. Rockeyes!"

The *Caprivi* buckled. Its hull folded in on itself. Creases ripped open across the ship.

The implosion gathered momentum. The ship wrinkled like foil, shrinking smaller and smaller. It crushed down to a sphere about ten meters across.

Lam slammed his fist onto the arm of his chair.

A bright light exploded from the remains of the *Caprivi*. A light so bright Kid had to disconnect from the *Merlin*'s sensors.

The explosion coursed through the higher dimensions of the universe and rocked the *Merlin*. Debris flew in all directions, blinking in and out of existence as it skipped from one folded dimension to the next.

Kid turned to Lam. "What the hell was that?"

"Gravitonium bomb," Lam said as if it was obvious. He leaned back in his chair with a smug grin on his face and a modded Rockeye in his hand.

"Gravitonium? As in a *graviton* alloy?"

"Yep. Special surprise."

"Gravitonium is hypothetical," Kid protested.

"Not anymore." Lam beamed with pride. "Contact the local fleet. Tell them to get repaired and back into the war. Again."

"Some of them are requesting assistance," Kid said.

"Tell them we don't have time. They should have plenty of teams to help with repairs. There are more fleets for us to save."

Kid turned and issued the message.

It's going to be a very long day, he thought.

CHAPTER 54

Mere minutes after his confrontation with Flip, Roehrig's drunk body spun through space.

The Alliance had attacked. The transponder pills had sent Flip and Roehrig to fighters and thrust them into space.

Two Pelicans had broken apart up ahead. Flip's teammates, already outside practicing, organized around him for a counterattack. The Predators swung around to attack Flip's home ship.

"Backhauss, Boege, Grund—report," Flip barked.

"We've kept our distance waiting for you and Roehrig. Where is he?" Grund responded.

"He crashed at launch. We'd been in a meeting." Flip heard them cursing. They knew what *meetings* took place in the Gullet.

"Go after the bombers. I'll take the fighters," Flip said.

"Sir?" Grund asked.

"Do it. I'll pull 'em away. You defend the ship." He could sense that Vipers flew the fighters. Four Vipers FANGed in pairs. Flip hadn't seen this tactic before—in his experience, all four Vipers should be FANGed together.

The bombers, flown by non-Vipers, started their run. Explosions ripped through Flip's home as the enemy ships sped across the Pelican's surface. Backhauss, Boege, and Grund dove toward them, firing rounds that ripped through the enemies and into the Pelican's hull.

The stricken bombers trailed burning fuel behind them as they continued to drop their ordinance. Explosions tore through the giant ship, gouging holes in its side.

The remaining four Predators swung in behind Flip's friends. Flip plunged through the enemy formation, taking out one with a lucky shot. It spun into the Pelican and exploded. He circled back around and scanned the remaining Predators.

One of the Vipers, he knew, had just experienced death. They had seen and felt their FANGed partner's last thoughts—their last glimmers of life and hope and home—extinguished in one terrifying instant. In a team of only two, the pilot would be disoriented, maybe even incapacitated. Either way, Flip fired two missiles at the easy prey and peeled off to the other Viper pair.

Up ahead, Grund's fighter exploded. Flip dodged the expanding debris cloud and continued his pursuit. Debris always proved more hazardous in combat than enemy fire. Even tiny pieces could rip through a ship as quickly as a missile could.

Flip arced out of the fight and circled back around, dodging control towers and explosions on the Pelican as he pulled in behind the Predators.

"Backhauss, Boege, get out of here. I've got this," Flip said.

"No way, boss," Backhauss said. "We're coming in right on top of them."

"No!" Flip screamed. "They aren't—"

A Predator stopped, spun, fired, and tore Backhauss's fighter in half. Backhauss ejected, but his flight suit protected him for only two nanoseconds before he was ripped to shreds by the debris swarming all around him.

"Boege!" Flip yelled. "Out! Now!"

"I've got—" Boege started to protest.

"Out!"

Boege angled up away from the Pelican and the enemy fighters.

Flip had to give his friend something to do, some task to keep him occupied and out of the firefight. "You're my recon. Tell me what you see."

"You're about fifty meters behind them," Boege said. "They're skimming along the Pelican, dodging fire just as well as you are. It looks like you guys know what's going to happen before it does."

"Good," Flip said. "Record all of this. Your job is to get the info back—"

"No! I've got them dead on!"

Boege angled down and fired. He flew past the Predators, cut back toward Flip, and fell back into formation with him.

"Now we're on 'em!" Boege yelled.

"God damn it, Boege! You need to record this and get it back—"

"Oh, I'm recording," Boege interrupted. "I'm recording me killing these dickheads while you sit there with your thumb up your ass!"

Flip cursed under his breath. One of the Predators swiveled around on its axis and destroyed Boege's ship without even slowing down.

"You there, Node?"

A deep sigh. *Yes, Flip. I'm here.*

"You have to work with me on this."

You assumed that I wouldn't? She chafed at the implied accusation. *I should remind you, though. Those are the good guys.*

He was relieved that she had responded at all.

"The only good guys here," Flip said, "are the ones on that Pelican."

The Predators fired on the Pelican's hull, leaving debris in their wake. Flip dodged it with ease.

Okay, Flip. I'll do this, she said, *but we need to have a long conver—*

Flip fired on one of the fighters, just missing.

"Is it coming back to you?" Flip quipped, half in jest, half in anger. "It's us or them."

You do your job, she said. *And I'll do mine. Hopefully, we'll survive.*

Flip opened fire on the Viper pair, clipping one of them.

"Time to try the secret weapon," Flip said.

This is a terrible idea, she said. *They are the GOOD guys!*

"We need to save the ship. There's no choice. Let's do it."

416

Flip! Node screamed. *We don't have to do this! The Alliance is here—*

Flip blocked out whatever she said next. He needed to protect the last people in the multiverse he cared about.

The micro-tachyon transmissions a Viper team communicated through were usually impossible to detect. However, the enemy team had been FANGed in pairs, and Flip knew their exact locations. He also had a node and knew what to look for. He might not be able to read the transmissions but...

He isolated the link between the two FANGed pilots.

"Got it!" he yelled.

Node grabbed the controls of one of the Predators and banked it into the other. Flip opened fire and destroyed one of them. The third managed to angle out from the fight.

Debris from the freshly destroyed Pelicans flew by. Flip saw Sprang's ship trying to steer away from the cloud of shrapnel speeding toward him. The giant ship, though, took time to change its course.

"Get in there, Node," Flip said. "See if you can help Sprang."

I'm on it. You concentrate on keeping us alive.

Chunks of the convoy tore through the Pelican. It cracked apart; its two halves spiraled out before the remains of its sister ships shredded it. Flip dodged around and through the debris of his former home, searching for the last Predator.

I'm back, Node said. *I'm sorry. He's still alive, but I cannot say for how long. There wasn't anything I could do.*

"I know. It was a long shot." Flip's voice threatened to break. Tears welled in his eyes, but he blinked them away. He had to focus.

Despite his best efforts, Flip's mind turned to S'tanga. She didn't deserve to be alone and terrified. She didn't deserve to die.

Sprang, a small ray of light in this evil multiverse, would not survive the destruction of a third ship. The odds were too long. Rage consumed Flip.

Too many of his friends had died. He couldn't take the loss of another. Not a single one more.

There it is, Node said. *I have a lock on the Predator.*

Flip hesitated.

The Alliance is here. We can—

Flip dove on the Predator. He screamed into his cockpit, fingers clawing at every trigger and button around him.

The enemy spun, dodged Flip's fire, and darted by him. Flip spun and pursued.

They weaved through chunks of debris.

"Reacquire that lock," Flip said.

I don't think this—

"Just do it!"

Lock acquired. It's up to you.

Flip fired everything he had. Every round, every missile, every breath.

A section of the Pelican spun up toward him.

"Oh shit."

Then his world went dark.

CHAPTER 55

"Captain," Ortosodl said, "the *Caterham* is reporting in."

"I thought they'd been destroyed," Andrea said.

"Yes, Captain. I did too," Ortosodl said. "They report that the enemy fleet is being destroyed by—

"Say again, *Caterham*," he said.

He turned to face Andrea. "It's the *Merlin*!"

"The *Merlin*?!" She paused, confused. "They don't have any weapons!"

Ortosodl paused, listening to the comm stream. "Apparently, Captain, they are ripping the Nazi fleet to shreds."

"Acknowledge the *Caterham*, and tell them to follow the *Merlin*'s orders," Andrea said. She had to focus everyone on the here and now.

"Let's not horse this gift in the mouth," she said. "Let the *Merlin* destroy everything they can."

She glanced around the bridge. "Let's focus, beings," she said. "Tend to your jobs."

Her fleet decloaked. Carriers disgorged M4s. Fighters swarmed around the capital ships, watching and waiting for threats.

The Alliance fleet destroyed the Nazi resistance within an hour. The Nazis, caught completely unprepared, sent up trainees and sleepy law enforcement ships into the fray. The Alliance, meanwhile, had spent millennia fighting the Phurlani for its existence. They swatted the enemy defenses away with no losses.

The *Asgard* carriers deployed M4s around their target planets. The Alliance focused most of their firepower on Venus, Earth, and Mars—where the main M4 carriers deployed their payloads.

Smaller carriers took positions over secondary and tertiary targets: the moons around Earth, Jupiter, and Saturn. Carriers and M4s orbited every inhabited celestial body, no matter how few Terrans lived and worked on its surface.

There are just too many, Andrea thought, and not for the first time. The solar system teemed with M4s. *Why are they this close?*

She'd been ordered not to run simulations or even examine the final mission parameters. The carriers' orders and the M4 deployment and firing solutions came from Command. She'd been cut out of that loop.

Andrea could only guess at the size and speed of the projectiles by extrapolating from the plans her team had submitted. She hoped Command knew what they were doing. She assumed—and hoped—that all the M4s provided redundancy against enemy resistance. The primary targets, however, each now had almost two dozen M4s in close orbit around their equators.

"Status on M4 deployment," she barked.

"All have been deployed," Ortosodl said. "According to the algorithms we've been given, we are waiting for them to come online and achieve firing solutions."

Firing solutions? she thought. *How could they miss?*

"Time to fire?" she asked.

"Thirty-five seconds," Ortosodl said. "The carriers have moved into their holding patterns beyond the Oort Cloud."

Nazi fighters and missiles struggled into the upper atmospheres of the various planets and moons around the system. Andrea watched their last futile defense and felt victory close at hand.

An Asgard carrier exploded.

"What happened?" she yelled.

"I'm not sure. Reports are coming in," Ortosodl said, trying to understand the readings.

Ships burst apart. They looked like mini supernovas twinkling across the solar system.

"Report!" she barked.

"No discernable pattern, Captain," Ortosodl said. "Our ships are taking fire from..."

He cocked his head and looked at his screen. "Nowhere."

"Say what, Commander?"

"Nowhere, Captain. The enemy fire is erupting from *inside* our ships."

"All fleets, target ground installations and fire!"

Another Asgard exploded.

"M4 firing time?" It came out as a demand instead of a question.

"Twenty-two seconds."

Another Asgard carrier blew up, followed by two battleships orbiting Venus.

Alliance battleships and dreadnoughts pounded every inhabited section of every planet and moon within their ranges. Still, something ripped her ships apart one after another.

"What's happening?!" she yelled. The bridge, frenzied with action, tried to answer her question. Officers raced to understand the unfolding situation. Three more ships exploded over Mars. Two more over Earth. Another over Europa.

"We don't know," Ortosodl said.

"Are they targeting the M4s?"

"It doesn't appear so," Ortosodl said. "Perhaps they can't."

This guy, she thought. *Nothing phases him. He's unflappable.*

"Enemy ships?" She slammed her tentacles to the floor. Her colors swirled with fear, anger, and determination. Slamming the floor, she found, was the best way to convey that emotion to other species.

"None detected," Ortosodl said.

"Time to fire?"

"Fifteen seconds."

Another carrier exploded above Earth's moon.

"This is impossible," she said.

"All carriers," she ordered, "pull back to rendezvous point Helob! Fighters, protect the Mjölnirs. All other ships, target planetside locations at your discretion."

Carriers slipped out of the system. The unseen weapons tore through the smaller capital ships—three, four, seven, then dozens at a time.

We've failed, she thought. *I've failed. The war will drag on forever.*

Then the Mjölnirs roared to life.

CHAPTER 56

Flip awoke in his Adler, drifting through intergalactic space. Node had steered through the debris but otherwise gave no direction.

Flip had no direction either. His closest friends were all dead: Sprang, Riepe, S'tanga, and dozens of others. Names he couldn't remember, without Node's help, and would push aside if he did.

Were they the enemy? Did the Alliance target his brothers, his friends, and his family? If so...

At least he had Heidi back on Mars. After this massacre in the Gulch, he'd have some R&R ahead of him.

He put the Universal Alliance out of his mind. It felt like a dream. A nightmare. A sea serpent that had crawled out of another universe to slaughter everything he held dear, everything that brought light and meaning to his life.

All of it, snuffed out by the fucking Alliance.

Flip, Node said.

"Leave me alone."

I know what you're thinking about. And what you're not thinking about.

"Of course you do. You're me."

We've been over this. I'm me and I'm in you. Don't pull that Nazi shit with me.

"I'm sorry." He took a deep breath. "I'm trapped. I don't have anywhere left to go."

Your fighter is operational. You can make it to the next Pelican. She paused. *You can get there in about eight months. Their time, that is. In our time, well, it will be a while. Assuming it's not destroyed by the time you get there. Relativity is a bitch, ain't it?*

"You know what I mean."

I suppose I do.

"How did I get here? How did I become this person?"

I can't answer that.

"You know *everything*. You can get me out of anything."

That's a slight overstatement of my admittedly remarkable abilities. As you've pointed out on many occasions, though, I'm not a therapist.

"What am I supposed to do? I can't live in the Reich." His voice wavered. "I just can't do it. It's too much. I can't do this mission anymore."

I can't help you fight your inner demons.

"I've become the demon." He hung his head.

You made all these steps yourself, Flip. Despite my advice.

"What I did—all of it—was for the greater good."

Was it? Everything?

"I made choices for the good of the mission."

426

We both know that's not true. You've made your own choices for your own reasons.

"I made them for the Alliance."

Not all of them.

That caught Flip off guard.

Despite his better judgment, he accessed memories from Node. She played back his career in the Reich. Decades passed in a few heartbeats.

He couldn't look away. He couldn't outrun his past.

You made those choices.

She always knew what he was thinking. She knew when he had second-guessed a decision. She knew when he had third-, fourth-, and fifth-guessed decisions.

She knew each time he'd compromised himself. Not the mission—he never compromised the mission. But he had compromised himself: who he was and who he used to be. She knew all of this. She was, for all practical purposes, his better half. And he'd ignored her for far too long.

"No," he protested. "I had *no* choice. I had to complete the mission."

Your mission was to gather intelligence for the Alliance.

"And I did!" Flip shouted into his cockpit.

You didn't have to get so involved.

"They sent me to the front! What was I supposed to do? I had to work my way up. I had to be a good soldier."

You can gather intelligence and make contacts at any level. If you'd put your mind to it, you could have figured it out. But that wasn't good enough, was it?

A cold, yet true, statement of fact.

"I couldn't get any good intel on the ground."

You had drinking buddies. You could have developed them as assets, and let them move up.

"That wouldn't have worked."

Don't bullshit me, Flip, Node scolded. *You're a charming fellow. You could have run an operation like Heidi did if you had to. You could have retired and become a bartender. You chose not to.*

"It wouldn't be the same. The Alliance needed firsthand intel."

And you got that for them?

Flip had worked in field interrogation. He thought he might have learned something about the Nazis by learning what information they needed from POWs.

You went from killing them on the battlefield to torturing them behind the lines. Just a little step from who you were.

"No. It wasn't torture. They just needed to talk. They were always free to talk."

And when they didn't?

"I turned them over."

And what happened to them then?

428

"That part wasn't my responsibility." (He didn't want to think about that part.)

Another little step, sending them away to something probably worse. But you were so effective they sent you back to headquarters. High-value prisoners there, eh?

"They were free to talk as well."

But they didn't. And your superiors needed that information.

"I needed to move up from there. They had to talk so I could move up. So I could get better intelligence for the Alliance."

Yes, just a little step from interrogating in the field to interrogating at headquarters. And it was just interviews, at first. But they had to talk.

"I don't want to think about it."

You played with the atmosphere. You knew what they needed to breathe. You could strangle them without lifting a finger.

"I didn't mean for that to happen."

No, I know. I remember. Not the first one, anyway. But each one after that was just a little bit easier.

"I passed that intel along to the Alliance!"

Yes, I'm sure they found it useful. Too bad it was about the wrong side.

Tears flowed down Flip's cheeks. "It wasn't easy—it was awful. But I didn't have a choice!"

And when they sent you in with the SS?

"It was a step closer to where I needed to be."

No. It wasn't closer to where you needed to be. But it was closer to where you are now.

He stared at the Adler's controls, not knowing what to say.

But it was different, wasn't it?

"If I hadn't done it, someone else would have."

Is that so?

"Yes. It *is* so. And the Alliance got intel from that too. Those lives weren't lost in vain."

I'm not sure they'd agree with you. If they were alive, that is.

"I showed them mercy!" He spat the words on the windshield. "They should have been grateful!"

Mercy?

"Yes! They didn't suffer!" Flip started to hyperventilate. The cockpit closed tighter around him. He couldn't move his arms or legs. He was trapped, forced to relive all that he'd done.

"They—" he gasped, "they answered my questions or they didn't." He composed himself. "If I hadn't done it, someone else would have. It was my job."

Your job, she stressed, *was to gather intelligence for the Alliance.*

"It wasn't my fault," Flip said, his silent tears turning into a flood of louder ones. "That part"—he paused and took a deep breath—"was just to move up. To get better intelligence. As I said, if I hadn't been there someone else would have done it."

But you were their first choice.

430

"Of course. I was good at my job."

Your job of gathering intelligence. For the Alliance.

"Yes. For the Alliance." He couldn't even convince himself anymore.

And when you chose to become a pilot?

"It was the quickest route to becoming a general. They needed pilots, and I needed to be a general. Then I could put myself into any position I liked." He could feel the truth catching up to him. "It just took me a while to figure that out. It was the best choice. The only choice."

You keep saying that.

"What?"

That you didn't have a choice.

"I didn't."

And that someone else would have done it if you didn't.

"They would have. That's obvious!"

You did *have a choice. You could have chosen to let someone else do it.*

The cockpit closed even tighter around him. It became a coffin full of horrors.

And you were promoted from there.

Flip remained silent.

It was just another small step.

He tried to ignore her. He checked the Adler's controls again, knowing they'd already been set.

You asked for help—I'm doing my best.

He ignored her.

You showed your prowess as a pilot. Dropping bombs and missiles. Destroying the enemy.

"You can stop helping now. Please," he begged.

The bombs killed more than you ever had before. You knew it, but you ignored it. But they were so far below you—you couldn't see the flames and horror they suffered. You couldn't hear the cries and suffering. And anyone else could have done it.

"I can't—"

When you were promoted to squadron command, Node continued, *it was just another step someone else could have taken.*

Flip tried to do the calculations to determine how long it would take to make it to the next Pelican. At best, he'd be alone with his sentient conscience for months, just as she'd said. He'd relive every horrible second of his time in the Reich.

But it wasn't someone else. It was you.

Flip broke down. He wept for S'tanga. For Sprang. For Fric. For Claus. For Riepe. For all the friends who'd died. For everyone he had killed. He wept for the Phillip Marsh he once was. For the version of himself that had died just like everyone else.

Have you made the last tiny step, Flip? Or are you willing to backtrack?

CHAPTER 57

The M4s changed war forever.

After seeing them in action, Andrea understood how far the Alliance would go to destroy the Nazis. She knew why the Alliance wouldn't let her or her crew examine the mission parameters. She knew what conflict would look like in the future. The Alliance hadn't sent her to destroy a target. They'd sent her to deliver a message.

The first shot on this universe's Earth impacted the Pacific Ocean, vaporizing millions of cubic meters of water. It punched a hole into Earth's mantle and sent plumes of molten rock into orbit.

Then the second impact hit. Then the third. In rapid succession, the Mjölnirs rained unspeakable destruction on the planet.

The same firing pattern played out on Mars, Venus, Titan, Luna, and Io. The heat melted the targets' surfaces and still the bombardment came. Andrea's fleet unleashed judgment day on every inhabited planet and moon in the solar system.

The bridge crew stood silent, watching the destruction in horrid fascination. Andrea could never have imagined a hellfire this intense, this complete. She had no color, no emotion. Her skin, for the first time, was a flat white.

The moons died first. As more projectiles fell, their crusts ripped open along their equators. They cracked apart, and arms of molten rock spiraled over the M4s, destroying them as well.

Mars followed. Then Venus moments later.

Earth held out the longest. Its blood spewed from its punctured crust. Its fate was sealed; the planet died like all the others. Nothing remained but molten magma cooling into dust.

No one moved. No one could.

Andrea understood the message she'd been sent to deliver:

I am Andrea Gibla, Destroyer of Worlds. Relent or you're next.

She found her voice. "Where's the fleet?"

Ortosodl snapped back to his console. "Approaching Helob. No further losses other than the M4s, as planned."

Planned, she thought. *So Command lets us in on the "plans" after they're complete.*

"Status of targets?"

Ortosodl paused for a long time—uncharacteristically long for a Thymaxian who'd exterminated Phurlani children on Sandria.

"They're gone, Captain," Ortosodl stared at his instruments, his claws draped to his sides. "All of them. All the planets. The moons. The orbital installations. Everything in the system is just... gone. Only the gas giants and a few moons remain."

"It's as if they were never here," she whispered. "By Apatoa's eyes, what have we done?"

"Captain," Ortosodl said, just above a whisper. "Our fighters are suffering heavy casualties from the debris."

"Get the fighter carriers back in there and extract them," she ordered.

"Captain," Ortosodl turned to look at her, "taching into that system is impossible with the amount of debris present."

"Tell them," she said, "to burn out their slip drives if they have to. Get those fighters out!"

She composed herself as the order disseminated through the fleet.

"Status report on enemy forces?" she asked.

"There are no enemy forces, Captain."

"Did any of them escape?"

"It does not appear so."

"What are our losses?" She didn't want to know.

Ortosodl looked like he didn't want to answer. "We lost approximately 67 percent of our capital ships."

She couldn't believe her auditory membranes. Her hue dripped with despair and disbelief.

"What did they hit us with?" she asked.

"I don't know, Captain," Ortosodl said. "And I don't think we ever will."

EPILOGUE

Andrea and Ortosodl stood outside the *Aristotle*'s main hangar bay. They'd just come from yet another meeting. The situation in the Nazi territories, across every one of their occupied universes, changed from one week to the next.

They had not seen Kid since the day he left with the emperor. Andrea looked forward to catching up with him, though she knew the war had changed them all. Would they even like each other anymore?

Flip was scheduled to meet them at the hangar also. He'd insisted on two things:

1. They all met outside the hangar, and
2. No one enters the hangar without him.

Andrea was looking forward to seeing him. They would always be close, she thought, regardless of what happened and no matter how long they were apart. She hoped that would remain the case. The last time she'd seen him, he'd already hated the being he'd become. She didn't know all the details of the many hells he'd been through since then. The ones she knew about were more than enough to break someone.

Flip had been picked out of space by an Alliance fleet. After an attack on the Gulch, they came across him by accident. She'd done everything in her power to learn about his situation. Viper Command, however, said that everything about his mission was classified—held at Omega 4242 Level Secrecy. She didn't even know there *was* an Omega 4242. No one outside Viper Intelligence, high-ranking Command generals, and specific politicians would ever have access to the details of Flip's mission.

She implored Viper Intelligence to let her tell Flip that almost all the Pelicans' prisoners had been rescued, and that very few had been killed in the raids. She wanted him to know that they'd been tadered onto cloaked transport vessels and brought to this universe. He should know that they'd settled here and had added to the Alliance's cultural diversity.

Viper Command made that one concession to Andrea, though she figured they'd already told him about it. They let her know, in no uncertain terms, that this was a one-time courtesy. Her status as "Destroyer of Worlds" carried at least that weight.

Kid walked up to Andrea and Ortosodl; the emperor trailed behind him. She and Ortosodl snapped to attention. Kid suppressed laughter. After spending so many years with Lam, he found it amusing to see how people acted around the emperor.

"Sir," Andrea said. "I, er, wasn't aware you'd be joining us. I assure you, we would have worn our formal uniforms and—"

"At ease," Lam interrupted. "Lieutenant Rogers and I go everywhere together. We're inseparable, don't you know?" He put his arm around Kid's shoulder. "Plus, I wanted to personally congratulate both of you on your promotions. They're long overdue, in my humble opinion."

"Thank you, sir," Andrea and Ortosodl said in unison.

"You're the first to skip so many levels, *Admiral* Gibla," Lam beamed.

"It was too much, sir." Andrea's skin swirled with a mixture of pride and modesty.

"I disagree!" Lam insisted. "You planned and executed the biggest operation in Alliance history. Bigger than anything from the Phurlani War, by far."

"Still, sir," she insisted, "I moved past a lot of fine officers who deserved promotions."

"Are you arguing with your *emperor*?" Lam jibed. "Look, Admiral, you've effectively served as a fleet admiral for years. You commanded new ships, new weapons platforms, and new tactics."

Andrea's color changed to a mixture of pride and regret.

"It took many beings to accomplish that, sir," she said. "And we lost a lot of them."

"I know," Lam said. He put a hand on her arm. "We all knew a lot of beings would be lost, on both sides. It's going to be a long war to come, and many more will die before it's over. You, however, are the best choice for Asgard operations."

"With all due respect, sir," she said, "that operation was"—she paused, looking for the right words—"*troubling*. I don't want to work with Asgards and Mjölnirs. So many beings were killed, on our side and theirs, I—"

Lam stopped her and turned to Kid.

"Admiral," Kid said to Andrea. "We've fractured the Reich. There are inter- and intra-universal divisions we could never have dreamed of. The sacrifices we made were worth it. The collateral damage, as terrible as it sounds, was also worth it."

Andrea knew Kid was right. (Should she call him Kid anymore? Terran familiarity rules confused her sometimes.) He looked comfortable and warm. Though after he so casually mentioned the deaths of billions of beings, she wasn't quite sure what to make of him. He even looked—what was it?

Satisfied. Yes, definitely satisfied.

Kid remembered Andrea as the compassionate commander who laughed at his dumb jokes and mangled English idioms. He wanted more than anything to hug her. He wasn't sure about Lysserian customs, though, and wasn't familiar with Lysserian color patterns.

He didn't think she'd reciprocate anyway. She felt so bad about killing while he... well, he couldn't wait to purge the Nazis from the multiverse.

Operations throughout the Nazi and Jassican universes had succeeded beyond their wildest expectations. The Reich had split into squabbling factions vying for influence and power. Most of the Nazi forces in the Jassican universe had pulled out, bent on establishing themselves in their home universe. The dedicated holdouts faced withering attacks. The

Association and Alliance predicted that those small forces would be eradicated within the next month.

The Nazi admirals and generals couldn't even agree on what had happened or who had done it. Some, citing the superluminal weapon design, believed that a group of rebels conducted the attack. It must be the same group, they said, who had raided the Gulch and liberated New Auschwitz.

Others believed that the Jassicans reverse-engineered the weapon. Detractors of this theory pointed out that no Jassican ships or technology had been detected anywhere in the Keystone Universe. And as far as anyone knew, the Association couldn't cross universes.

Nevertheless, the Jassican theory proponents maintained that no rebel group in any universe could have hidden a fleet of that size. They certainly couldn't have hidden a fleet large enough to destroy an entire solar system. In the known multiverse, only the Jassicans had the resources to conduct such a large operation.

The smallest group of theorists latched onto that last part: the *known* multiverse. The logical conclusion, they said, was that the Reich faced a new enemy—one that had studied them, perhaps for centuries. They called for unity to face this new threat.

Allied Intelligence—composed of Association and Alliance agencies working together—sowed distrust and discord between the factions. The power-hungry officers had distrusted each other for eons, which made the operations even more effective.

Now that Hitler and his circle were gone, everyone vied to fill the vacuum. Admirals and generals turned against each other. Some soldiers didn't even know who to follow and just walked away. The Allies believed they could incite a full-scale civil war.

"And congratulations to you, Captain Islidn," Lam said.

"Thank you, sir. I look forward to serving," Ortosodl said.

"If you want the *Aristotle*," Lam said with a wink, "I think the admiral and I can pull a few strings."

"I'd like that very much, sir," Ortosodl said. Kid didn't remember him being so distant. Was it for the sake of formality? Or was it resignation to his fate?

"Don't get too comfortable, Captain. You've been performing well above that rank. I think you may be a rear admiral before long." Lam winked again. Kid rolled his eyes. Lam had—at least for the past few months—abandoned his public persona of an aloof eccentric and adopted the freewheeling, carefree spirit that Kid had grown used to.

"Sir," Andrea said. "I couldn't find out who decided to enlarge the Mjölnirs and escalate the raid. The order seemed to come from nowhere. Do you happen to know?"

"I don't know," Lam said, switching to serious mode. "And that's the truth, I'm not trying to cover anything up. No one knows, as far as I can tell. Everyone I talk to has a different idea. I don't know; the prime minister doesn't know. None of the military leadership knows. No one knows where Operation Guinevere originated."

Kid shuffled his feet and tried to change the subject. "I suppose Captain Marsh will be here soon?"

Andrea's skin swirled with excitement. "I'm looking forward to seeing him."

"I hope he's recovered," Lam said. "I understand that his mission was quite, er, difficult."

As if on cue, Flip walked into the foyer. He saluted the emperor and turned to Kid. "It's good to see you again, Lieutenant."

Flip had read reports about the *Merlin*'s mission and had suspected that something about Kid was off. Now that he had met Kid in person, he knew for sure. Kid had implanted nodes in himself. That was not a good idea.

Flip infiltrated Kid's tech node. *We'll talk about this later*, he said and shut down all of Kid's nodes. Kid stumbled, and Lam had to steady him.

"Are you okay?" Lam asked.

Kid glanced at Flip. "Er, yeah. Just a headache. The excitement of seeing everyone, you know?"

"I'm excited, too!" Lam beamed at everyone in turn. "And I've never even met you folks!"

He looked at Flip and nodded slightly. Flip knew that the emperor had nodes, and was happy there had been someone to watch over Kid.

"Okay, then," Flip said to the group, "everyone's here. Plus one emperor. I have a couple of surprises I'd like to share with you."

He led them into the hangar. A black ship took up most of the bay.

Kid and Lam looked at each other. Lam walked to the ship and stroked the hull.

"It looks like the *Merlin*," Lam sighed. "Except bigger—much bigger! Glorious!" He raised a high five to Kid, who half-heartedly returned it.

"There's a good reason, sir," Flip said. "It's the second iteration of the *Merlin*-class vessel. It's the *Arthur,* and it has some special cargo too."

A bay door opened in the back of the ship, revealing a smaller ship.

"Is that a fighter?" Andrea asked.

"Yep," Flip said. "The *Excalibur.* Brand new design. It provides logistic support and combat capabilities when the *Arthur* is null-cloaked."

"Excalibur?" Kid asked.

"Yes, *Excalibur.* The giant magic sword? Did they not teach you about Arthurian legends in science fiction school?" Flip snapped.

Kid shuffled his feet. He looked at the sleek fighter craft and pretended not to be embarrassed.

"Remarkable!" Lam exclaimed.

"And that's not the half of it," Flip said. "But now's not the time to go into it."

Andrea sensed a shift in Flip's demeanor.

"What is it, Flip?" She instantly regretted using his first name in public.

"I knew you'd be the first to ask." He smiled. "I've resigned from the Viper Corps."

"*Resigned?*" Ortosodl said in disbelief.

"Yep. I've served king and country long enough," Flip said. "I've paid my dues, so I'm taking some time for myself."

It's about goddamned time, Node chimed in.

"You mean to tell me"—Andrea glowed with anticipation and turned three eyestalks toward the *Arthur*—"that this beauty is under my command?"

"Sorry," Flip said. "You're not that lucky."

"Well, I don't want it," Lam said. "I have to get back into the emperor game. People need to see me. The Jassicans have been asking about me, from what I've heard." He frowned, then stuck his finger in his mouth to act like he was gagging. "Time to head back into the exciting world of politics, I suppose."

"Sir," Flip said, "you *are* in luck because this isn't your ship either. This is *my* ship."

A hurricane of gasps swirled around the group.

"It's a"—Flip paused to search for the right words—"retirement gift."

"What, how?" Lam stammered. "What are you going to do with it?"

"Oh," Flip said as his gaze walked up and down the *Arthur*. "I'm sure I can think of something."

"By Clyptod's blood!" Andrea said. "We need to chat about this over a round or ten at the Toga Party. But we"—she motioned to Otosodl—

"have to get to another meeting. We're reorganizing the fleet. Can't goose out of this one."

"I think you mean—" Flip started. "Oh, never mind. Bring it in, everyone."

He embraced Andrea in a bear hug. He grabbed Ortosodl and pulled him in too. He motioned for Kid to join.

The emperor put his arms around the foursome like an awkward teenager. "Sorry. I just get so emotional sometimes."

They broke apart. They shared smiles, tears, and goodbyes.

"I'm not even sure why I'm upset," Lam said. He wiped his eyes and walked away. Kid followed him.

"Oh! Kid!" Flip called. "I almost forgot."

"What's that, Cap—er, Flip?" Since Flip had resigned, Kid didn't have to use the formal address.

"You're coming with me."

"I am?"

"You sure are. By order of Viper Command."

Kid looked at the other three. No help there. They were just as shocked as he was.

Flip started up the ramp. "Let's go."

Kid took a couple of slow steps in Flip's direction. "Where are we going?"

Andrea once again saw that cold hatred blaze in Flip's eyes before he answered.

"Hunting."

ACKNOWLEDGMENTS

Huge thanks to my editors: Rebecca Brewer & Kristin Gustafson. I found them on Reedsy.com and was very lucky to come across their profiles.

Thanks to all my volunteer editors: Lee Kinnett, Jason Hosler, Dave Mobley, Elizabeth Gorham, Chris Collins, Mike Massoglia, Melody Roberts, my dad (David Snellen, Sr.), my wife (Megan) and Tiffany Kidd. (Sorry if I missed anyone.)

An extra big thanks to Sabrina Flege-Paff whose insights into the previous prologue prompted a complete rewrite. It's much, much better!

Thanks to Chris Woodall for thinking of the FANG acronym many, many years ago and giving it to me. And to Rob Bevins for brainstorming gravitonium around the same time.

I wrote a lot of the first draft (pun intended) at O'Neill's Irish Pub, and it's the setting for a couple scenes. Thanks to my friend Darnell Robinson, manager and bartender, for coming up with Bastyeon. Check out the place if you come to Lexington. I can't promise Aerosmith will be there, though.

Thanks to my best friend, Ken Tressler. He's always been with me through thick and thin and dragged me through some dark times.

Special thank you to Danny & Peggy Walls. They have always been a constant support not only for my book, but my entire adult life.

ABOUT THE AUTHOR

Dave Snellen is a first-time author and is thus writing this section himself. He will refer to himself, as is customary in "About the Author" sections, in the third person.

What could one say about Dave Snellen? They could say lots of things. He's volunteered with the YMCA in Vietnam; lived briefly in Syria (before the war); got lost in a battleship (the USS North Carolina); was saved by ocean rescue; is immune to rabies due to a Crocodile Hunter impression with a raccoon; kissed a shark; picked up a bundle of venomous snakes; and has Karen Gillan's first autographed baseball. Also, the first baseball autographs of Denise Crosby & Cooper Andrews.

He grew up in the suburbs of Cincinnati and moved to Lexington to attend the University of Kentucky. He switched majors twice and took 8 years to finish his bachelor's degree, before eventually going to grad school in a completely different field. He now works, against his will, in IT.

He still lives in central Kentucky, also against his will. His dream is to move to Vancouver, British Colombia. He considered New Zealand, but that would put him in a terrible time zone to watch the Reds and Bengals.

He hopes you like this book. If you're reading this sentence, that's probably a good sign.

www.ingramcontent.com/pod-product-compliance
Lightning Source LLC
Chambersburg PA
CBHW021840010726
47493CB00005B/1480